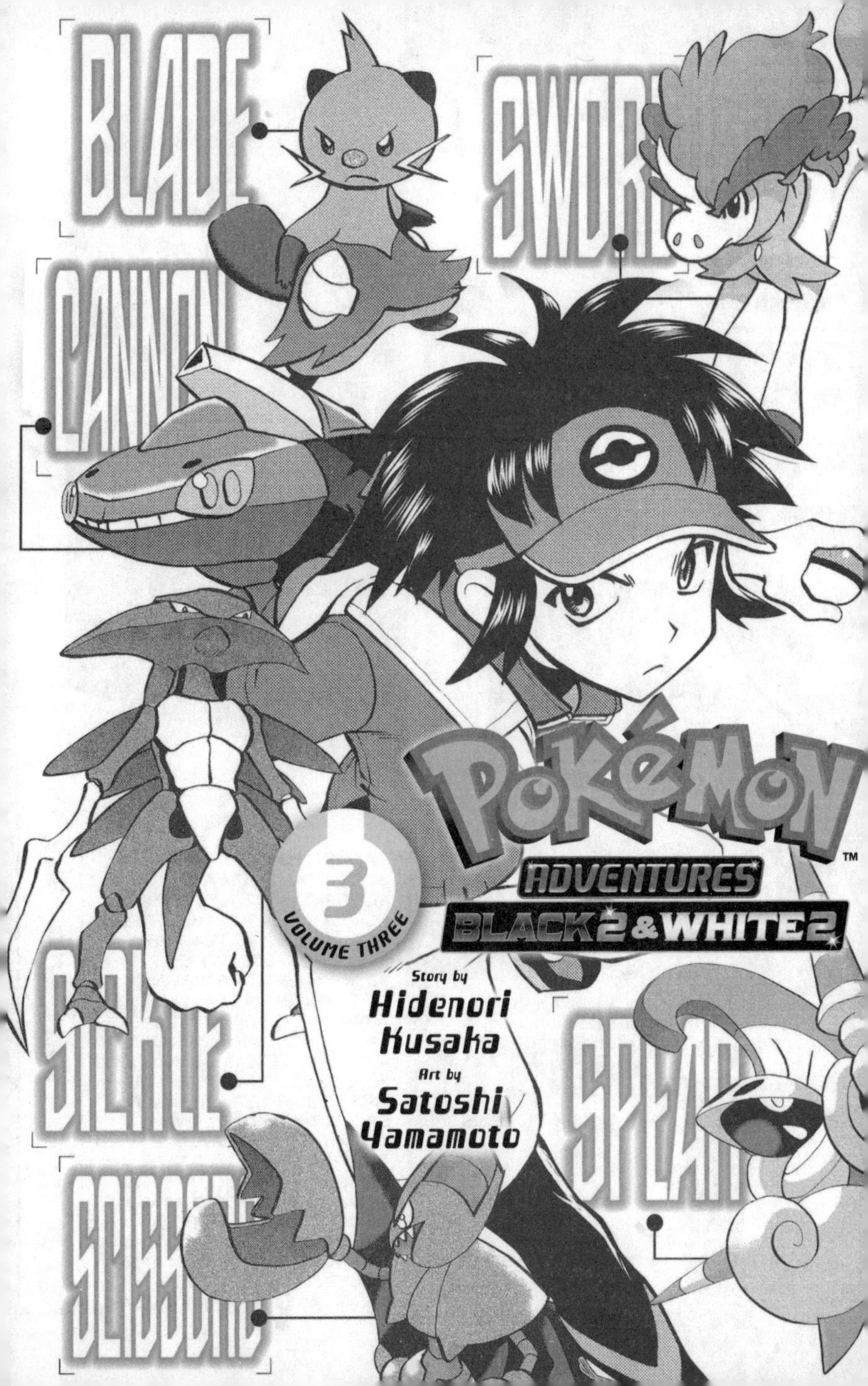
BLADE
POKéMON™
ADVENTURES
BLACK 2 & WHITE 2
3
VOLUME THREE
Story by
Hidenori Kusaka
Art by
Satoshi Yamamoto

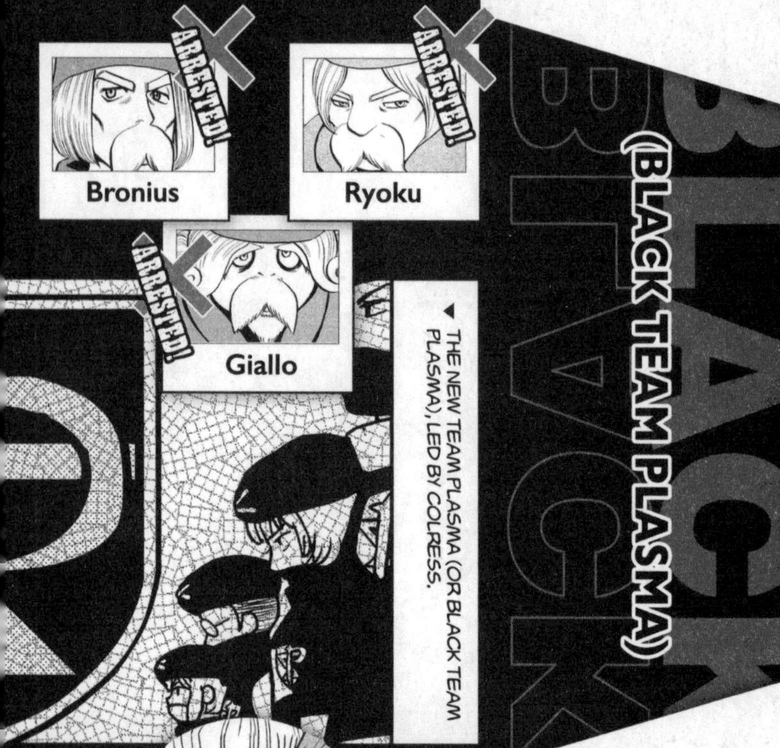
BLACK
(BLACK TEAM PLASMA)
ARRESTED!
Ryoku
ARRESTED!
Bronius
ARRESTED!
Giallo
▼ THE NEW TEAM PLASMA (OR BLACK TEAM PLASMA), LED BY COLRESS.

The Story Thus Far

THE UNOVA REGION.

TWO YEARS HAVE PASSED SINCE TEAM PLASMA'S NOTORIOUS ATTACK ON THE POKÉMON LEAGUE. THE CITIZENS OF THE UNOVA REGION ARE STILL RECOVERING WHEN YOUNG INVESTIGATOR BLAKE OF THE INTERNATIONAL POLICE ARRIVES IN ASPERTIA CITY. HE HAS ASSUMED ANOTHER IDENTITY AND ENROLLED AT THE TRAINERS' SCHOOL FOR TWO REASONS: FIRST, TO ARREST THE SEVEN SAGES, THE TEAM PLASMA EXECUTIVES WHO HAVE SCATTERED ALL OVER THE REGION; SECOND, TO FIND THE MEMORY CARD HIDDEN BY WHITE TEAM PLASMA, A GROUP OF TEAM PLASMA MEMBERS WHO HAVE REBELLED AGAINST THE CURRENT MEMBERS, NOW KNOWN AS BLACK TEAM PLASMA.

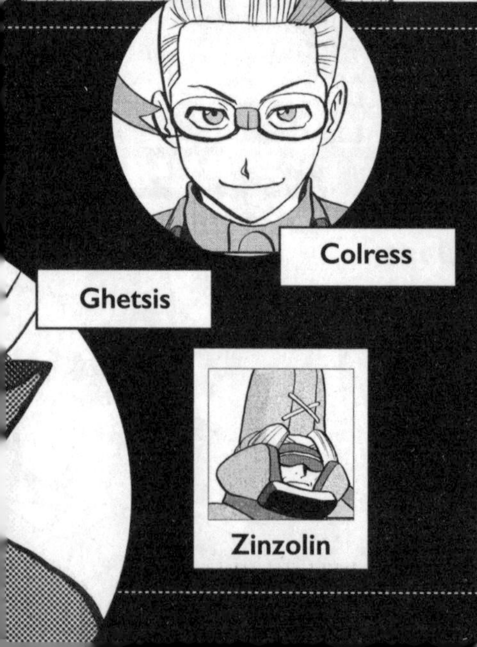
Colress
Ghetsis
Zinzolin

WHITE
(WHITE TEAM PLASMA)

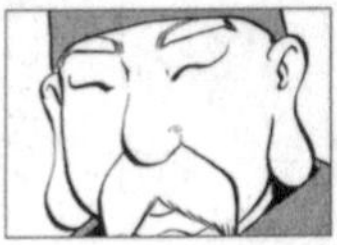

Gorm

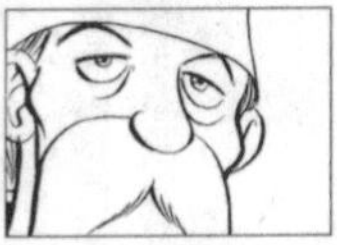

Rood

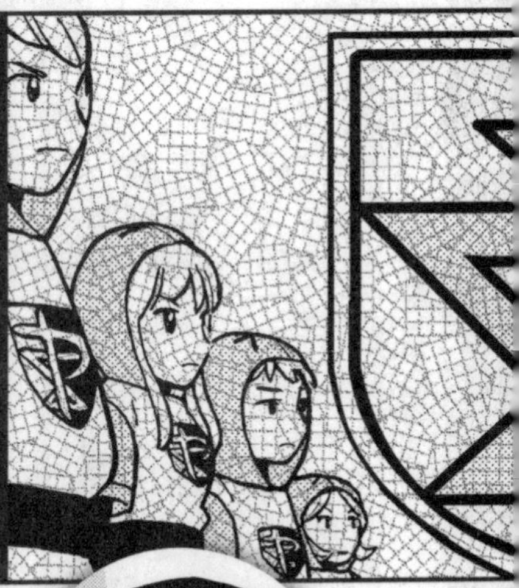

A GROUP OF TEAM PLASMA MEMBERS LED BY N WHO HAVE NOW SEEN THE ERROR OF THEIR WAYS.

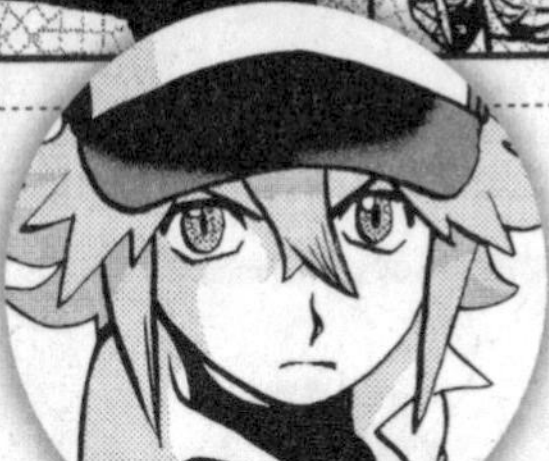

N

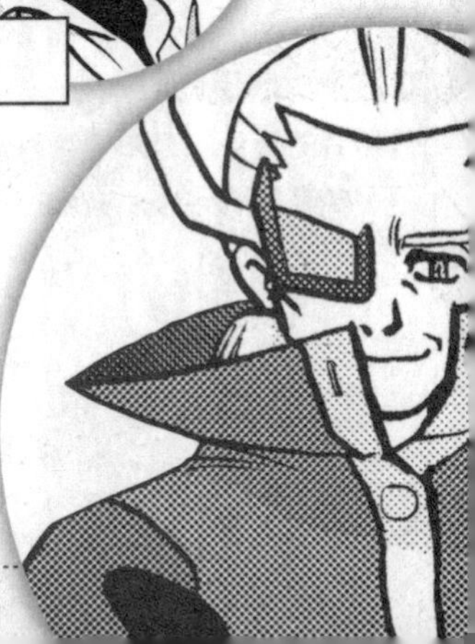

BLAKE AND HIS SUBORDINATE OFFICER LOOKER SUCCESSFULLY ARREST TEAM PLASMA MEMBERS GIALLO, BRONIUS, AND RYOKU. TOGETHER, THEY INFILTRATE TEAM PLASMA'S FLYING HEADQUARTERS, THE PLASMA FRIGATE, IN ORDER TO ARREST GHETSIS, THE LEADER OF THE SEVEN SAGES. MEANWHILE, FORMER TEAM PLASMA MEMBER WHITLEY FINDS A MEMORY CARD HIDDEN INSIDE HER PENDANT JUST BEFORE SHE IS CAPTURED BY TEAM PLASMA. BLAKE AND WHITLEY ARE REUNITED INSIDE THE PLASMA FRIGATE. THEY DECIDE TO TRY TO SAVE KYUREM, A POKÉMON CAPTURED BY TEAM PLASMA. BUT BLAKE AND WHITLEY BOTH END UP BEING FROZEN SOLID BY COLRESS!

The Characters...

Blake

A young International Police investigator whose rank is Inspector. He's a perfectionist who excels in Pokémon battles and capturing both Pokémon and criminals alike. He's currently working undercover in the Unova region.

Whitley

A girl who recently transferred to the Trainers' School. She is a former member of Team Plasma and wears a locket with N's photo inside it.

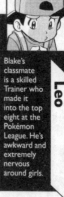

Looker

A veteran International Police investigator. Currently serving under Blake to help apprehend the Seven Sages.

Leo

Blake's classmate is a skilled Trainer who made it into the top eight at the Pokémon League. He's awkward and extremely nervous around girls.

Hugh

Another of Blake's classmates. He harbors a deep-seated hatred of Team Plasma because they kid-napped his little sister's Pokémon, a Purrloin.

Cheren

Black's childhood friend who has taken a post as a rookie teacher at Aspertia City's Trainers' School.

Bianca

Black's childhood friend who is currently working as an assistant at Professor Juniper's laboratory in Nuvema Town.

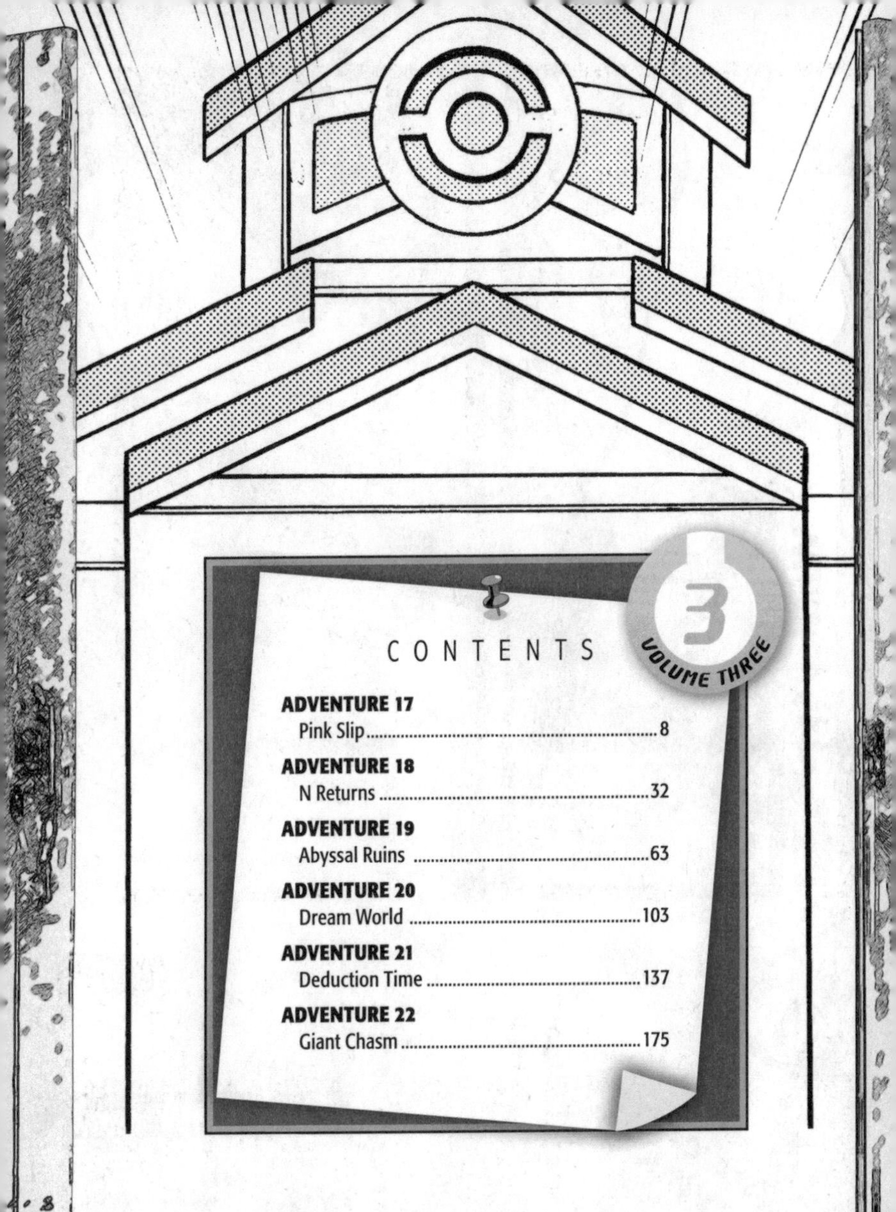
3
VOLUME THREE

CONTENTS

Pokémon Adventures the 11th Chapter B2·W2
eleventh

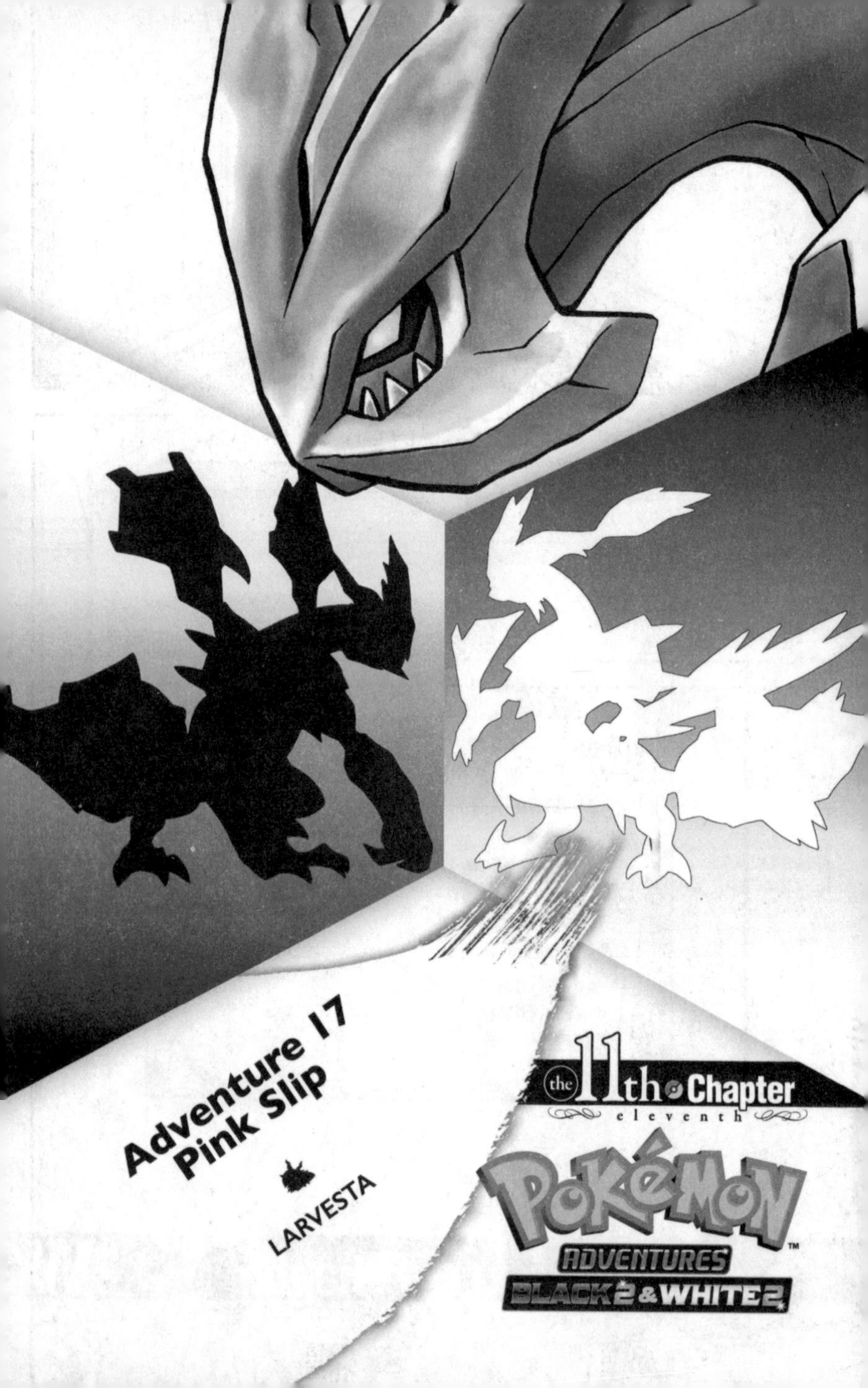
Adventure 17
Pink Slip
LARVESTA
the 11th Chapter
eleventh
POKéMON
ADVENTURES
BLACK 2 & WHITE 2

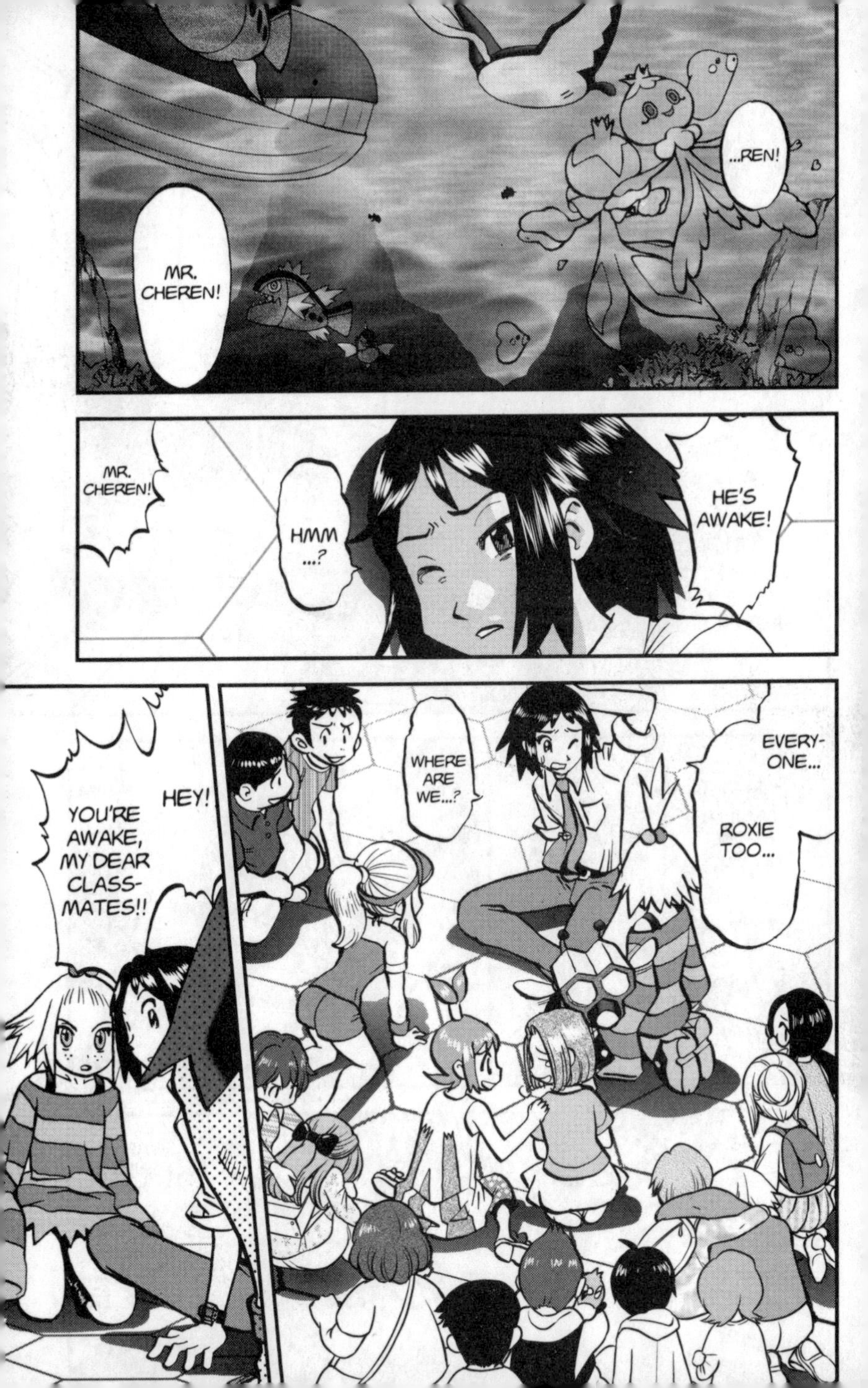
...REN!
MR. CHEREN!
HE'S AWAKE!
HMM ...?
MR. CHEREN!
EVERY-ONE...
ROXIE TOO...
WHERE ARE WE...?
HEY!
YOU'RE AWAKE, MY DEAR CLASS-MATES!!

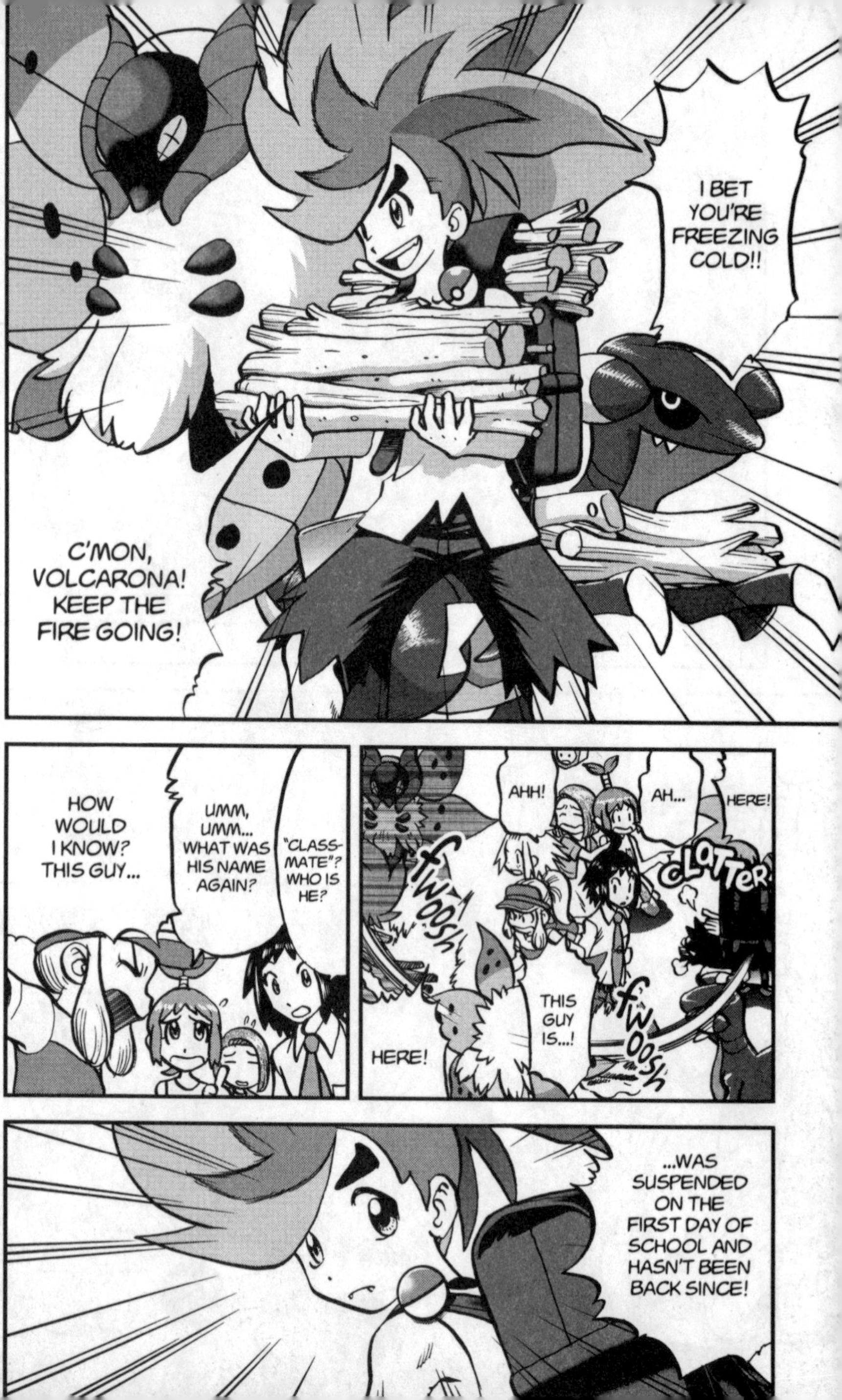
I BET YOU'RE FREEZING COLD!!
C'MON, VOLCARONA! KEEP THE FIRE GOING!
HERE!
AH...
AHH!
CLATTER
FWOOSH
THIS GUY IS...!
FWOOSH
HERE!
"CLASSMATE"? WHO IS HE?
UMM, UMM... WHAT WAS HIS NAME AGAIN?
HOW WOULD I KNOW? THIS GUY...
...WAS SUSPENDED ON THE FIRST DAY OF SCHOOL AND HASN'T BEEN BACK SINCE!

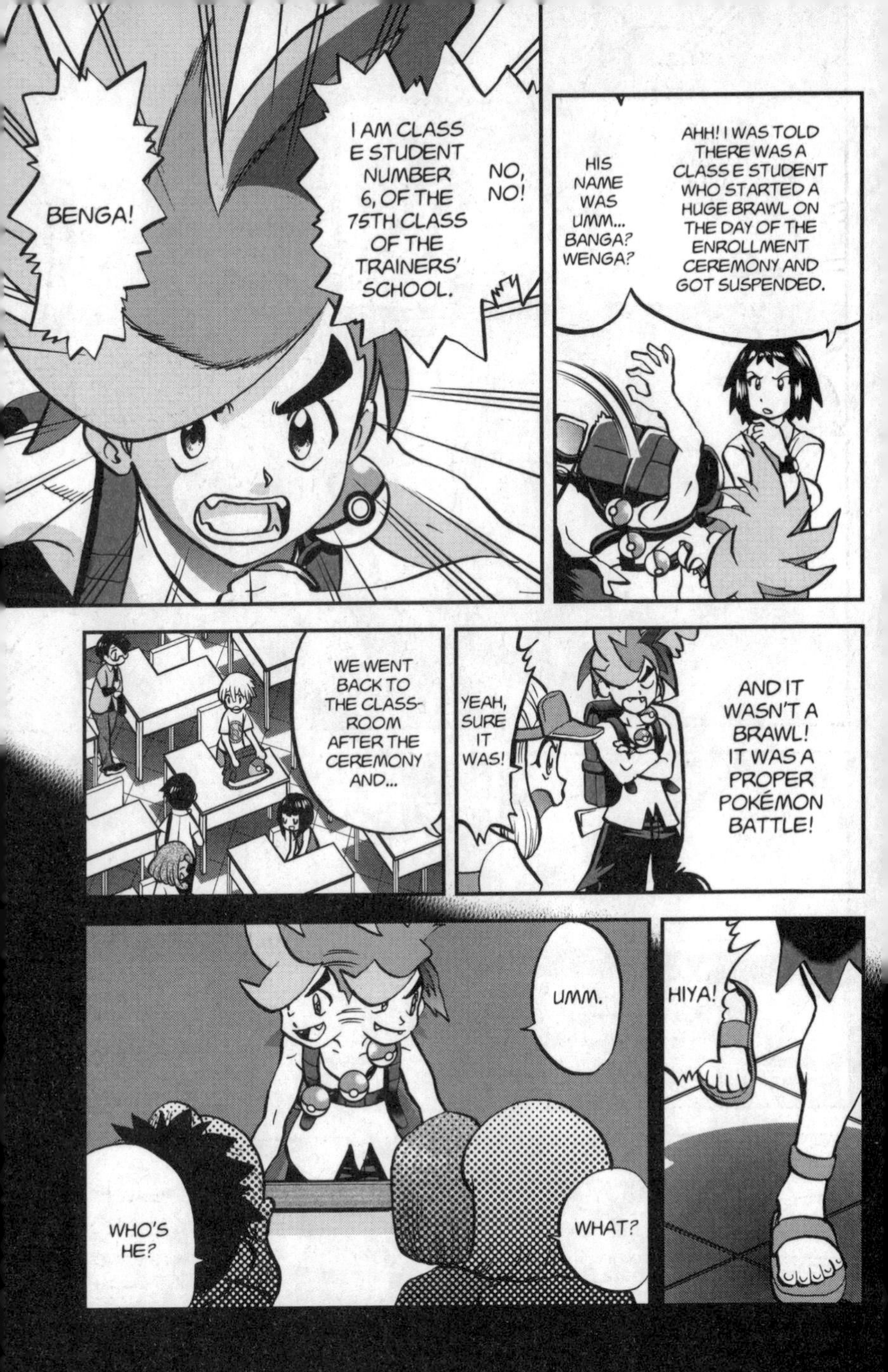
AHH! I WAS TOLD THERE WAS A CLASS E STUDENT WHO STARTED A HUGE BRAWL ON THE DAY OF THE ENROLLMENT CEREMONY AND GOT SUSPENDED.
HIS NAME WAS UMM... BANGA? WENGA?
NO, NO!
I AM CLASS E STUDENT NUMBER 6, OF THE 75TH CLASS OF THE TRAINERS' SCHOOL.
BENGA!
AND IT WASN'T A BRAWL! IT WAS A PROPER POKÉMON BATTLE!
YEAH, SURE IT WAS!
WE WENT BACK TO THE CLASS-ROOM AFTER THE CEREMONY AND...
HIYA!
UMM.
WHAT?
WHO'S HE?

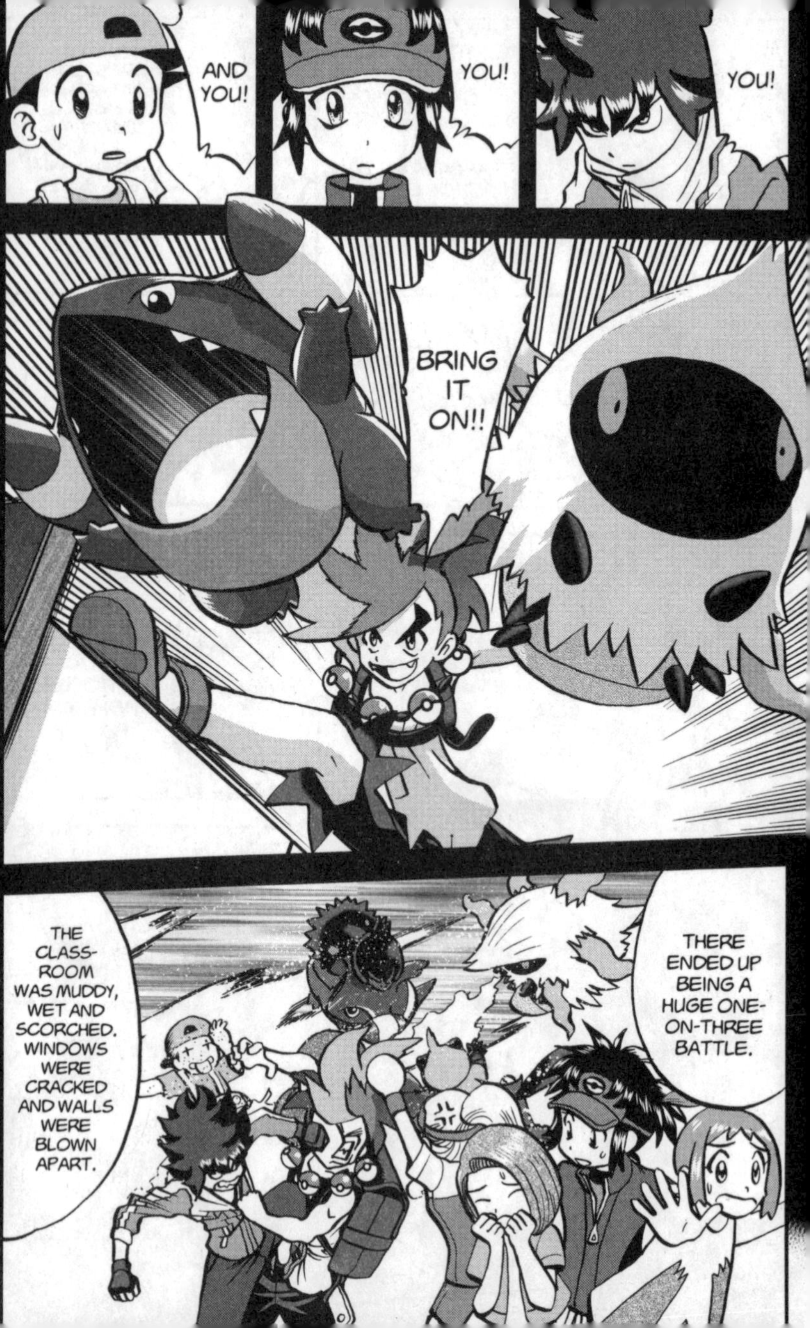
YOU!
YOU!
AND YOU!
BRING IT ON!!
THERE ENDED UP BEING A HUGE ONE-ON-THREE BATTLE.
THE CLASS-ROOM WAS MUDDY, WET AND SCORCHED. WINDOWS WERE CRACKED AND WALLS WERE BLOWN APART.

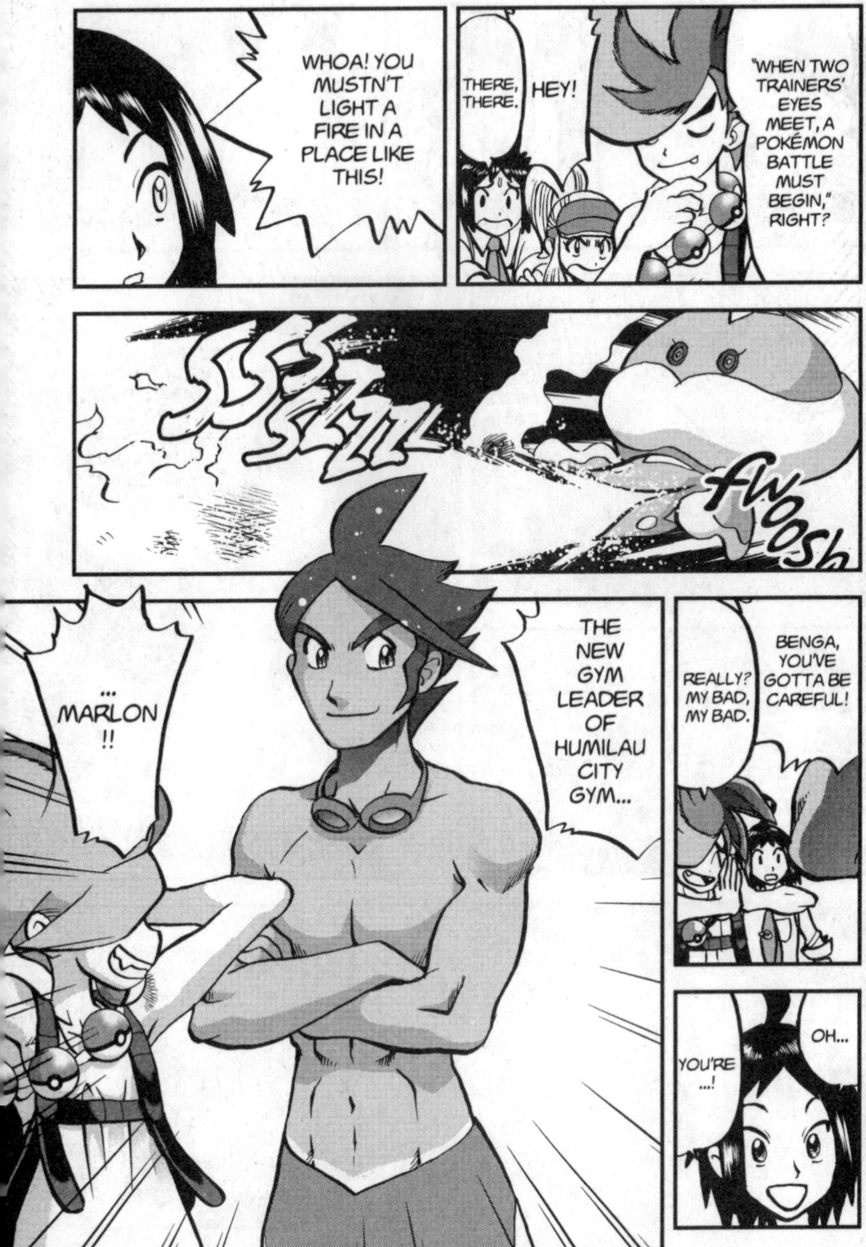

"WHEN TWO TRAINERS' EYES MEET, A POKÉMON BATTLE MUST BEGIN," RIGHT?
HEY!
THERE, THERE.
WHOA! YOU MUSTN'T LIGHT A FIRE IN A PLACE LIKE THIS!
fwoosh
BENGA, YOU'VE GOTTA BE CAREFUL!
REALLY? MY BAD, MY BAD.
OH...
YOU'RE ...!
THE NEW GYM LEADER OF HUMILAU CITY GYM...
... MARLON !!

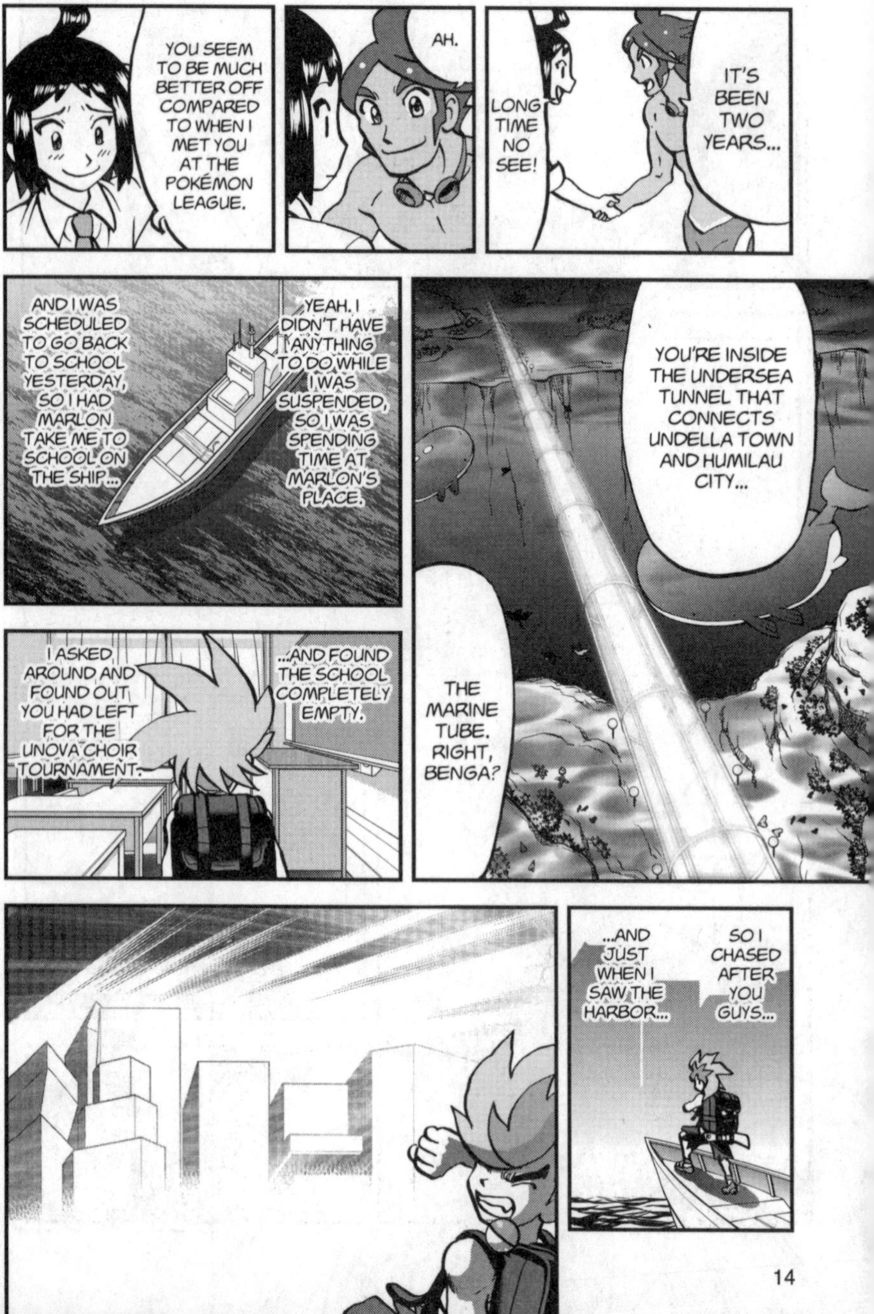
IT'S BEEN TWO YEARS...
LONG TIME NO SEE!
AH.
YOU SEEM TO BE MUCH BETTER OFF COMPARED TO WHEN I MET YOU AT THE POKÉMON LEAGUE.
YOU'RE INSIDE THE UNDERSEA TUNNEL THAT CONNECTS UNDELLA TOWN AND HUMILAU CITY...
THE MARINE TUBE. RIGHT, BENGA?
YEAH. I DIDN'T HAVE ANYTHING TO DO WHILE I WAS SUSPENDED, SO I WAS SPENDING TIME AT MARLON'S PLACE.
AND I WAS SCHEDULED TO GO BACK TO SCHOOL YESTERDAY, SO I HAD MARLON TAKE ME TO SCHOOL ON THE SHIP...
...AND FOUND THE SCHOOL COMPLETELY EMPTY.
I ASKED AROUND AND FOUND OUT YOU HAD LEFT FOR THE UNOVA CHOIR TOURNAMENT.
SO I CHASED AFTER YOU GUYS...
...AND JUST WHEN I SAW THE HARBOR...

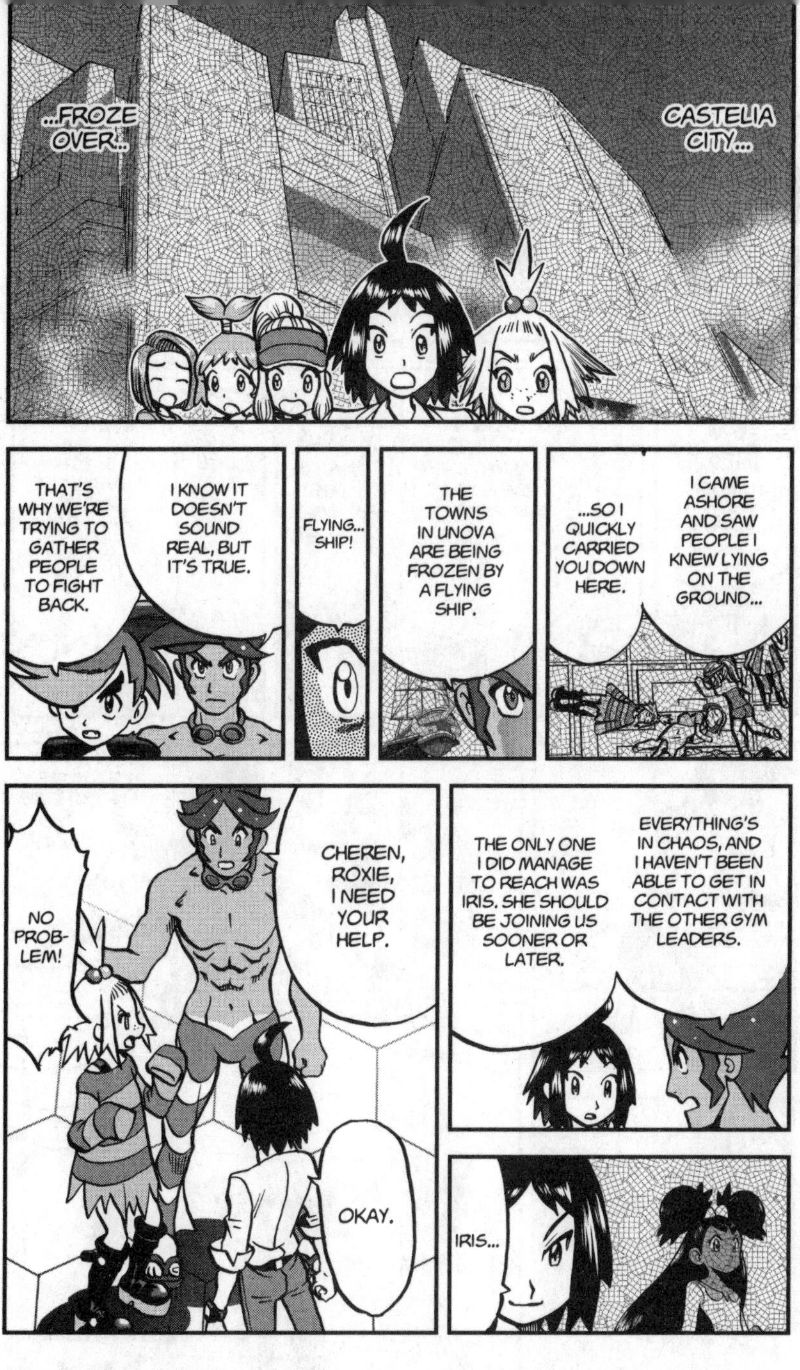
CASTELIA CITY...
...FROZE OVER...
I CAME ASHORE AND SAW PEOPLE I KNEW LYING ON THE GROUND...
...SO I QUICKLY CARRIED YOU DOWN HERE.
THE TOWNS IN UNOVA ARE BEING FROZEN BY A FLYING SHIP.
FLYING... SHIP!
I KNOW IT DOESN'T SOUND REAL, BUT IT'S TRUE.
THAT'S WHY WE'RE TRYING TO GATHER PEOPLE TO FIGHT BACK.
EVERYTHING'S IN CHAOS, AND I HAVEN'T BEEN ABLE TO GET IN CONTACT WITH THE OTHER GYM LEADERS.
THE ONLY ONE I DID MANAGE TO REACH WAS IRIS. SHE SHOULD BE JOINING US SOONER OR LATER.
IRIS...
CHEREN, ROXIE, I NEED YOUR HELP.
NO PROB-LEM!
OKAY.

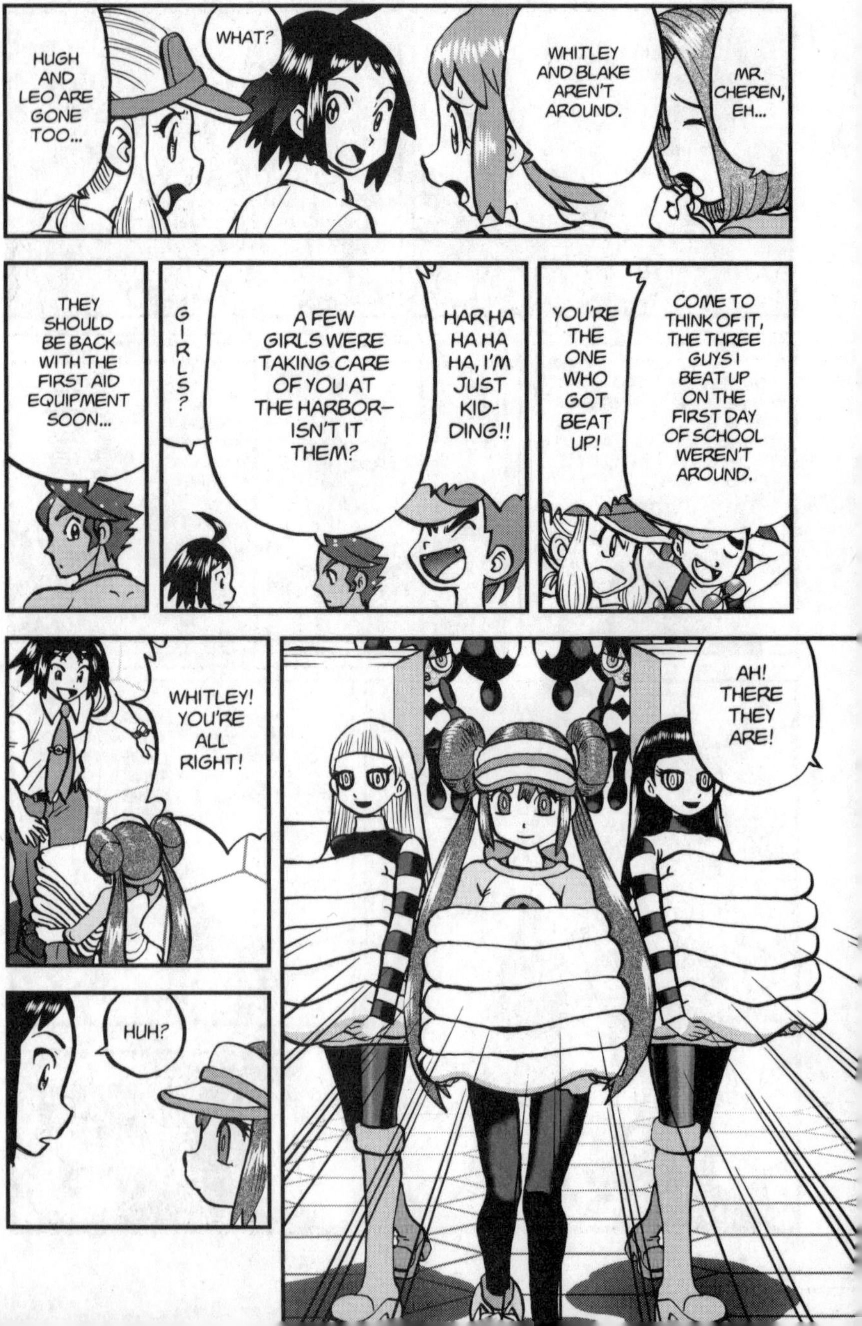
MR. CHEREN, EH...
WHITLEY AND BLAKE AREN'T AROUND.
WHAT?
HUGH AND LEO ARE GONE TOO...
COME TO THINK OF IT, THE THREE GUYS I BEAT UP ON THE FIRST DAY OF SCHOOL WEREN'T AROUND.
YOU'RE THE ONE WHO GOT BEAT UP!
HAR HA HA HA HA, I'M JUST KID-DING!!
A FEW GIRLS WERE TAKING CARE OF YOU AT THE HARBOR– ISN'T IT THEM?
GIRLS?
THEY SHOULD BE BACK WITH THE FIRST AID EQUIPMENT SOON...
AH! THERE THEY ARE!
WHITLEY! YOU'RE ALL RIGHT!
HUH?

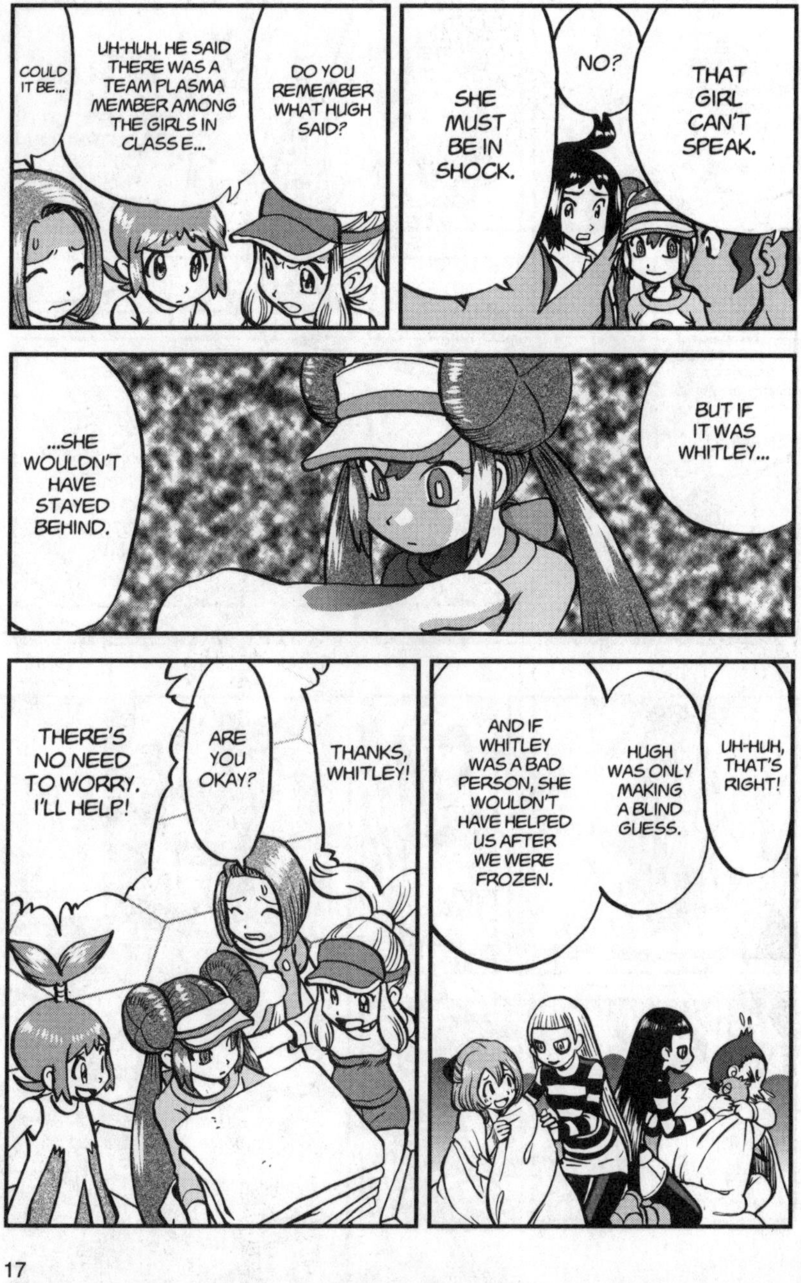
THAT GIRL CAN'T SPEAK.
NO?
SHE MUST BE IN SHOCK.
DO YOU REMEMBER WHAT HUGH SAID?
UH-HUH. HE SAID THERE WAS A TEAM PLASMA MEMBER AMONG THE GIRLS IN CLASS E...
COULD IT BE...
BUT IF IT WAS WHITLEY...
...SHE WOULDN'T HAVE STAYED BEHIND.
UH-HUH, THAT'S RIGHT!
HUGH WAS ONLY MAKING A BLIND GUESS.
AND IF WHITLEY WAS A BAD PERSON, SHE WOULDN'T HAVE HELPED US AFTER WE WERE FROZEN.
THANKS, WHITLEY!
ARE YOU OKAY?
THERE'S NO NEED TO WORRY. I'LL HELP!

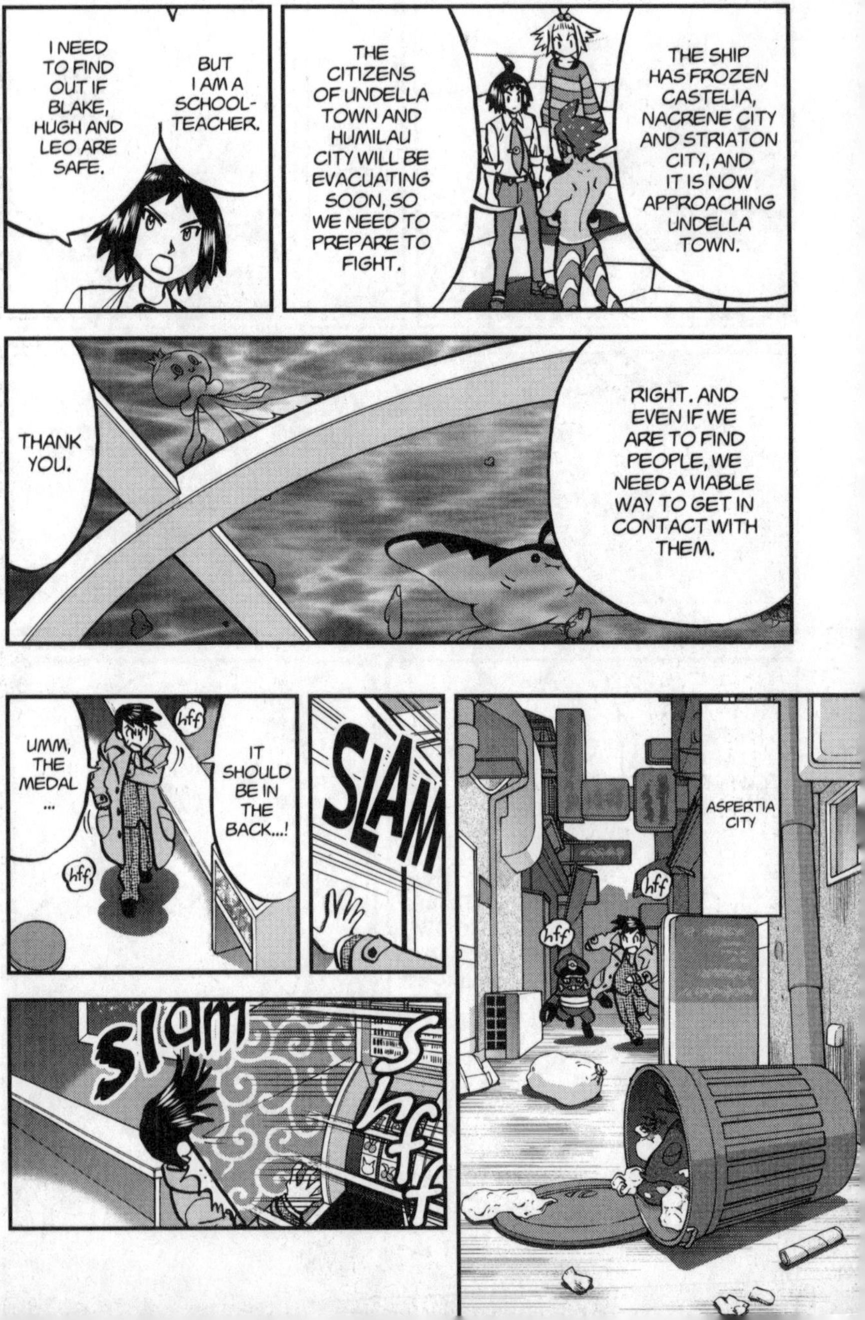
THE SHIP HAS FROZEN CASTELIA, NACRENE CITY AND STRIATON CITY, AND IT IS NOW APPROACHING UNDELLA TOWN.
THE CITIZENS OF UNDELLA TOWN AND HUMILAU CITY WILL BE EVACUATING SOON, SO WE NEED TO PREPARE TO FIGHT.
BUT I AM A SCHOOL-TEACHER.
I NEED TO FIND OUT IF BLAKE, HUGH AND LEO ARE SAFE.
RIGHT. AND EVEN IF WE ARE TO FIND PEOPLE, WE NEED A VIABLE WAY TO GET IN CONTACT WITH THEM.
THANK YOU.
ASPERTIA CITY
hff
hff
SLAM
hff
IT SHOULD BE IN THE BACK...!
UMM, THE MEDAL ...
hff
slam
hff

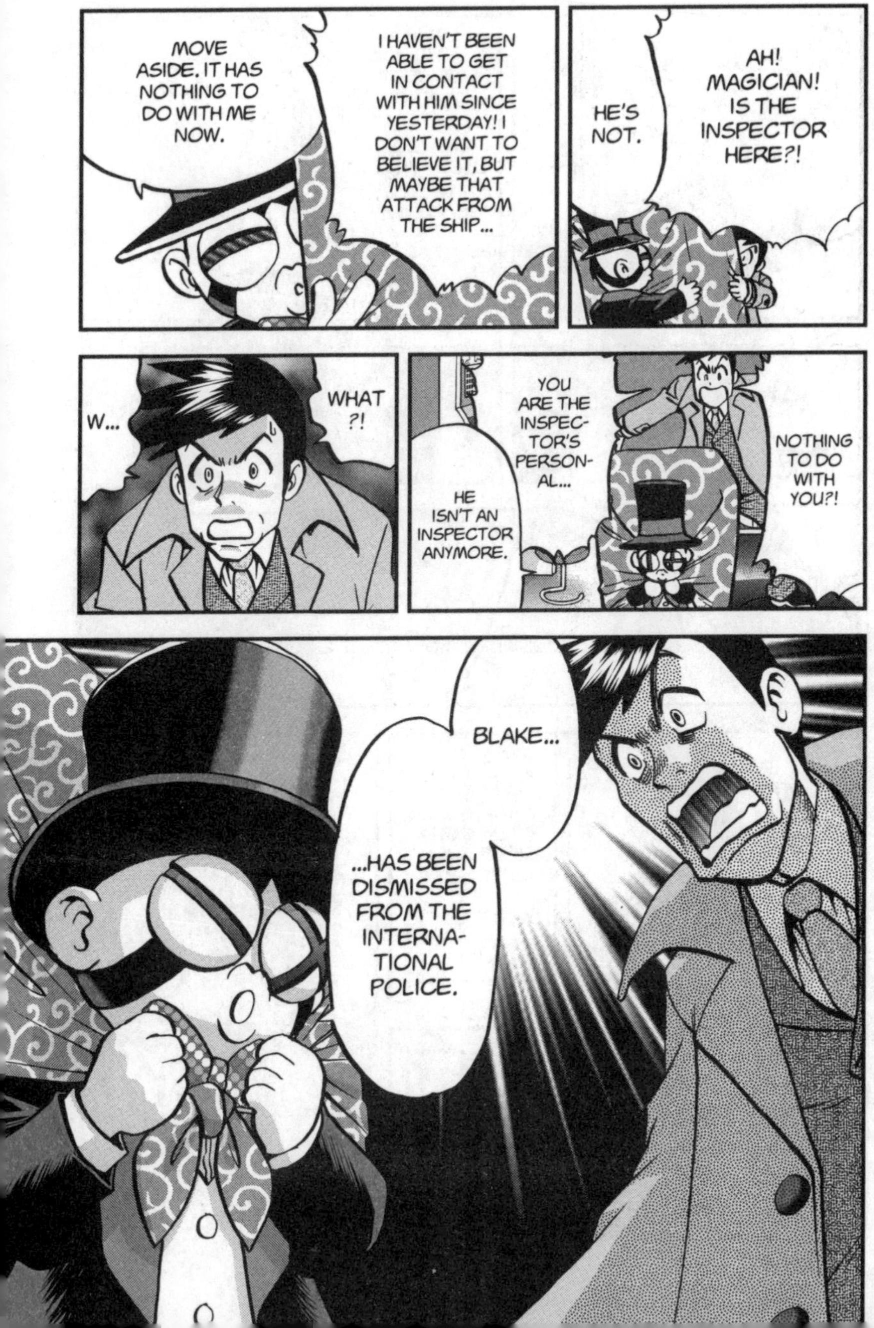
AH! MAGICIAN! IS THE INSPECTOR HERE?!
HE'S NOT.
I HAVEN'T BEEN ABLE TO GET IN CONTACT WITH HIM SINCE YESTERDAY! I DON'T WANT TO BELIEVE IT, BUT MAYBE THAT ATTACK FROM THE SHIP...
MOVE ASIDE. IT HAS NOTHING TO DO WITH ME NOW.
NOTHING TO DO WITH YOU?!
YOU ARE THE INSPECTOR'S PERSONAL...
HE ISN'T AN INSPECTOR ANYMORE.
WHAT ?!
W...
BLAKE...
...HAS BEEN DISMISSED FROM THE INTERNATIONAL POLICE.

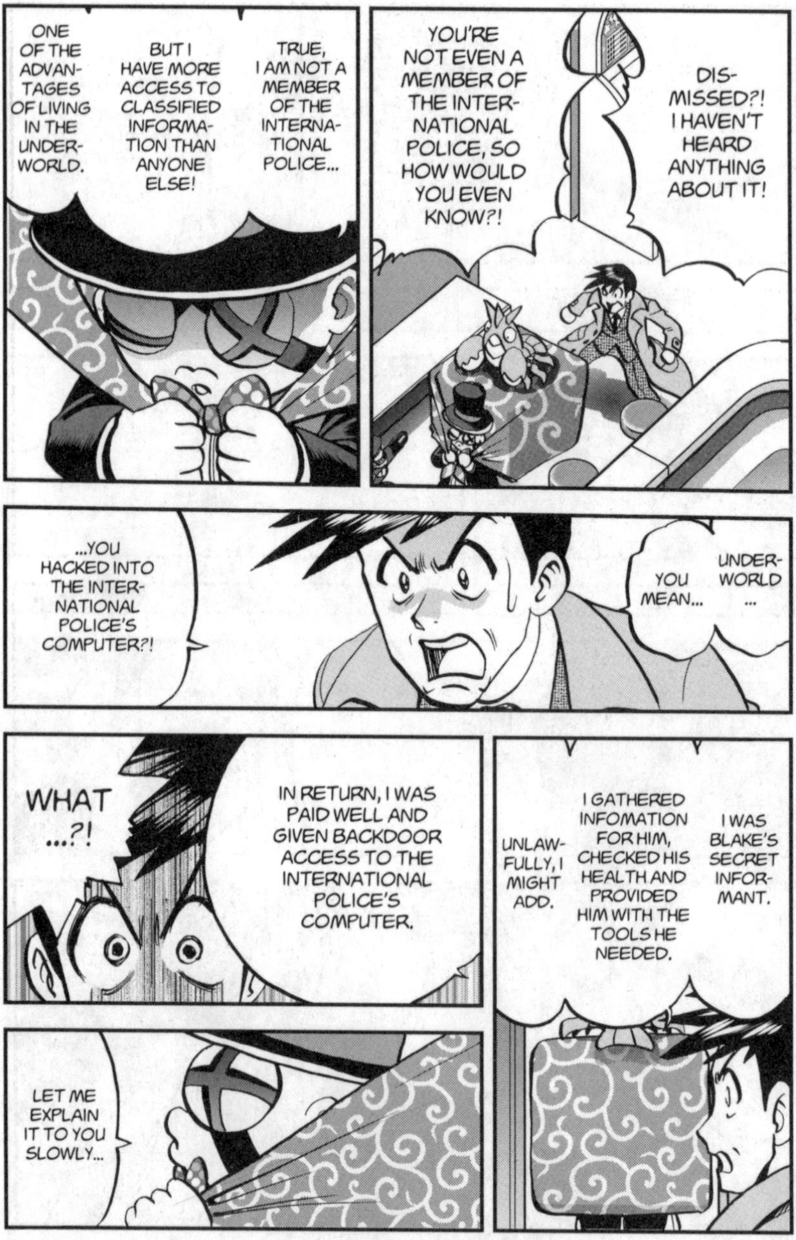
DISMISSED?! I HAVEN'T HEARD ANYTHING ABOUT IT!
YOU'RE NOT EVEN A MEMBER OF THE INTERNATIONAL POLICE, SO HOW WOULD YOU EVEN KNOW?!
TRUE, I AM NOT A MEMBER OF THE INTERNATIONAL POLICE...
BUT I HAVE MORE ACCESS TO CLASSIFIED INFORMATION THAN ANYONE ELSE!
ONE OF THE ADVANTAGES OF LIVING IN THE UNDERWORLD.
UNDERWORLD...
YOU MEAN...
...YOU HACKED INTO THE INTERNATIONAL POLICE'S COMPUTER?!
I WAS BLAKE'S SECRET INFORMANT.
I GATHERED INFOMATION FOR HIM, CHECKED HIS HEALTH AND PROVIDED HIM WITH THE TOOLS HE NEEDED.
UNLAWFULLY, I MIGHT ADD.
IN RETURN, I WAS PAID WELL AND GIVEN BACKDOOR ACCESS TO THE INTERNATIONAL POLICE'S COMPUTER.
WHAT...?!
LET ME EXPLAIN IT TO YOU SLOWLY...

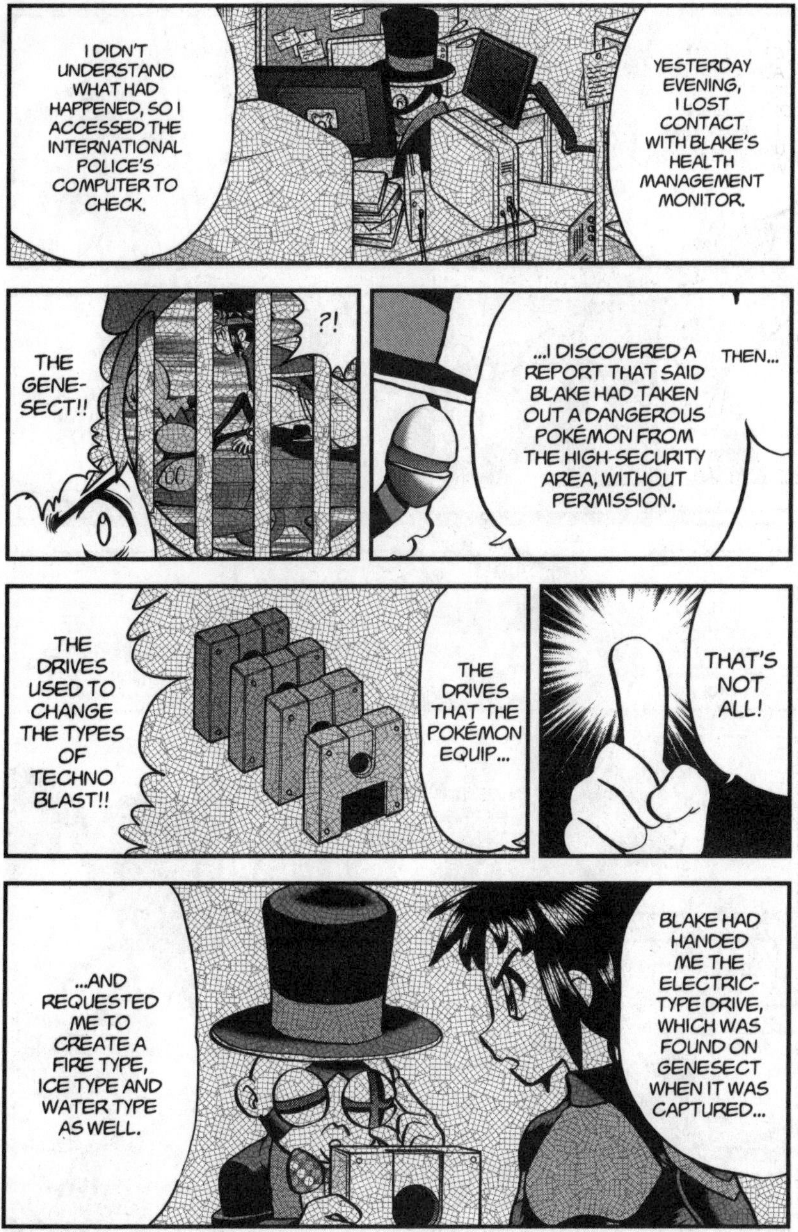
YESTERDAY EVENING, I LOST CONTACT WITH BLAKE'S HEALTH MANAGEMENT MONITOR.
I DIDN'T UNDERSTAND WHAT HAD HAPPENED, SO I ACCESSED THE INTERNATIONAL POLICE'S COMPUTER TO CHECK.
THEN...
...I DISCOVERED A REPORT THAT SAID BLAKE HAD TAKEN OUT A DANGEROUS POKÉMON FROM THE HIGH-SECURITY AREA, WITHOUT PERMISSION.
?!
THE GENE-SECT!!
THAT'S NOT ALL!
THE DRIVES THAT THE POKÉMON EQUIP...
THE DRIVES USED TO CHANGE THE TYPES OF TECHNO BLAST!!
BLAKE HAD HANDED ME THE ELECTRIC-TYPE DRIVE, WHICH WAS FOUND ON GENESECT WHEN IT WAS CAPTURED...
...AND REQUESTED ME TO CREATE A FIRE TYPE, ICE TYPE AND WATER TYPE AS WELL.

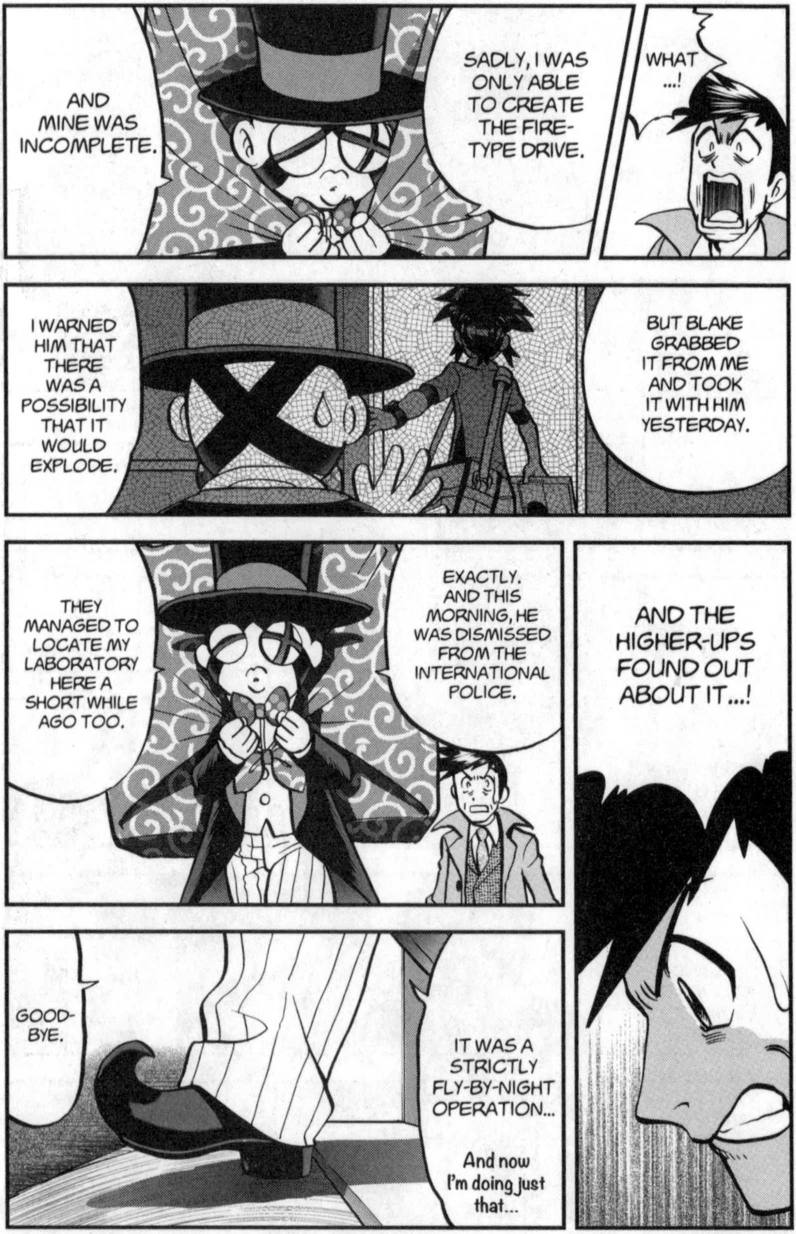
WHAT...!
SADLY, I WAS ONLY ABLE TO CREATE THE FIRE-TYPE DRIVE.
AND MINE WAS INCOMPLETE.
BUT BLAKE GRABBED IT FROM ME AND TOOK IT WITH HIM YESTERDAY.
I WARNED HIM THAT THERE WAS A POSSIBILITY THAT IT WOULD EXPLODE.
AND THE HIGHER-UPS FOUND OUT ABOUT IT...!
EXACTLY. AND THIS MORNING, HE WAS DISMISSED FROM THE INTERNATIONAL POLICE.
THEY MANAGED TO LOCATE MY LABORATORY HERE A SHORT WHILE AGO TOO.
IT WAS A STRICTLY FLY-BY-NIGHT OPERATION...
And now I'm doing just that...
GOOD-BYE.

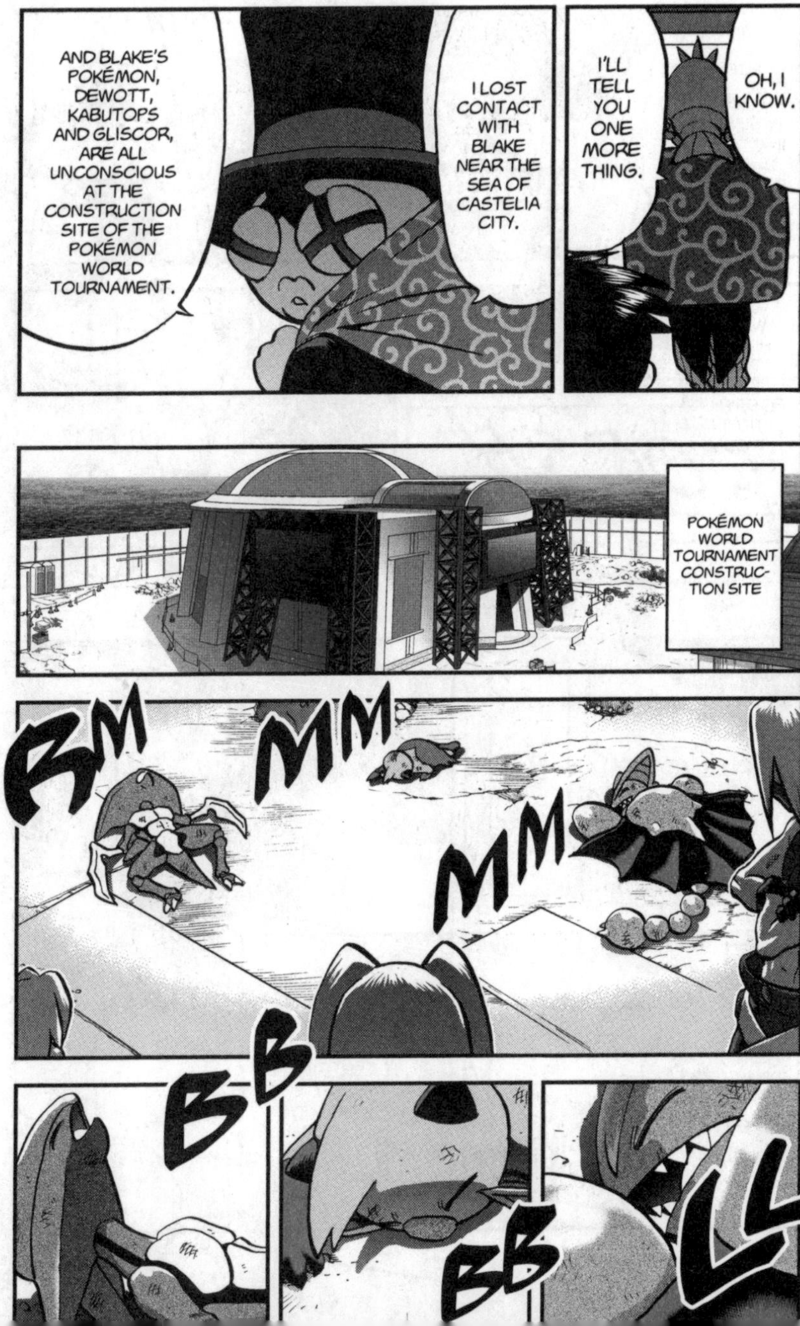
I'LL TELL YOU ONE MORE THING.
OH, I KNOW.
I LOST CONTACT WITH BLAKE NEAR THE SEA OF CASTELIA CITY.
AND BLAKE'S POKÉMON, DEWOTT, KABUTOPS AND GLISCOR, ARE ALL UNCONSCIOUS AT THE CONSTRUCTION SITE OF THE POKÉMON WORLD TOURNAMENT.
POKÉMON WORLD TOURNAMENT CONSTRUCTION SITE
RMMMMM
BB
BB
LL

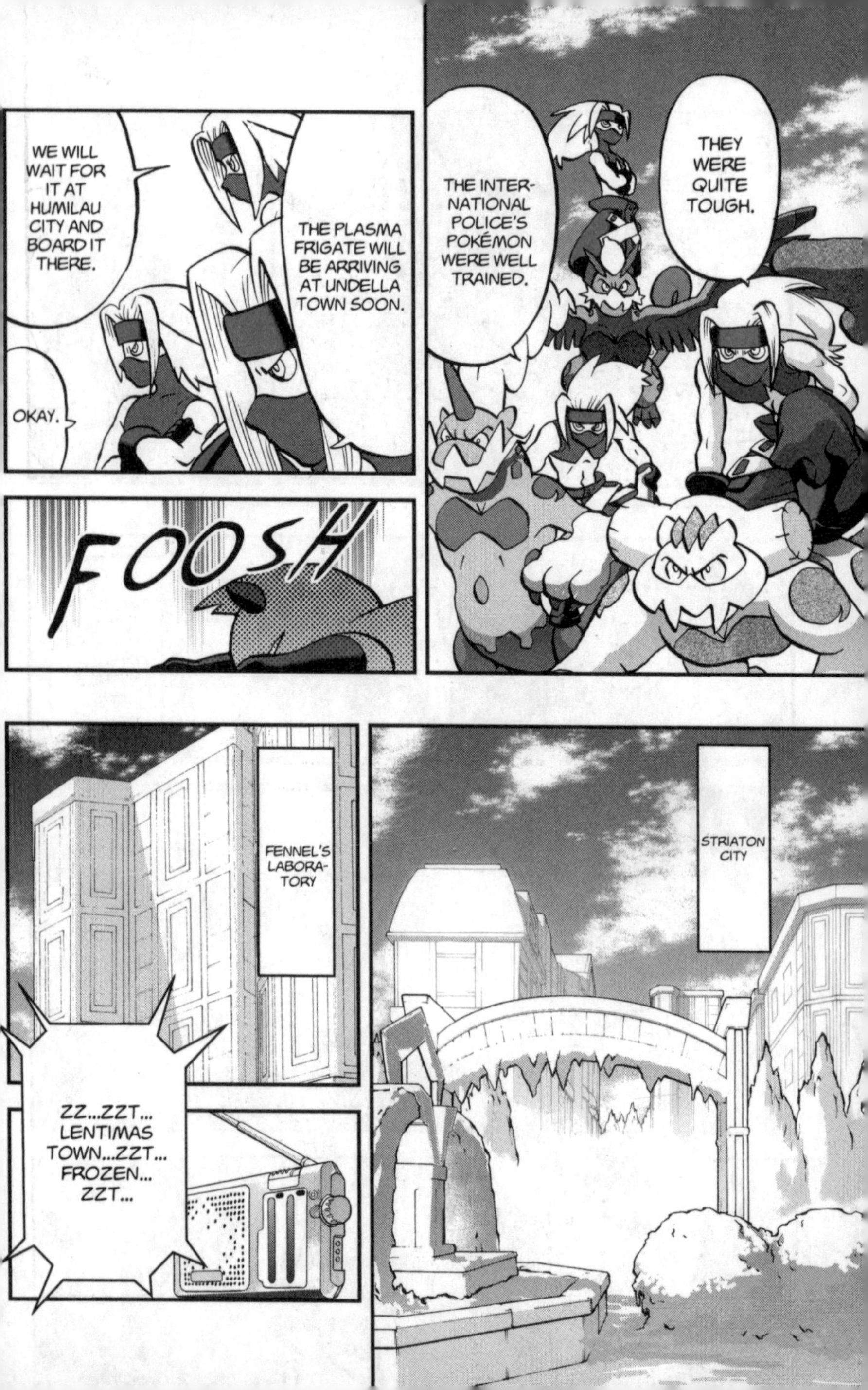
THEY WERE QUITE TOUGH.
THE INTERNATIONAL POLICE'S POKÉMON WERE WELL TRAINED.
THE PLASMA FRIGATE WILL BE ARRIVING AT UNDELLA TOWN SOON.
WE WILL WAIT FOR IT AT HUMILAU CITY AND BOARD IT THERE.
OKAY.
FOOSH
STRIATON CITY
FENNEL'S LABORATORY
ZZ...ZZT... LENTIMAS TOWN...ZZT... FROZEN... ZZT...

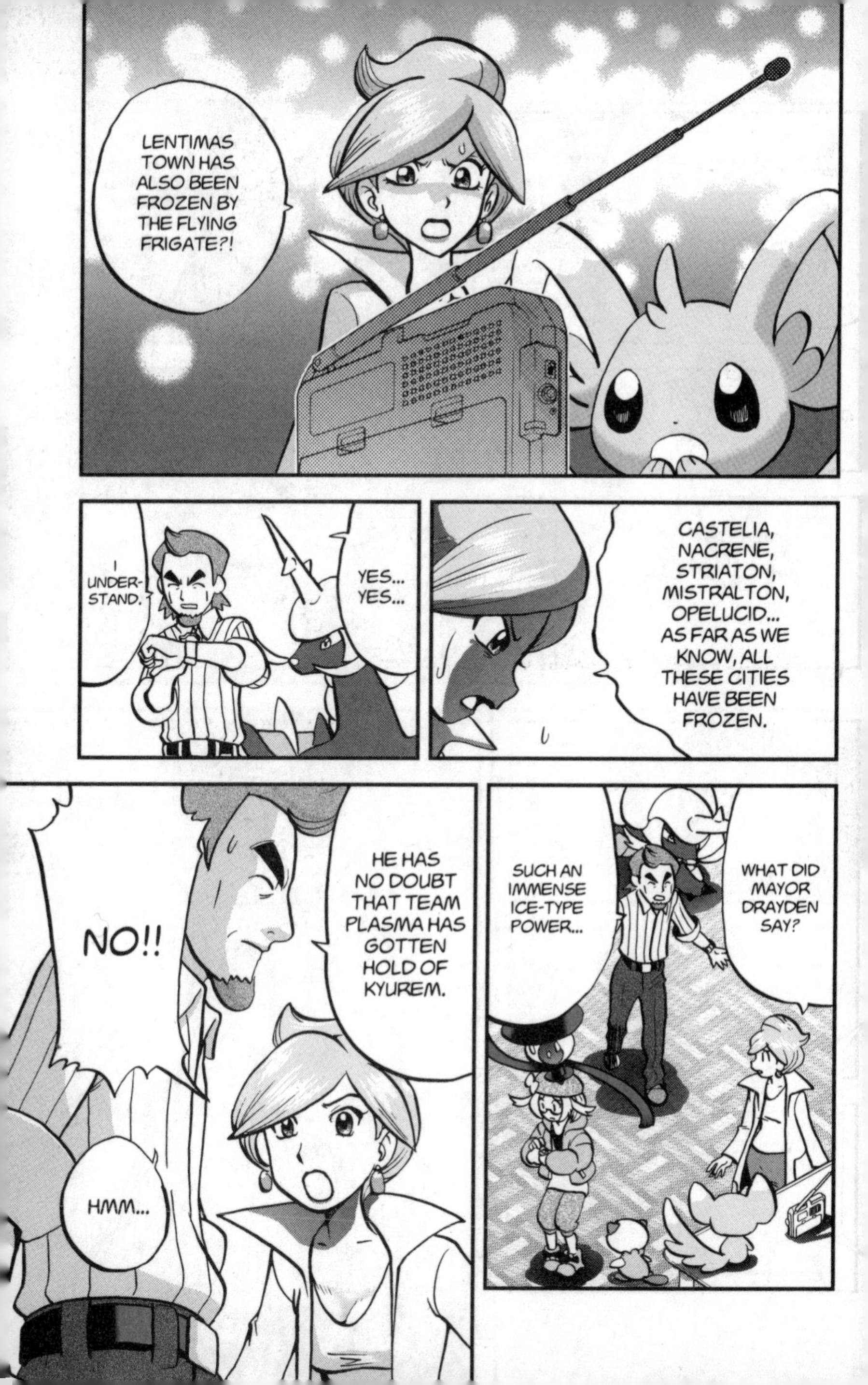
LENTIMAS TOWN HAS ALSO BEEN FROZEN BY THE FLYING FRIGATE?!
CASTELIA, NACRENE, STRIATON, MISTRALTON, OPELUCID... AS FAR AS WE KNOW, ALL THESE CITIES HAVE BEEN FROZEN.
YES... YES...
I UNDER-STAND.
WHAT DID MAYOR DRAYDEN SAY?
SUCH AN IMMENSE ICE-TYPE POWER...
HE HAS NO DOUBT THAT TEAM PLASMA HAS GOTTEN HOLD OF KYUREM.
NO!!
HMM...

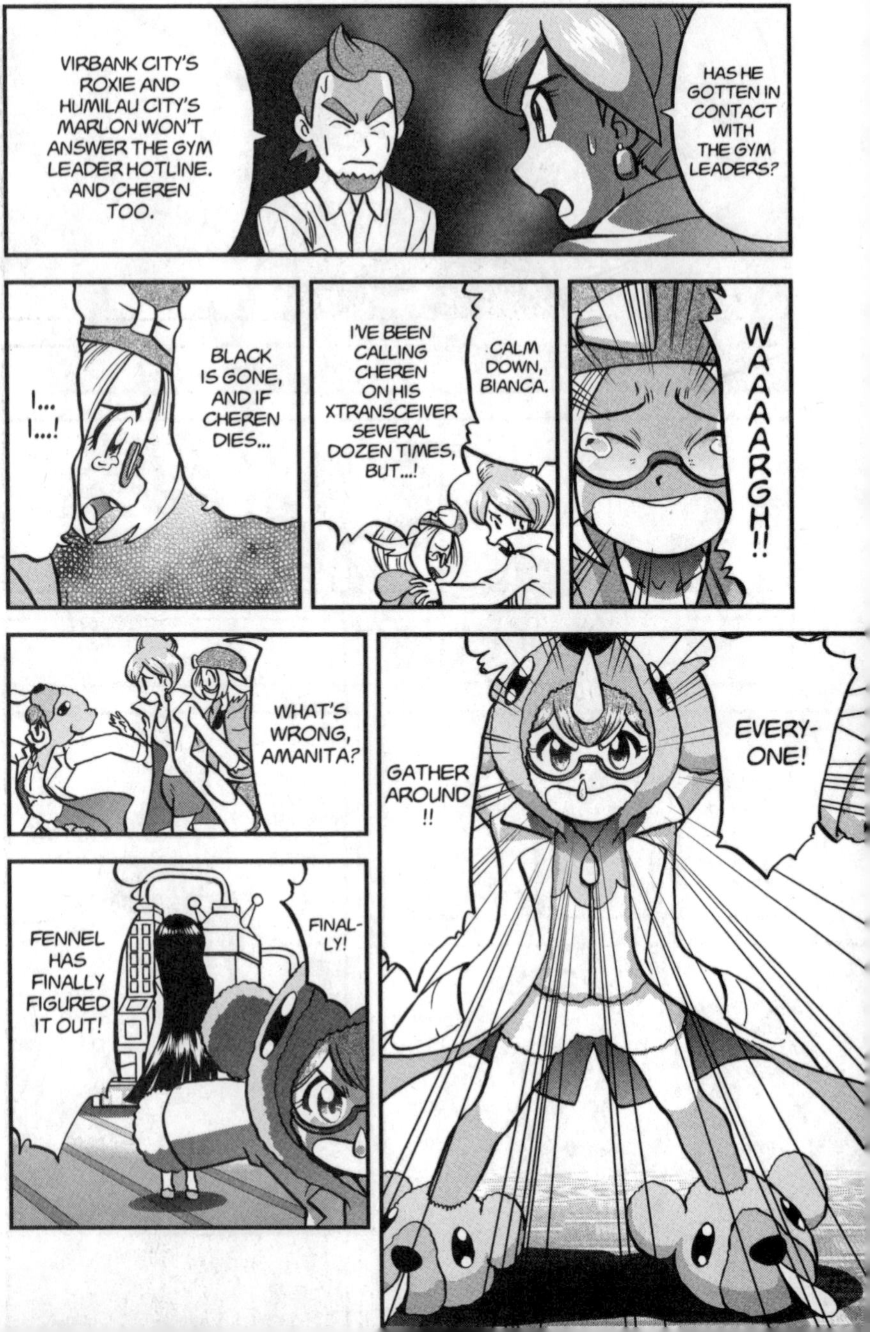
HAS HE GOTTEN IN CONTACT WITH THE GYM LEADERS?
VIRBANK CITY'S ROXIE AND HUMILAU CITY'S MARLON WON'T ANSWER THE GYM LEADER HOTLINE. AND CHEREN TOO.
WAAAAARGH!!
CALM DOWN, BIANCA.
I'VE BEEN CALLING CHEREN ON HIS XTRANSCEIVER SEVERAL DOZEN TIMES, BUT...!
BLACK IS GONE, AND IF CHEREN DIES...
I... I...!
EVERY-ONE!
GATHER AROUND!!
WHAT'S WRONG, AMANITA?
FINAL-LY!
FENNEL HAS FINALLY FIGURED IT OUT!

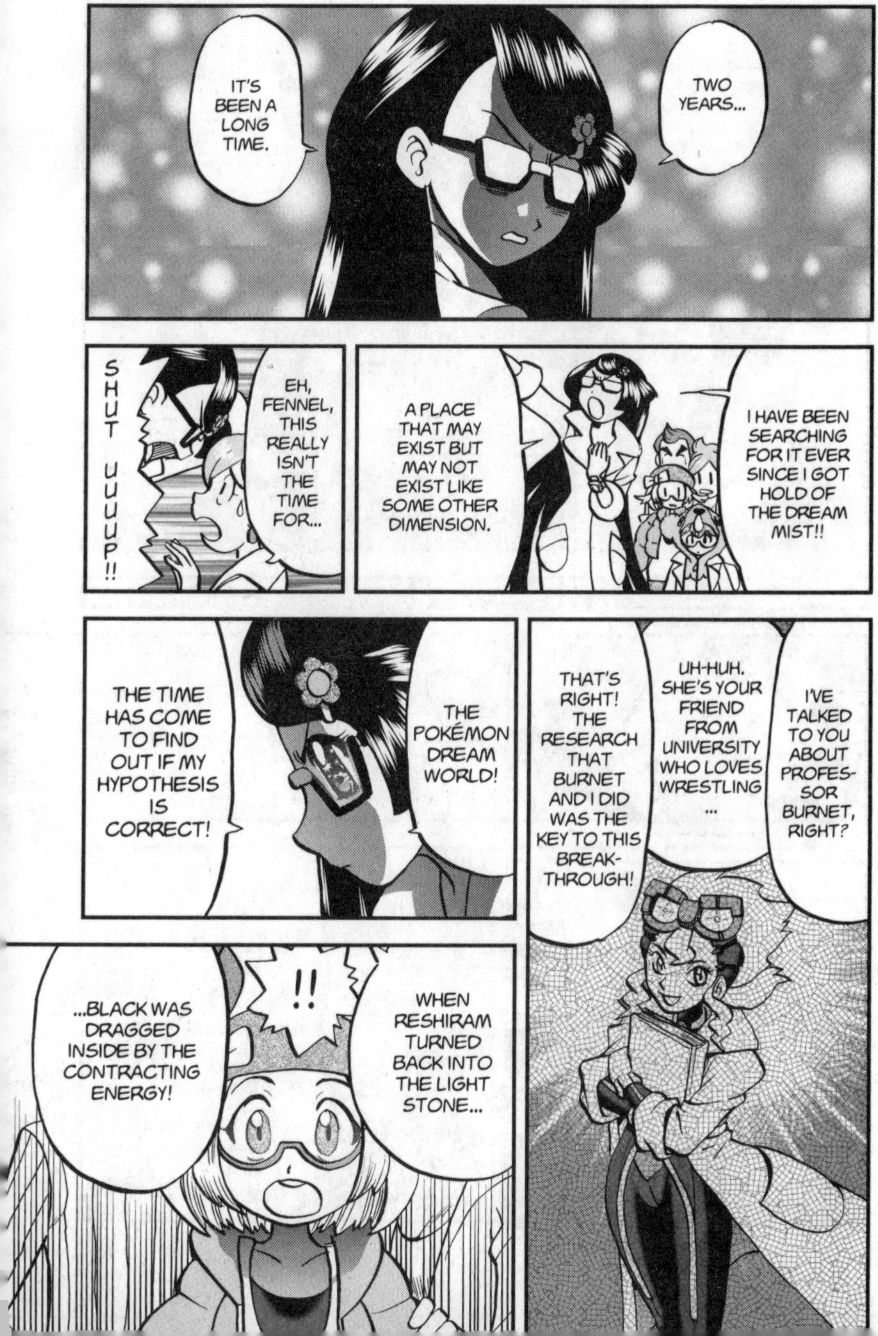
TWO YEARS...
IT'S BEEN A LONG TIME.
I HAVE BEEN SEARCHING FOR IT EVER SINCE I GOT HOLD OF THE DREAM MIST!!
A PLACE THAT MAY EXIST BUT MAY NOT EXIST LIKE SOME OTHER DIMENSION.
EH, FENNEL, THIS REALLY ISN'T THE TIME FOR...
SHUT UUUUUP!!
I'VE TALKED TO YOU ABOUT PROFES-SOR BURNET, RIGHT?
UH-HUH. SHE'S YOUR FRIEND FROM UNIVERSITY WHO LOVES WRESTLING ...
THAT'S RIGHT! THE RESEARCH THAT BURNET AND I DID WAS THE KEY TO THIS BREAK-THROUGH!
THE POKÉMON DREAM WORLD!
THE TIME HAS COME TO FIND OUT IF MY HYPOTHESIS IS CORRECT!
WHEN RESHIRAM TURNED BACK INTO THE LIGHT STONE...
!!
...BLACK WAS DRAGGED INSIDE BY THE CONTRACTING ENERGY!

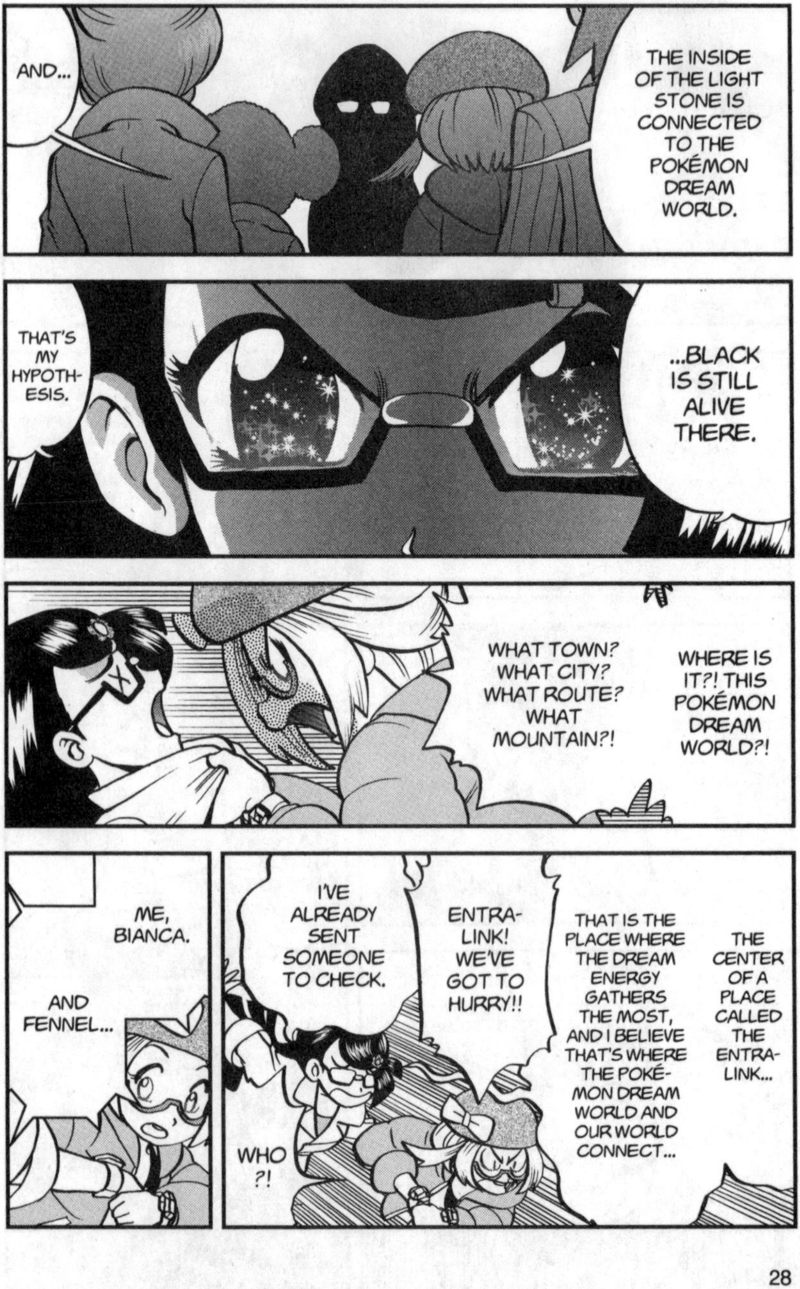
THE INSIDE OF THE LIGHT STONE IS CONNECTED TO THE POKÉMON DREAM WORLD.
AND...
...BLACK IS STILL ALIVE THERE.
THAT'S MY HYPOTHESIS.
WHERE IS IT?! THIS POKÉMON DREAM WORLD?!
WHAT TOWN? WHAT CITY? WHAT ROUTE? WHAT MOUNTAIN?!
THE CENTER OF A PLACE CALLED THE ENTRALINK...
THAT IS THE PLACE WHERE THE DREAM ENERGY GATHERS THE MOST, AND I BELIEVE THAT'S WHERE THE POKÉMON DREAM WORLD AND OUR WORLD CONNECT...
ENTRALINK! WE'VE GOT TO HURRY!!
I'VE ALREADY SENT SOMEONE TO CHECK.
WHO?!
ME, BIANCA.
AND FENNEL...

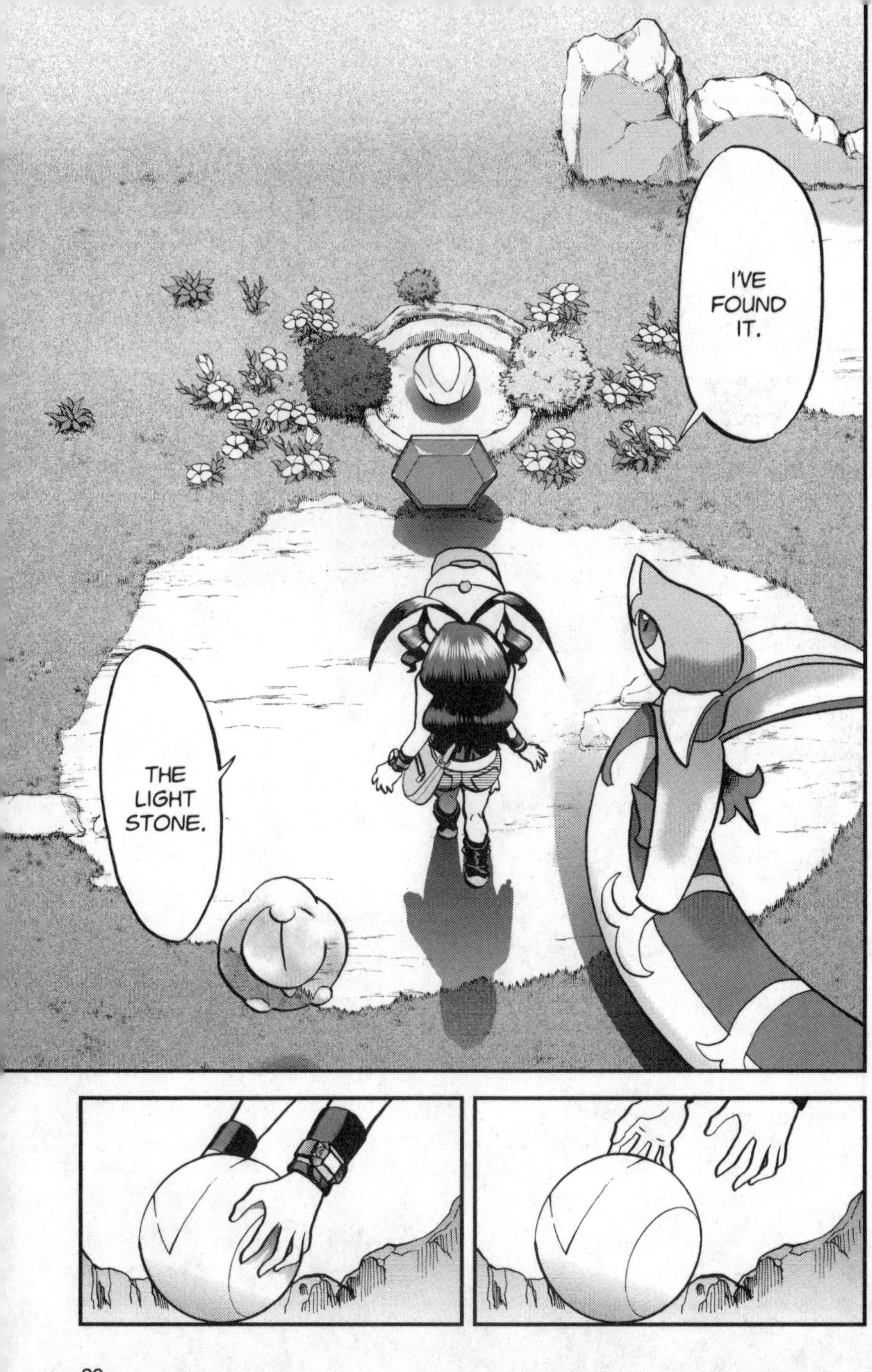
I'VE FOUND IT.
THE LIGHT STONE.

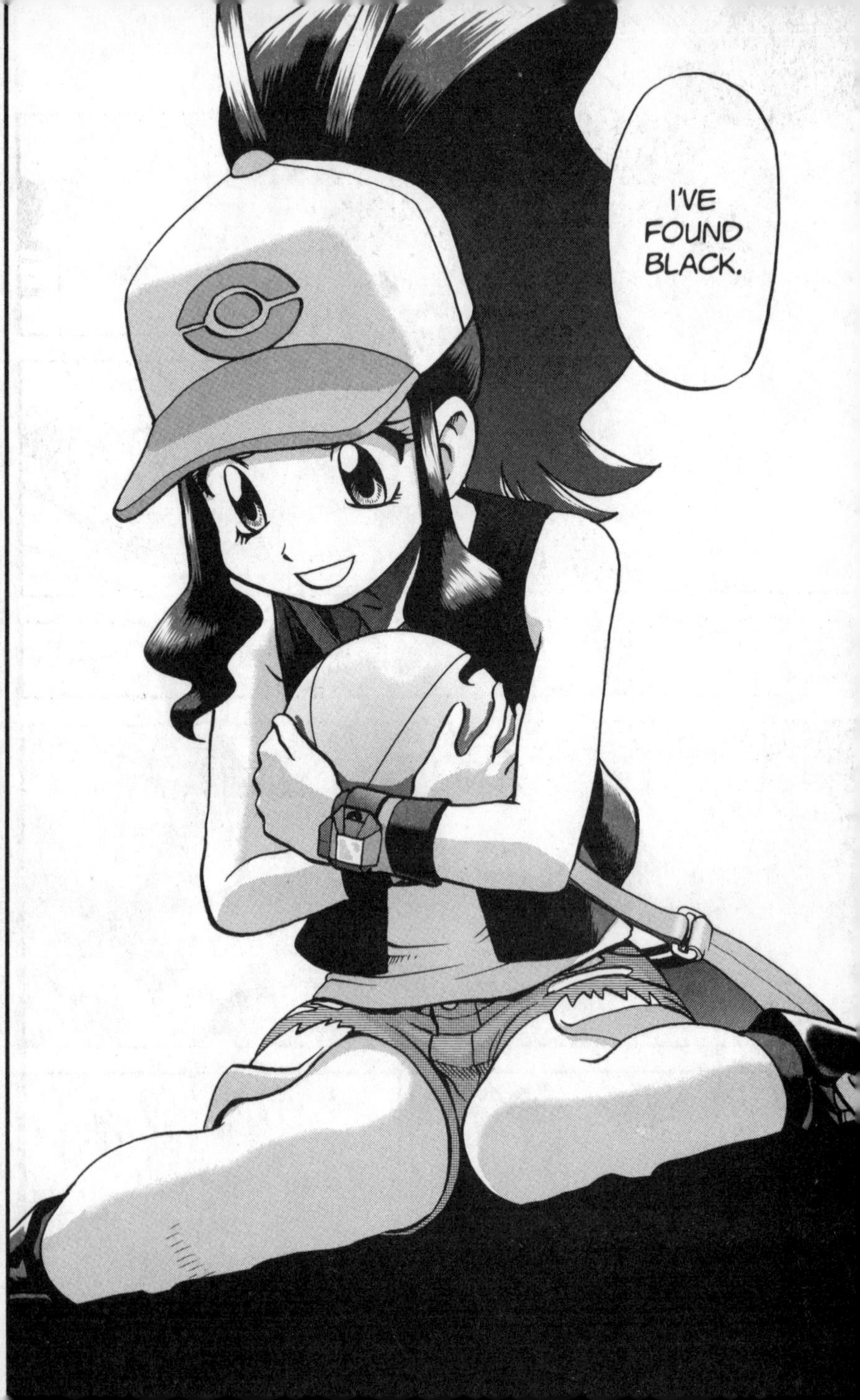
I'VE FOUND BLACK.

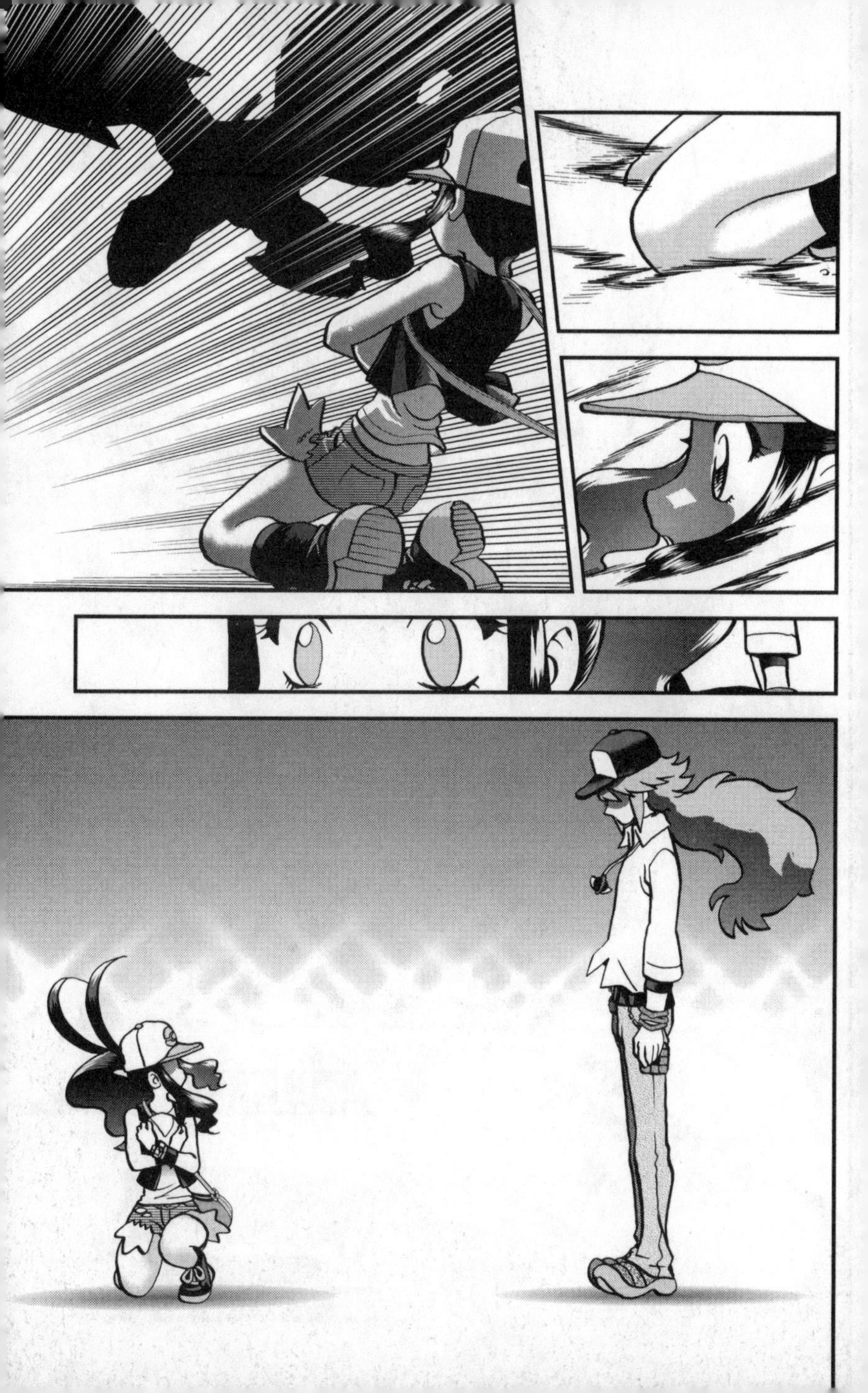

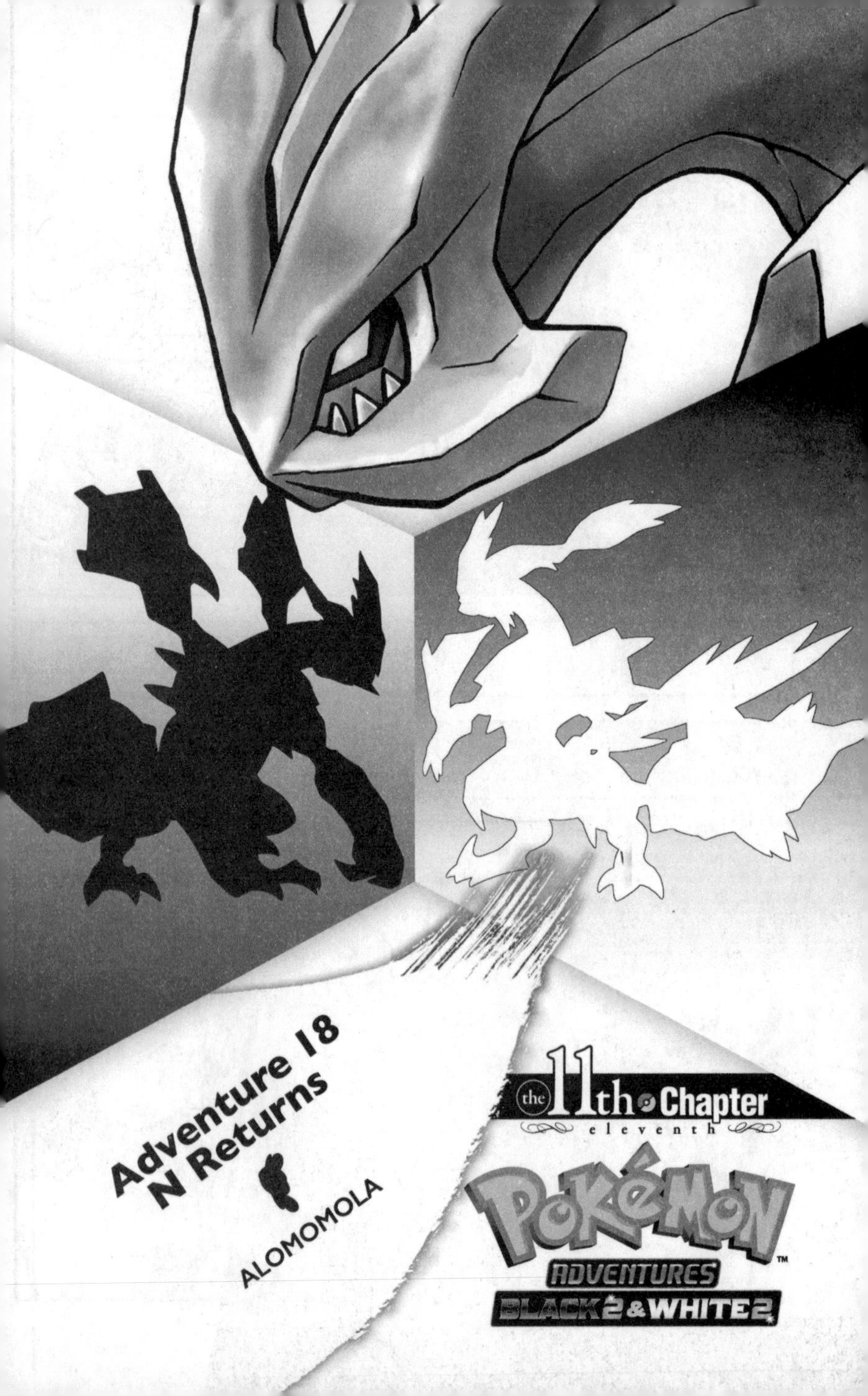
Adventure 18
N Returns
ALOMOMOLA
the 11th Chapter
eleventh
POKÉMON
ADVENTURES
BLACK 2 & WHITE 2

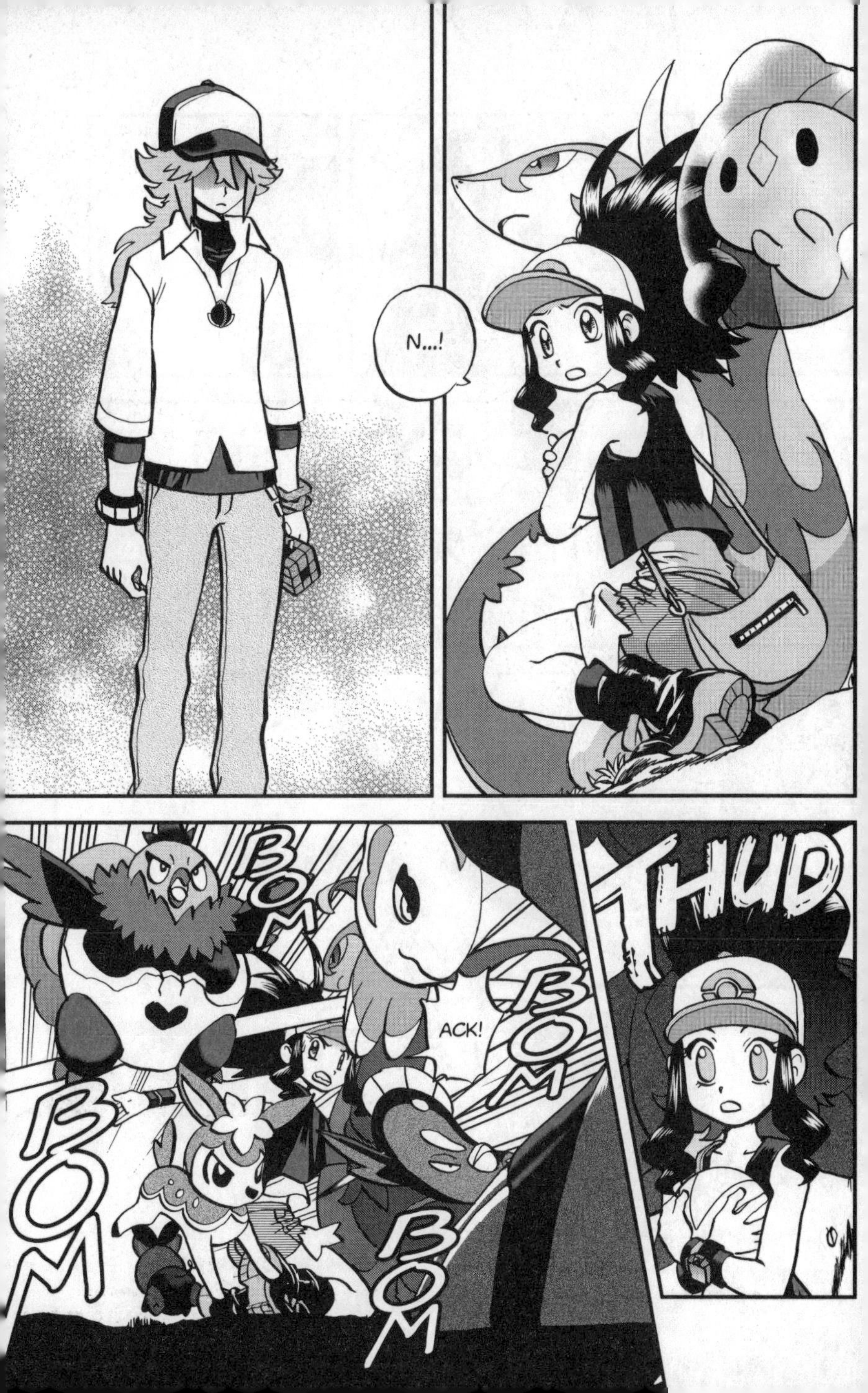
N...!
THUD
BOOM
BOOM
ACK!
BOOM
BOOM

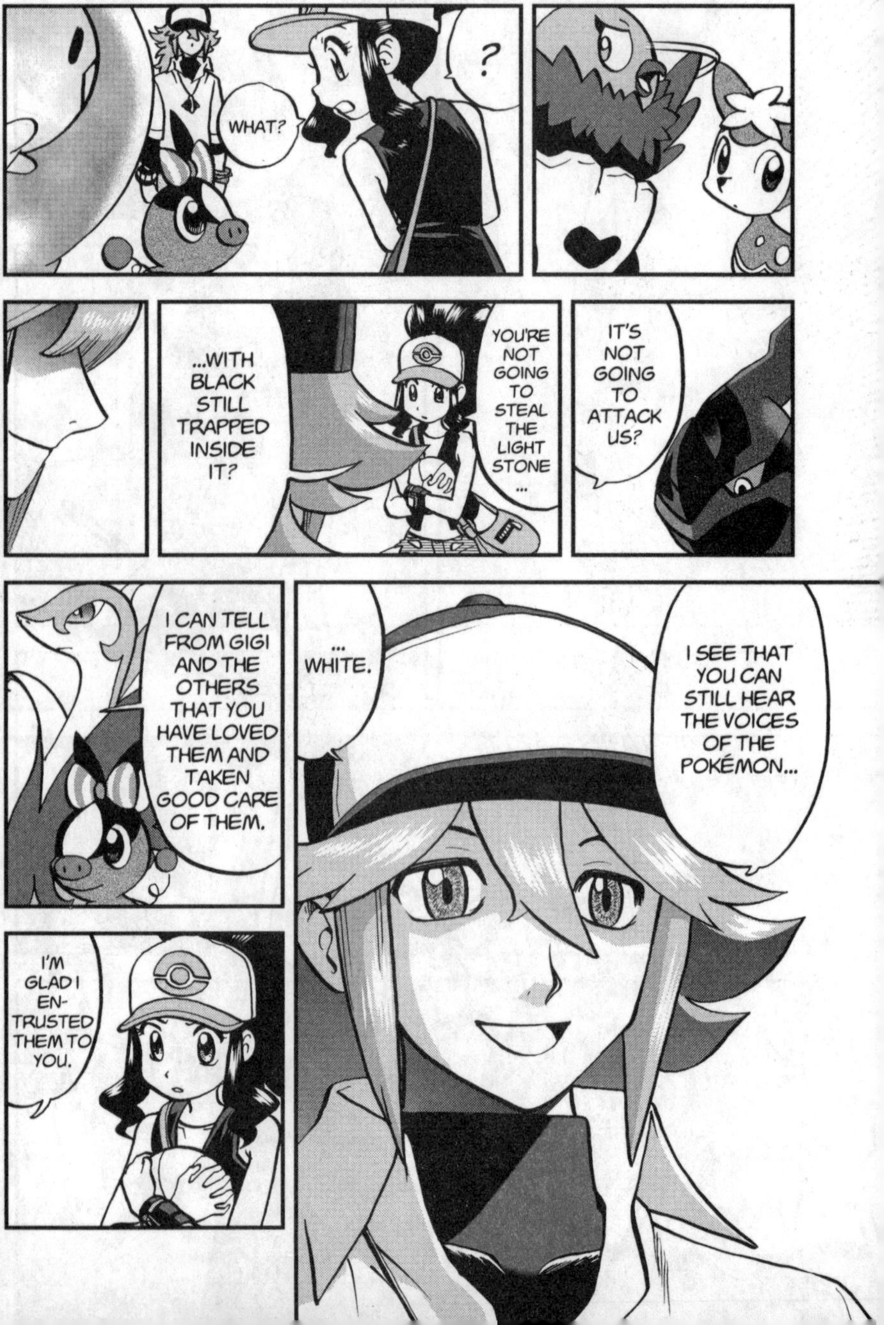
?
WHAT?
IT'S NOT GOING TO ATTACK US?
YOU'RE NOT GOING TO STEAL THE LIGHT STONE ...
...WITH BLACK STILL TRAPPED INSIDE IT?
I SEE THAT YOU CAN STILL HEAR THE VOICES OF THE POKÉMON...
... WHITE.
I CAN TELL FROM GIGI AND THE OTHERS THAT YOU HAVE LOVED THEM AND TAKEN GOOD CARE OF THEM.
I'M GLAD I EN-TRUSTED THEM TO YOU.

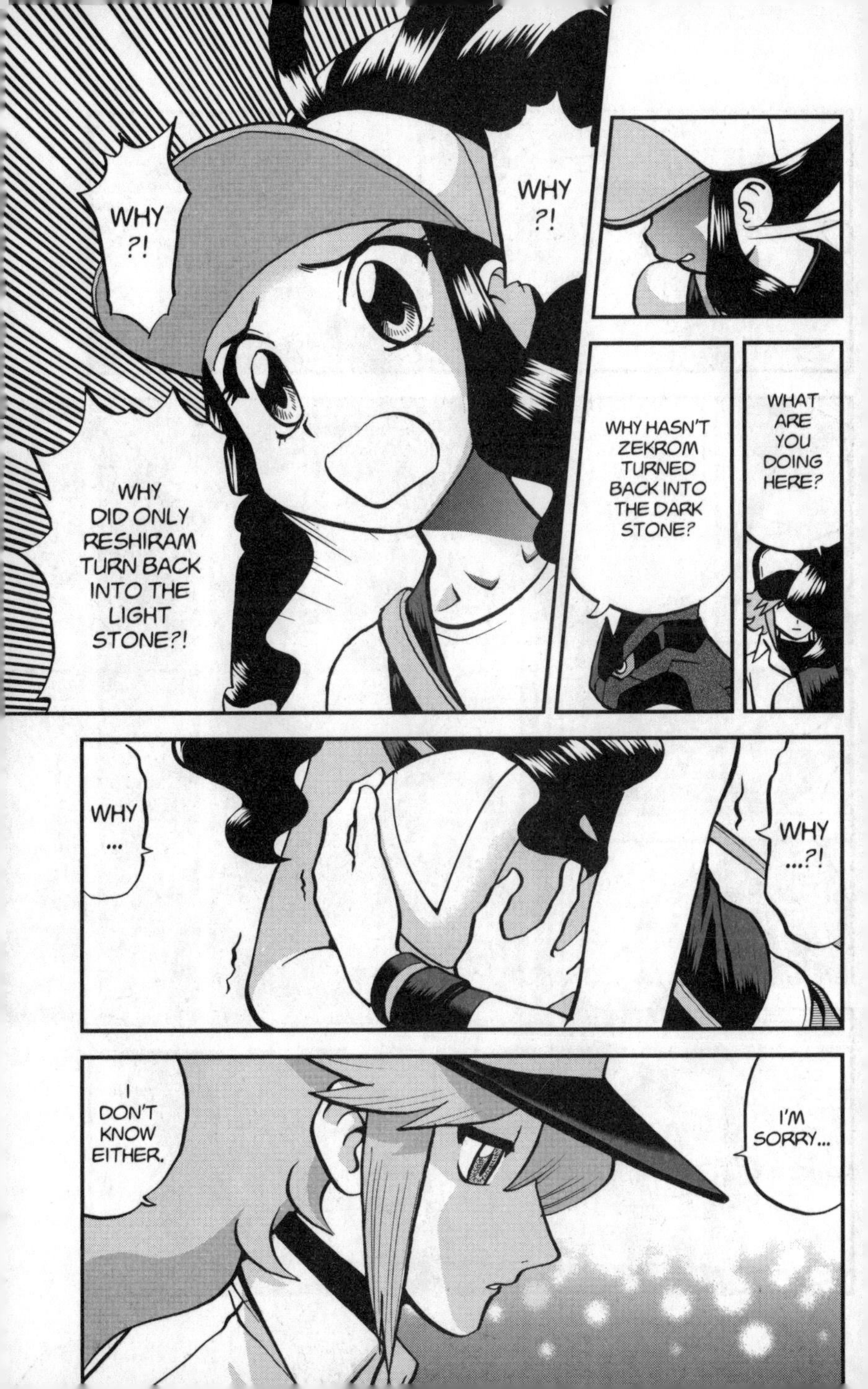
WHY ?!
WHY ?!
WHY DID ONLY RESHIRAM TURN BACK INTO THE LIGHT STONE?!
WHAT ARE YOU DOING HERE?
WHY HASN'T ZEKROM TURNED BACK INTO THE DARK STONE?
WHY ...?!
WHY ...
I'M SORRY...
I DON'T KNOW EITHER.

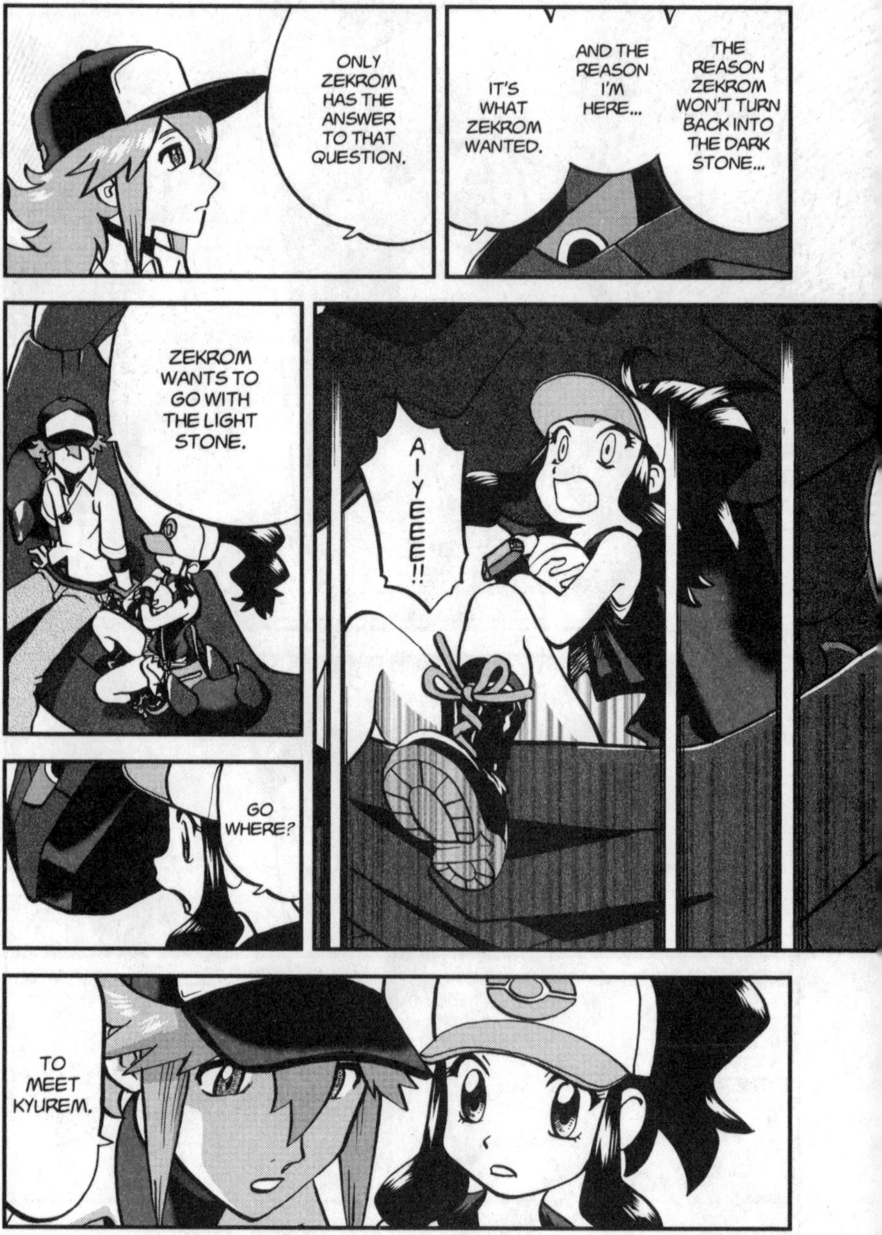

THE REASON ZEKROM WON'T TURN BACK INTO THE DARK STONE...
AND THE REASON I'M HERE...
IT'S WHAT ZEKROM WANTED.
ONLY ZEKROM HAS THE ANSWER TO THAT QUESTION.
AIYEEE!!
ZEKROM WANTS TO GO WITH THE LIGHT STONE.
GO WHERE?
TO MEET KYUREM.

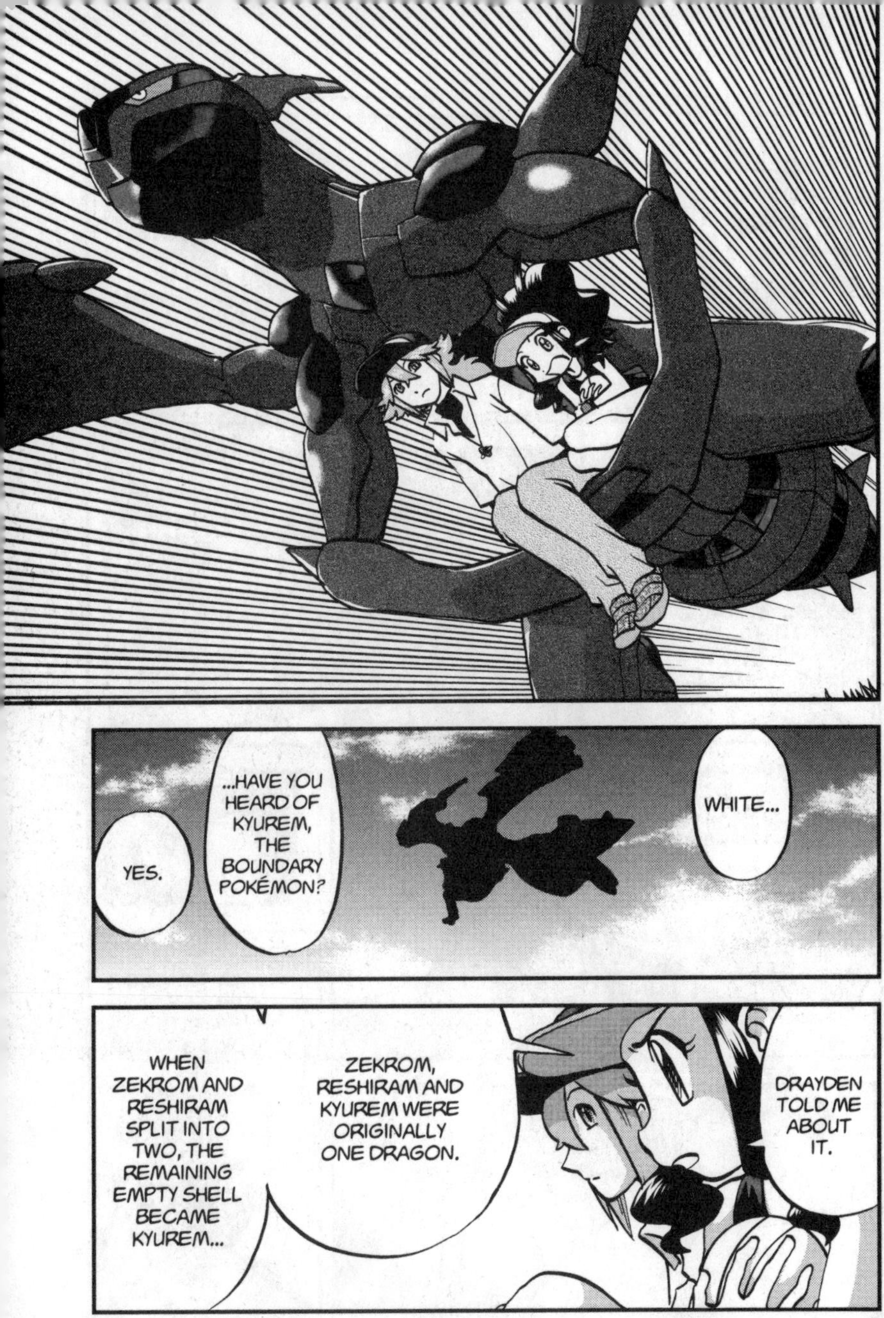
WHITE...
...HAVE YOU HEARD OF KYUREM, THE BOUNDARY POKÉMON?
YES.
DRAYDEN TOLD ME ABOUT IT.
ZEKROM, RESHIRAM AND KYUREM WERE ORIGINALLY ONE DRAGON.
WHEN ZEKROM AND RESHIRAM SPLIT INTO TWO, THE REMAINING EMPTY SHELL BECAME KYUREM...

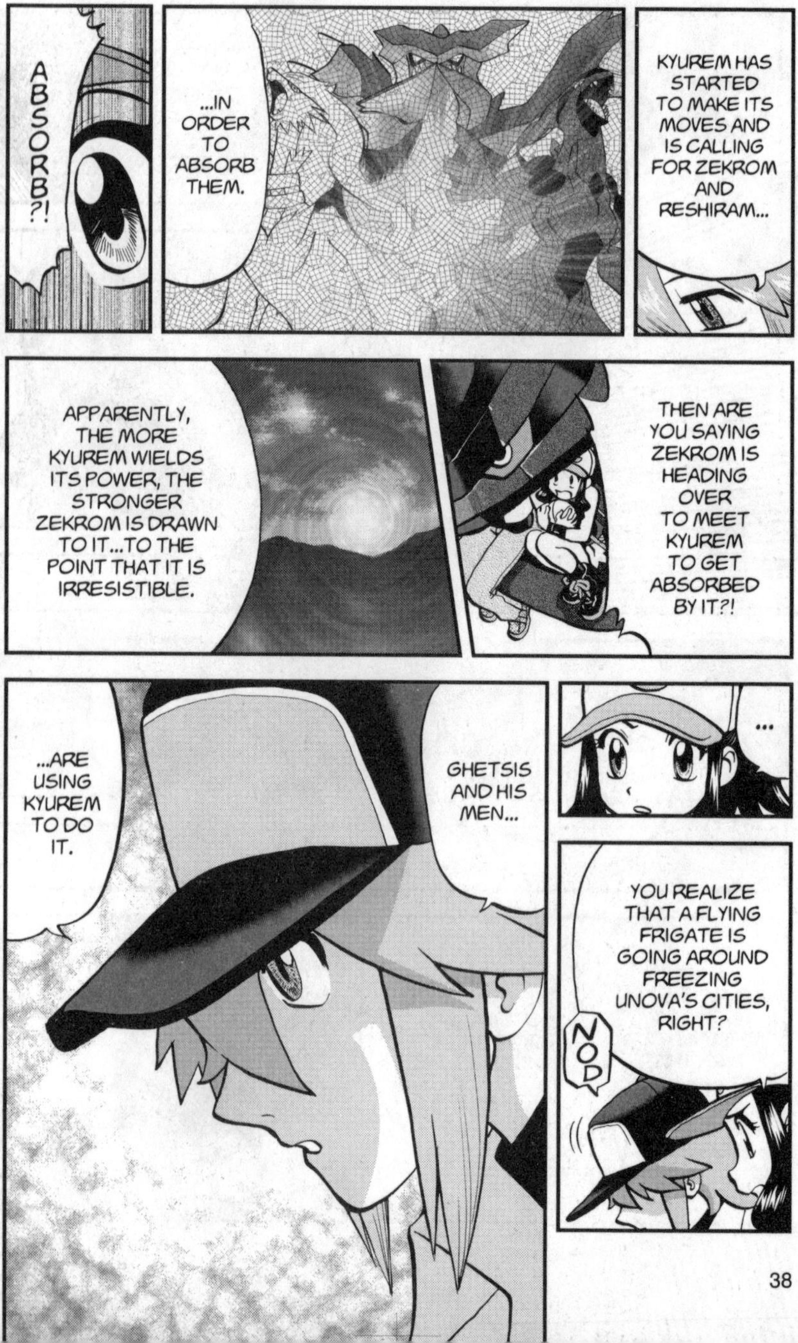
KYUREM HAS STARTED TO MAKE ITS MOVES AND IS CALLING FOR ZEKROM AND RESHIRAM...
...IN ORDER TO ABSORB THEM.
ABSORB?!
THEN ARE YOU SAYING ZEKROM IS HEADING OVER TO MEET KYUREM TO GET ABSORBED BY IT?!
APPARENTLY, THE MORE KYUREM WIELDS ITS POWER, THE STRONGER ZEKROM IS DRAWN TO IT...TO THE POINT THAT IT IS IRRESISTIBLE.
...
YOU REALIZE THAT A FLYING FRIGATE IS GOING AROUND FREEZING UNOVA'S CITIES, RIGHT?
NOD
GHETSIS AND HIS MEN...
...ARE USING KYUREM TO DO IT.

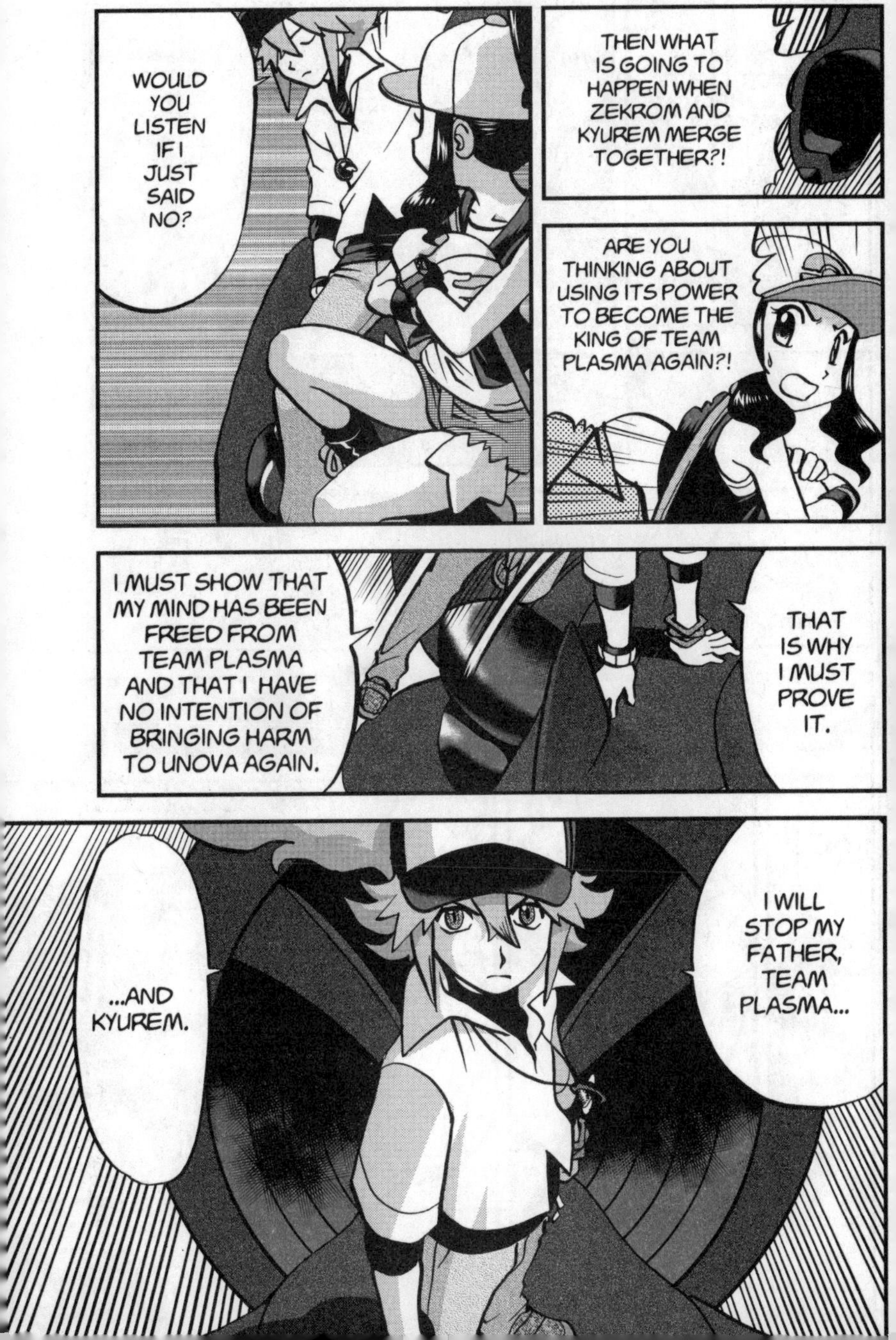
THEN WHAT IS GOING TO HAPPEN WHEN ZEKROM AND KYUREM MERGE TOGETHER?!
ARE YOU THINKING ABOUT USING ITS POWER TO BECOME THE KING OF TEAM PLASMA AGAIN?!
WOULD YOU LISTEN IF I JUST SAID NO?
THAT IS WHY I MUST PROVE IT.
I MUST SHOW THAT MY MIND HAS BEEN FREED FROM TEAM PLASMA AND THAT I HAVE NO INTENTION OF BRINGING HARM TO UNOVA AGAIN.
I WILL STOP MY FATHER, TEAM PLASMA...
...AND KYUREM.

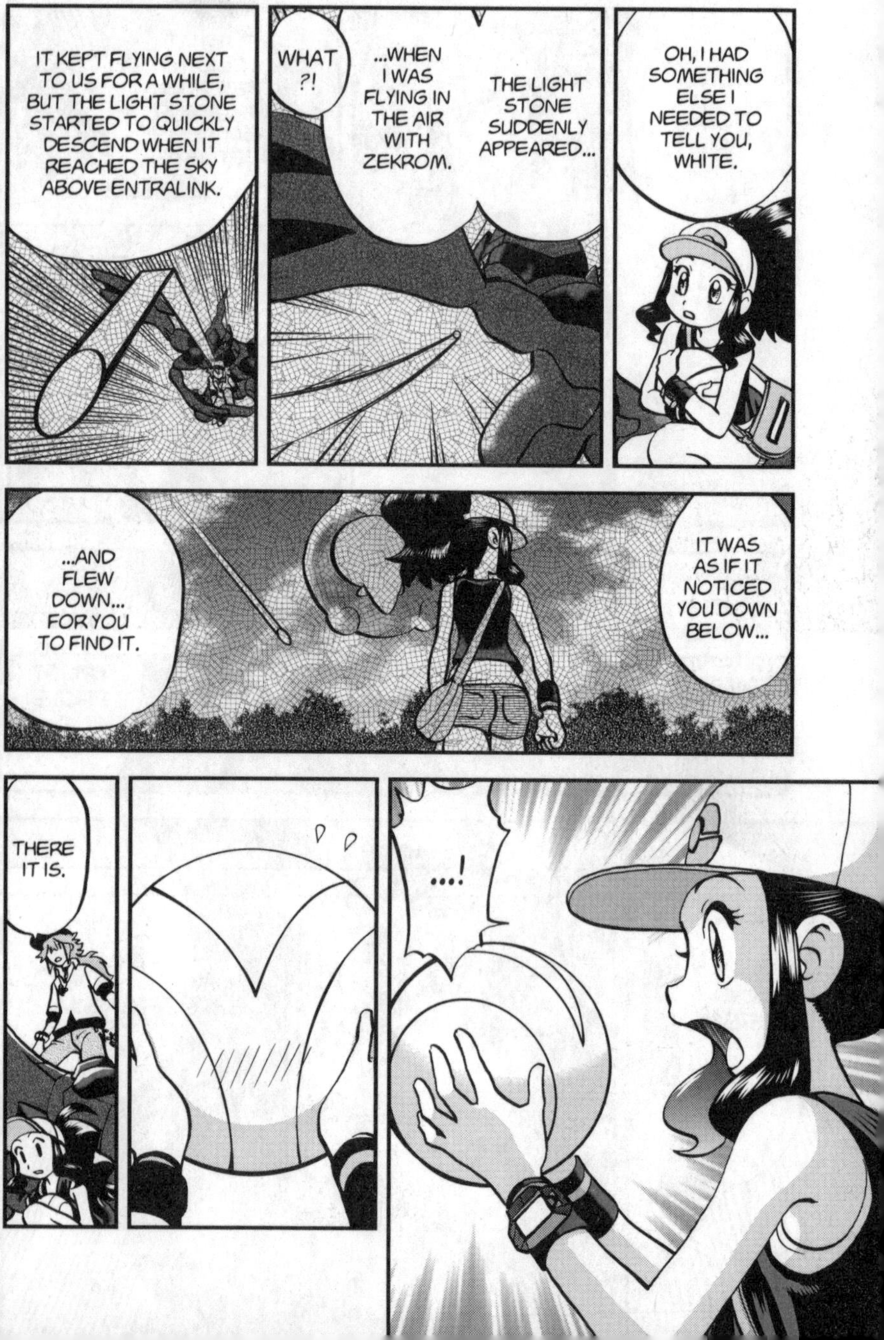
OH, I HAD SOMETHING ELSE I NEEDED TO TELL YOU, WHITE.
THE LIGHT STONE SUDDENLY APPEARED...
...WHEN I WAS FLYING IN THE AIR WITH ZEKROM.
WHAT?!
IT KEPT FLYING NEXT TO US FOR A WHILE, BUT THE LIGHT STONE STARTED TO QUICKLY DESCEND WHEN IT REACHED THE SKY ABOVE ENTRALINK.
IT WAS AS IF IT NOTICED YOU DOWN BELOW...
...AND FLEW DOWN... FOR YOU TO FIND IT.
...!
THERE IT IS.

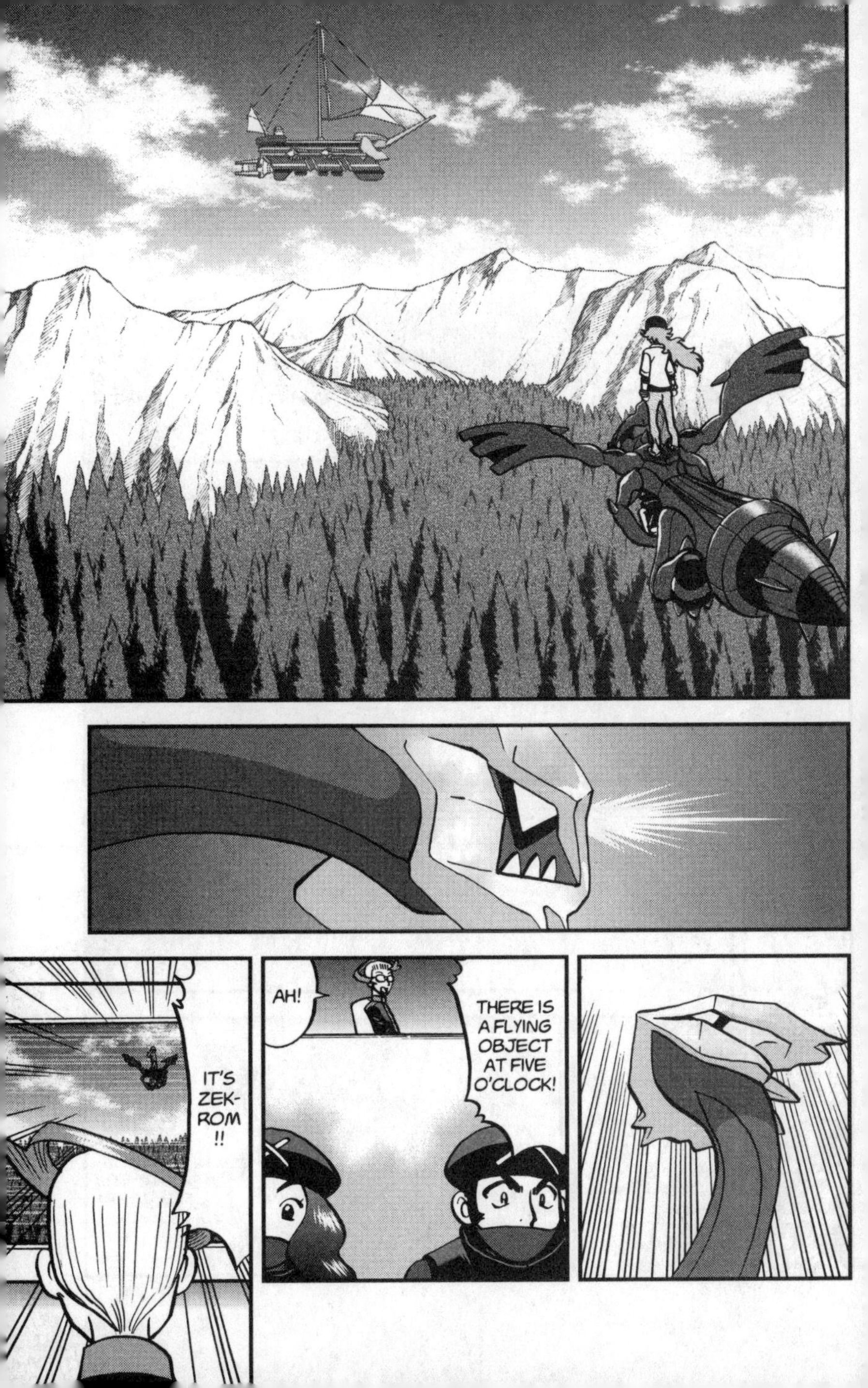
THERE IS A FLYING OBJECT AT FIVE O'CLOCK!
AH!
IT'S ZEK-ROM!!

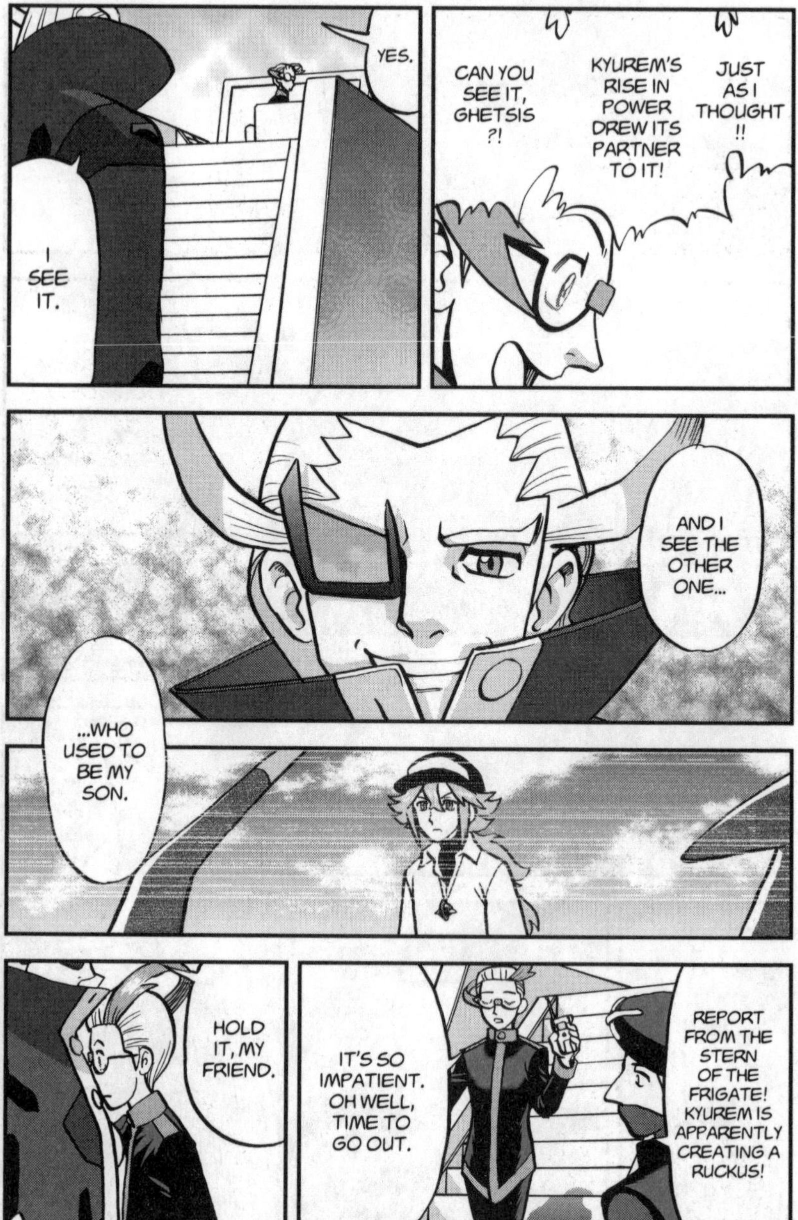
JUST AS I THOUGHT!!
KYUREM'S RISE IN POWER DREW ITS PARTNER TO IT!
CAN YOU SEE IT, GHETSIS?!
YES.
I SEE IT.
AND I SEE THE OTHER ONE...
...WHO USED TO BE MY SON.
REPORT FROM THE STERN OF THE FRIGATE! KYUREM IS APPARENTLY CREATING A RUCKUS!
IT'S SO IMPATIENT. OH WELL, TIME TO GO OUT.
HOLD IT, MY FRIEND.

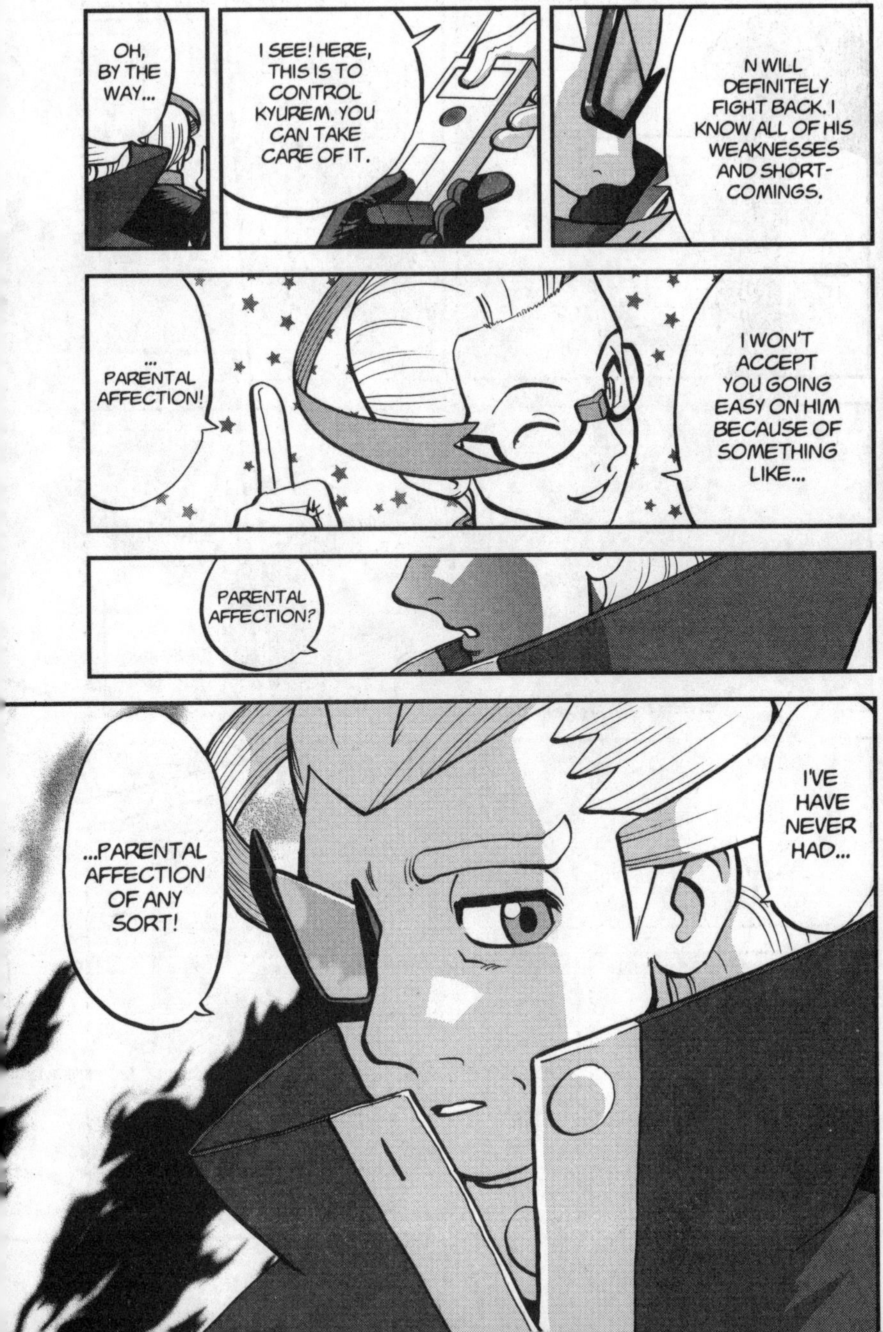
N WILL DEFINITELY FIGHT BACK. I KNOW ALL OF HIS WEAKNESSES AND SHORT-COMINGS.
I SEE! HERE, THIS IS TO CONTROL KYUREM. YOU CAN TAKE CARE OF IT.
OH, BY THE WAY...
I WON'T ACCEPT YOU GOING EASY ON HIM BECAUSE OF SOMETHING LIKE...
...PARENTAL AFFECTION!
PARENTAL AFFECTION?
I'VE HAVE NEVER HAD...
...PARENTAL AFFECTION OF ANY SORT!

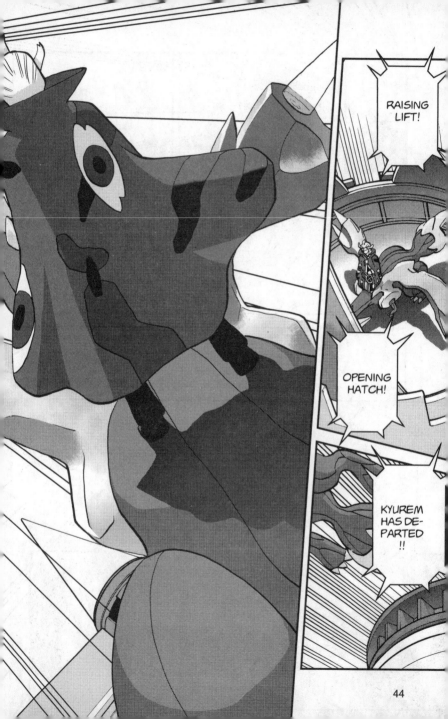

RAISING LIFT!

OPENING HATCH!

KYUREM HAS DE-PARTED !!

44

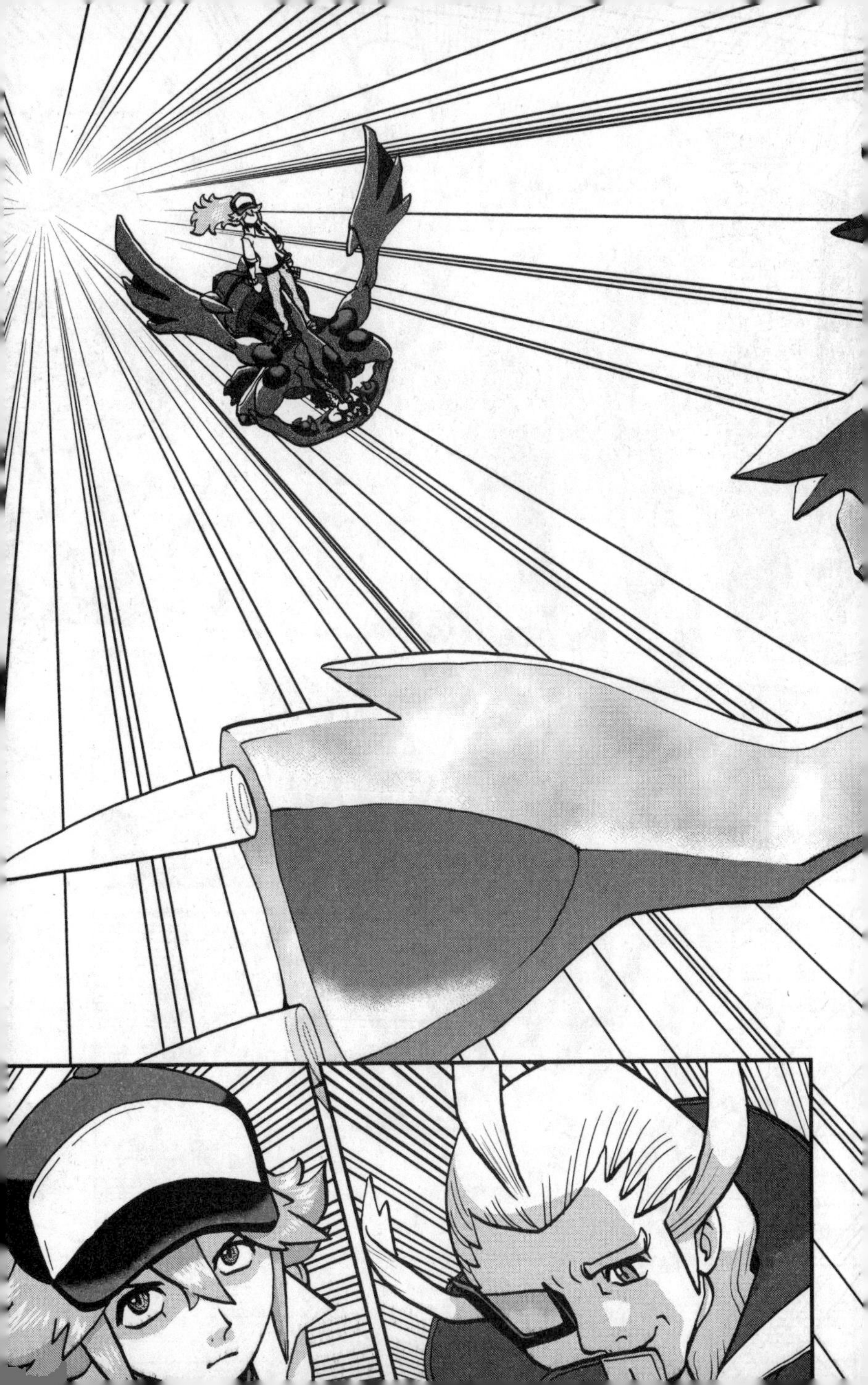

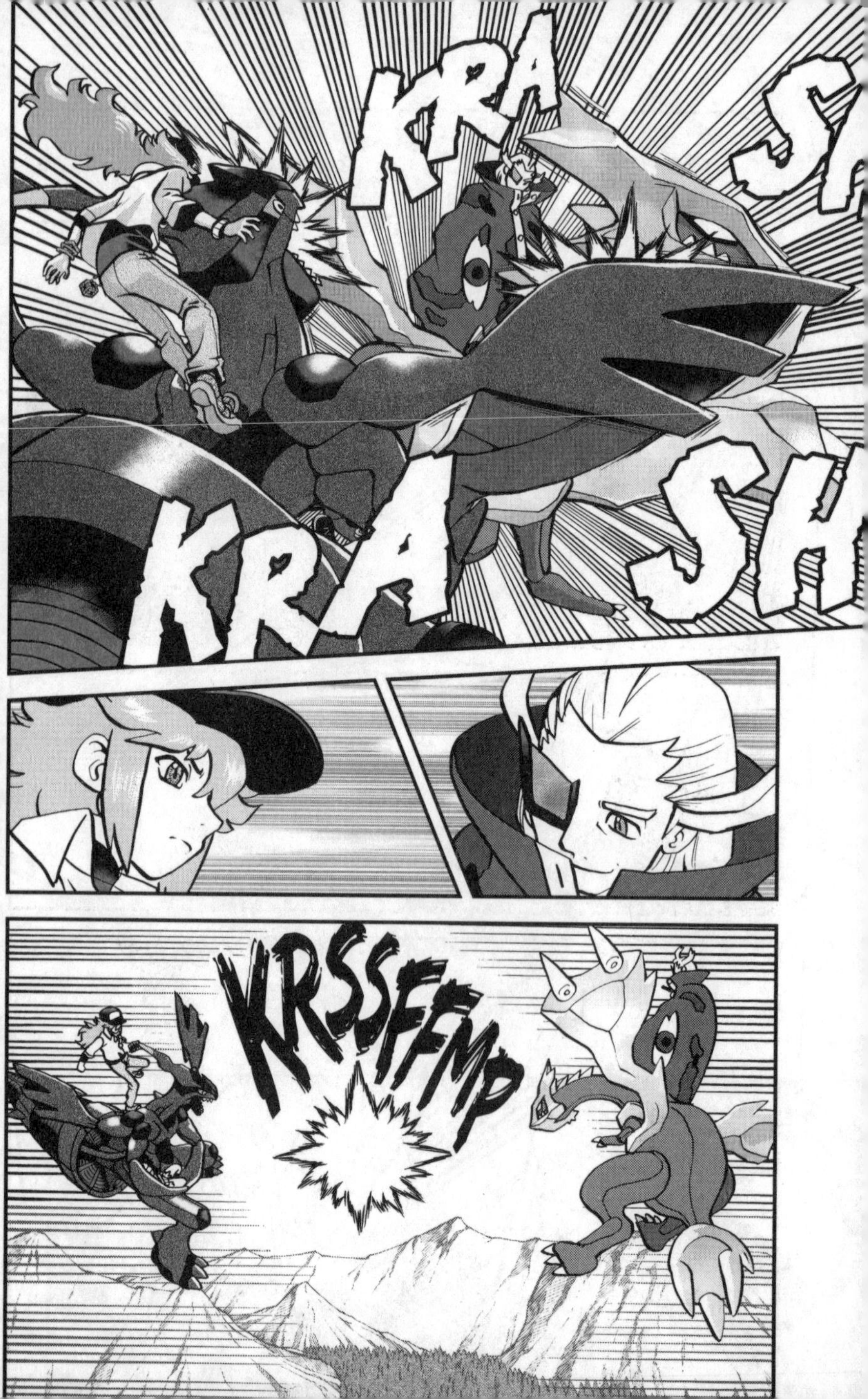
KRA
S
KRA
SH
KRSSFFMP

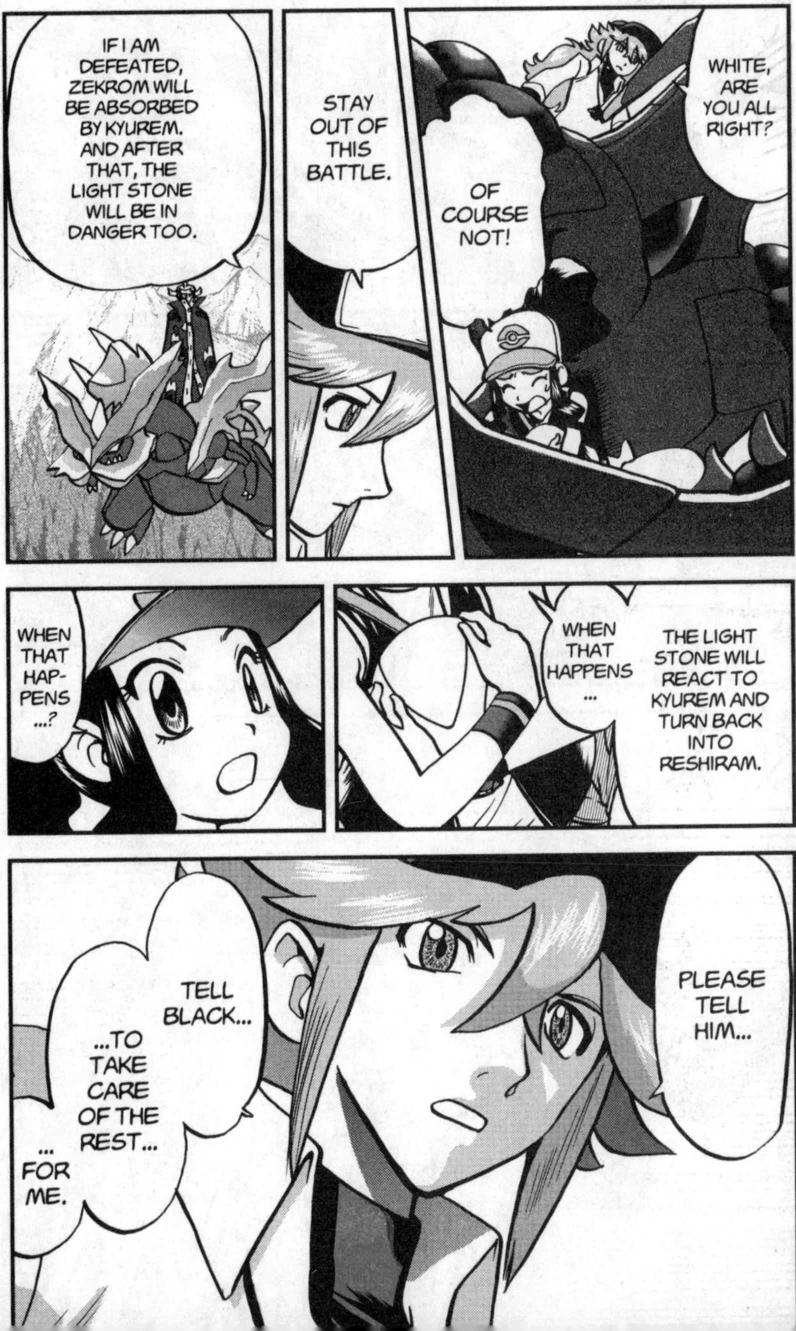
WHITE, ARE YOU ALL RIGHT?
OF COURSE NOT!
STAY OUT OF THIS BATTLE.
IF I AM DEFEATED, ZEKROM WILL BE ABSORBED BY KYUREM. AND AFTER THAT, THE LIGHT STONE WILL BE IN DANGER TOO.
WHEN THAT HAPPENS ...
THE LIGHT STONE WILL REACT TO KYUREM AND TURN BACK INTO RESHIRAM.
WHEN THAT HAP-PENS ...?
PLEASE TELL HIM...
TELL BLACK...
...TO TAKE CARE OF THE REST...
... FOR ME.

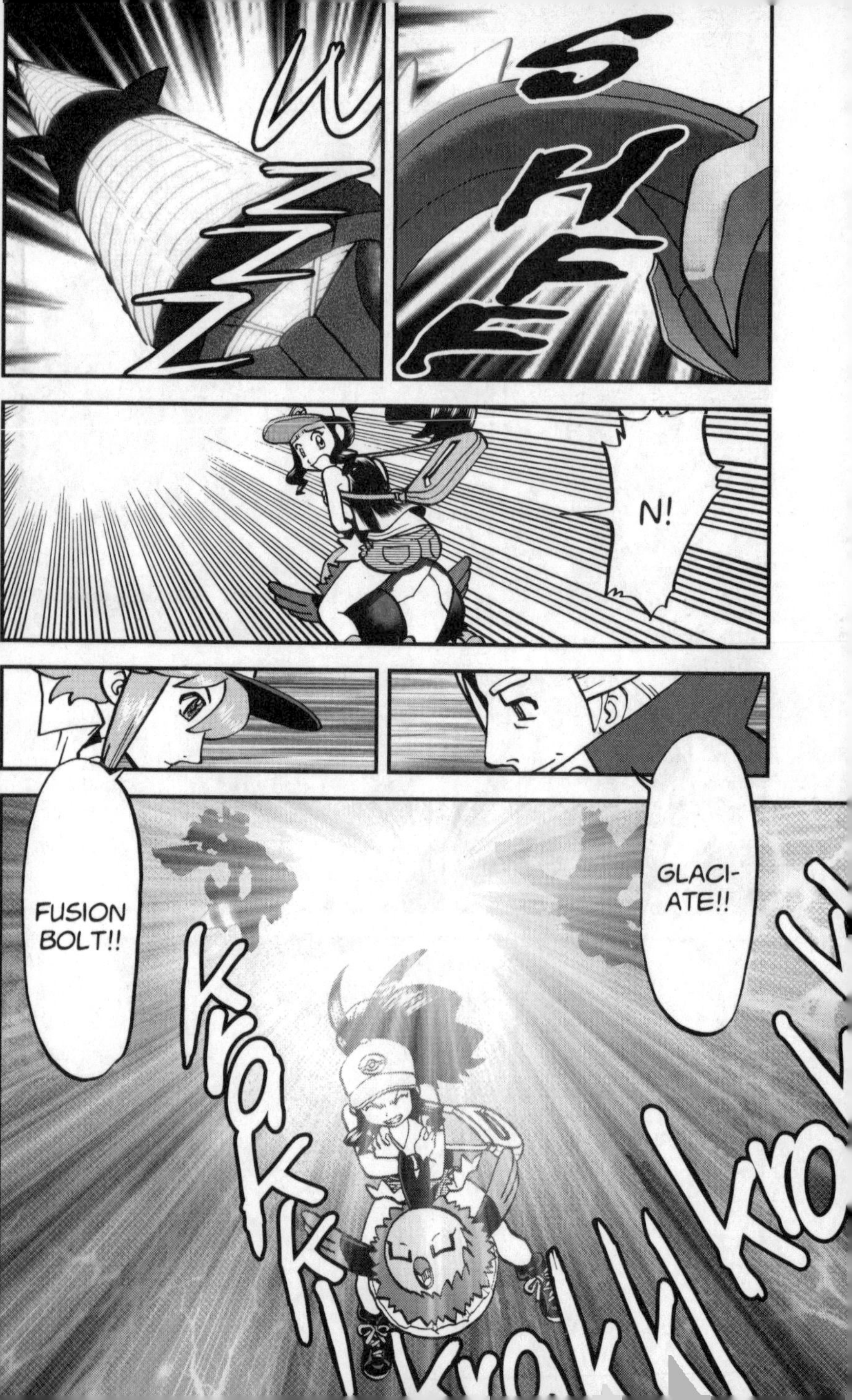

N!
GLACI-
ATE!!
FUSION
BOLT!!

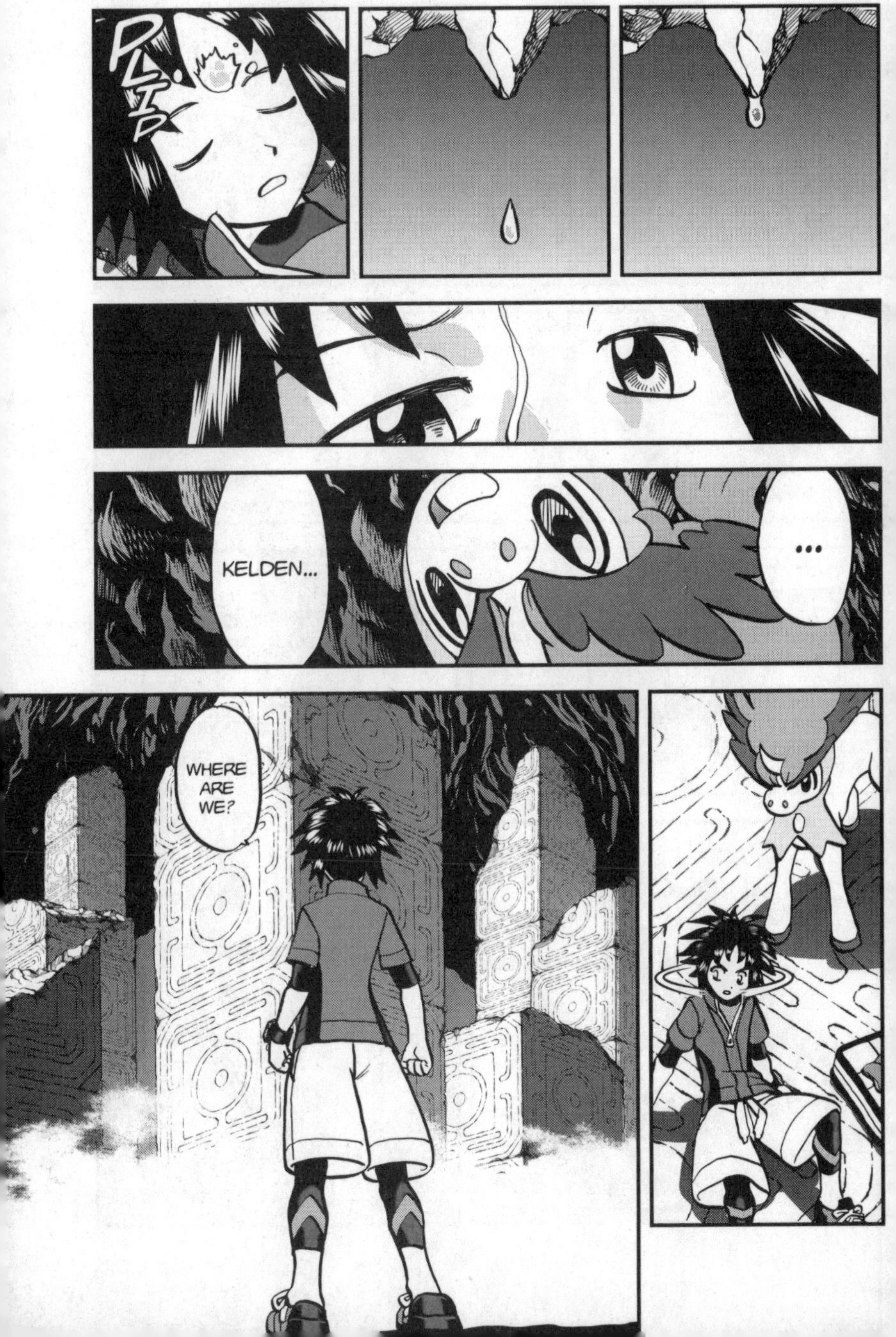
PLIP
...
KELDEN...
WHERE ARE WE?

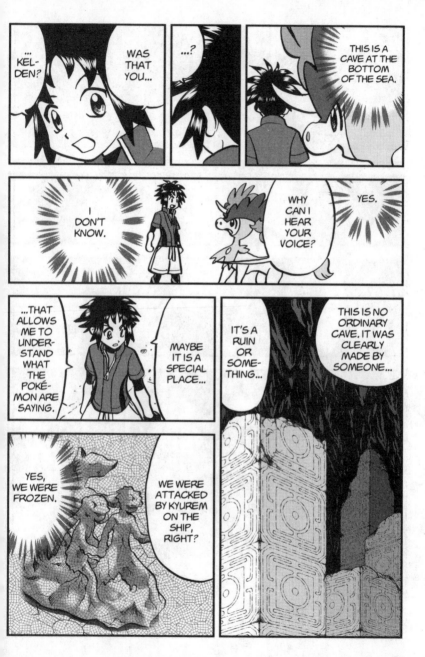

THIS IS A CAVE AT THE BOTTOM OF THE SEA.
...?
WAS THAT YOU...
... KEL-DEN?
YES.
WHY CAN I HEAR YOUR VOICE?
I DON'T KNOW.
THIS IS NO ORDINARY CAVE. IT WAS CLEARLY MADE BY SOMEONE...
IT'S A RUIN OR SOME-THING...
MAYBE IT IS A SPECIAL PLACE...
...THAT ALLOWS ME TO UNDER-STAND WHAT THE POKÉ-MON ARE SAYING.
WE WERE ATTACKED BY KYUREM ON THE SHIP, RIGHT?
YES, WE WERE FROZEN.

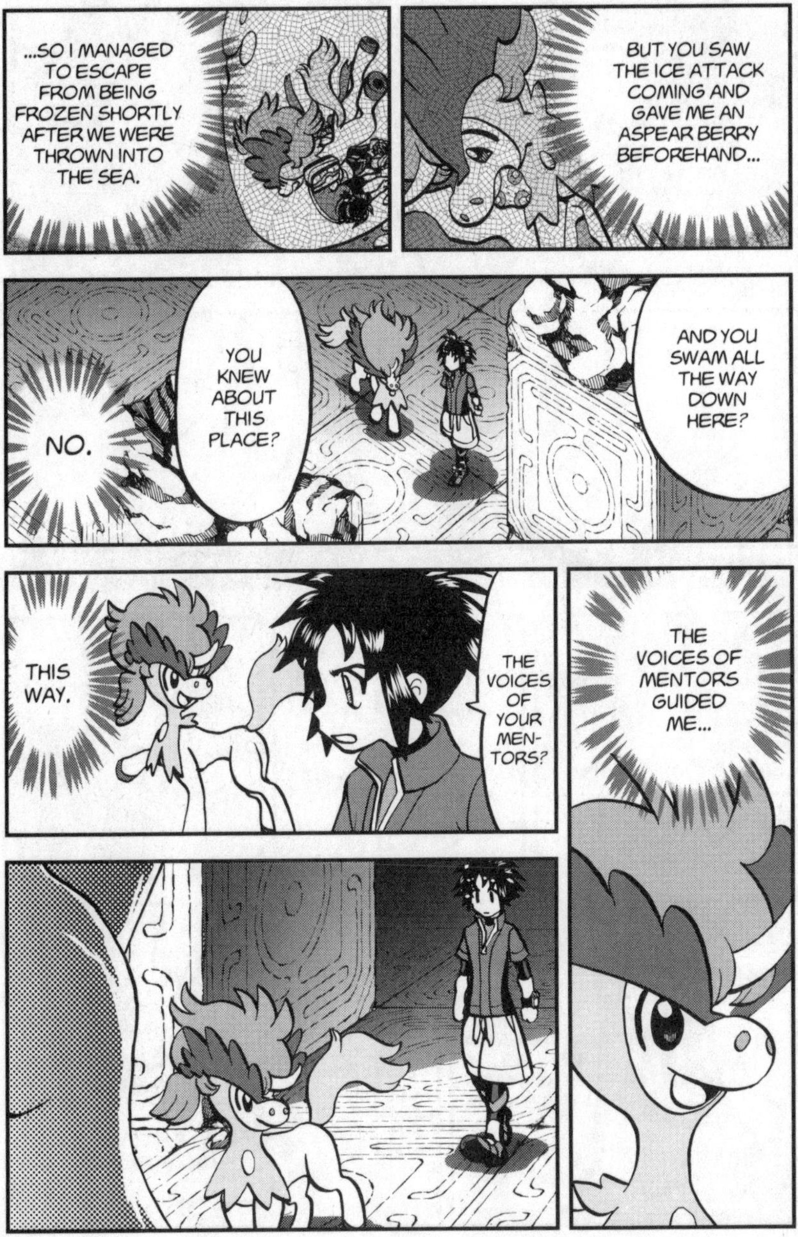
BUT YOU SAW THE ICE ATTACK COMING AND GAVE ME AN ASPEAR BERRY BEFOREHAND...
...SO I MANAGED TO ESCAPE FROM BEING FROZEN SHORTLY AFTER WE WERE THROWN INTO THE SEA.
AND YOU SWAM ALL THE WAY DOWN HERE?
YOU KNEW ABOUT THIS PLACE?
NO.
THE VOICES OF MENTORS GUIDED ME...
THE VOICES OF YOUR MEN-TORS?
THIS WAY.

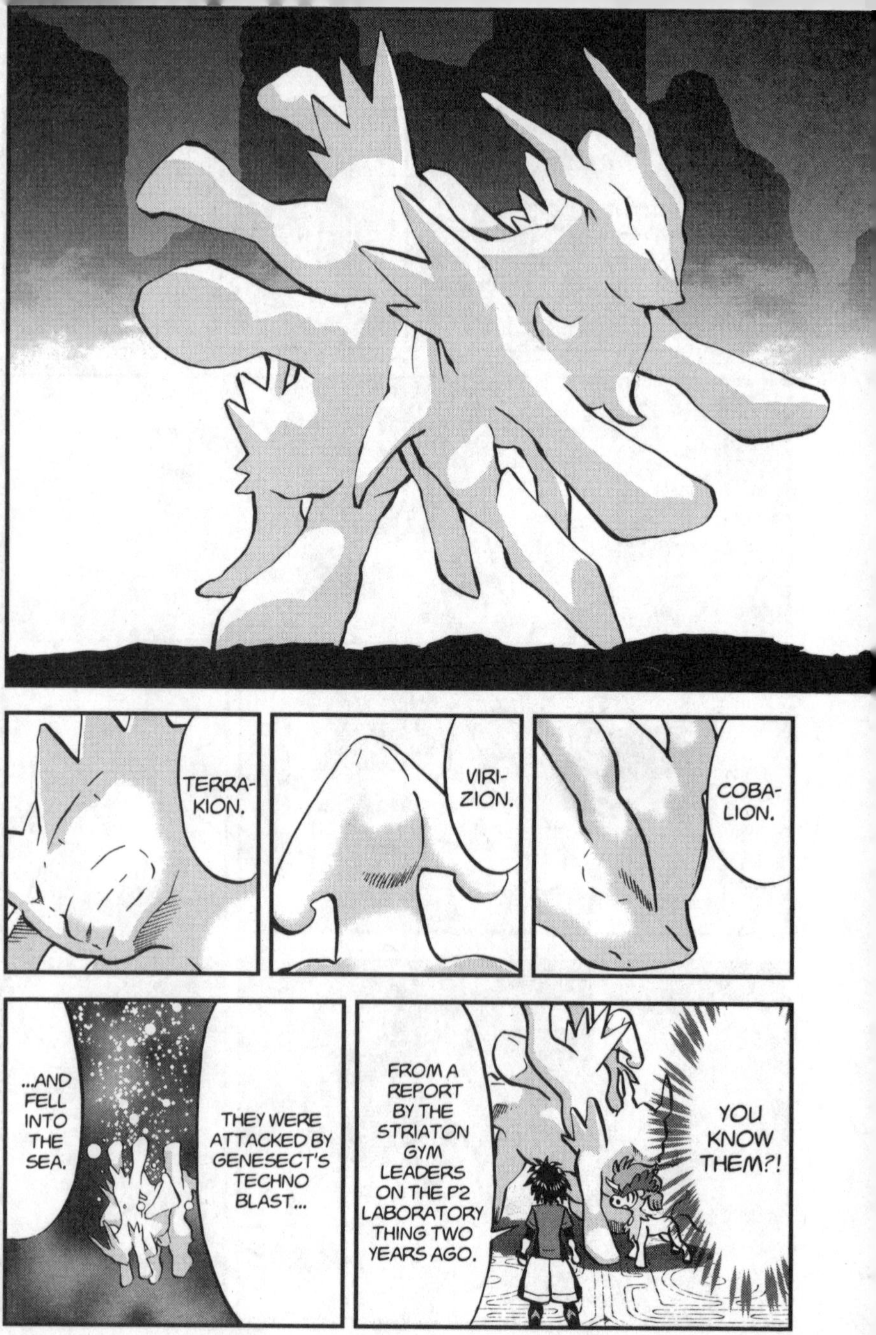
COBA-LION.
VIRI-ZION.
TERRA-KION.
YOU KNOW THEM?!
FROM A REPORT BY THE STRIATON GYM LEADERS ON THE P2 LABORATORY THING TWO YEARS AGO.
THEY WERE ATTACKED BY GENESECT'S TECHNO BLAST...
...AND FELL INTO THE SEA.

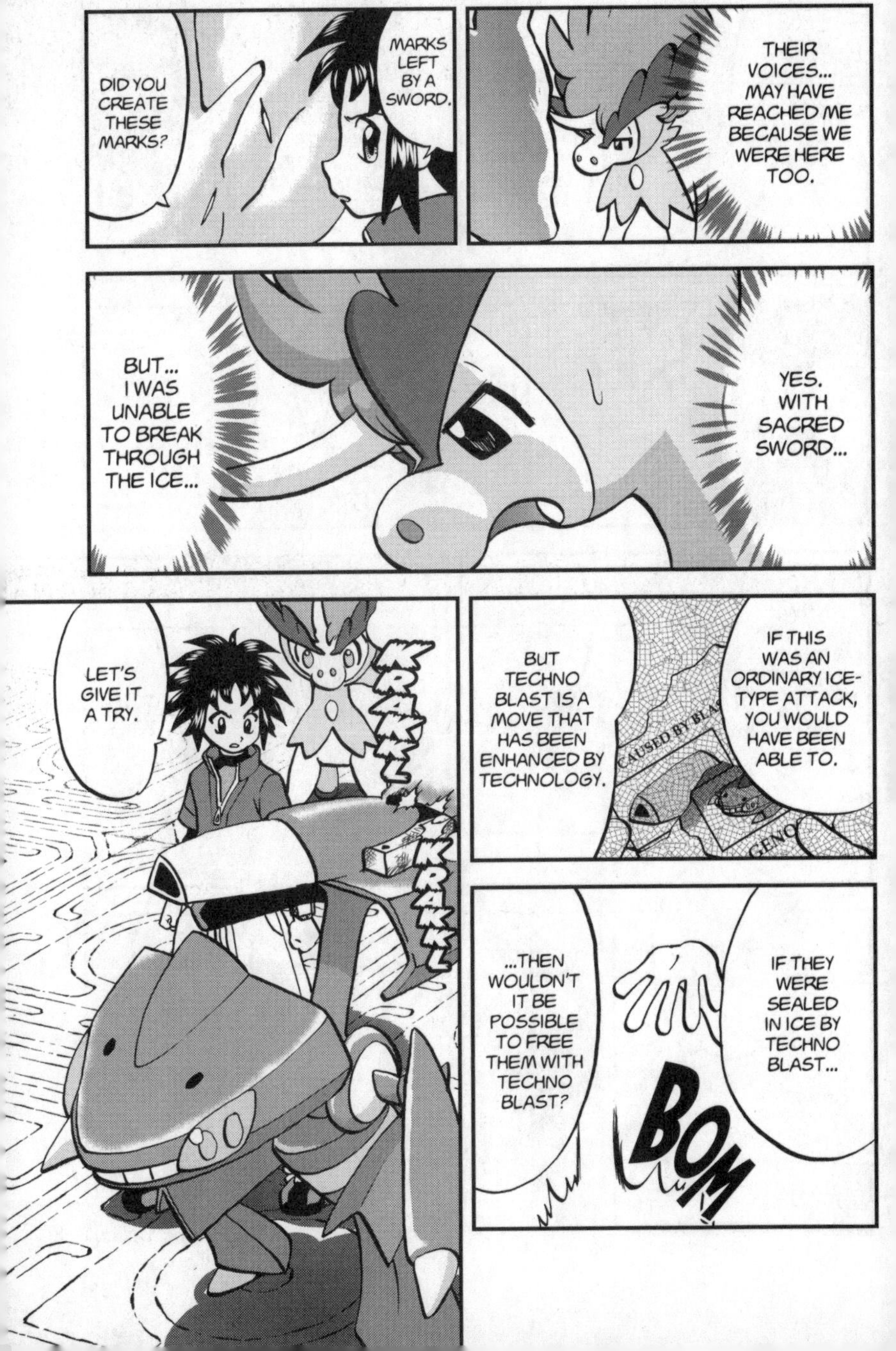
THEIR VOICES... MAY HAVE REACHED ME BECAUSE WE WERE HERE TOO.
MARKS LEFT BY A SWORD.
DID YOU CREATE THESE MARKS?
YES. WITH SACRED SWORD...
BUT... I WAS UNABLE TO BREAK THROUGH THE ICE...
IF THIS WAS AN ORDINARY ICE-TYPE ATTACK, YOU WOULD HAVE BEEN ABLE TO.
BUT TECHNO BLAST IS A MOVE THAT HAS BEEN ENHANCED BY TECHNOLOGY.
IF THEY WERE SEALED IN ICE BY TECHNO BLAST...
...THEN WOULDN'T IT BE POSSIBLE TO FREE THEM WITH TECHNO BLAST?
BOM
LET'S GIVE IT A TRY.
KRAKKL
KRAKKL

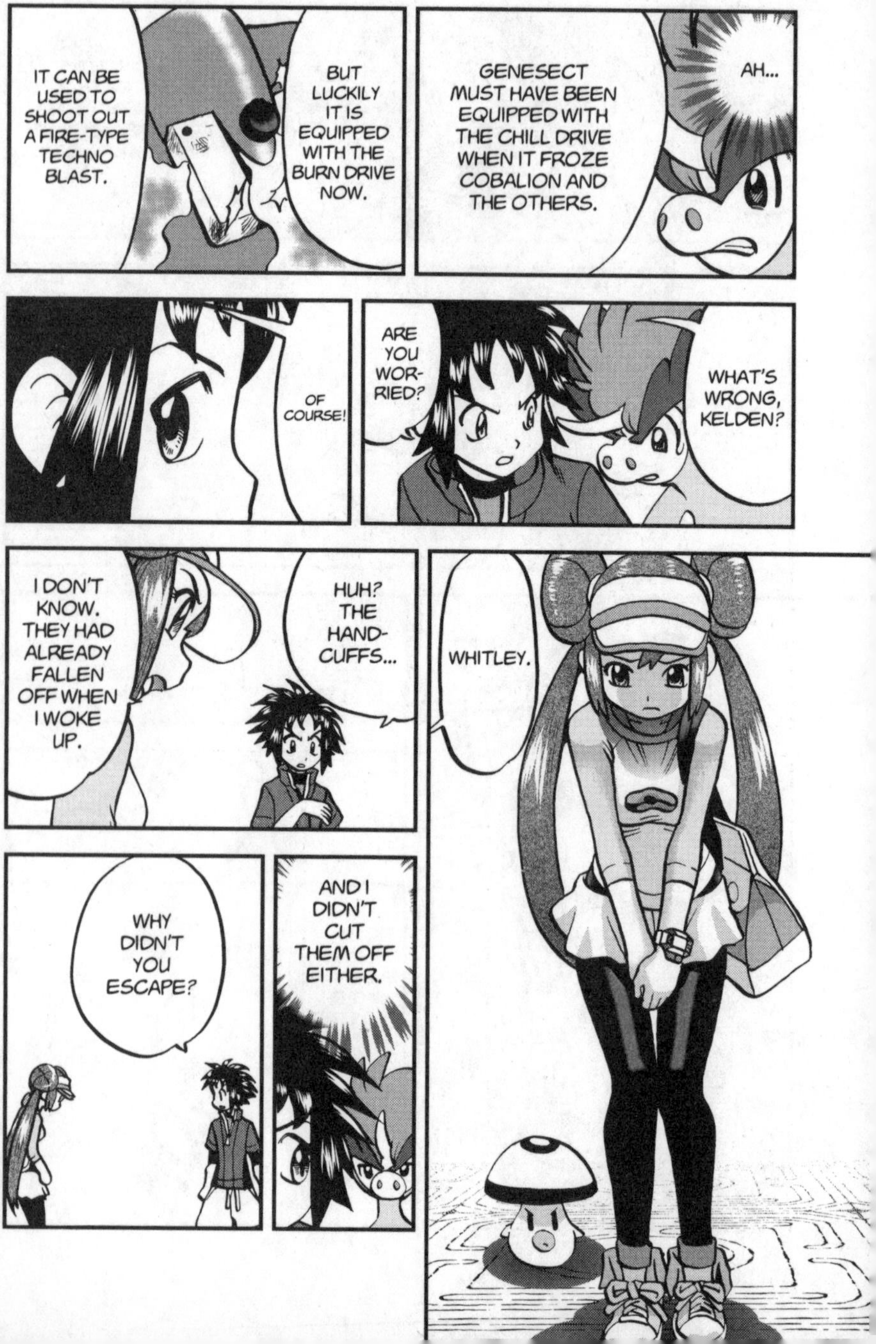
AH...
GENESECT MUST HAVE BEEN EQUIPPED WITH THE CHILL DRIVE WHEN IT FROZE COBALION AND THE OTHERS.
BUT LUCKILY IT IS EQUIPPED WITH THE BURN DRIVE NOW.
IT CAN BE USED TO SHOOT OUT A FIRE-TYPE TECHNO BLAST.
WHAT'S WRONG, KELDEN?
ARE YOU WORRIED?
OF COURSE!
WHITLEY.
HUH? THE HANDCUFFS...
I DON'T KNOW. THEY HAD ALREADY FALLEN OFF WHEN I WOKE UP.
AND I DIDN'T CUT THEM OFF EITHER.
WHY DIDN'T YOU ESCAPE?

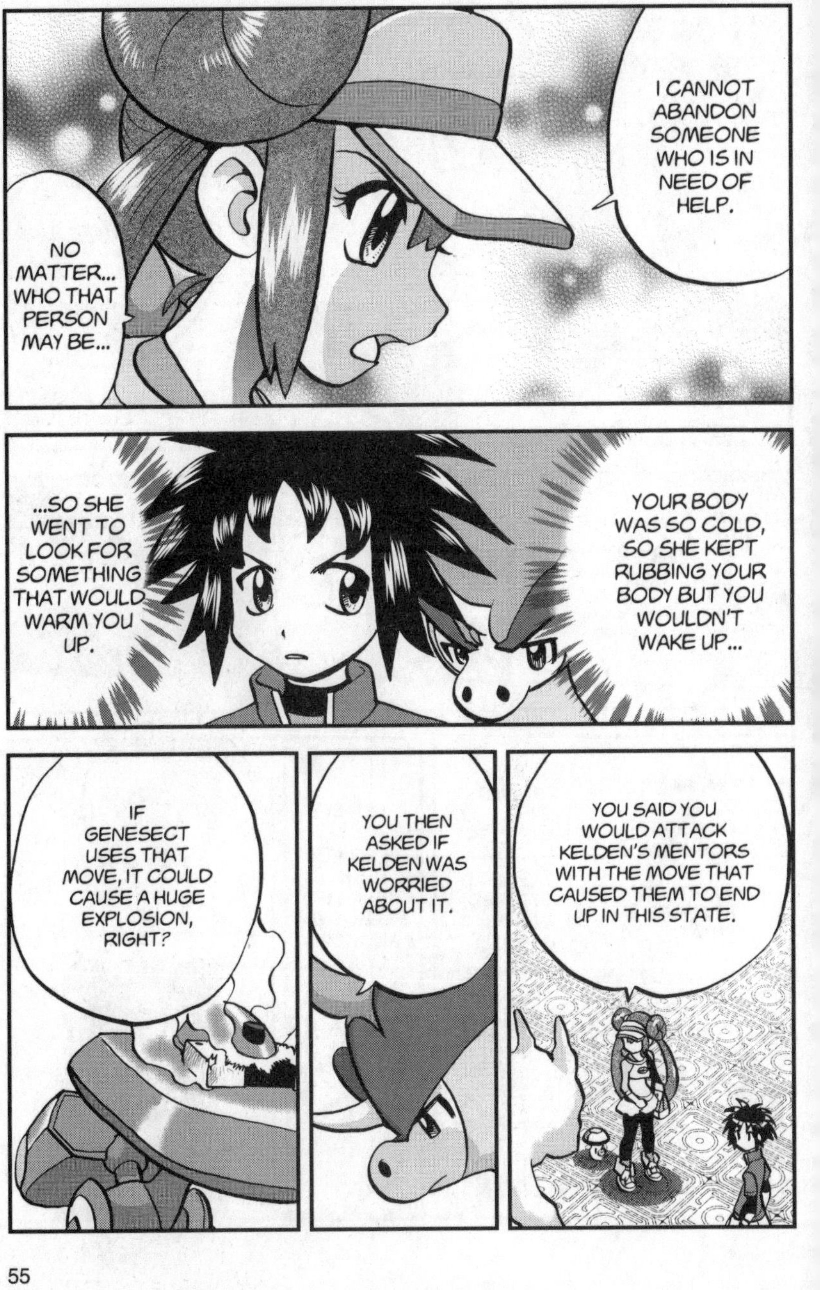
I CANNOT ABANDON SOMEONE WHO IS IN NEED OF HELP.
NO MATTER... WHO THAT PERSON MAY BE...
YOUR BODY WAS SO COLD, SO SHE KEPT RUBBING YOUR BODY BUT YOU WOULDN'T WAKE UP...
...SO SHE WENT TO LOOK FOR SOMETHING THAT WOULD WARM YOU UP.
YOU SAID YOU WOULD ATTACK KELDEN'S MENTORS WITH THE MOVE THAT CAUSED THEM TO END UP IN THIS STATE.
YOU THEN ASKED IF KELDEN WAS WORRIED ABOUT IT.
IF GENESECT USES THAT MOVE, IT COULD CAUSE A HUGE EXPLOSION, RIGHT?

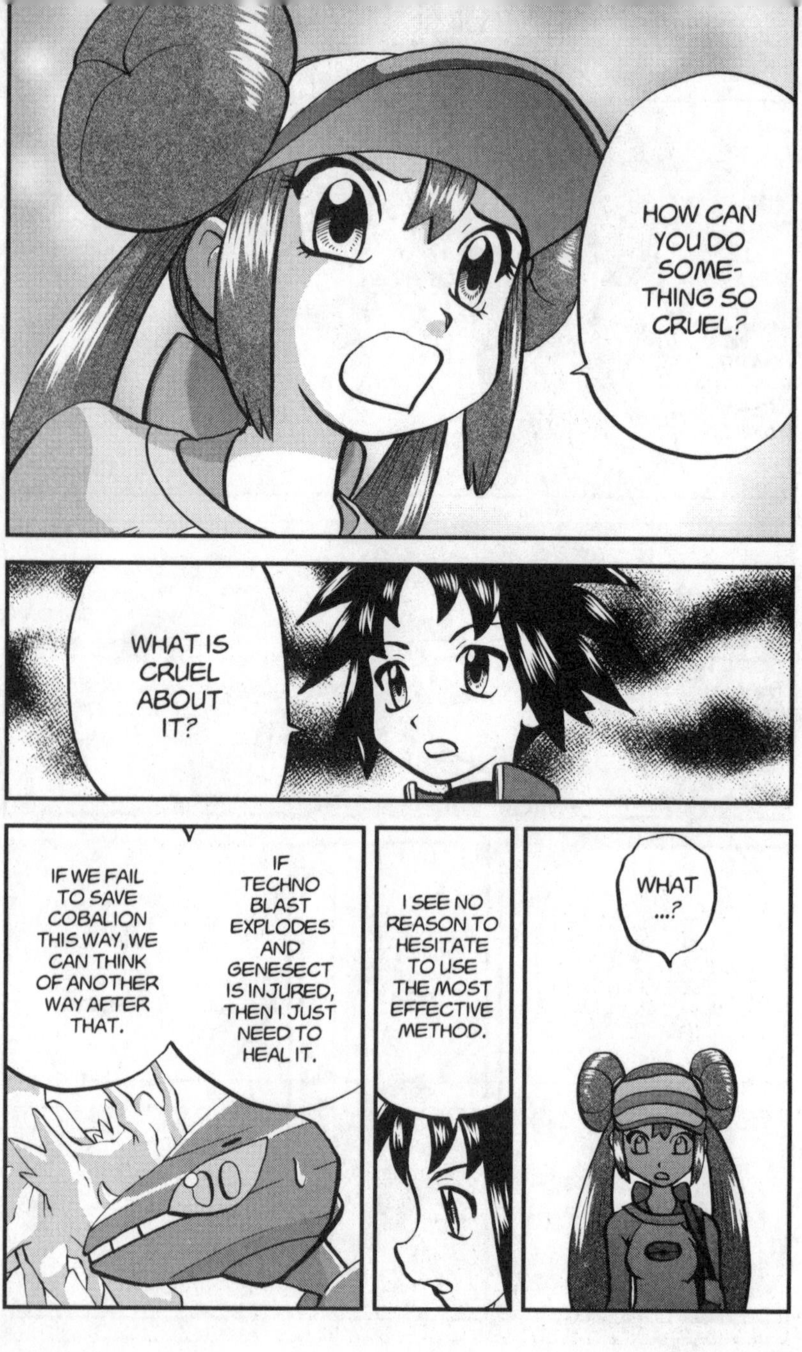
HOW CAN YOU DO SOME-THING SO CRUEL?
WHAT IS CRUEL ABOUT IT?
I SEE NO REASON TO HESITATE TO USE THE MOST EFFECTIVE METHOD.
IF TECHNO BLAST EXPLODES AND GENESECT IS INJURED, THEN I JUST NEED TO HEAL IT.
IF WE FAIL TO SAVE COBALION THIS WAY, WE CAN THINK OF ANOTHER WAY AFTER THAT.
WHAT ...?

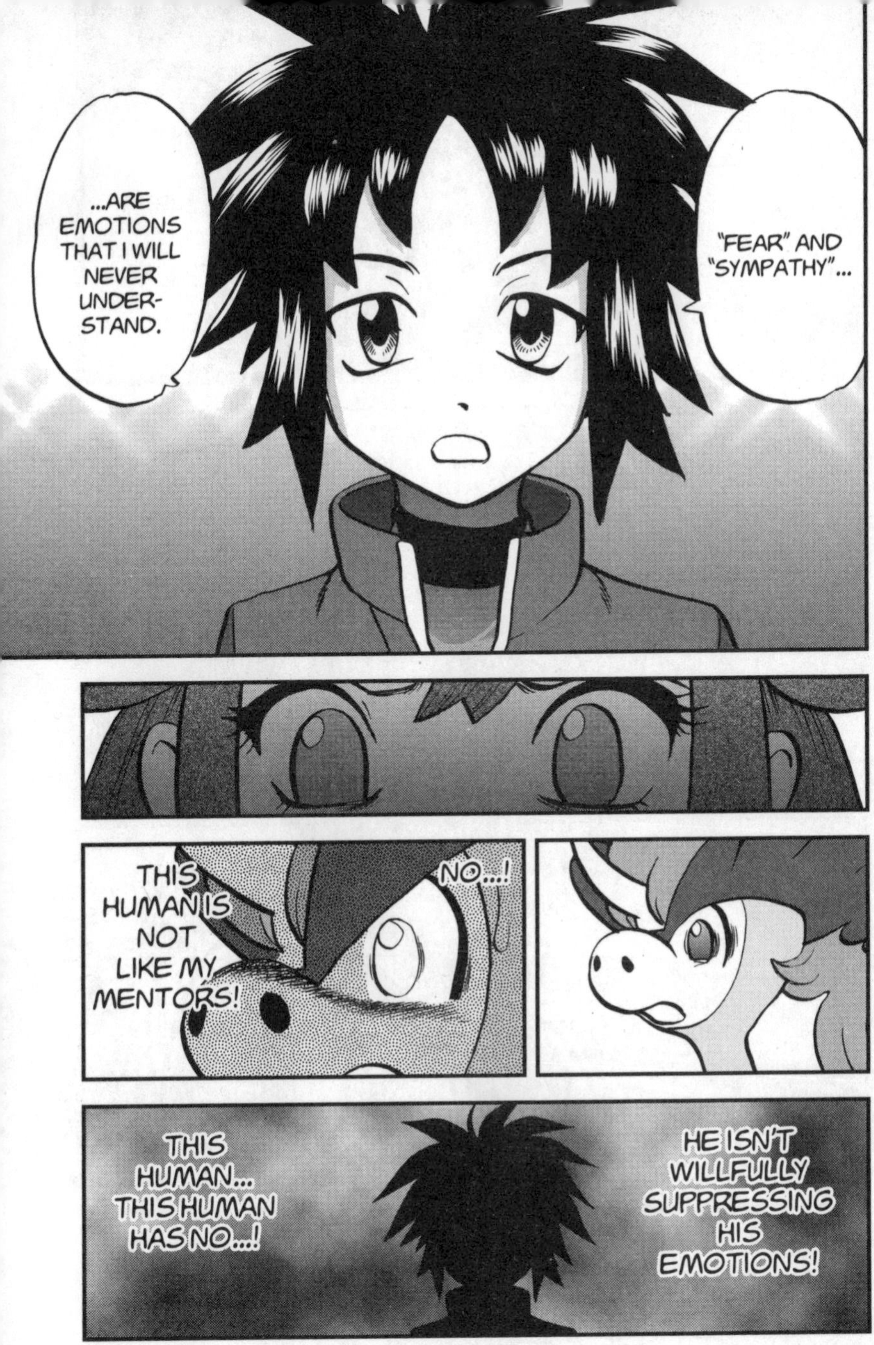
"FEAR" AND "SYMPATHY"...
...ARE EMOTIONS THAT I WILL NEVER UNDER-STAND.
NO...!
THIS HUMAN IS NOT LIKE MY MENTORS!
HE ISN'T WILLFULLY SUPPRESSING HIS EMOTIONS!
THIS HUMAN... THIS HUMAN HAS NO...!

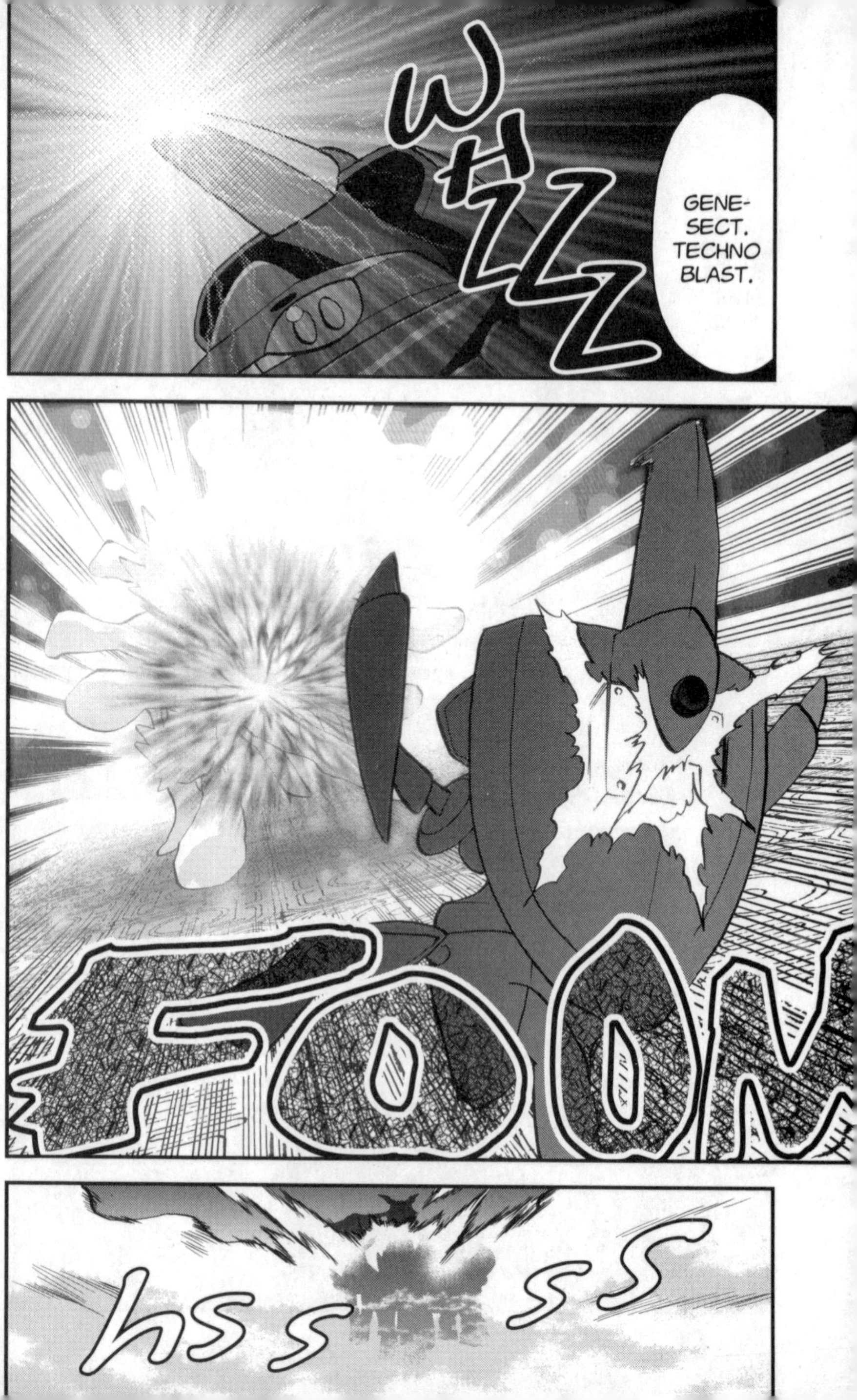

GENE-SECT. TECHNO BLAST.
WHIZZZ
FOOM
hssss

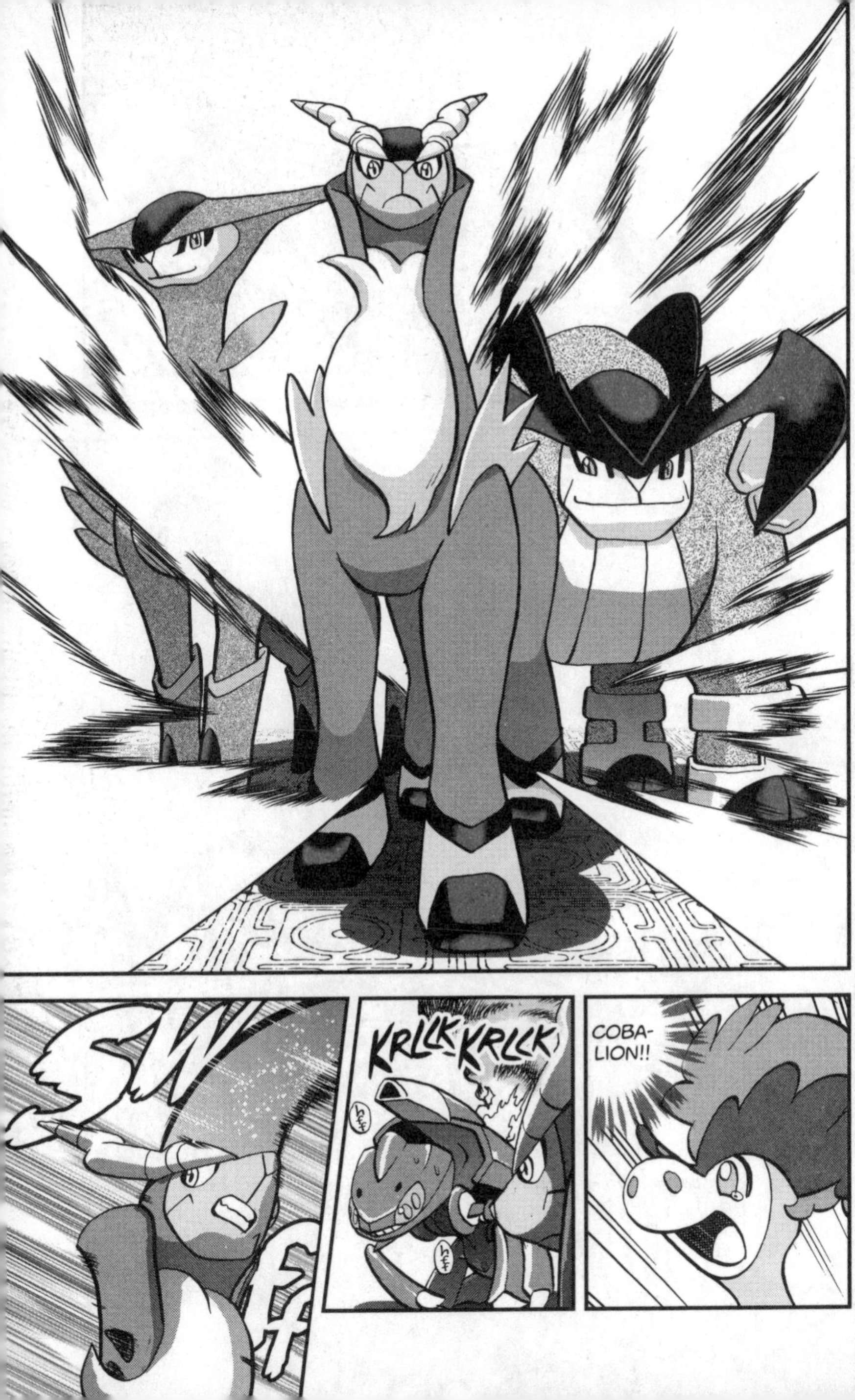
COBA-
LION!!
KRLCK-KRLCK
hff
hff

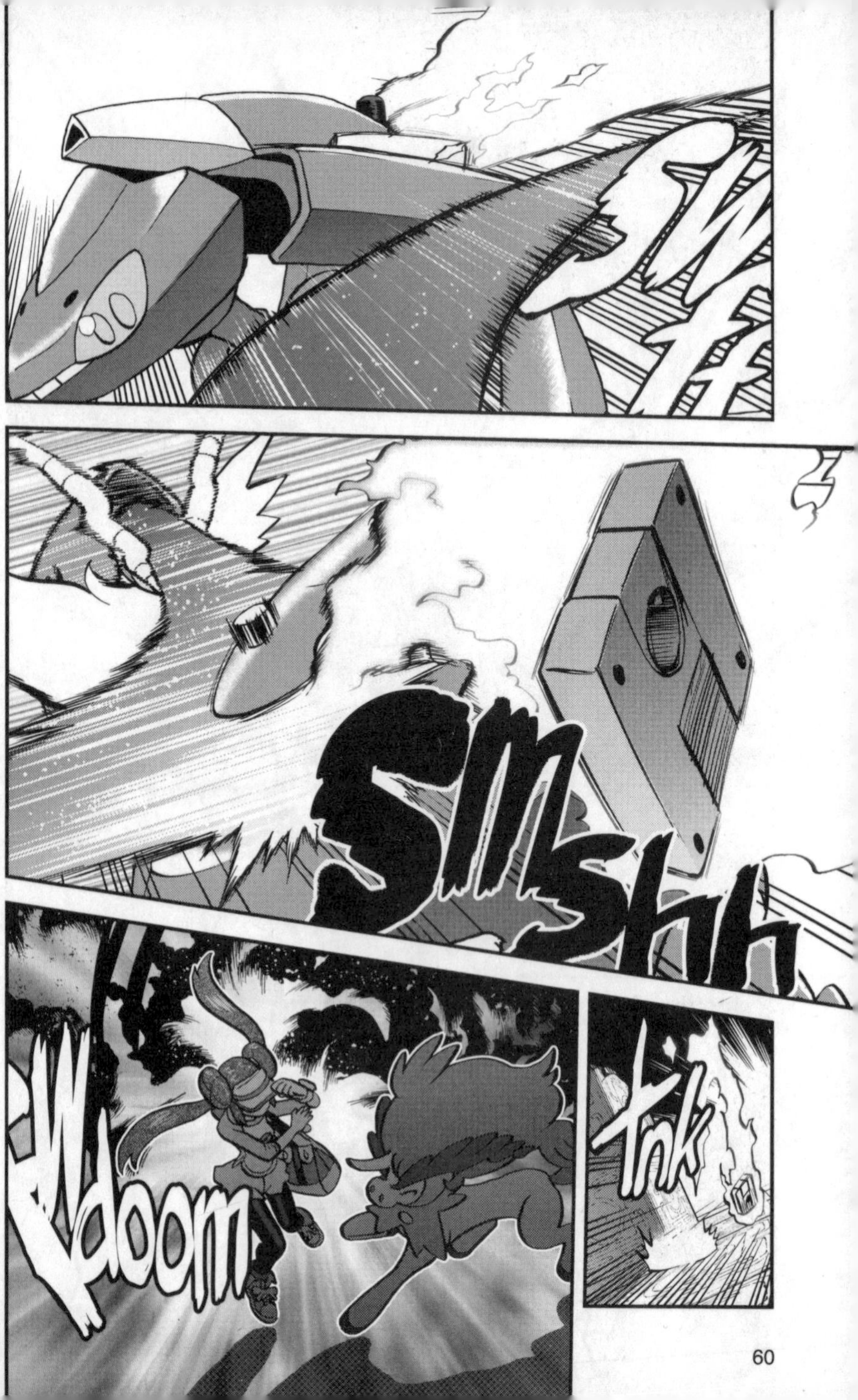
Smshh
Tnk
Vdoom

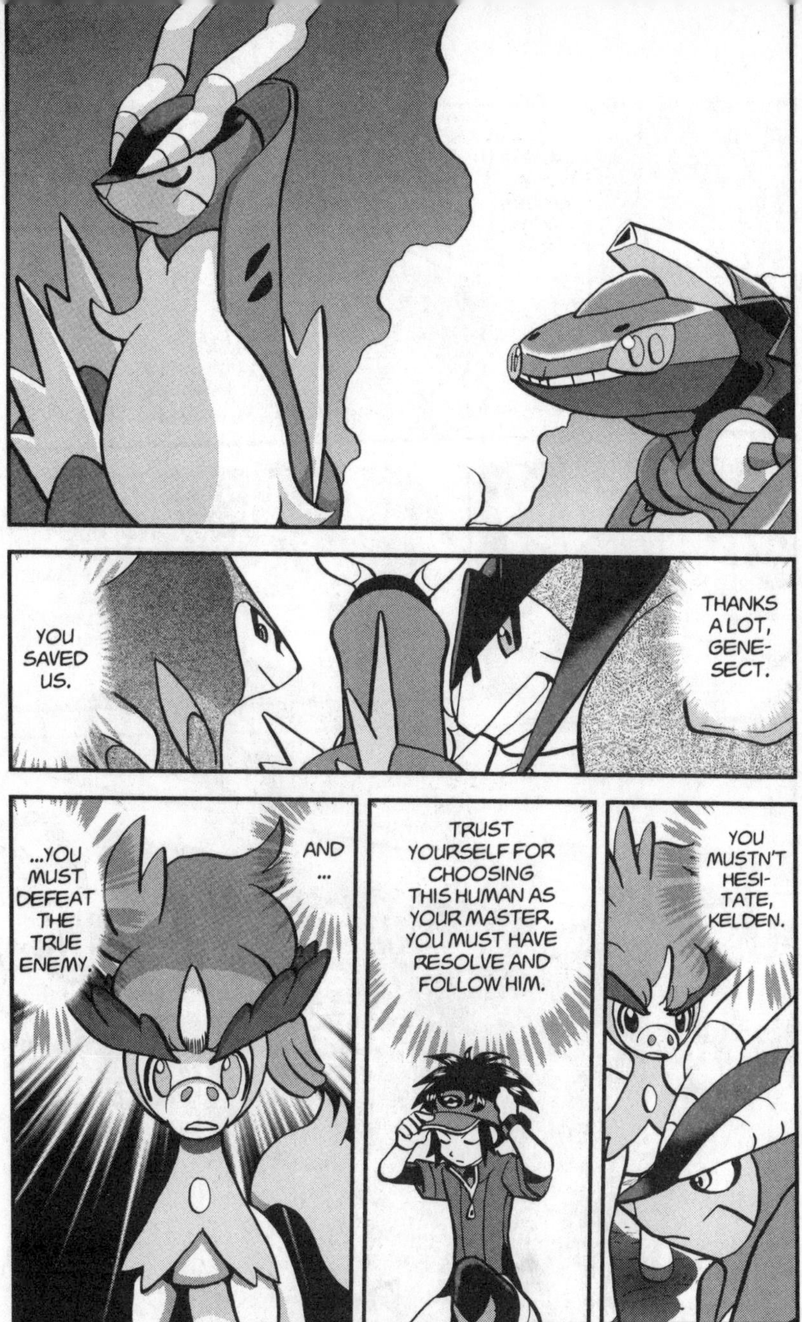
THANKS A LOT, GENESECT.
YOU SAVED US.
YOU MUSTN'T HESITATE, KELDEN.
TRUST YOURSELF FOR CHOOSING THIS HUMAN AS YOUR MASTER. YOU MUST HAVE RESOLVE AND FOLLOW HIM.
AND ...
...YOU MUST DEFEAT THE TRUE ENEMY.

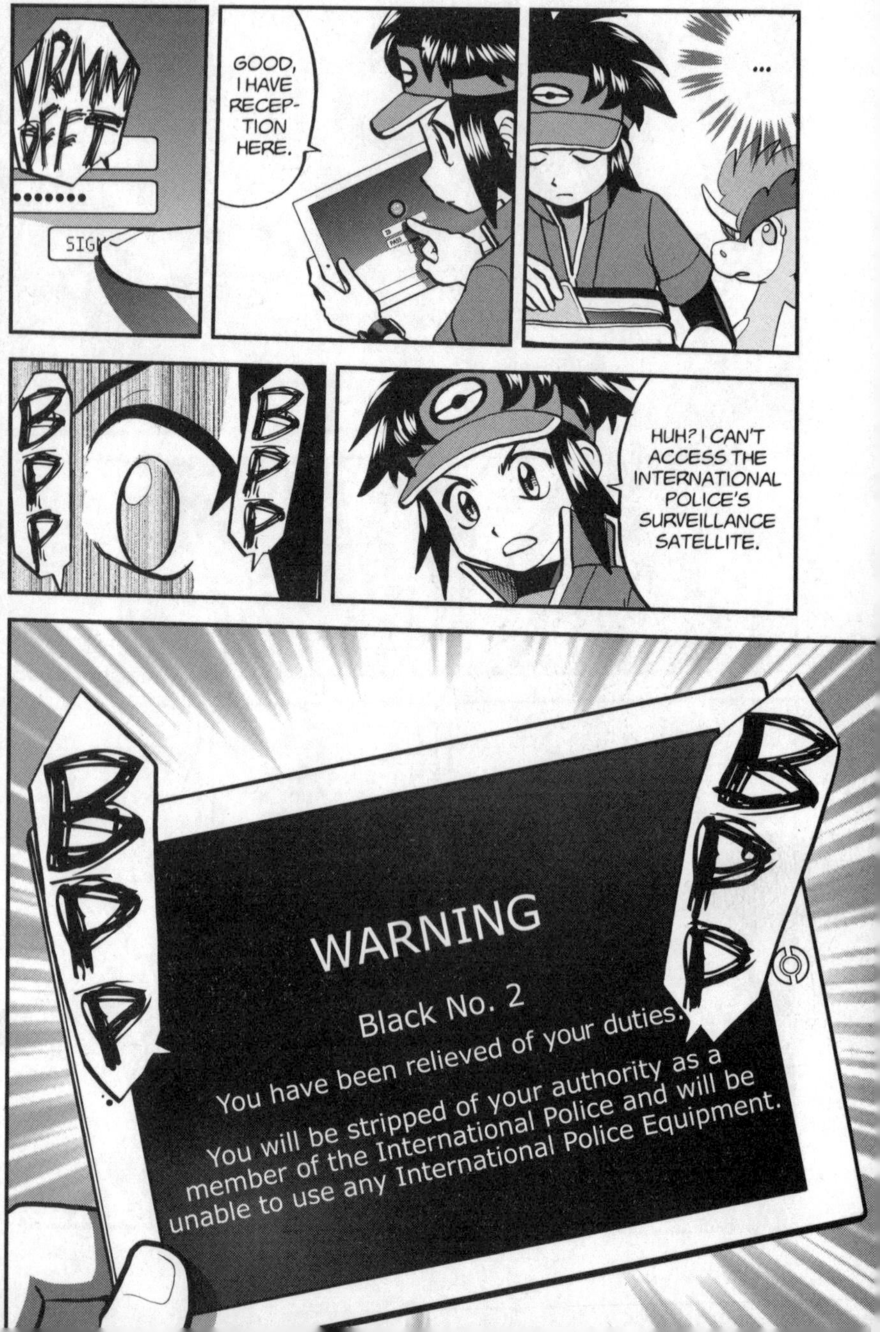
VRMM OFFT
GOOD, I HAVE RECEPTION HERE.
...
BPPP
BPPP
HUH? I CAN'T ACCESS THE INTERNATIONAL POLICE'S SURVEILLANCE SATELLITE.
BPPP
WARNING
Black No. 2
You have been relieved of your duties.
You will be stripped of your authority as a member of the International Police and will be unable to use any International Police Equipment.
BPPP

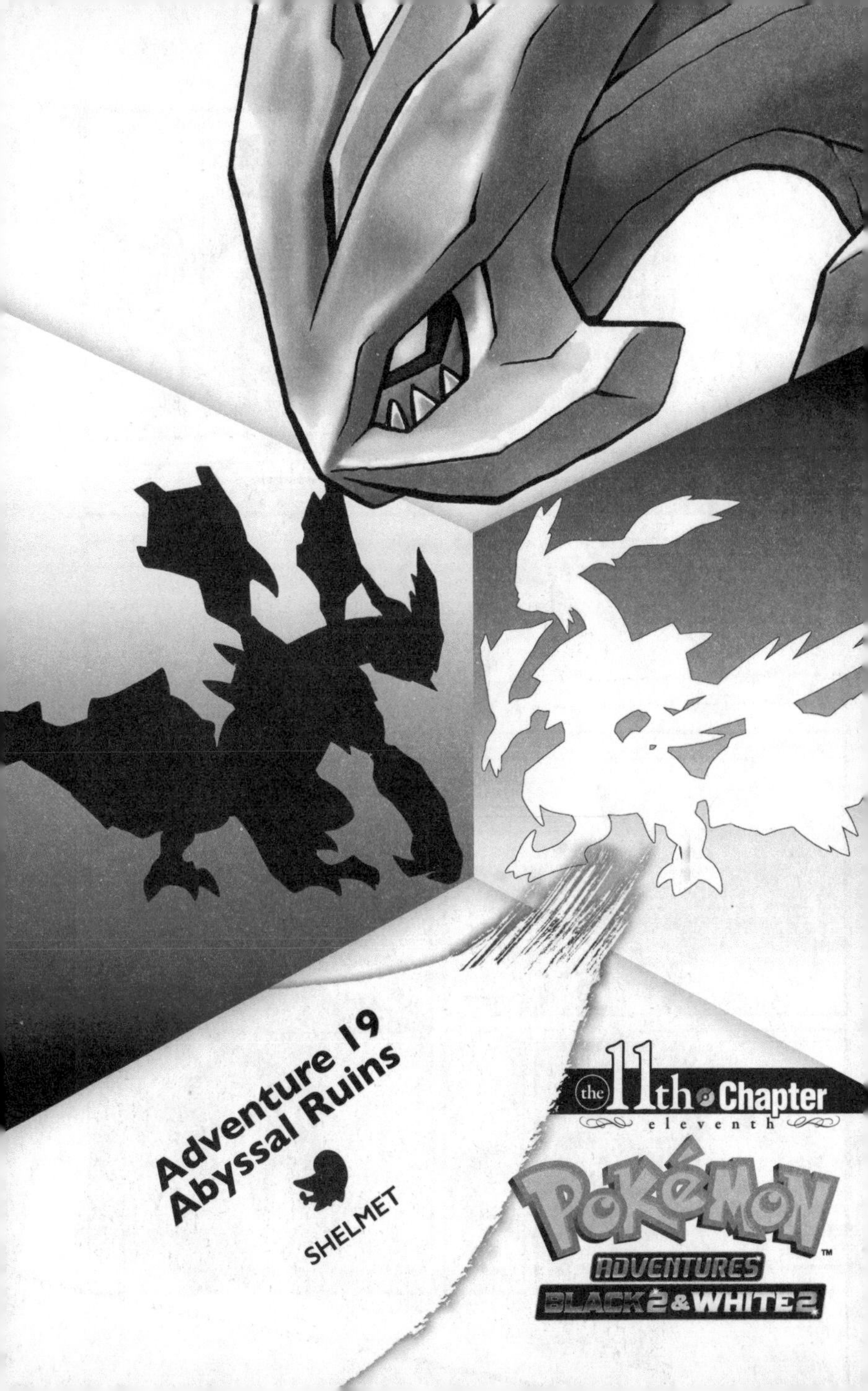
Adventure 19
Abyssal Ruins
SHELMET
the 11th Chapter
eleventh
POKÉMON™
ADVENTURES
BLACK 2 & WHITE 2

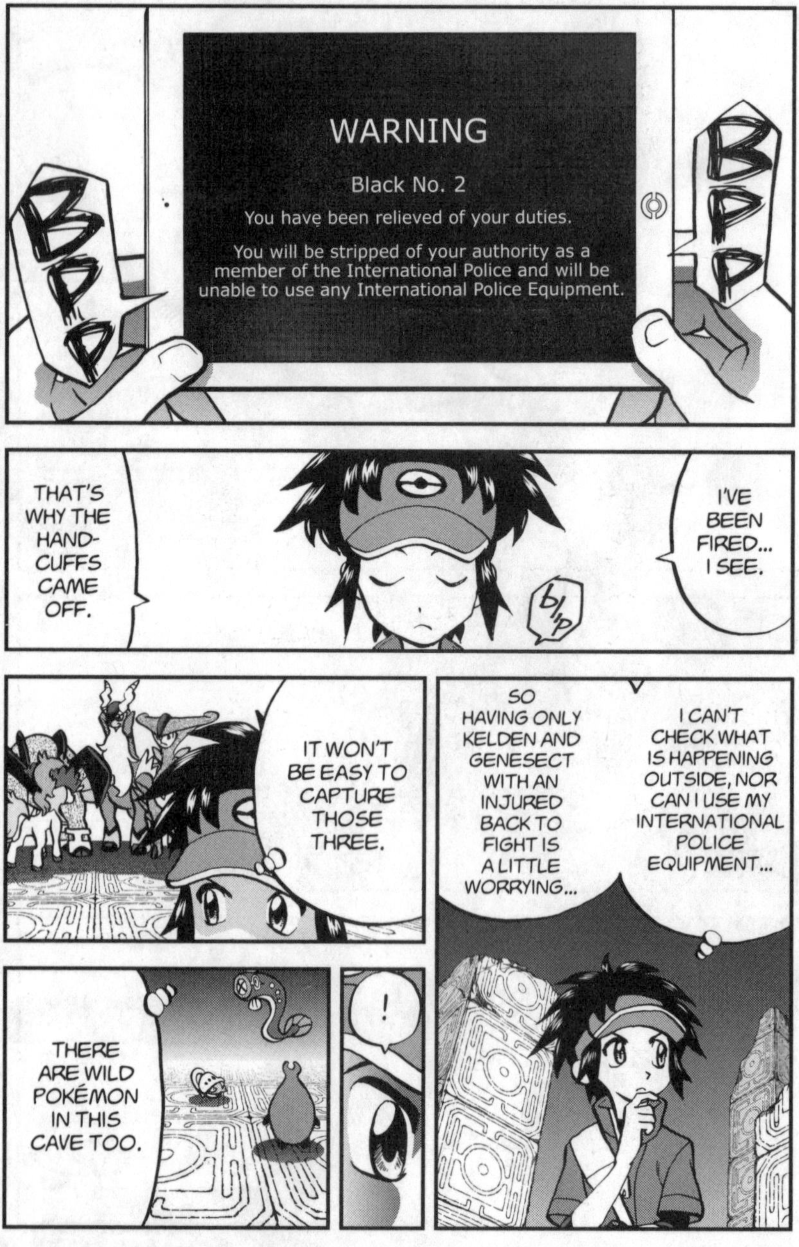
BPP
WARNING
Black No. 2
You have been relieved of your duties.
You will be stripped of your authority as a member of the International Police and will be unable to use any International Police Equipment.
BPP
I'VE BEEN FIRED... I SEE.
blip
THAT'S WHY THE HAND-CUFFS CAME OFF.
I CAN'T CHECK WHAT IS HAPPENING OUTSIDE, NOR CAN I USE MY INTERNATIONAL POLICE EQUIPMENT...
SO HAVING ONLY KELDEN AND GENESECT WITH AN INJURED BACK TO FIGHT IS A LITTLE WORRYING...
IT WON'T BE EASY TO CAPTURE THOSE THREE.
!
THERE ARE WILD POKÉMON IN THIS CAVE TOO.

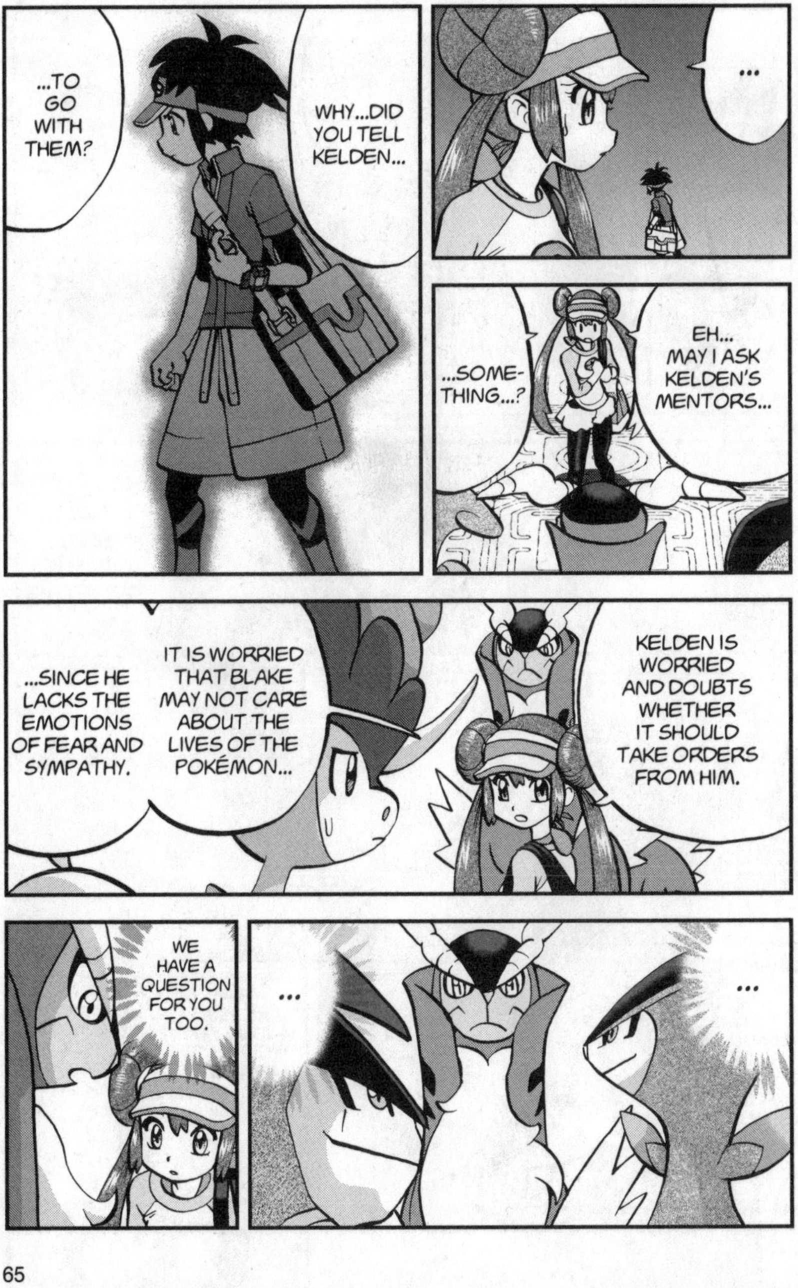
...
EH... MAY I ASK KELDEN'S MENTORS...
...SOME-THING...?
WHY...DID YOU TELL KELDEN...
...TO GO WITH THEM?
KELDEN IS WORRIED AND DOUBTS WHETHER IT SHOULD TAKE ORDERS FROM HIM.
IT IS WORRIED THAT BLAKE MAY NOT CARE ABOUT THE LIVES OF THE POKÉMON...
...SINCE HE LACKS THE EMOTIONS OF FEAR AND SYMPATHY.
...
...
WE HAVE A QUESTION FOR YOU TOO.

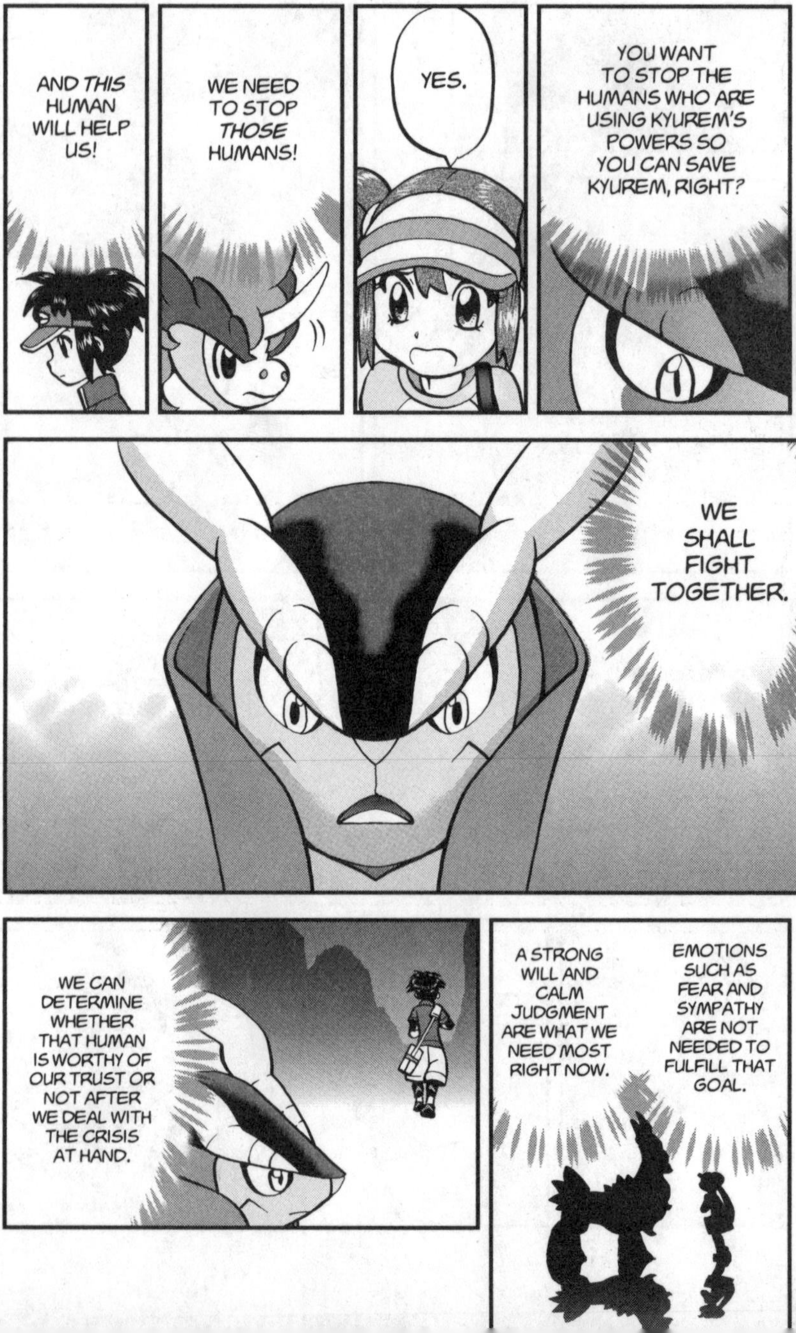
YOU WANT TO STOP THE HUMANS WHO ARE USING KYUREM'S POWERS SO YOU CAN SAVE KYUREM, RIGHT?
YES.
WE NEED TO STOP *THOSE* HUMANS!
AND *THIS* HUMAN WILL HELP US!
WE SHALL FIGHT TOGETHER.
EMOTIONS SUCH AS FEAR AND SYMPATHY ARE NOT NEEDED TO FULFILL THAT GOAL.
A STRONG WILL AND CALM JUDGMENT ARE WHAT WE NEED MOST RIGHT NOW.
WE CAN DETERMINE WHETHER THAT HUMAN IS WORTHY OF OUR TRUST OR NOT AFTER WE DEAL WITH THE CRISIS AT HAND.

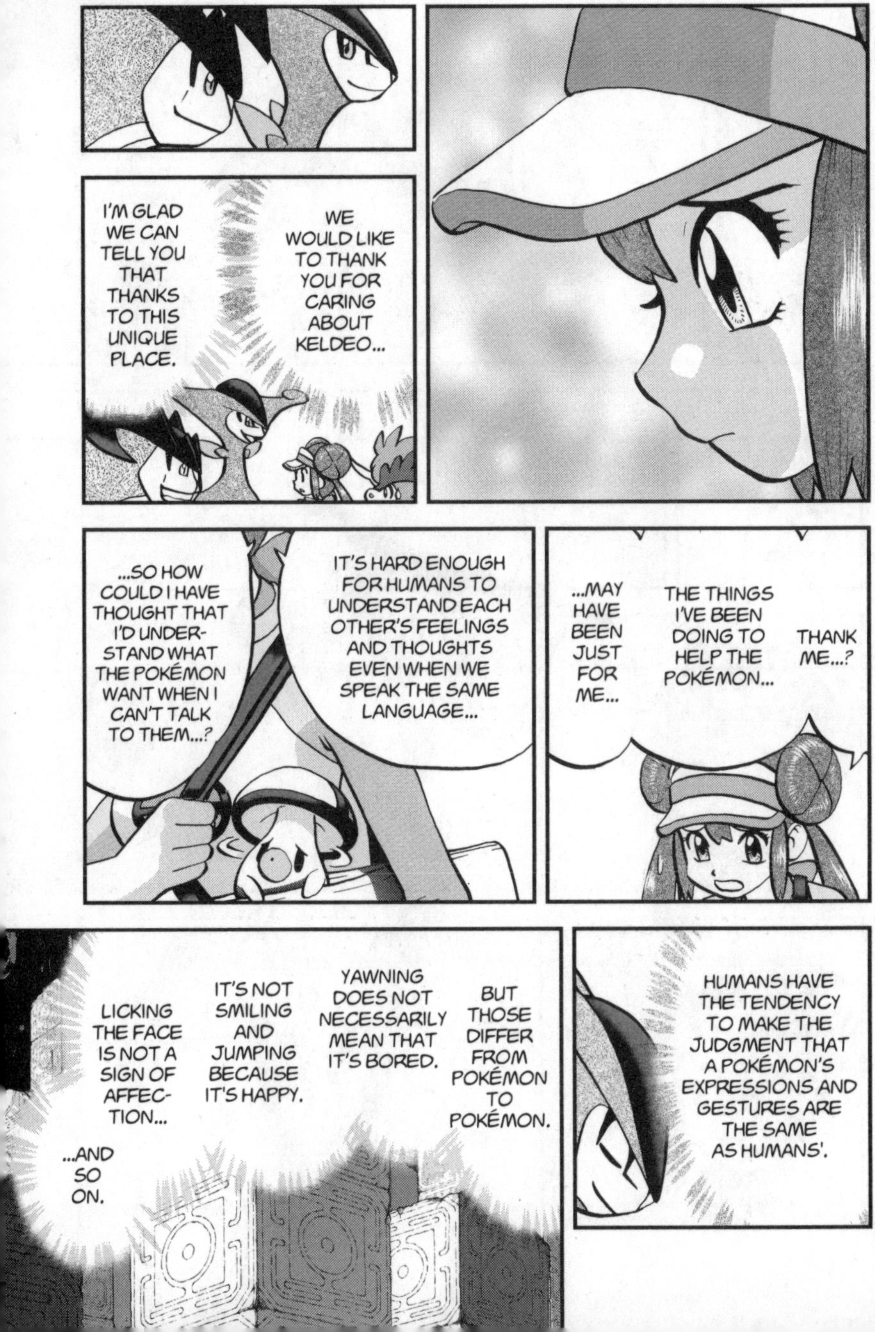
WE WOULD LIKE TO THANK YOU FOR CARING ABOUT KELDEO...
I'M GLAD WE CAN TELL YOU THAT THANKS TO THIS UNIQUE PLACE.
THANK ME...?
THE THINGS I'VE BEEN DOING TO HELP THE POKÉMON...
...MAY HAVE BEEN JUST FOR ME...
IT'S HARD ENOUGH FOR HUMANS TO UNDERSTAND EACH OTHER'S FEELINGS AND THOUGHTS EVEN WHEN WE SPEAK THE SAME LANGUAGE...
...SO HOW COULD I HAVE THOUGHT THAT I'D UNDER-STAND WHAT THE POKÉMON WANT WHEN I CAN'T TALK TO THEM...?
HUMANS HAVE THE TENDENCY TO MAKE THE JUDGMENT THAT A POKÉMON'S EXPRESSIONS AND GESTURES ARE THE SAME AS HUMANS'.
BUT THOSE DIFFER FROM POKÉMON TO POKÉMON.
YAWNING DOES NOT NECESSARILY MEAN THAT IT'S BORED.
IT'S NOT SMILING AND JUMPING BECAUSE IT'S HAPPY.
LICKING THE FACE IS NOT A SIGN OF AFFEC-TION...
...AND SO ON.

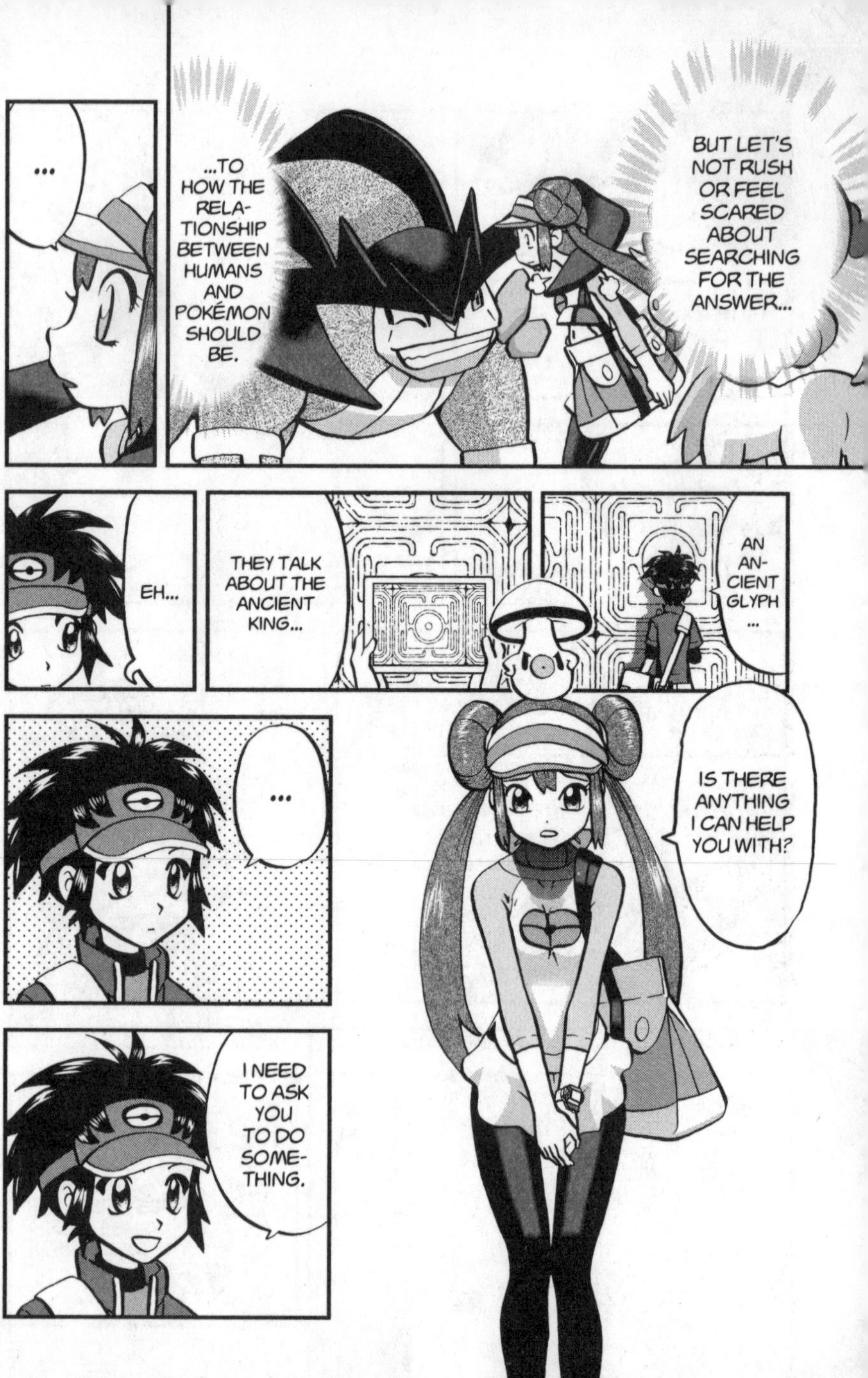
...TO HOW THE RELA-TIONSHIP BETWEEN HUMANS AND POKÉMON SHOULD BE.
BUT LET'S NOT RUSH OR FEEL SCARED ABOUT SEARCHING FOR THE ANSWER...
...
AN AN-CIENT GLYPH ...
THEY TALK ABOUT THE ANCIENT KING...
EH...
IS THERE ANYTHING I CAN HELP YOU WITH?
...
I NEED TO ASK YOU TO DO SOME-THING.

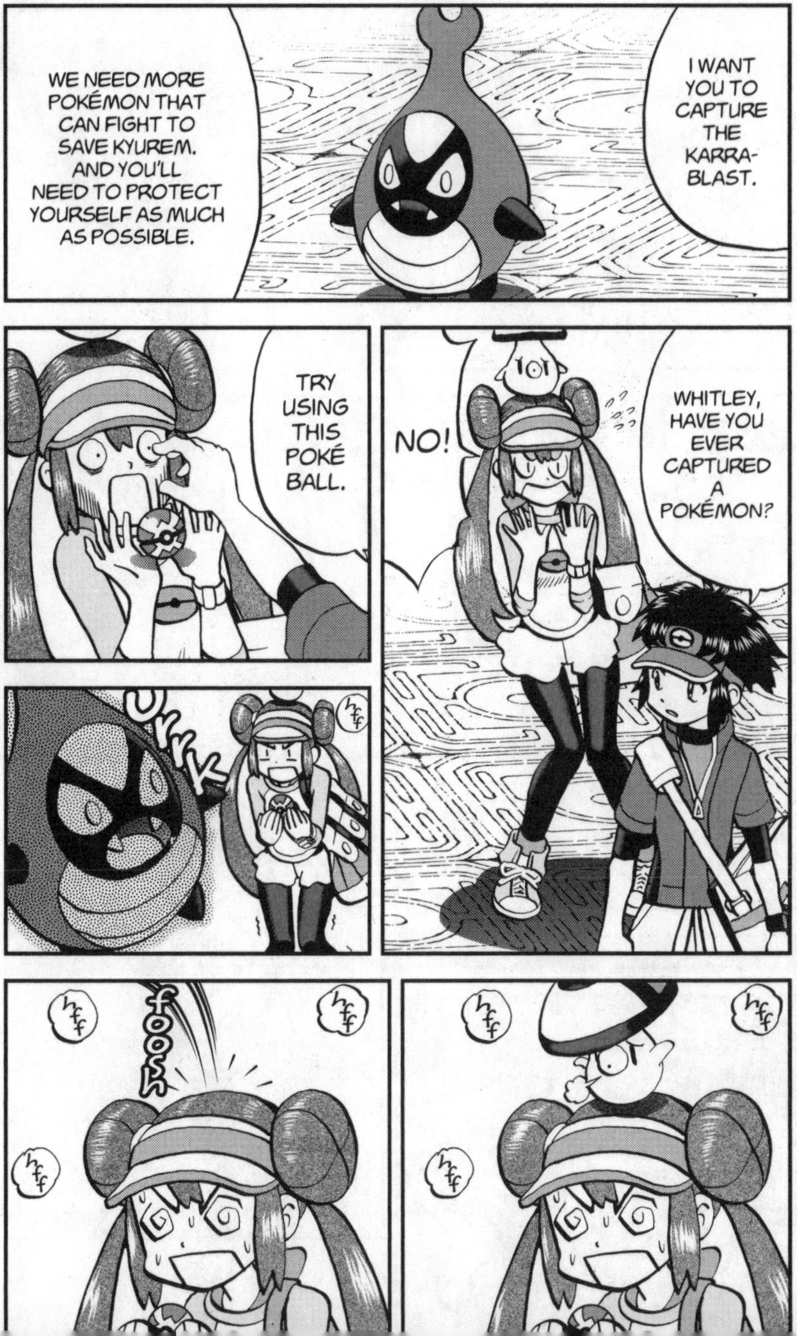
I WANT YOU TO CAPTURE THE KARRA-BLAST.
WE NEED MORE POKÉMON THAT CAN FIGHT TO SAVE KYUREM. AND YOU'LL NEED TO PROTECT YOURSELF AS MUCH AS POSSIBLE.
WHITLEY, HAVE YOU EVER CAPTURED A POKÉMON?
NO!
TRY USING THIS POKÉ BALL.
hff
urrk
hff
hff
hff
foosh
hff

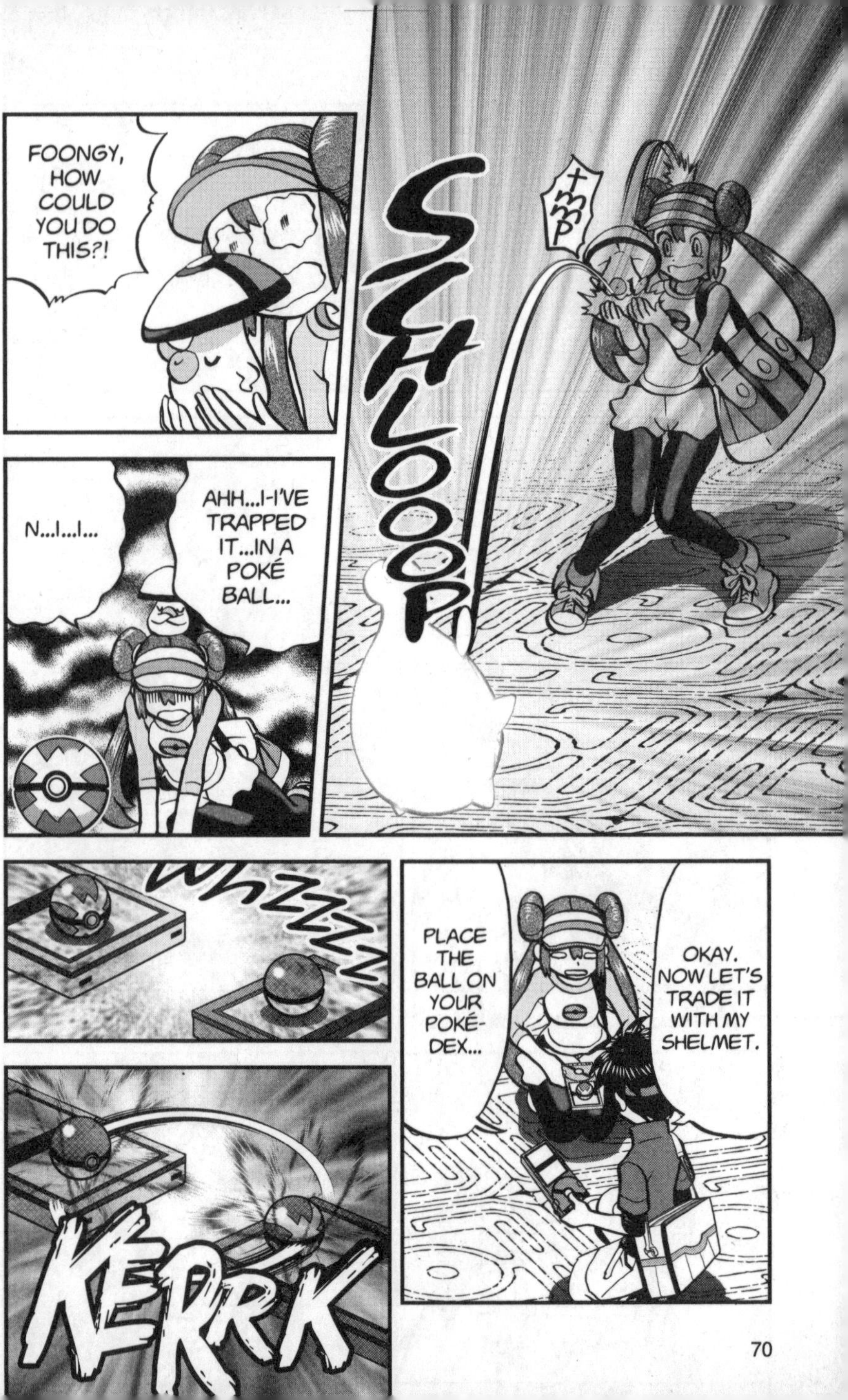
tmmp
SHLOOOP
FOONGY, HOW COULD YOU DO THIS?!
AHH...I-I'VE TRAPPED IT...IN A POKÉ BALL...
N...I...I...
OKAY. NOW LET'S TRADE IT WITH MY SHELMET.
PLACE THE BALL ON YOUR POKÉ-DEX...
WHZZZZN
KERRK

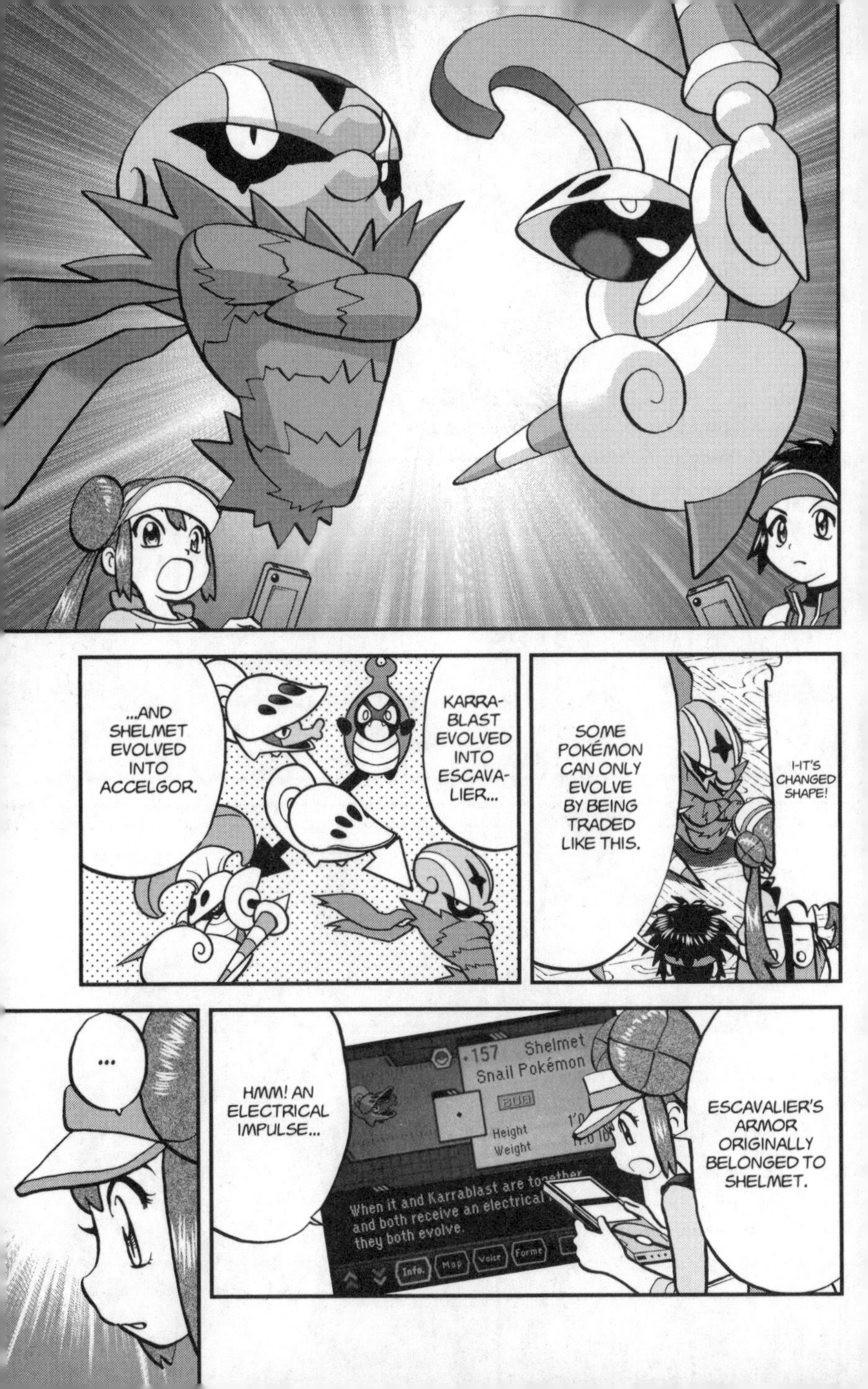
I-IT'S CHANGED SHAPE!
SOME POKÉMON CAN ONLY EVOLVE BY BEING TRADED LIKE THIS.
KARRA-BLAST EVOLVED INTO ESCAVA-LIER...
...AND SHELMET EVOLVED INTO ACCELGOR.
ESCAVALIER'S ARMOR ORIGINALLY BELONGED TO SHELMET.
157 Shelmet
Snail Pokémon
Height
Weight
When it and Karrablast are together and both receive an electrical
they both evolve.
Info.
Map
Voice
Forme
HMM! AN ELECTRICAL IMPULSE...
...

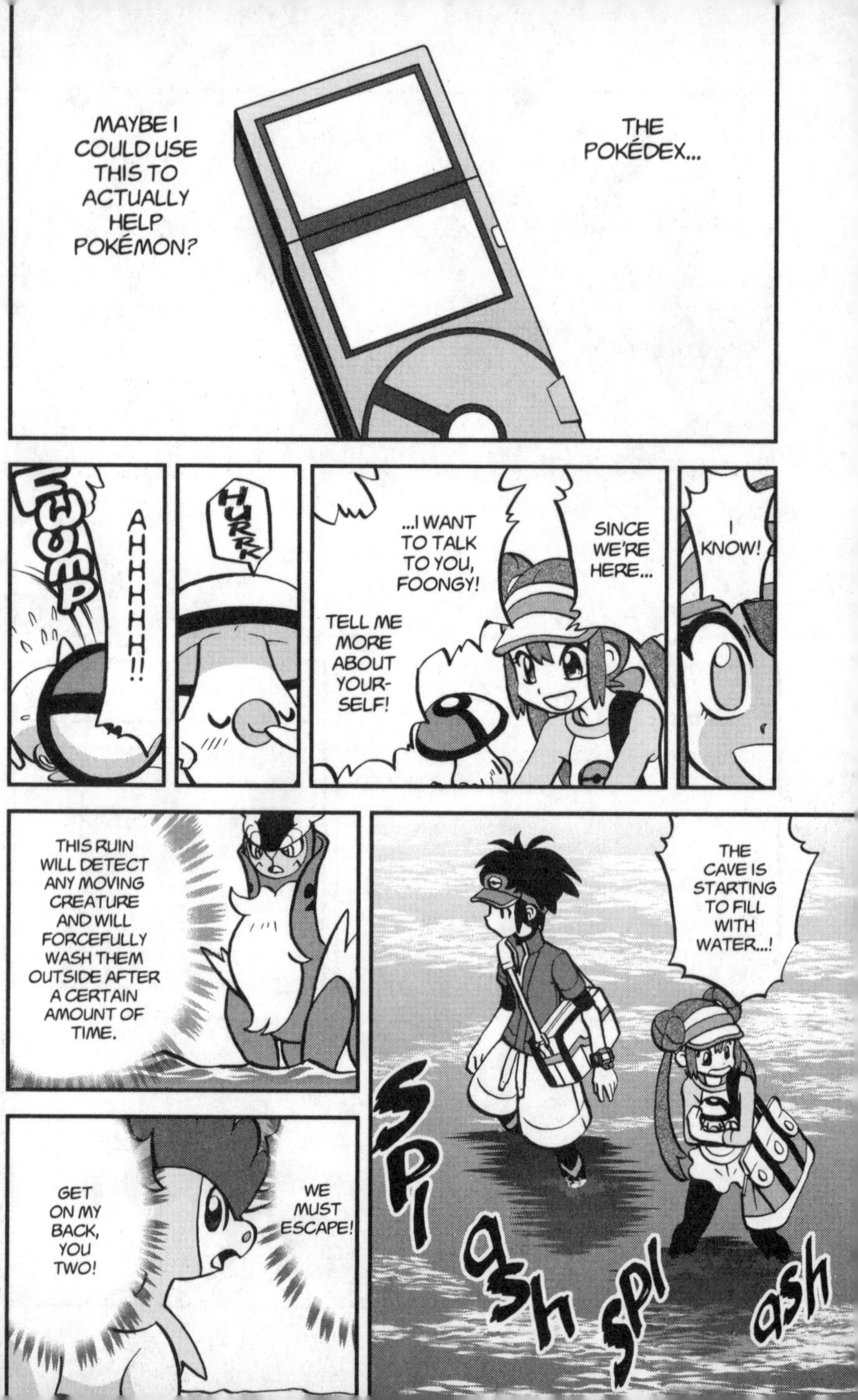
THE POKÉDEX...
MAYBE I COULD USE THIS TO ACTUALLY HELP POKÉMON?
I KNOW!
SINCE WE'RE HERE...
...I WANT TO TALK TO YOU, FOONGY!
TELL ME MORE ABOUT YOUR-SELF!
HURRK
AHHHHHH!!
FWUMP
THE CAVE IS STARTING TO FILL WITH WATER...!
SPLASH SPLASH
THIS RUIN WILL DETECT ANY MOVING CREATURE AND WILL FORCEFULLY WASH THEM OUTSIDE AFTER A CERTAIN AMOUNT OF TIME.
WE MUST ESCAPE!
GET ON MY BACK, YOU TWO!

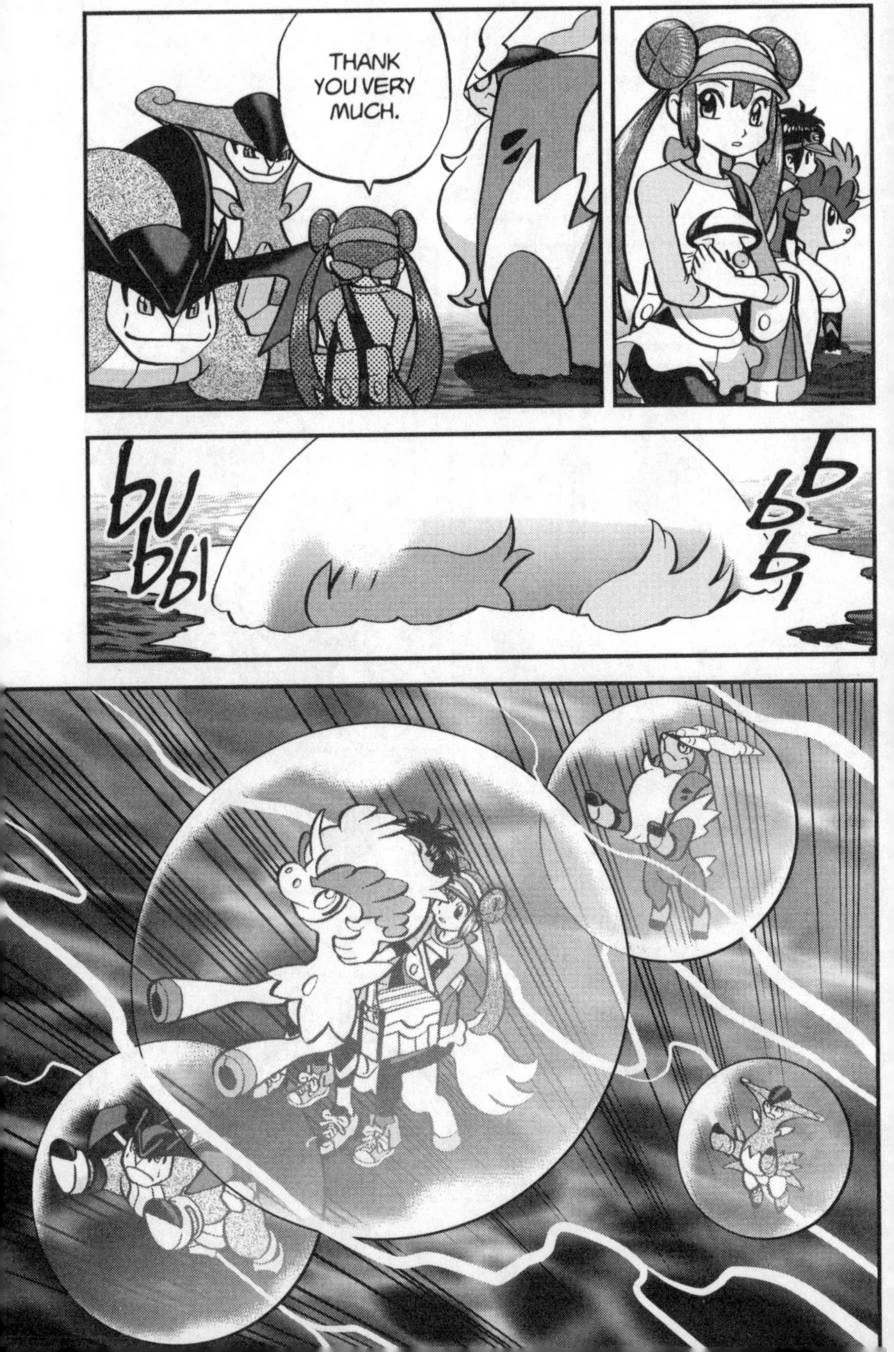
THANK YOU VERY MUCH.
bubbl

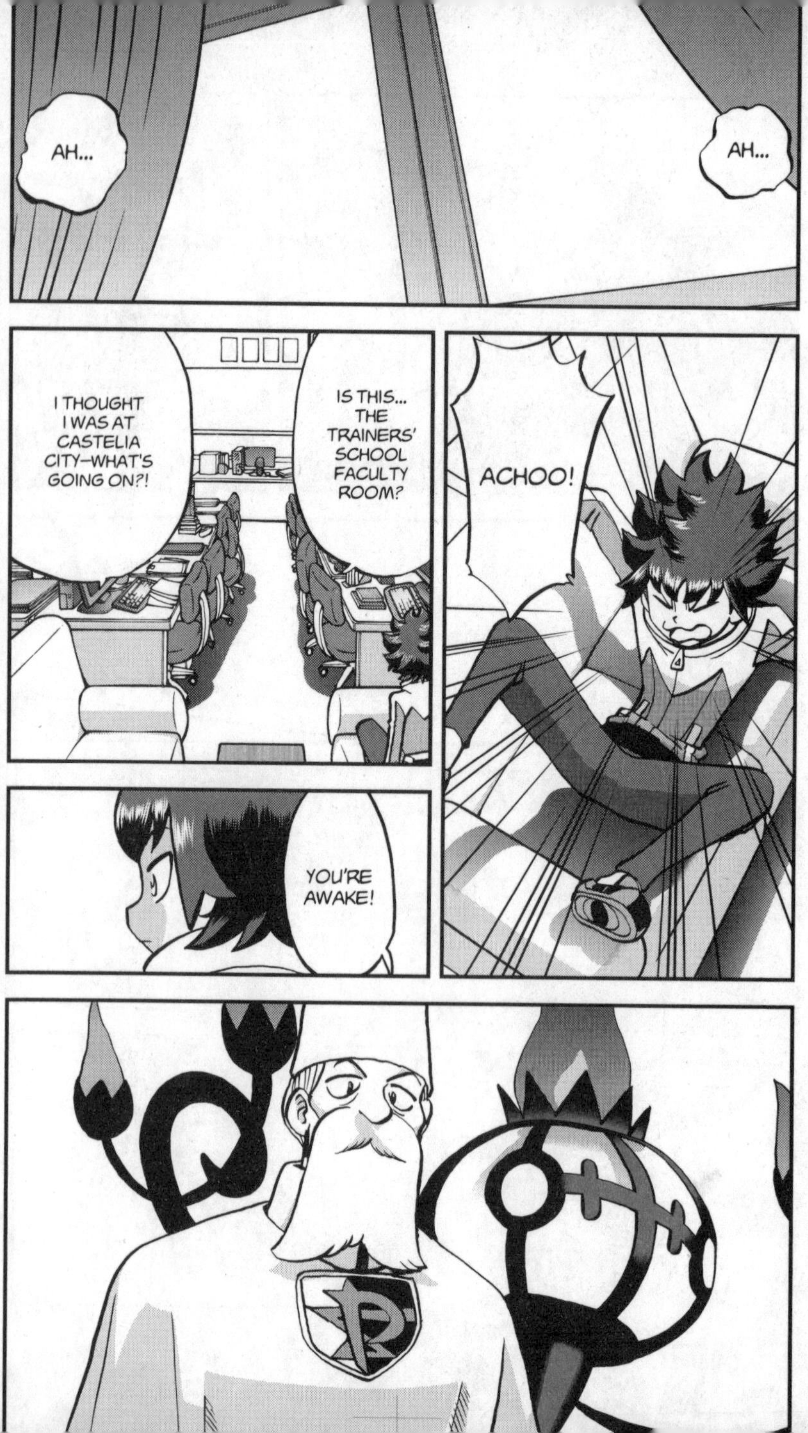
AH...
AH...
ACHOO!
IS THIS... THE TRAINERS' SCHOOL FACULTY ROOM?
I THOUGHT I WAS AT CASTELIA CITY—WHAT'S GOING ON?!
YOU'RE AWAKE!

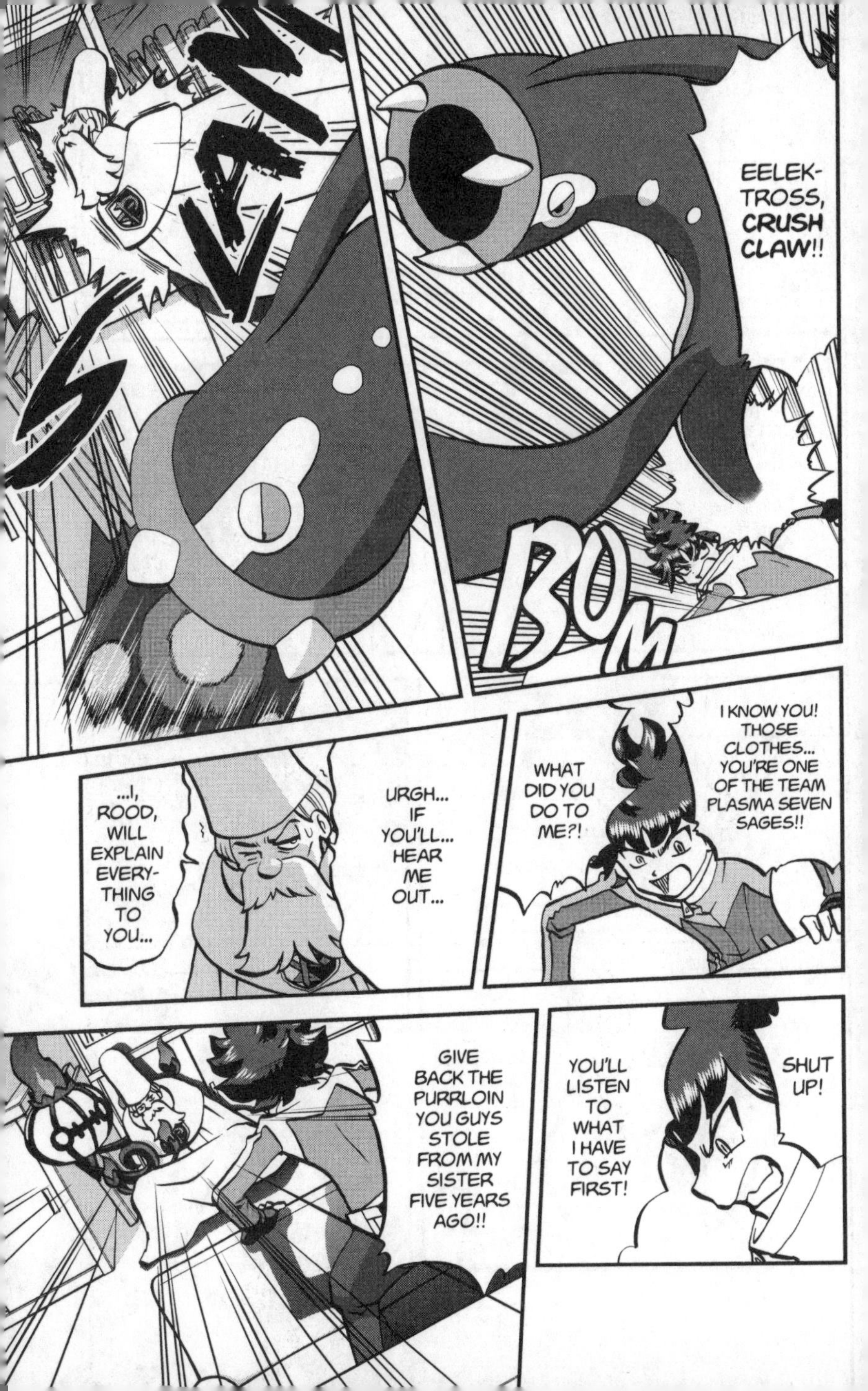
EELEKTROSS, CRUSH CLAW!!
BOM
SLAM
I KNOW YOU! THOSE CLOTHES... YOU'RE ONE OF THE TEAM PLASMA SEVEN SAGES!!
WHAT DID YOU DO TO ME?!
URGH... IF YOU'LL... HEAR ME OUT...
...I, ROOD, WILL EXPLAIN EVERYTHING TO YOU...
SHUT UP!
YOU'LL LISTEN TO WHAT I HAVE TO SAY FIRST!
GIVE BACK THE PURRLOIN YOU GUYS STOLE FROM MY SISTER FIVE YEARS AGO!!

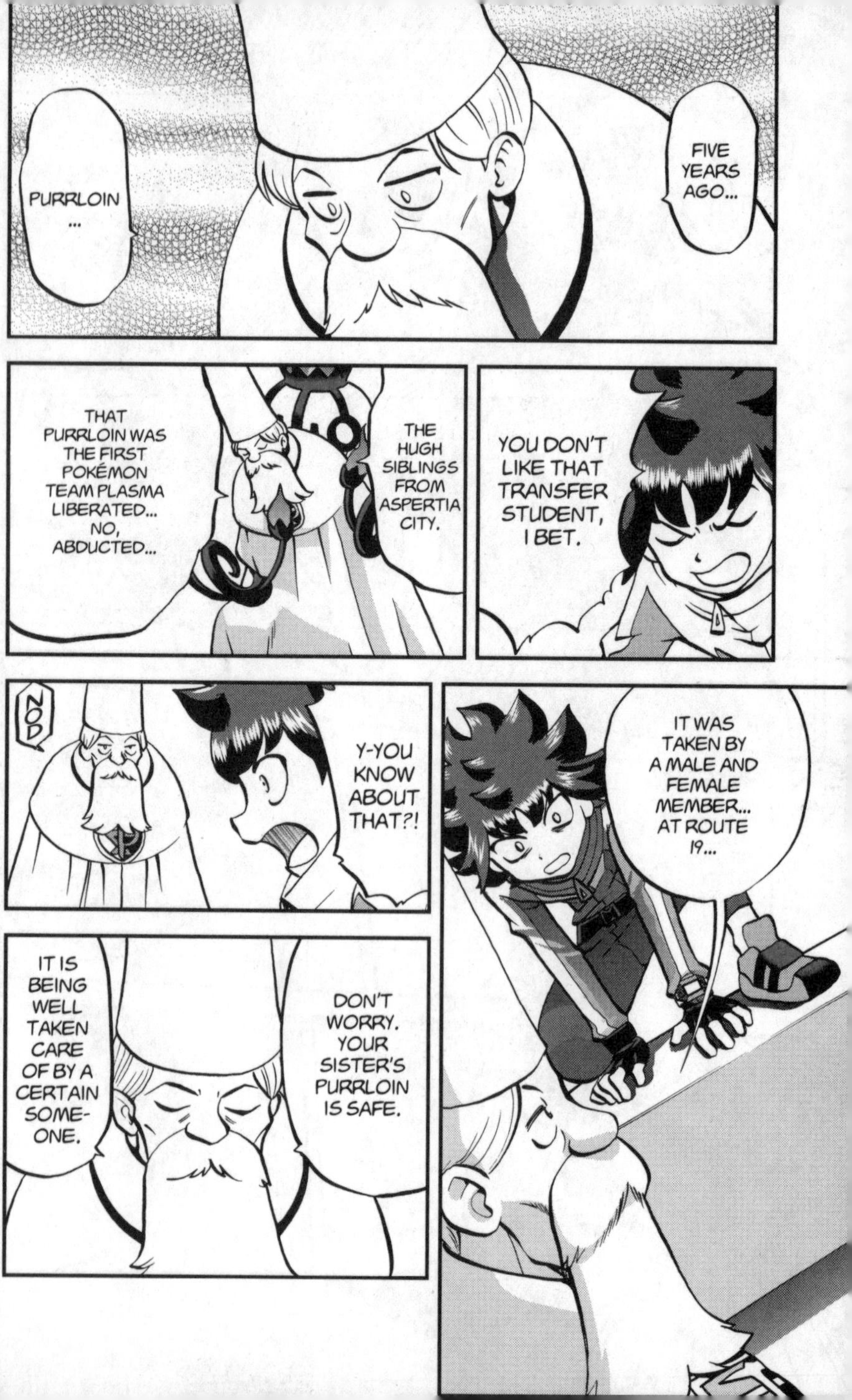
FIVE YEARS AGO...
PURRLOIN ...
YOU DON'T LIKE THAT TRANSFER STUDENT, I BET.
THE HUGH SIBLINGS FROM ASPERTIA CITY.
THAT PURRLOIN WAS THE FIRST POKÉMON TEAM PLASMA LIBERATED... NO, ABDUCTED...
IT WAS TAKEN BY A MALE AND FEMALE MEMBER... AT ROUTE 19...
NOD
Y-YOU KNOW ABOUT THAT?!
DON'T WORRY. YOUR SISTER'S PURRLOIN IS SAFE.
IT IS BEING WELL TAKEN CARE OF BY A CERTAIN SOME-ONE.

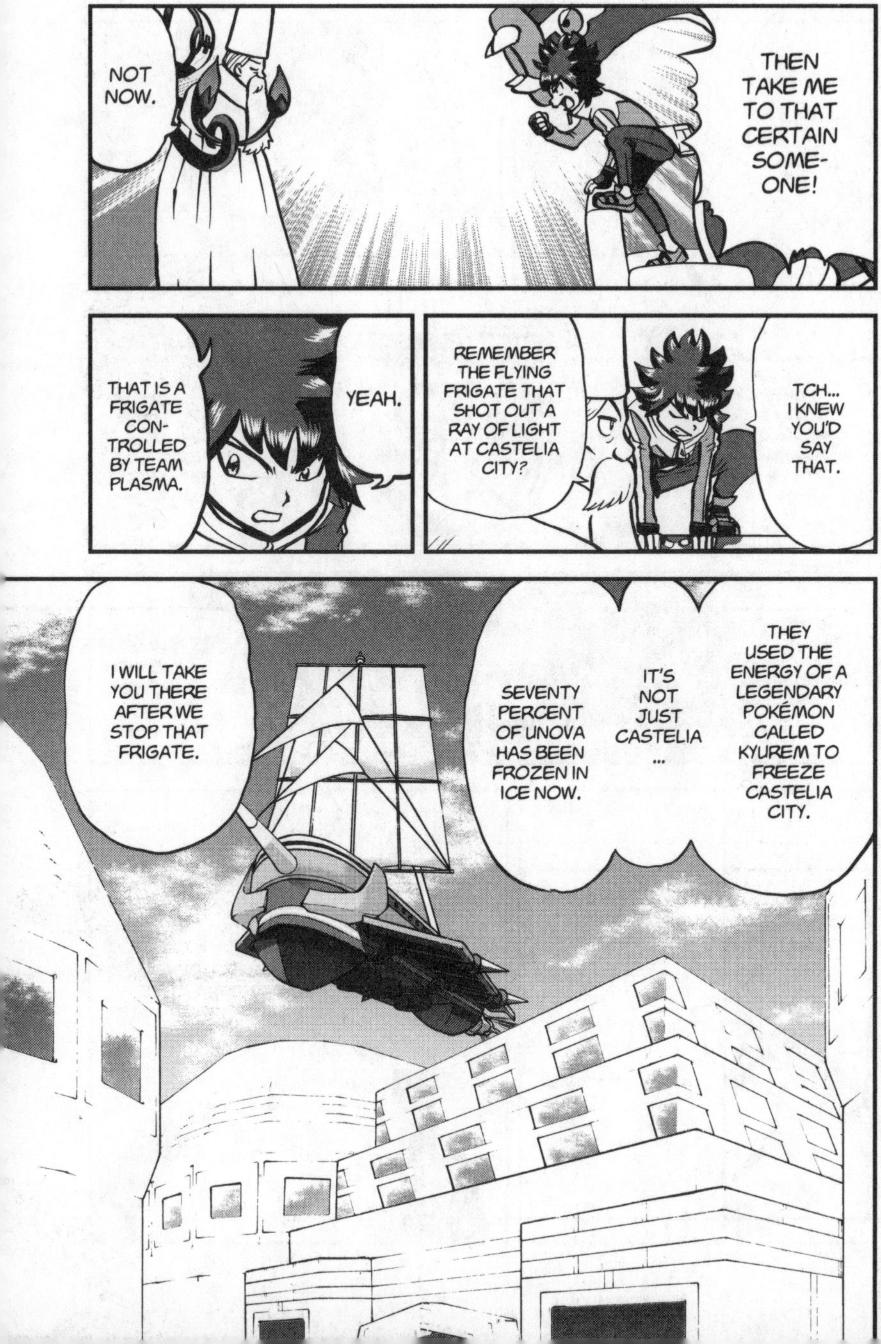
THEN TAKE ME TO THAT CERTAIN SOME-ONE!
NOT NOW.
TCH... I KNEW YOU'D SAY THAT.
REMEMBER THE FLYING FRIGATE THAT SHOT OUT A RAY OF LIGHT AT CASTELIA CITY?
YEAH.
THAT IS A FRIGATE CON-TROLLED BY TEAM PLASMA.
THEY USED THE ENERGY OF A LEGENDARY POKÉMON CALLED KYUREM TO FREEZE CASTELIA CITY.
IT'S NOT JUST CASTELIA...
SEVENTY PERCENT OF UNOVA HAS BEEN FROZEN IN ICE NOW.
I WILL TAKE YOU THERE AFTER WE STOP THAT FRIGATE.

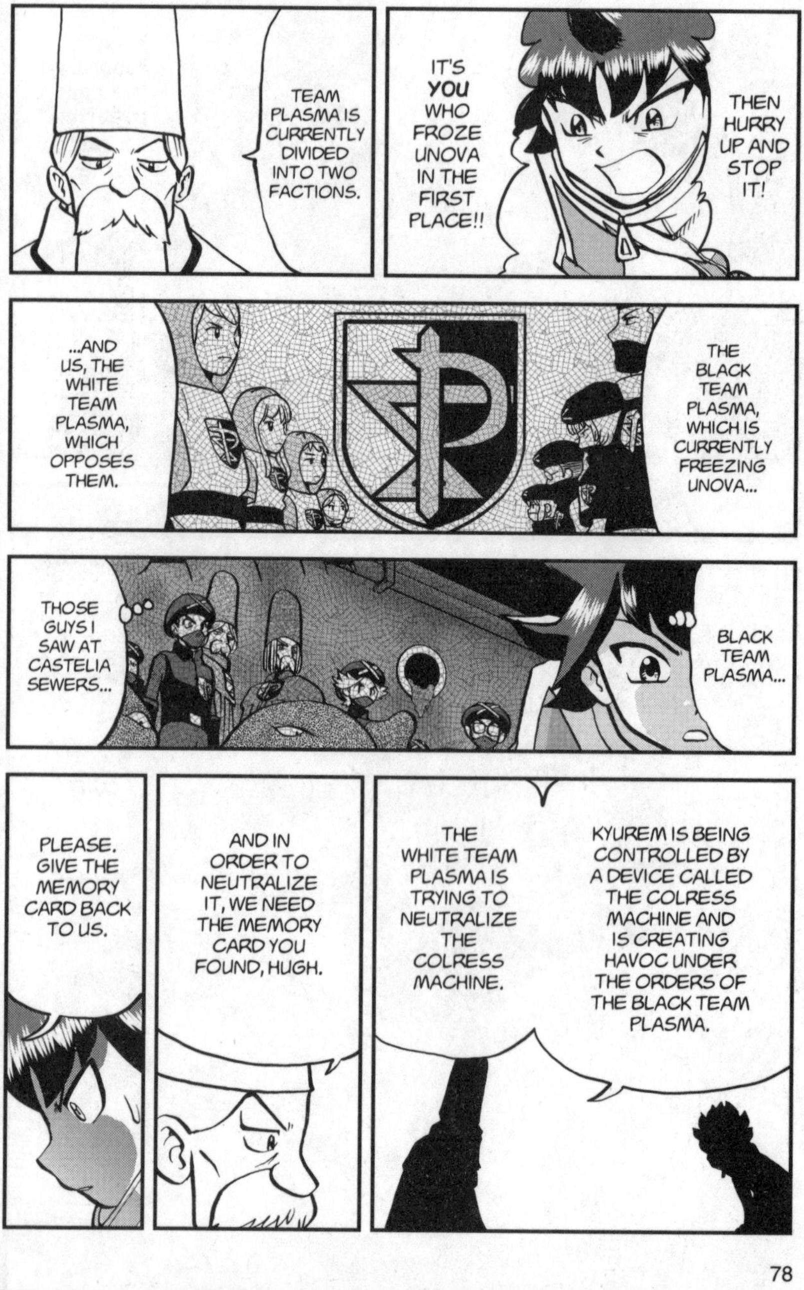
IT'S **YOU** WHO FROZE UNOVA IN THE FIRST PLACE!!
THEN HURRY UP AND STOP IT!
TEAM PLASMA IS CURRENTLY DIVIDED INTO TWO FACTIONS.
THE BLACK TEAM PLASMA, WHICH IS CURRENTLY FREEZING UNOVA...
...AND US, THE WHITE TEAM PLASMA, WHICH OPPOSES THEM.
BLACK TEAM PLASMA...
THOSE GUYS I SAW AT CASTELIA SEWERS...
KYUREM IS BEING CONTROLLED BY A DEVICE CALLED THE COLRESS MACHINE AND IS CREATING HAVOC UNDER THE ORDERS OF THE BLACK TEAM PLASMA.
THE WHITE TEAM PLASMA IS TRYING TO NEUTRALIZE THE COLRESS MACHINE.
AND IN ORDER TO NEUTRALIZE IT, WE NEED THE MEMORY CARD YOU FOUND, HUGH.
PLEASE. GIVE THE MEMORY CARD BACK TO US.

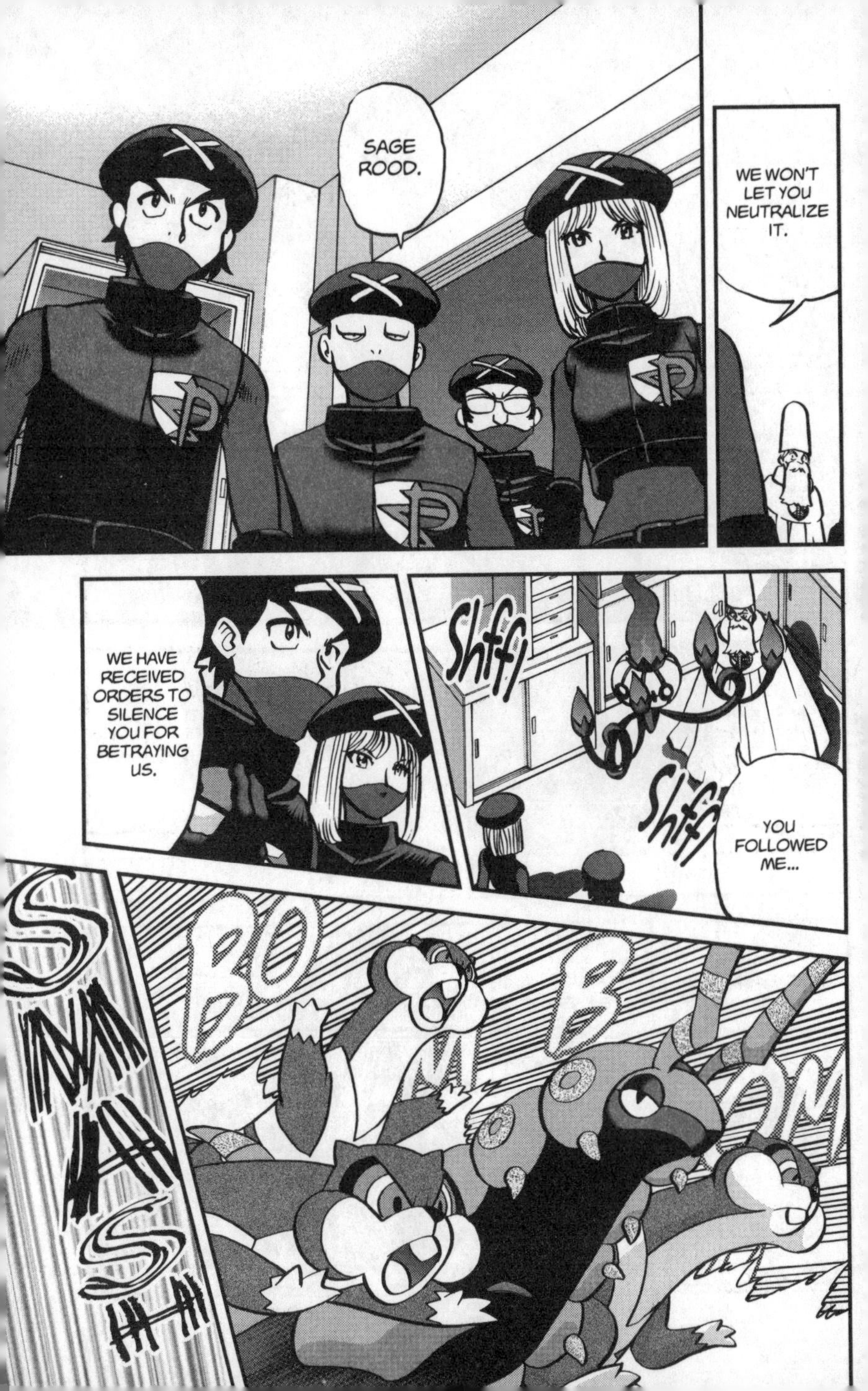
WE WON'T LET YOU NEUTRALIZE IT.
SAGE ROOD.
Shff
Shff
YOU FOLLOWED ME...
WE HAVE RECEIVED ORDERS TO SILENCE YOU FOR BETRAYING US.
BOOM
SMASH

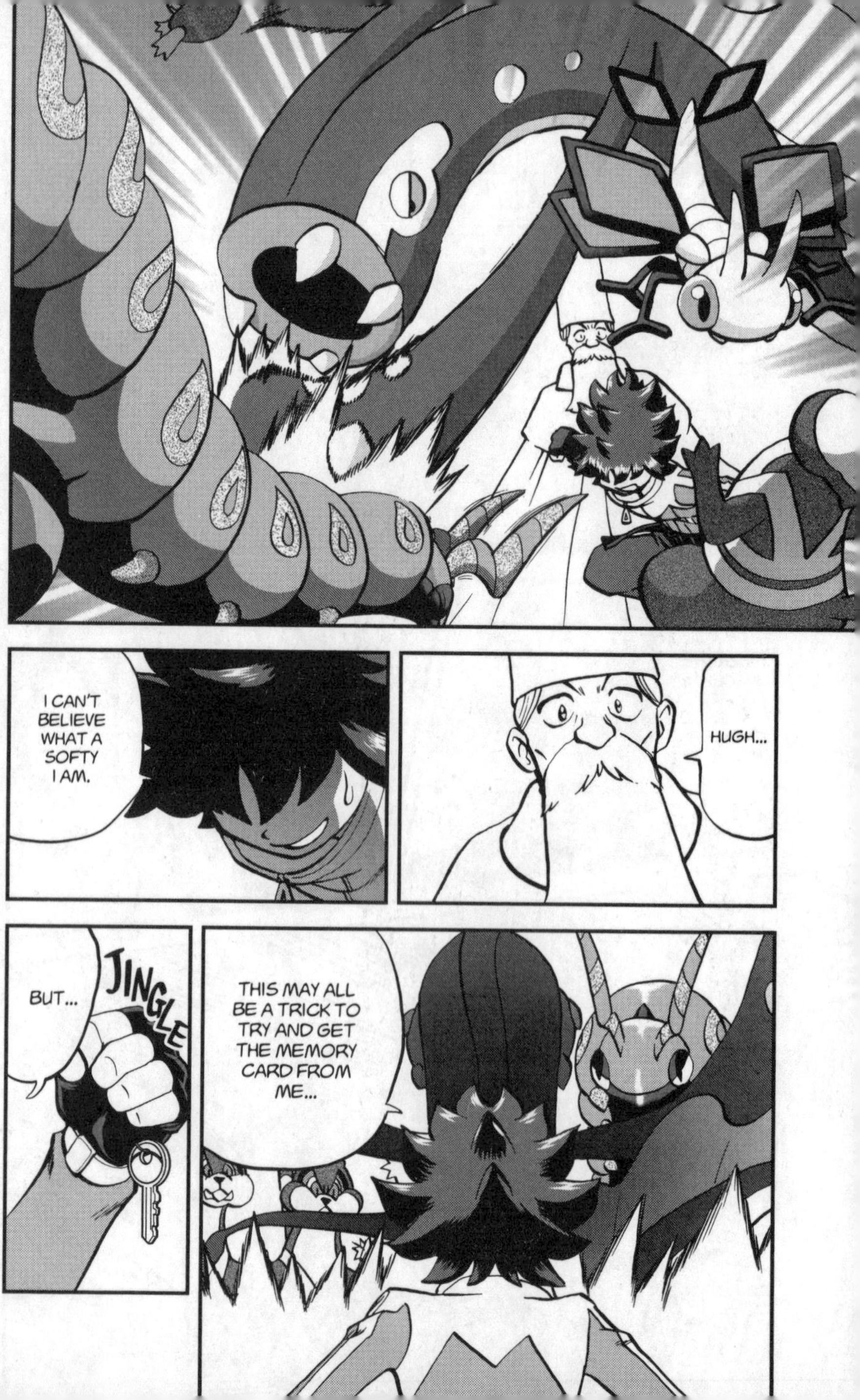
HUGH...
I CAN'T BELIEVE WHAT A SOFTY I AM.
THIS MAY ALL BE A TRICK TO TRY AND GET THE MEMORY CARD FROM ME...
BUT...
JINGLE

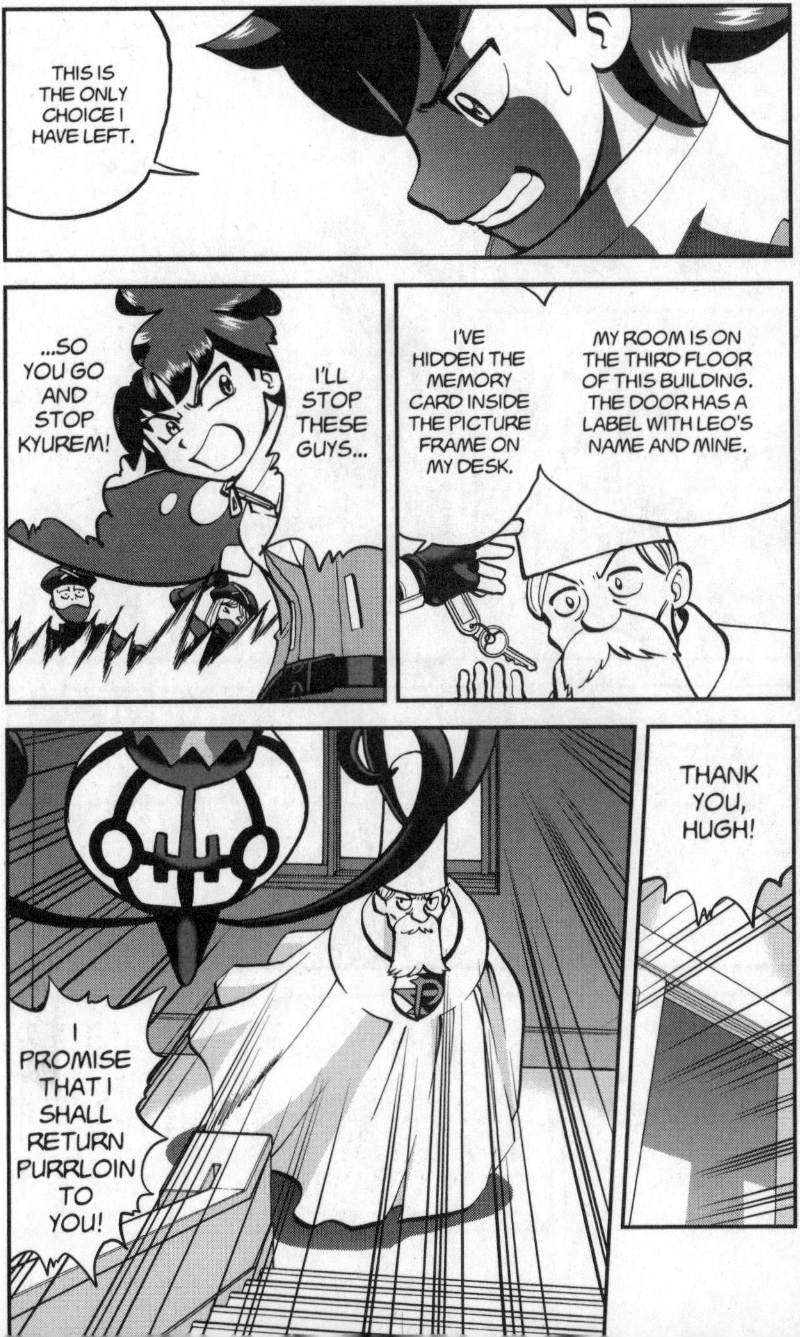
THIS IS THE ONLY CHOICE I HAVE LEFT.
MY ROOM IS ON THE THIRD FLOOR OF THIS BUILDING. THE DOOR HAS A LABEL WITH LEO'S NAME AND MINE.
I'VE HIDDEN THE MEMORY CARD INSIDE THE PICTURE FRAME ON MY DESK.
I'LL STOP THESE GUYS...
...SO YOU GO AND STOP KYUREM!
THANK YOU, HUGH!
I PROMISE THAT I SHALL RETURN PURRLOIN TO YOU!

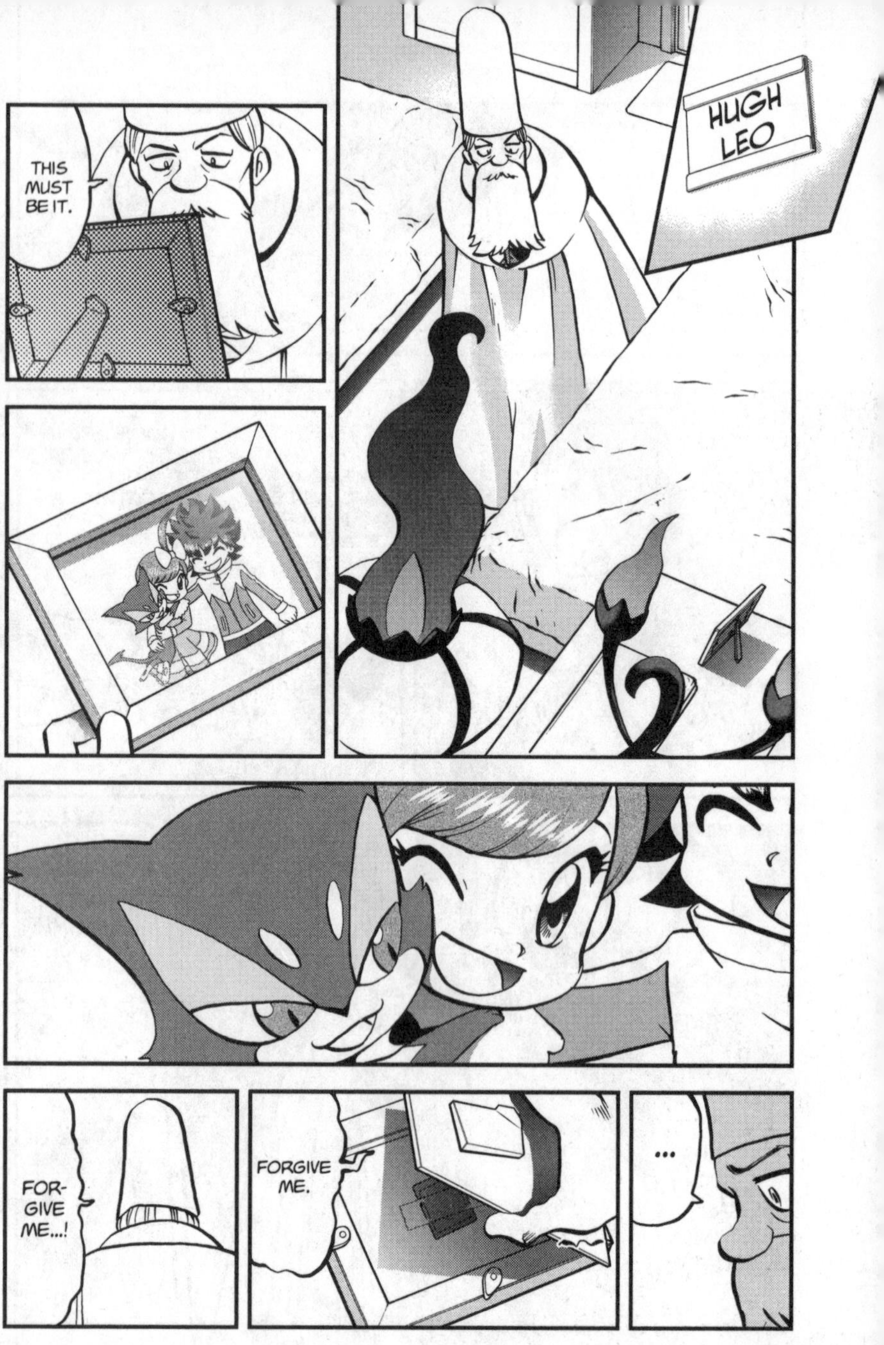
HUGH LEO
THIS MUST BE IT.
...
FORGIVE ME.
FOR-GIVE ME...!

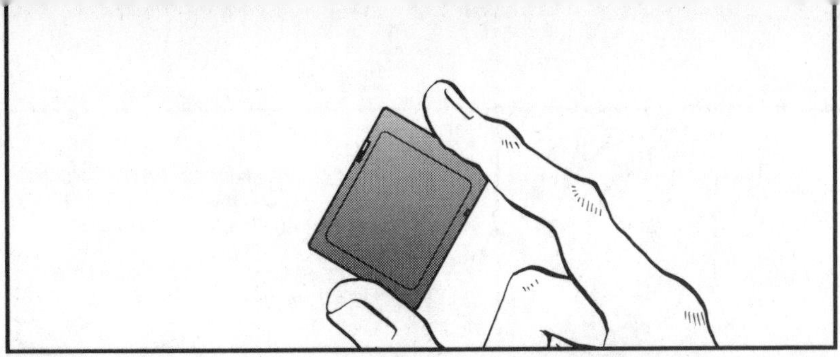

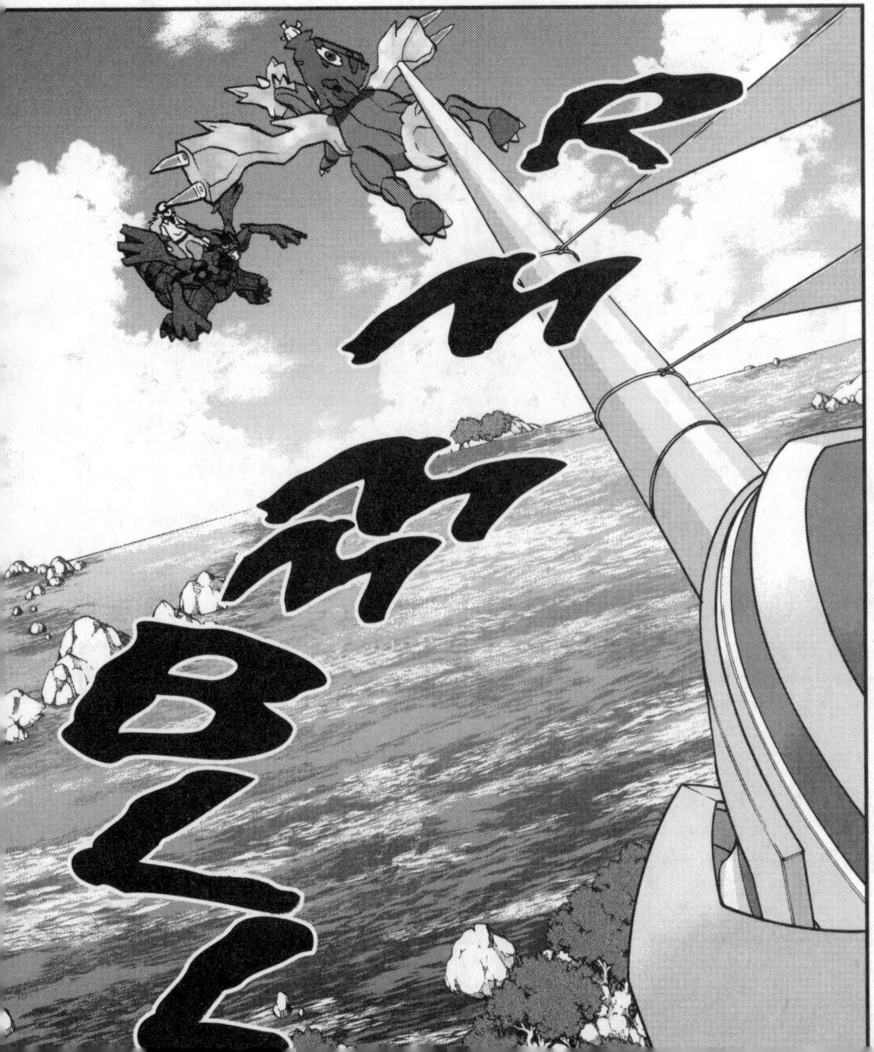
RMMMBL

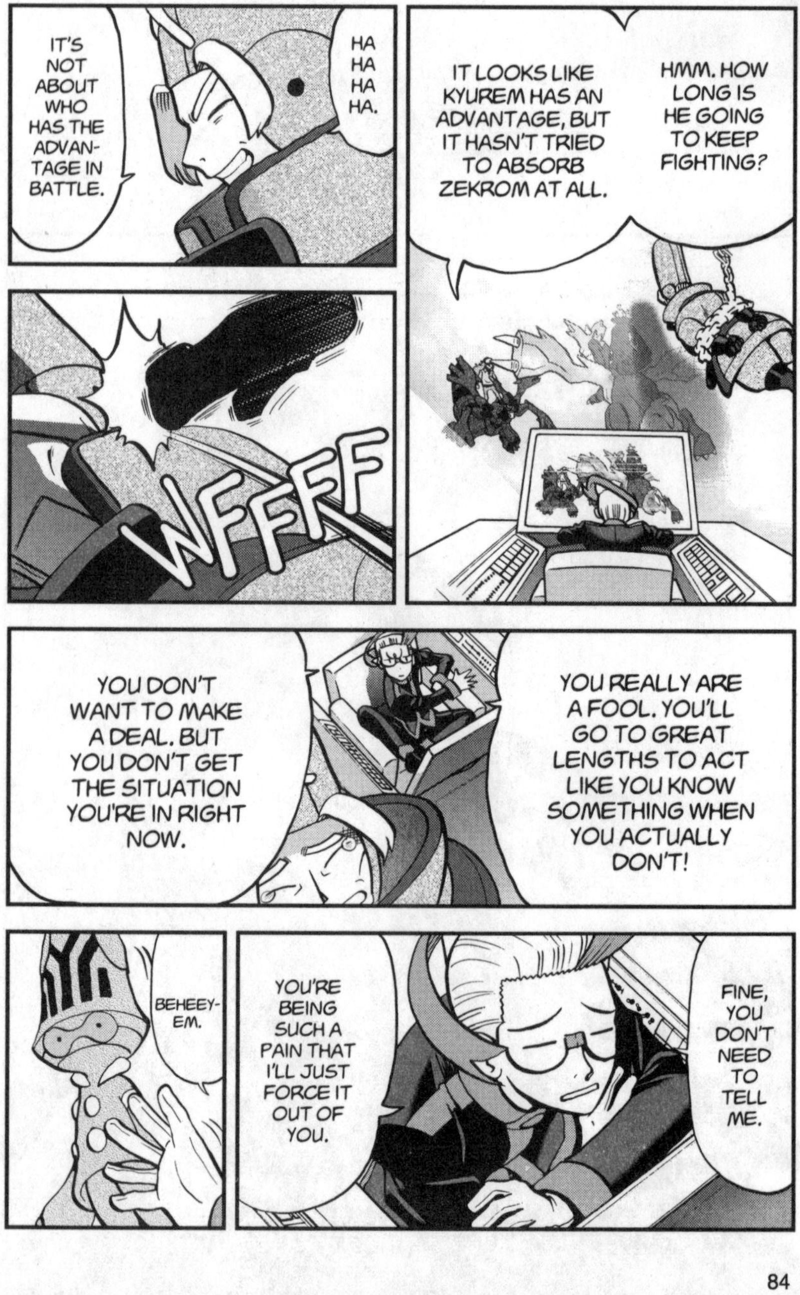
HMM. HOW LONG IS HE GOING TO KEEP FIGHTING?
IT LOOKS LIKE KYUREM HAS AN ADVANTAGE, BUT IT HASN'T TRIED TO ABSORB ZEKROM AT ALL.
HA HA HA HA.
IT'S NOT ABOUT WHO HAS THE ADVAN-TAGE IN BATTLE.
WFFFF
YOU REALLY ARE A FOOL. YOU'LL GO TO GREAT LENGTHS TO ACT LIKE YOU KNOW SOMETHING WHEN YOU ACTUALLY DON'T!
YOU DON'T WANT TO MAKE A DEAL. BUT YOU DON'T GET THE SITUATION YOU'RE IN RIGHT NOW.
FINE, YOU DON'T NEED TO TELL ME.
YOU'RE BEING SUCH A PAIN THAT I'LL JUST FORCE IT OUT OF YOU.
BEHEEY-EM.

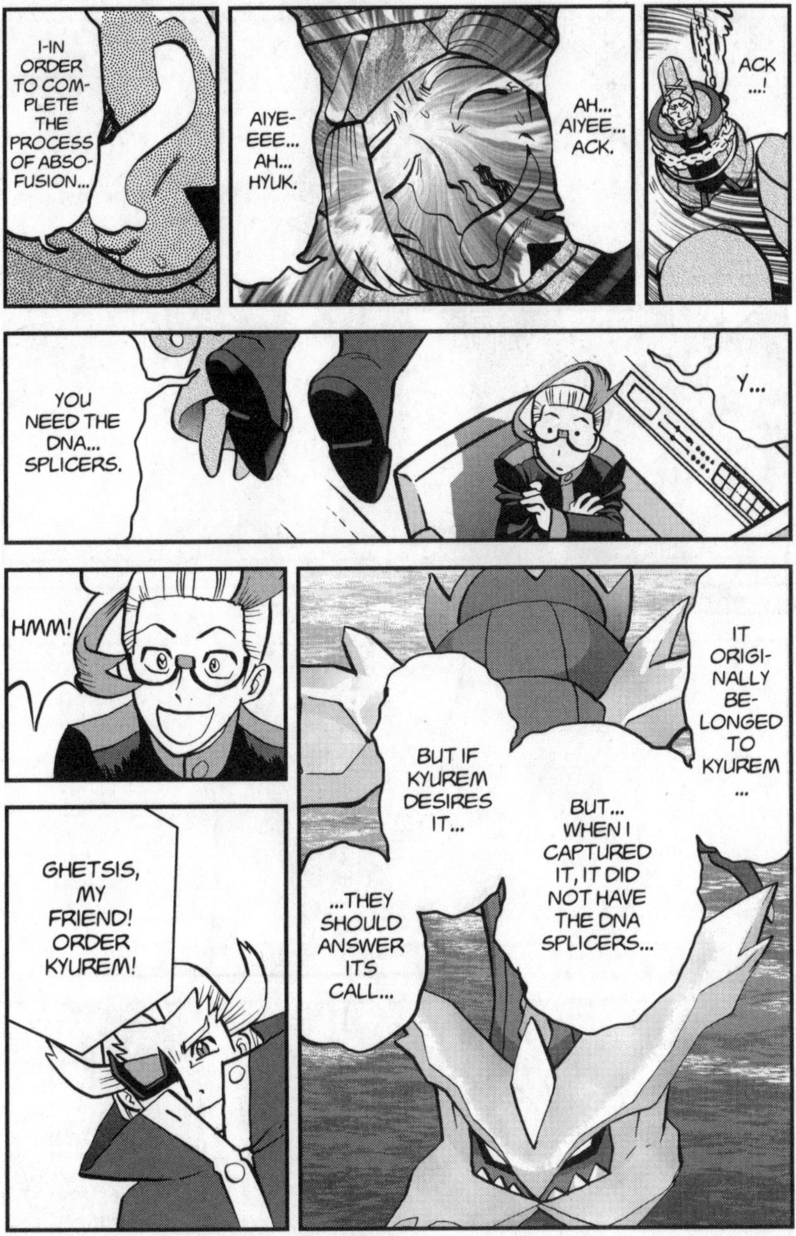
ACK ...!
AH... AIYEE... ACK.
AIYEEEE... AH... HYUK.
I-IN ORDER TO COMPLETE THE PROCESS OF ABSOFUSION...
Y...
YOU NEED THE DNA... SPLICERS.
IT ORIGINALLY BELONGED TO KYUREM ...
BUT... WHEN I CAPTURED IT, IT DID NOT HAVE THE DNA SPLICERS...
BUT IF KYUREM DESIRES IT...
...THEY SHOULD ANSWER ITS CALL...
HMM!
GHETSIS, MY FRIEND! ORDER KYUREM!

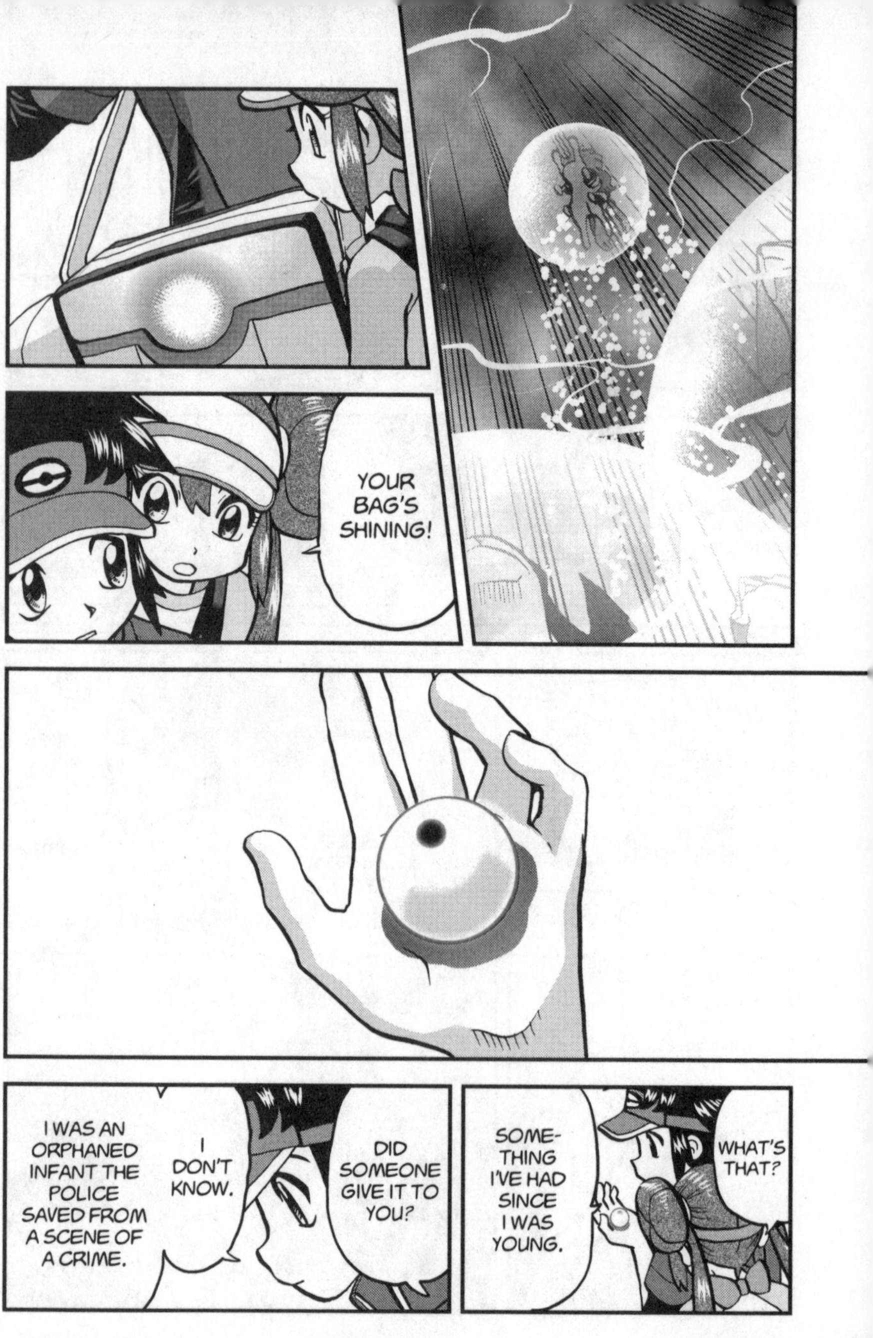

YOUR BAG'S SHINING!
WHAT'S THAT?
SOME-THING I'VE HAD SINCE I WAS YOUNG.
DID SOMEONE GIVE IT TO YOU?
I DON'T KNOW.
I WAS AN ORPHANED INFANT THE POLICE SAVED FROM A SCENE OF A CRIME.

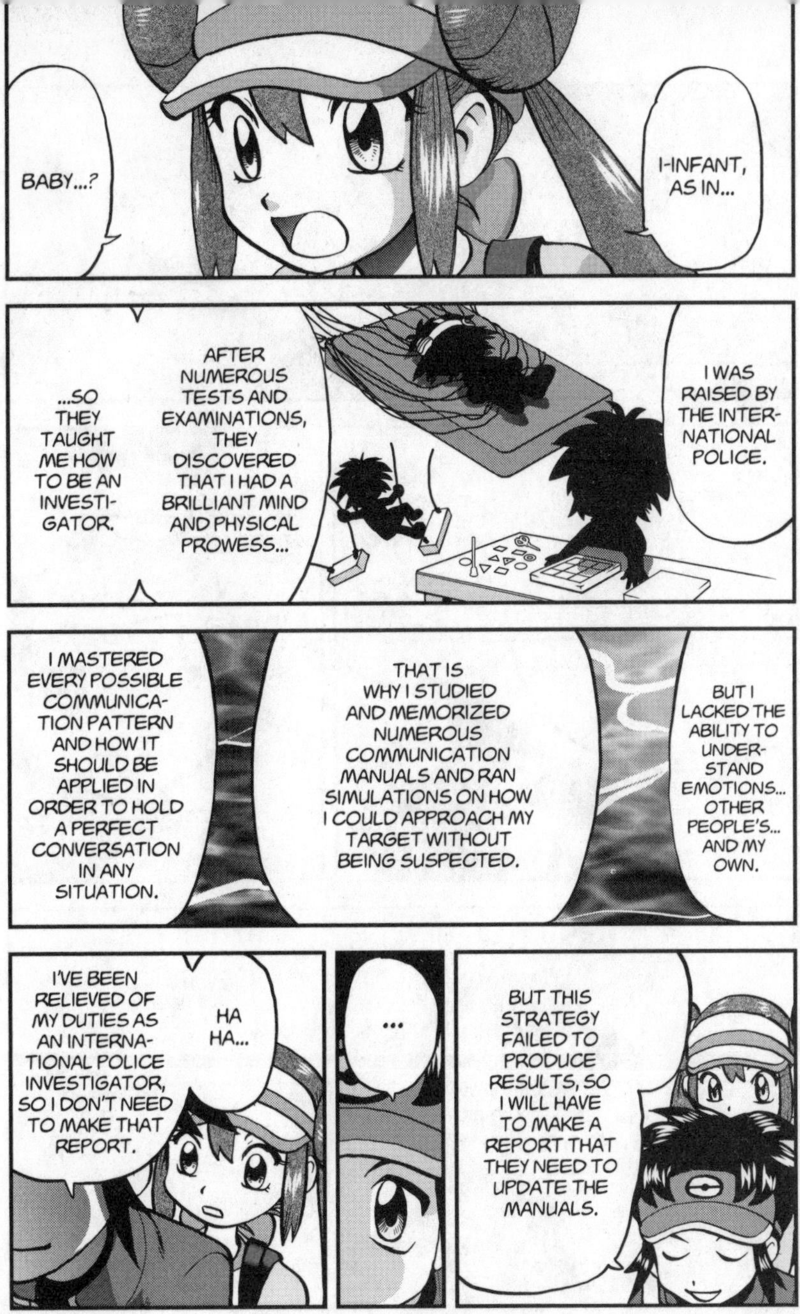
I-INFANT, AS IN...
BABY...?
I WAS RAISED BY THE INTER-NATIONAL POLICE.
AFTER NUMEROUS TESTS AND EXAMINATIONS, THEY DISCOVERED THAT I HAD A BRILLIANT MIND AND PHYSICAL PROWESS...
...SO THEY TAUGHT ME HOW TO BE AN INVESTI-GATOR.
BUT I LACKED THE ABILITY TO UNDER-STAND EMOTIONS... OTHER PEOPLE'S... AND MY OWN.
THAT IS WHY I STUDIED AND MEMORIZED NUMEROUS COMMUNICATION MANUALS AND RAN SIMULATIONS ON HOW I COULD APPROACH MY TARGET WITHOUT BEING SUSPECTED.
I MASTERED EVERY POSSIBLE COMMUNICA-TION PATTERN AND HOW IT SHOULD BE APPLIED IN ORDER TO HOLD A PERFECT CONVERSATION IN ANY SITUATION.
BUT THIS STRATEGY FAILED TO PRODUCE RESULTS, SO I WILL HAVE TO MAKE A REPORT THAT THEY NEED TO UPDATE THE MANUALS.
...
HA HA...
I'VE BEEN RELIEVED OF MY DUTIES AS AN INTERNA-TIONAL POLICE INVESTIGATOR, SO I DON'T NEED TO MAKE THAT REPORT.

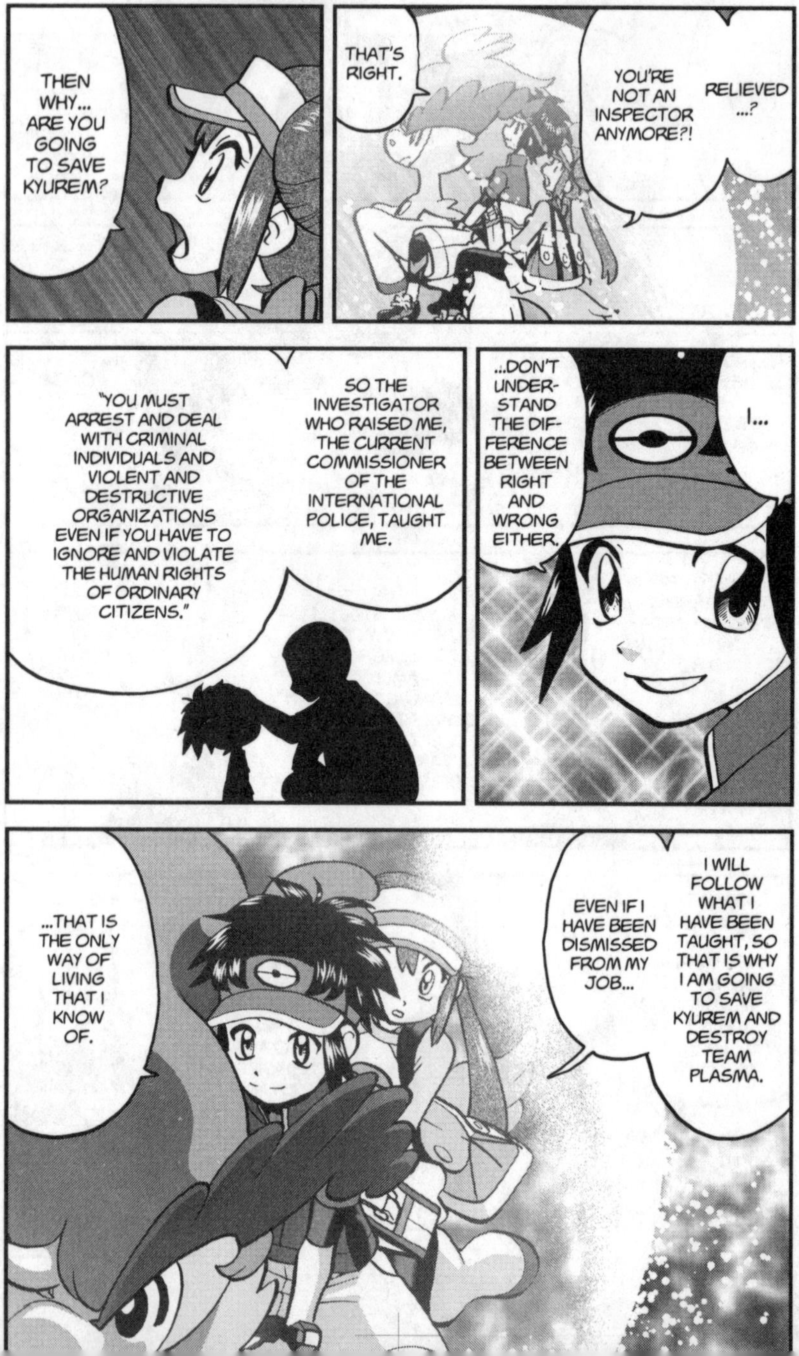
RELIEVED ...?
YOU'RE NOT AN INSPECTOR ANYMORE?!
THAT'S RIGHT.
THEN WHY... ARE YOU GOING TO SAVE KYUREM?
I...
...DON'T UNDER-STAND THE DIF-FERENCE BETWEEN RIGHT AND WRONG EITHER.
SO THE INVESTIGATOR WHO RAISED ME, THE CURRENT COMMISSIONER OF THE INTERNATIONAL POLICE, TAUGHT ME.
"YOU MUST ARREST AND DEAL WITH CRIMINAL INDIVIDUALS AND VIOLENT AND DESTRUCTIVE ORGANIZATIONS EVEN IF YOU HAVE TO IGNORE AND VIOLATE THE HUMAN RIGHTS OF ORDINARY CITIZENS."
I WILL FOLLOW WHAT I HAVE BEEN TAUGHT, SO THAT IS WHY I AM GOING TO SAVE KYUREM AND DESTROY TEAM PLASMA.
EVEN IF I HAVE BEEN DISMISSED FROM MY JOB...
...THAT IS THE ONLY WAY OF LIVING THAT I KNOW OF.

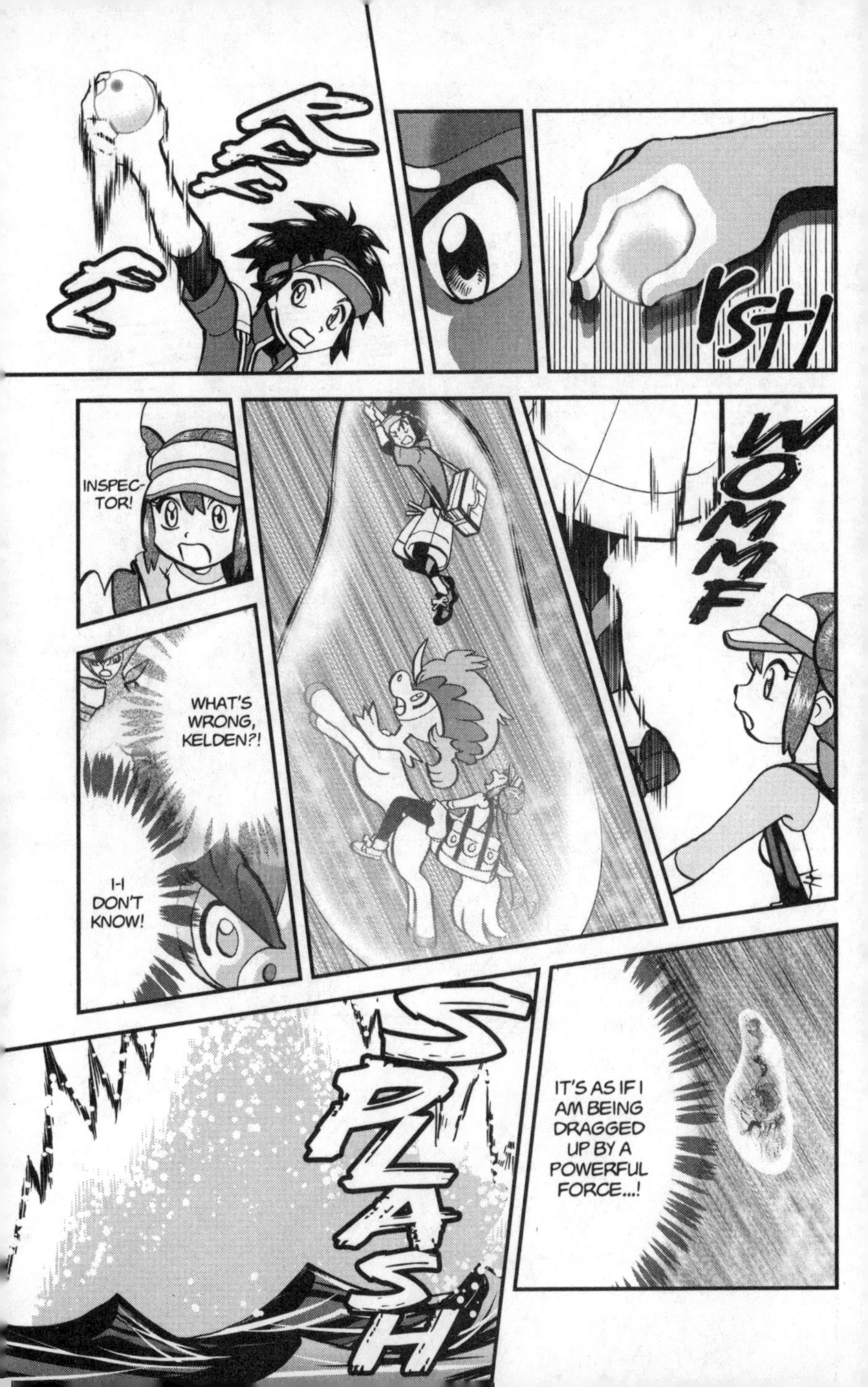

RST!
WOMMF
INSPEC-TOR!
WHAT'S WRONG, KELDEN?!
I-I DON'T KNOW!
IT'S AS IF I AM BEING DRAGGED UP BY A POWERFUL FORCE...!
SPLASH

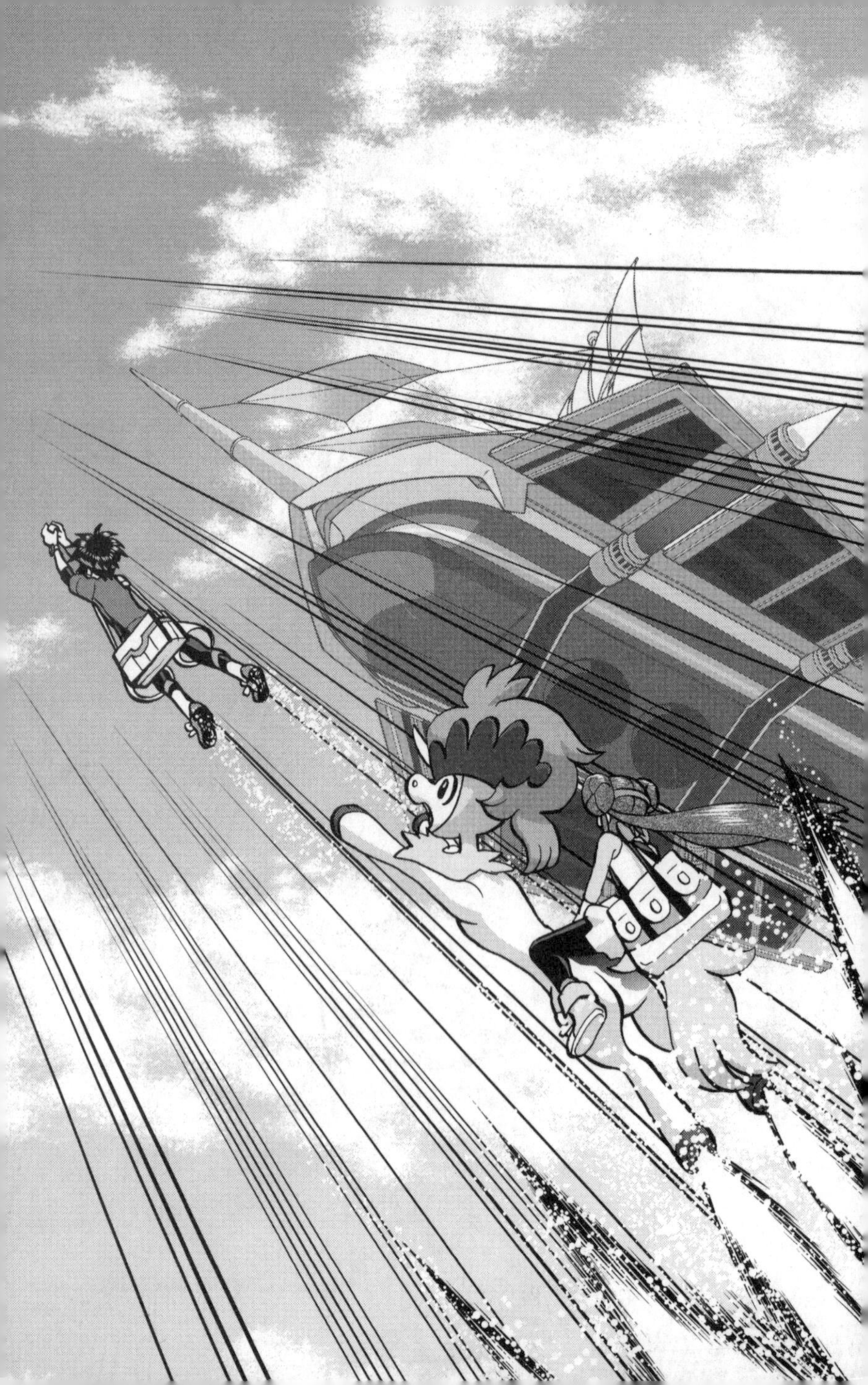

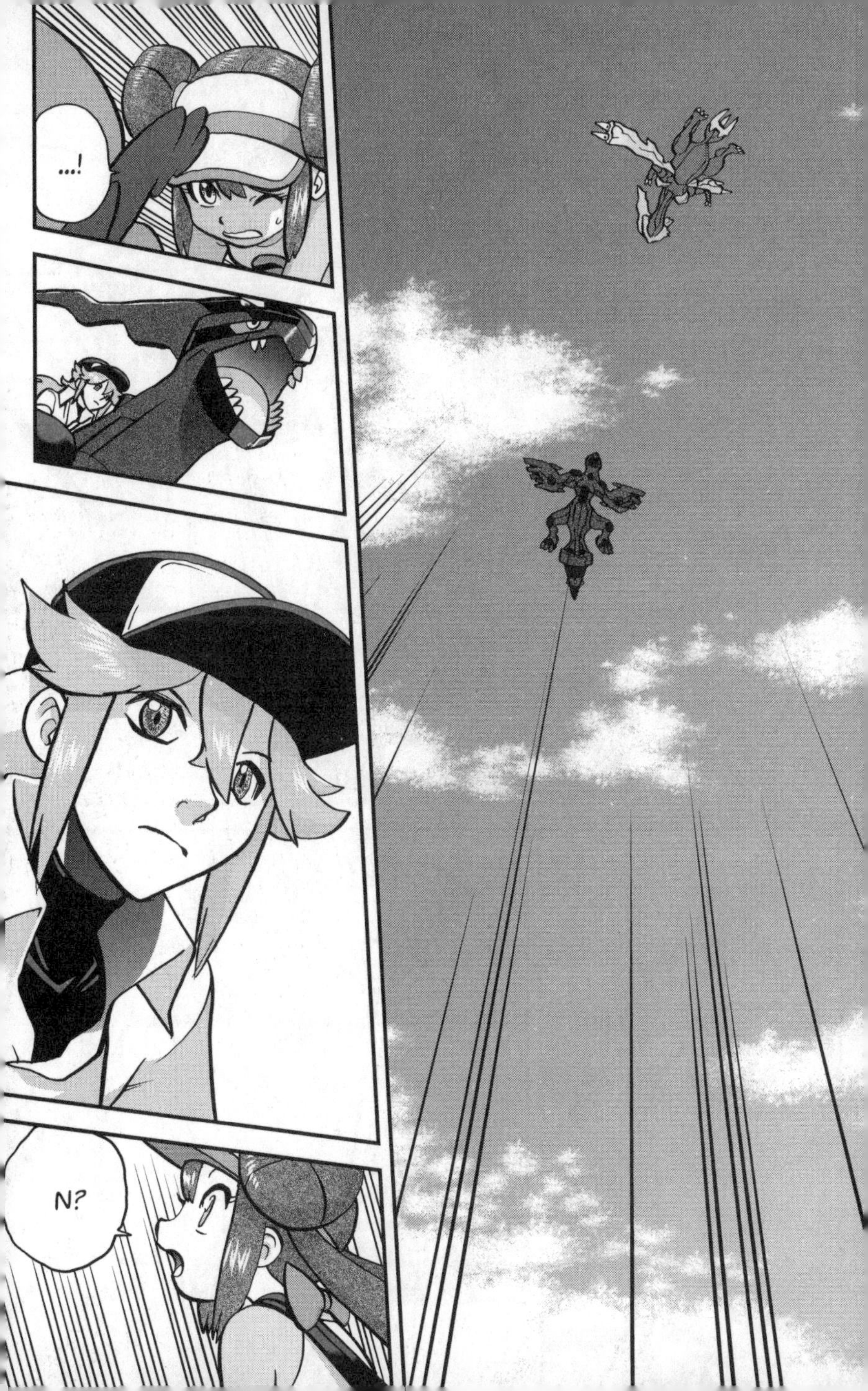
...!
N?

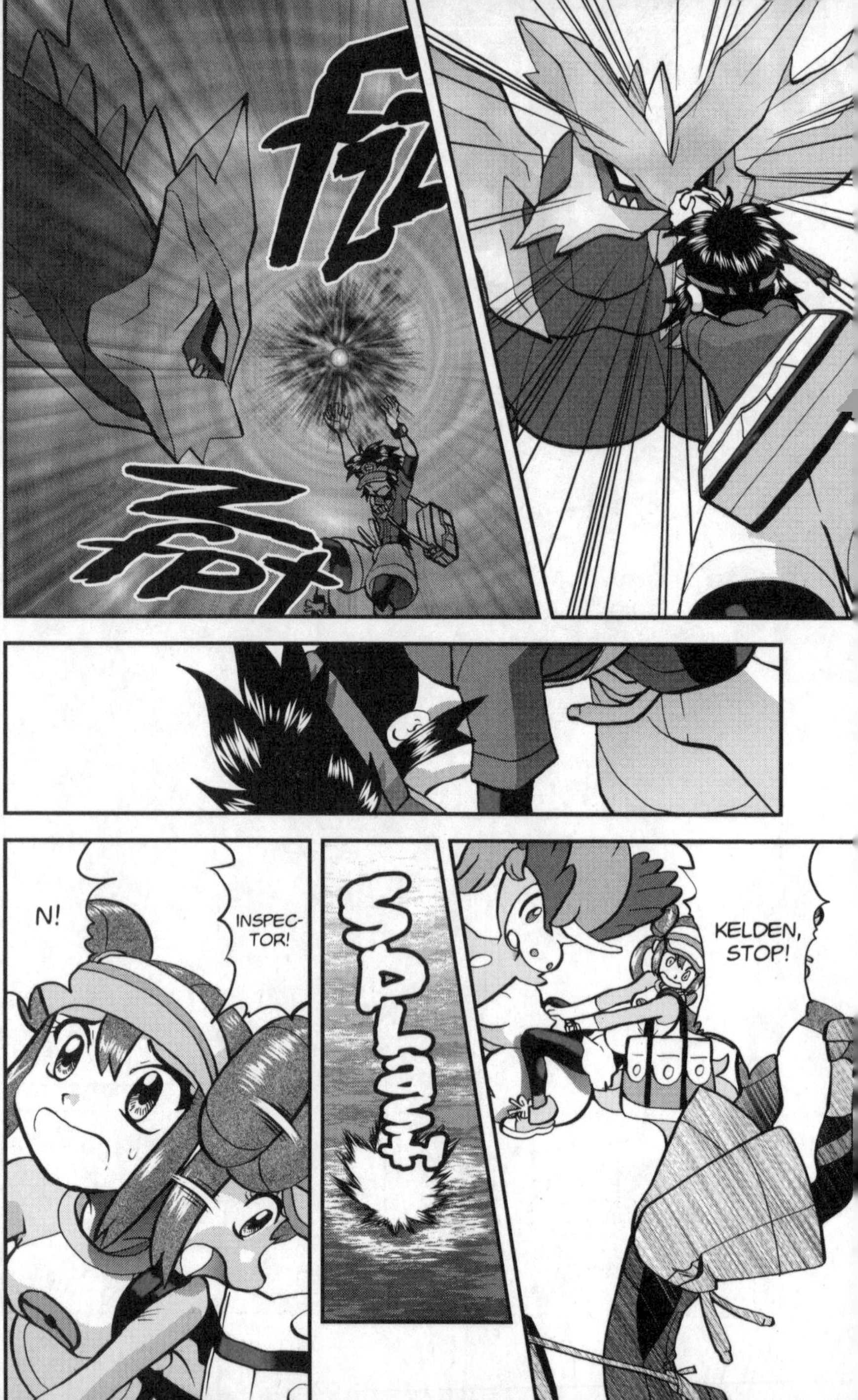
KELDEN, STOP!
SPLASH
INSPECTOR!
N!

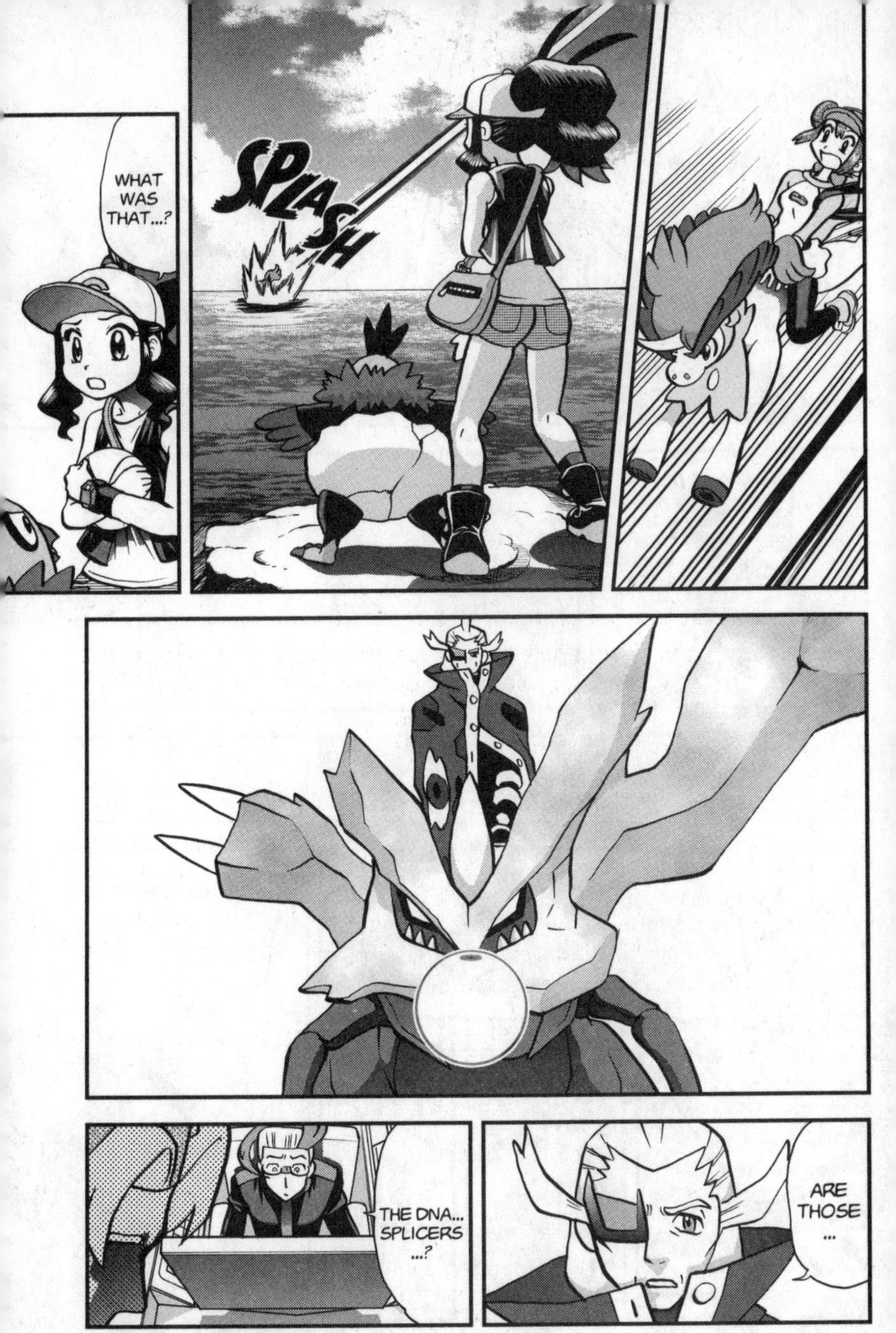
SPLASH
WHAT WAS THAT...?
ARE THOSE ...
THE DNA... SPLICERS ...?

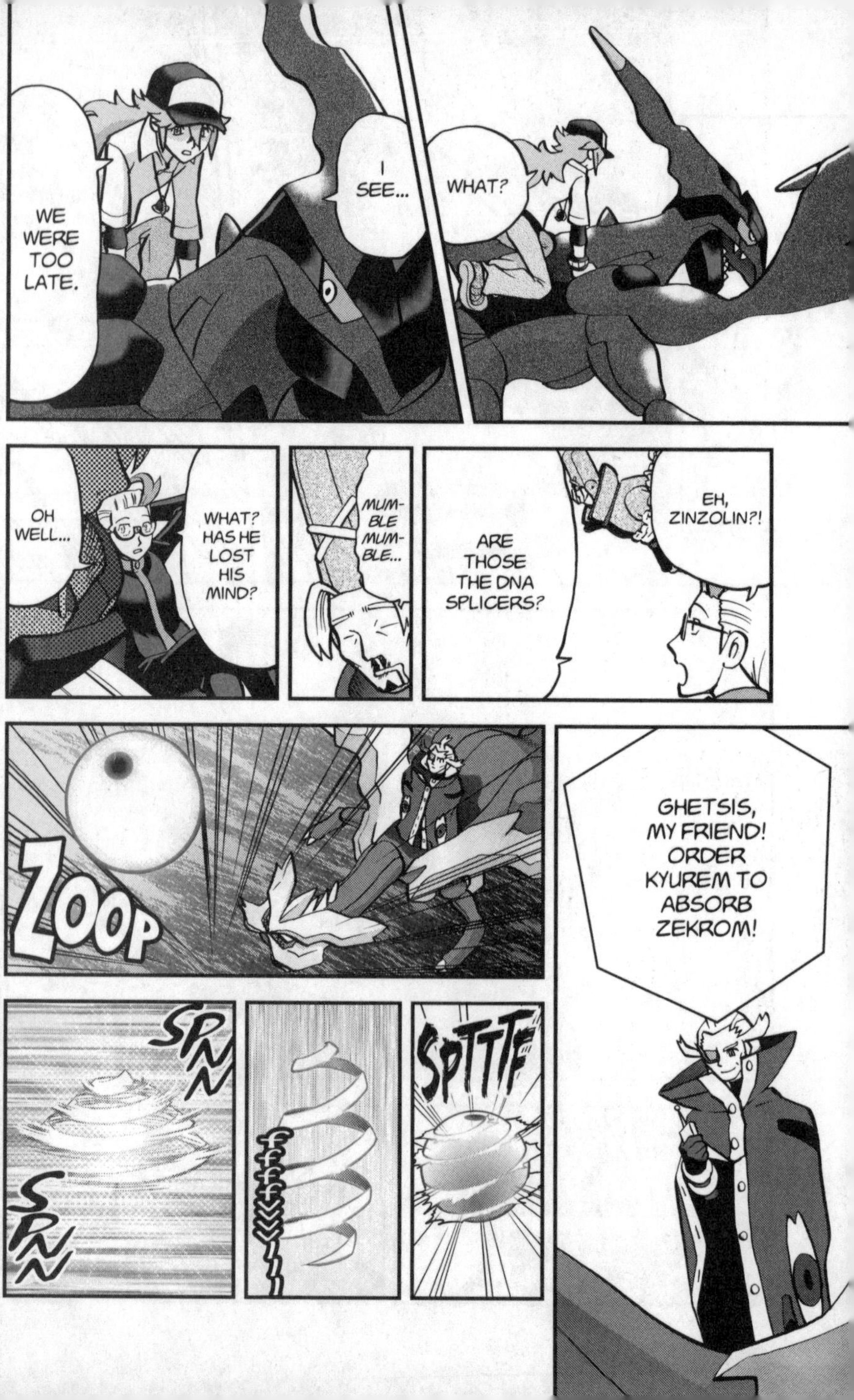
WHAT?
I SEE...
WE WERE TOO LATE.
EH, ZINZOLIN?!
ARE THOSE THE DNA SPLICERS?
MUMBLE MUMBLE...
WHAT? HAS HE LOST HIS MIND?
OH WELL...
GHETSIS, MY FRIEND! ORDER KYUREM TO ABSORB ZEKROM!
ZOOP
SPTTF
SPNN
SPNN

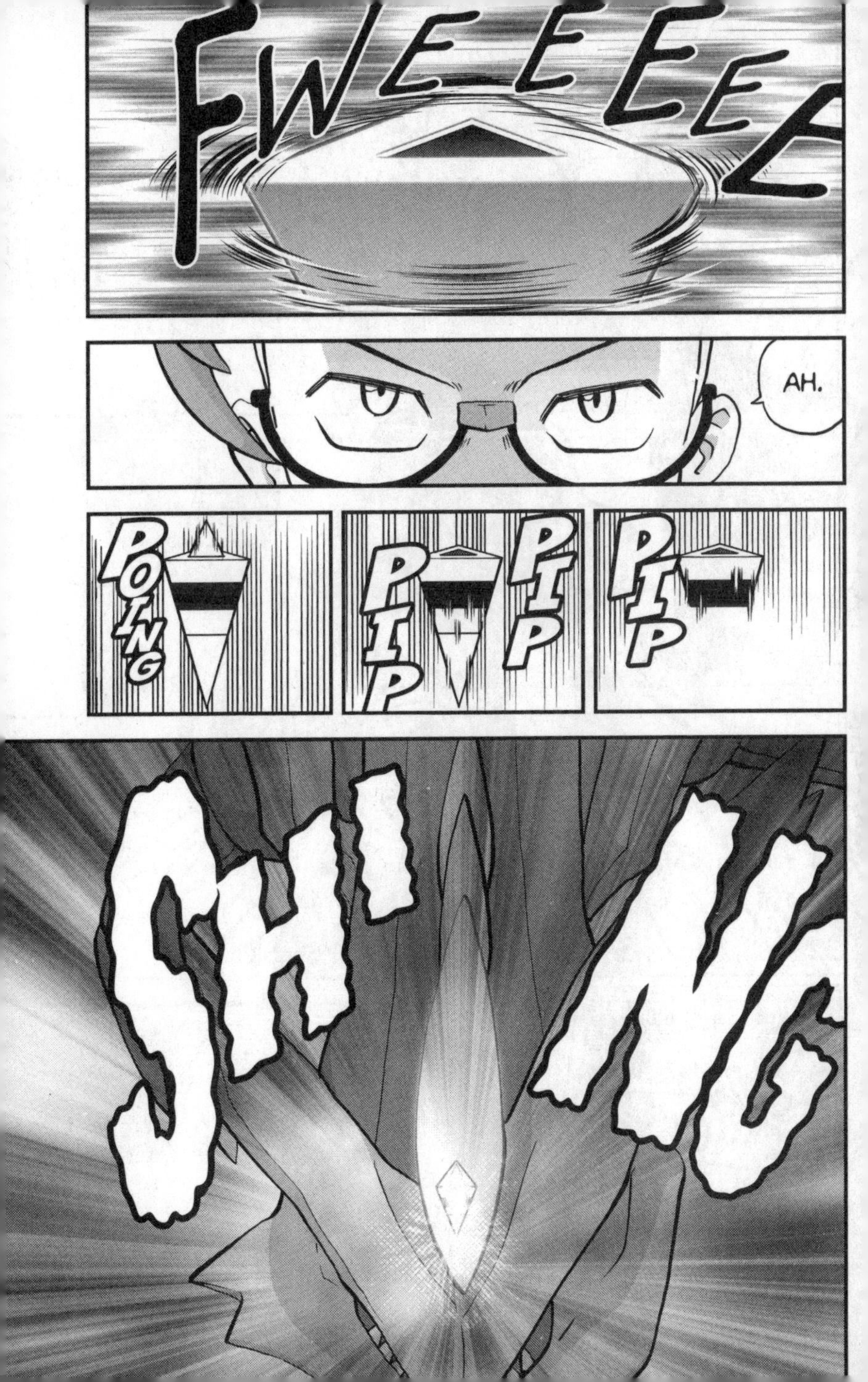

FWEEEE
AH.
PIP
PIP
PIP
POING
SHING

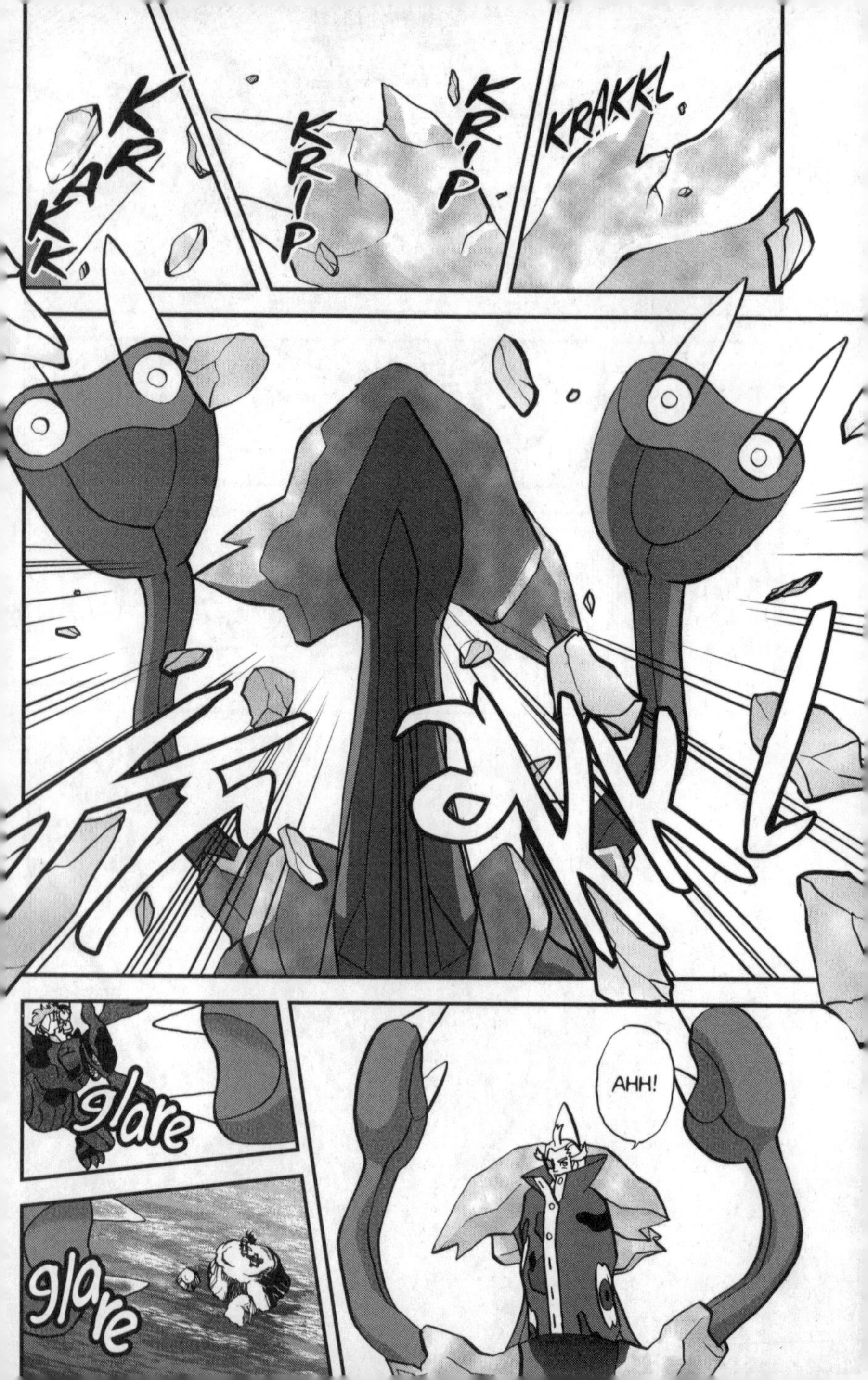
KRAKKL
KRIP
KRIP
KKARK
AHH!
glare
glare

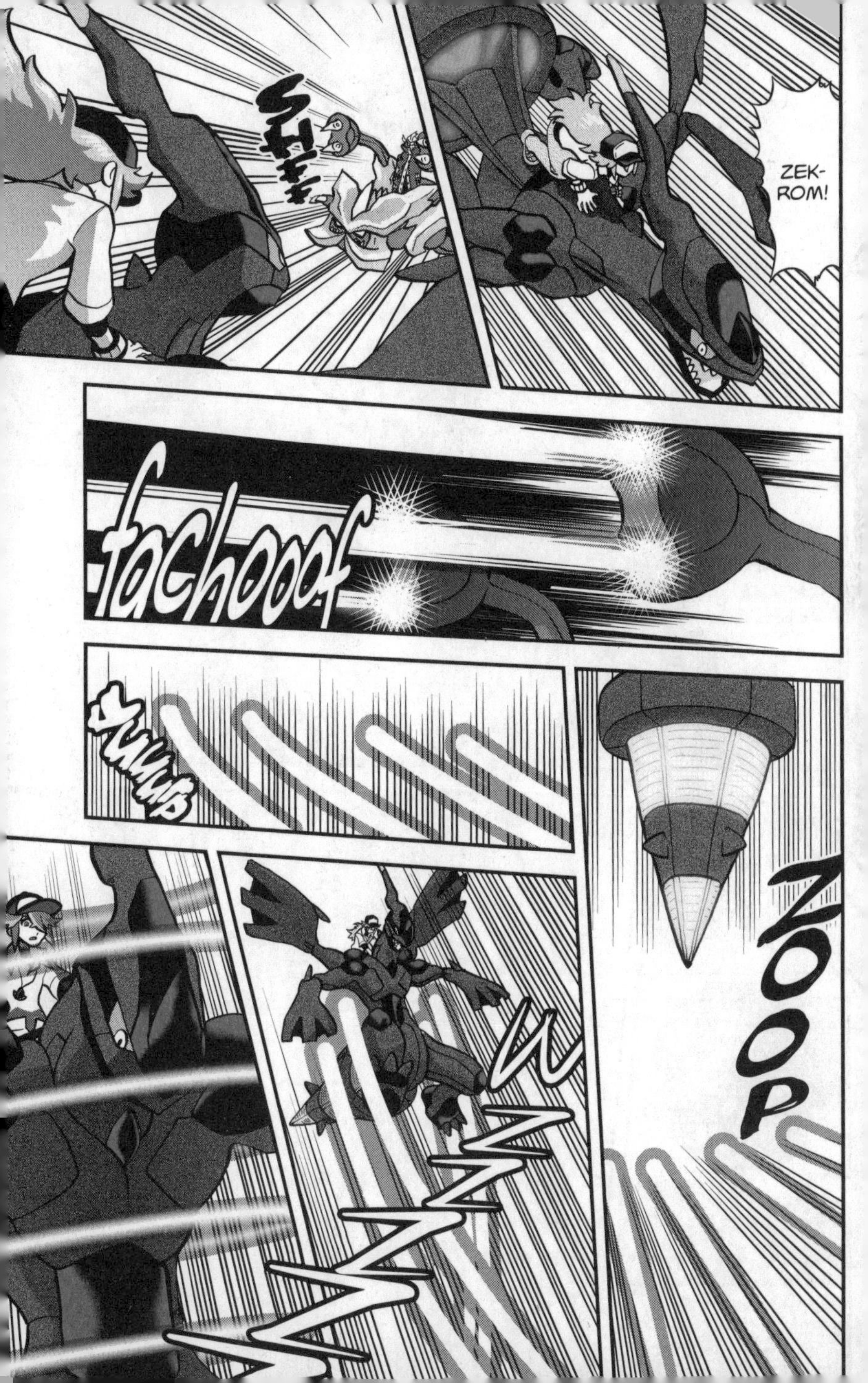
ZEK-
ROM!
SHFF
fachooof
ZOOOP

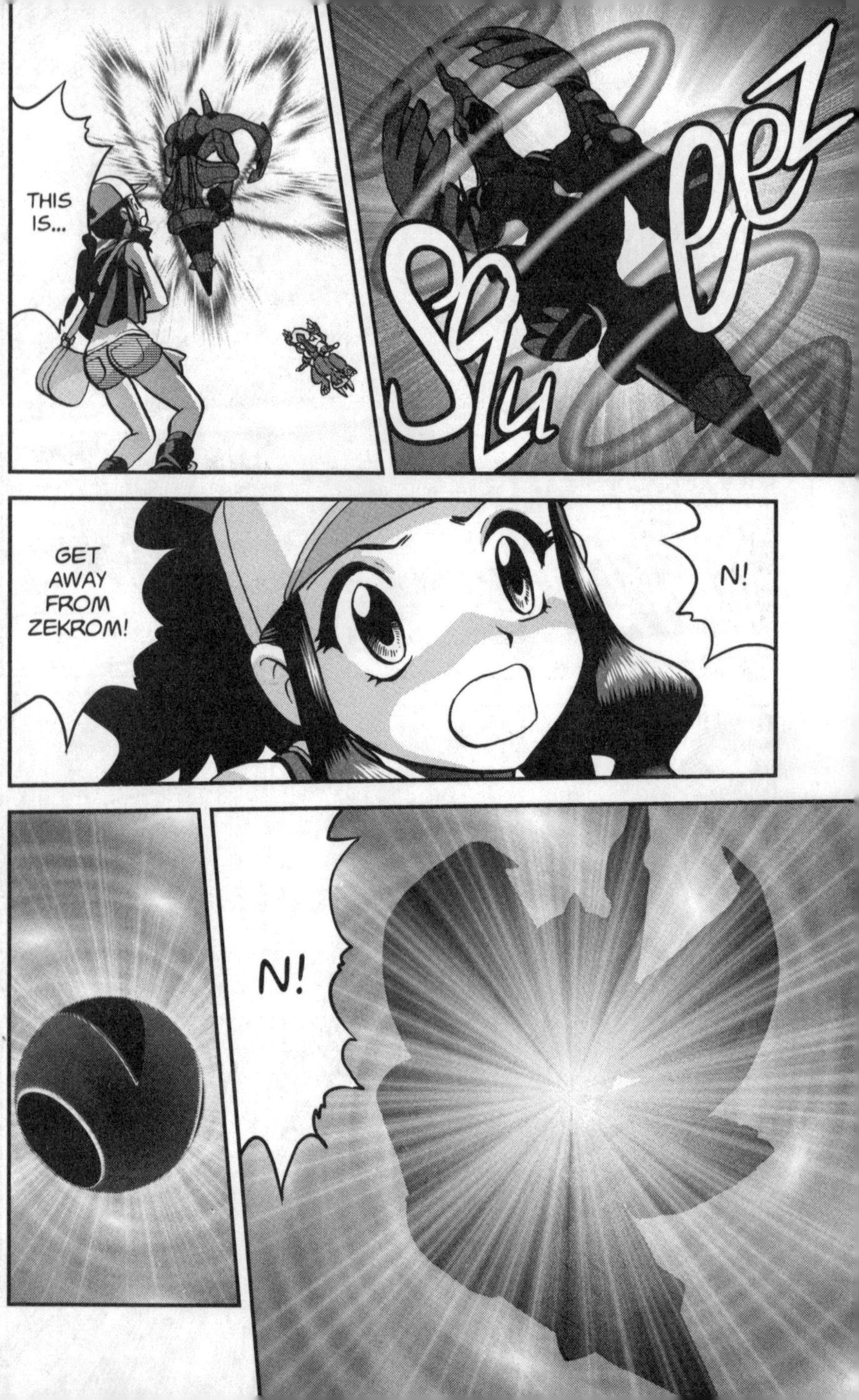
SQUEEZ
THIS IS...
N!
GET AWAY FROM ZEKROM!
N!

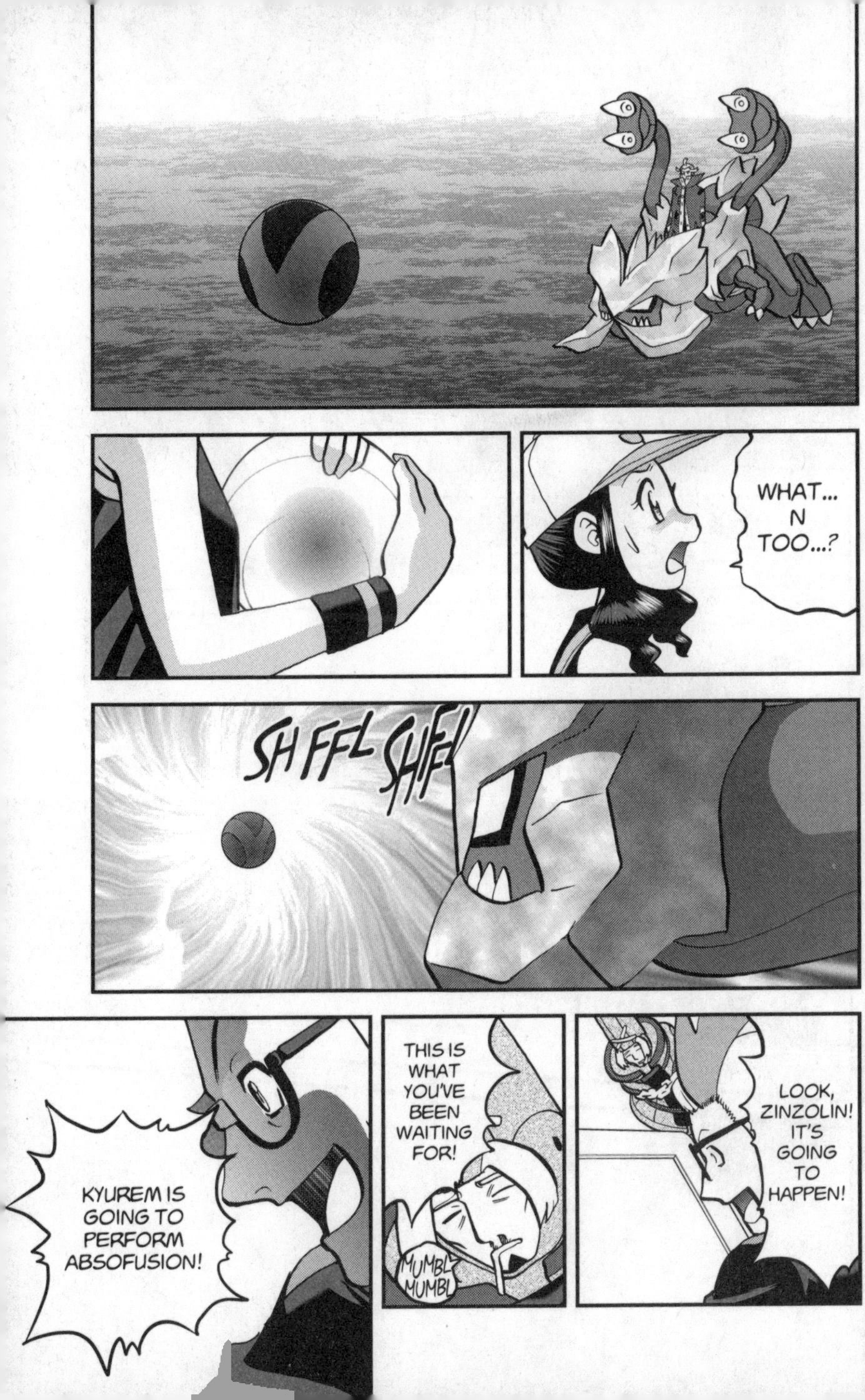
WHAT... N TOO...?
SHFFL
LOOK, ZINZOLIN! IT'S GOING TO HAPPEN!
THIS IS WHAT YOU'VE BEEN WAITING FOR!
MUMBL MUMBL
KYUREM IS GOING TO PERFORM ABSOFUSION!

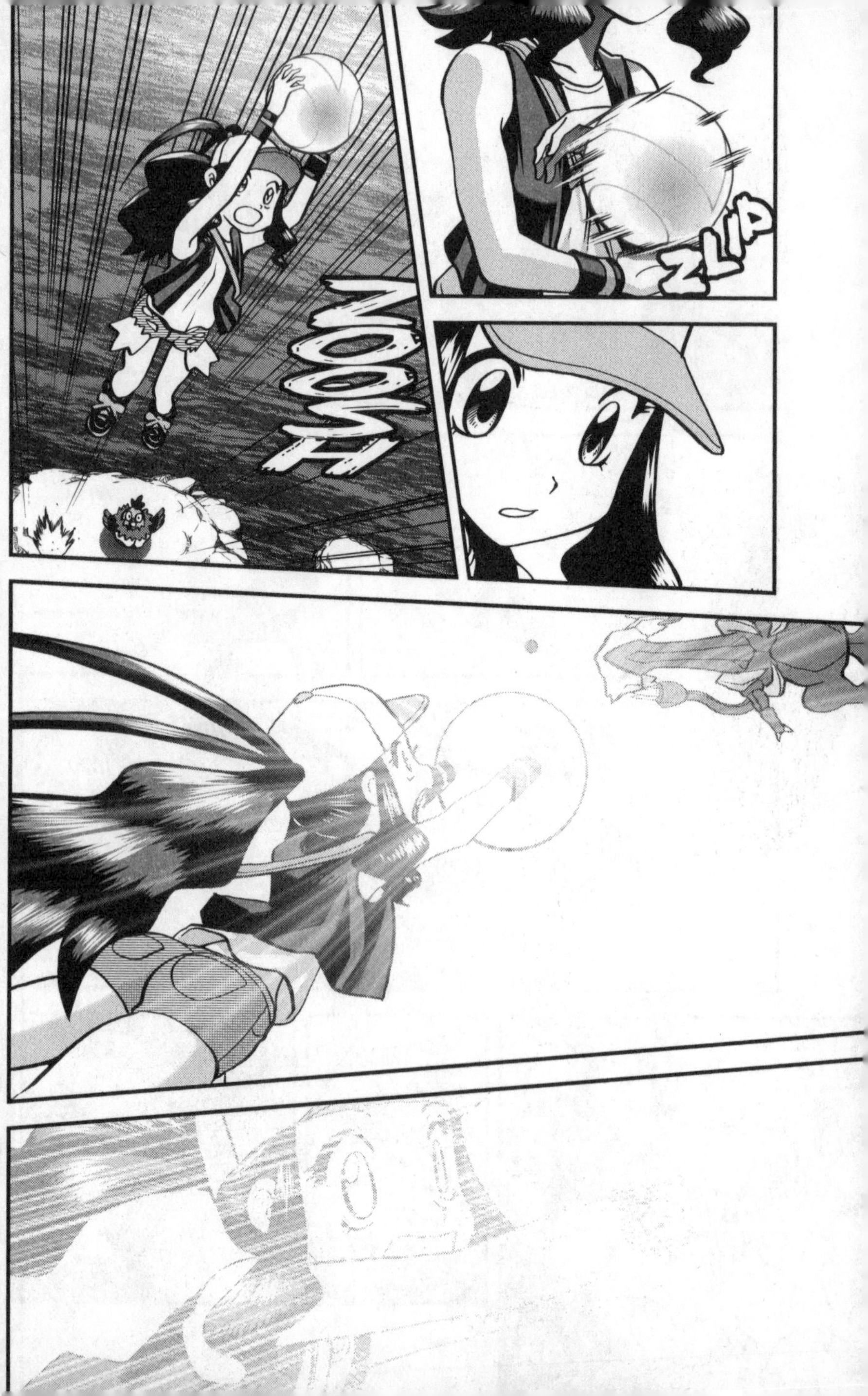
ZLIP
WOOMF

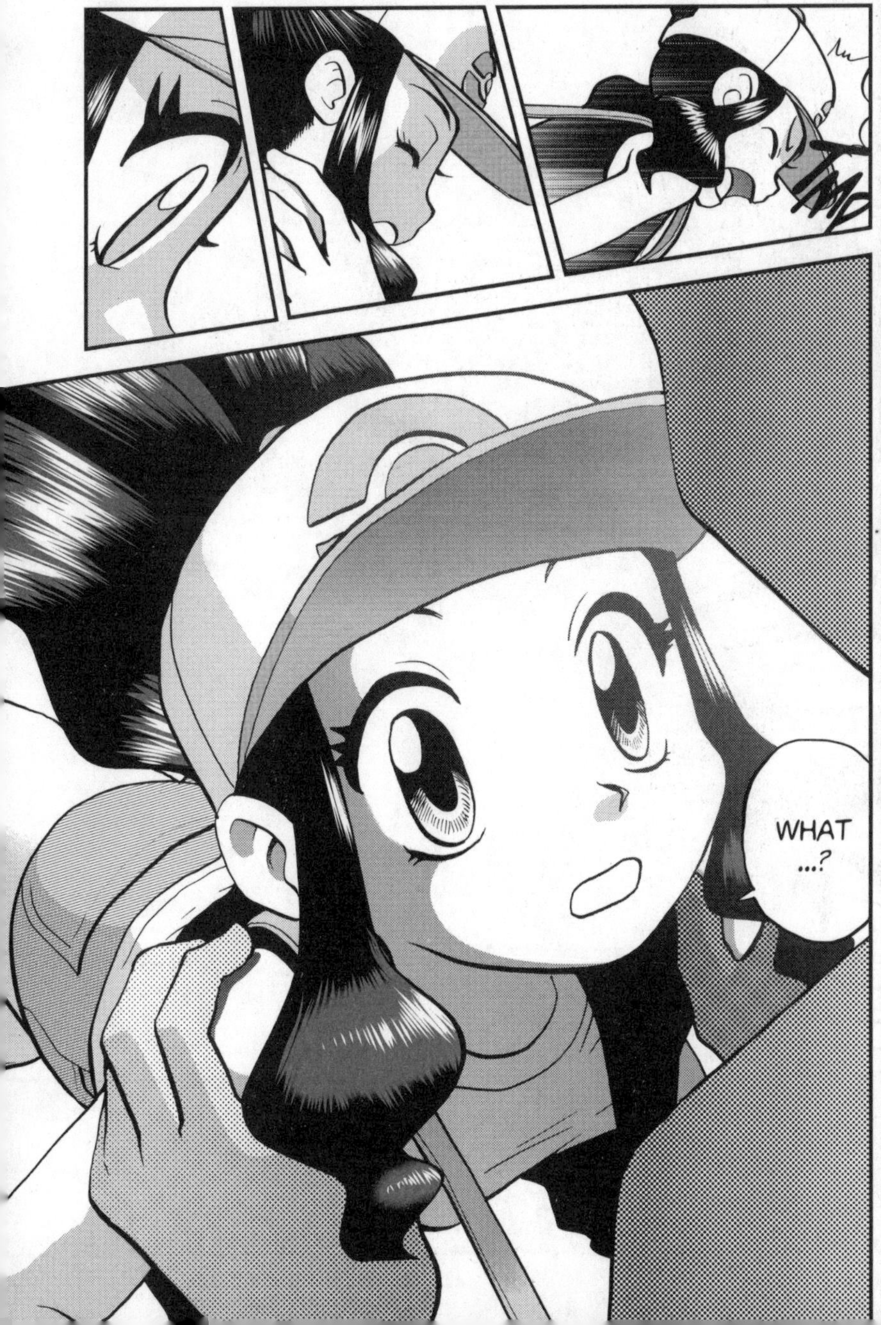
WHAT ...?

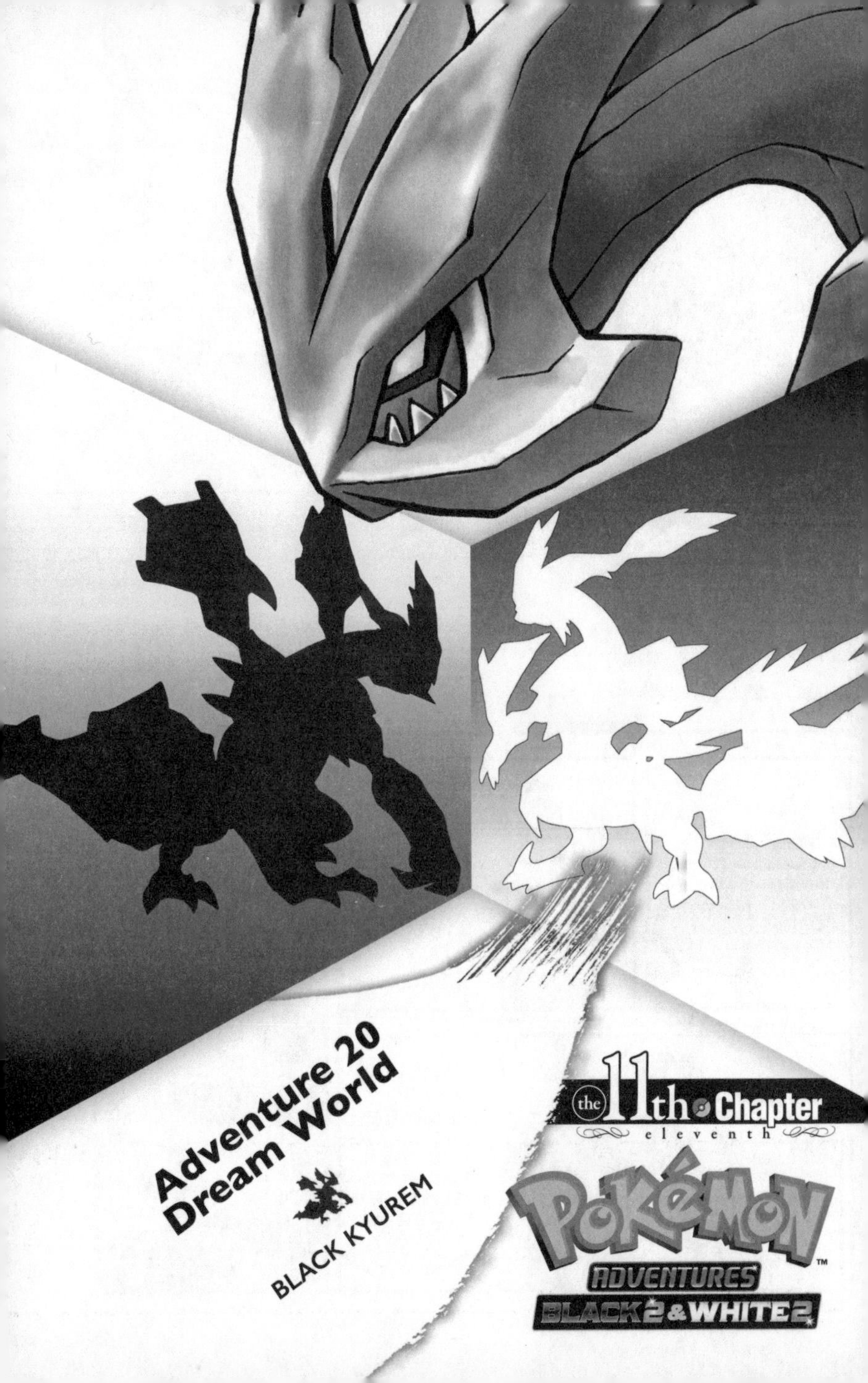

Adventure 20
Dream World
BLACK KYUREM
the 11th Chapter
eleventh
POKÉMON
ADVENTURES
BLACK 2 & WHITE 2

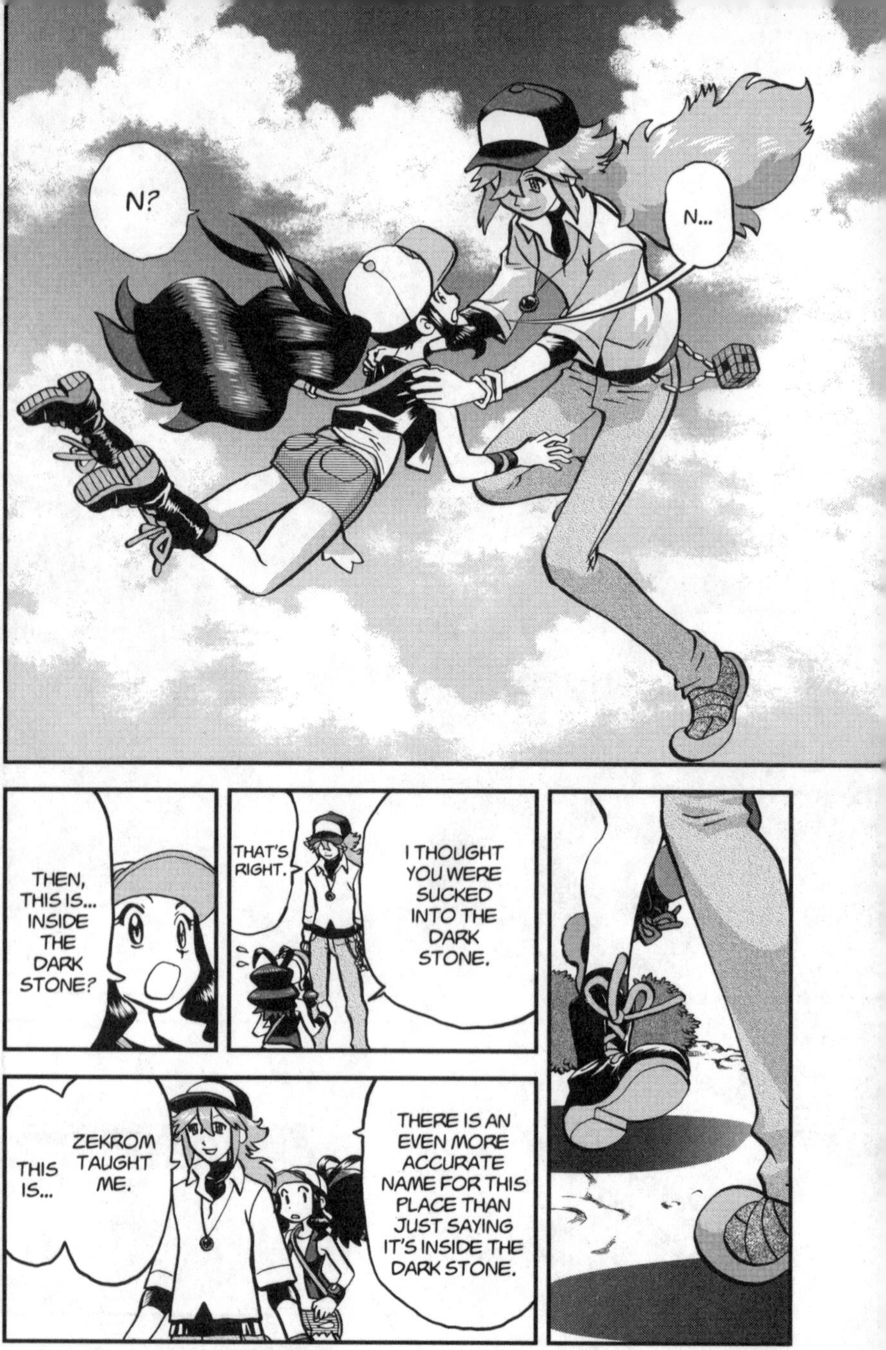
N...
N?
I THOUGHT YOU WERE SUCKED INTO THE DARK STONE.
THAT'S RIGHT.
THEN, THIS IS... INSIDE THE DARK STONE?
THERE IS AN EVEN MORE ACCURATE NAME FOR THIS PLACE THAN JUST SAYING IT'S INSIDE THE DARK STONE.
ZEKROM TAUGHT ME.
THIS IS...

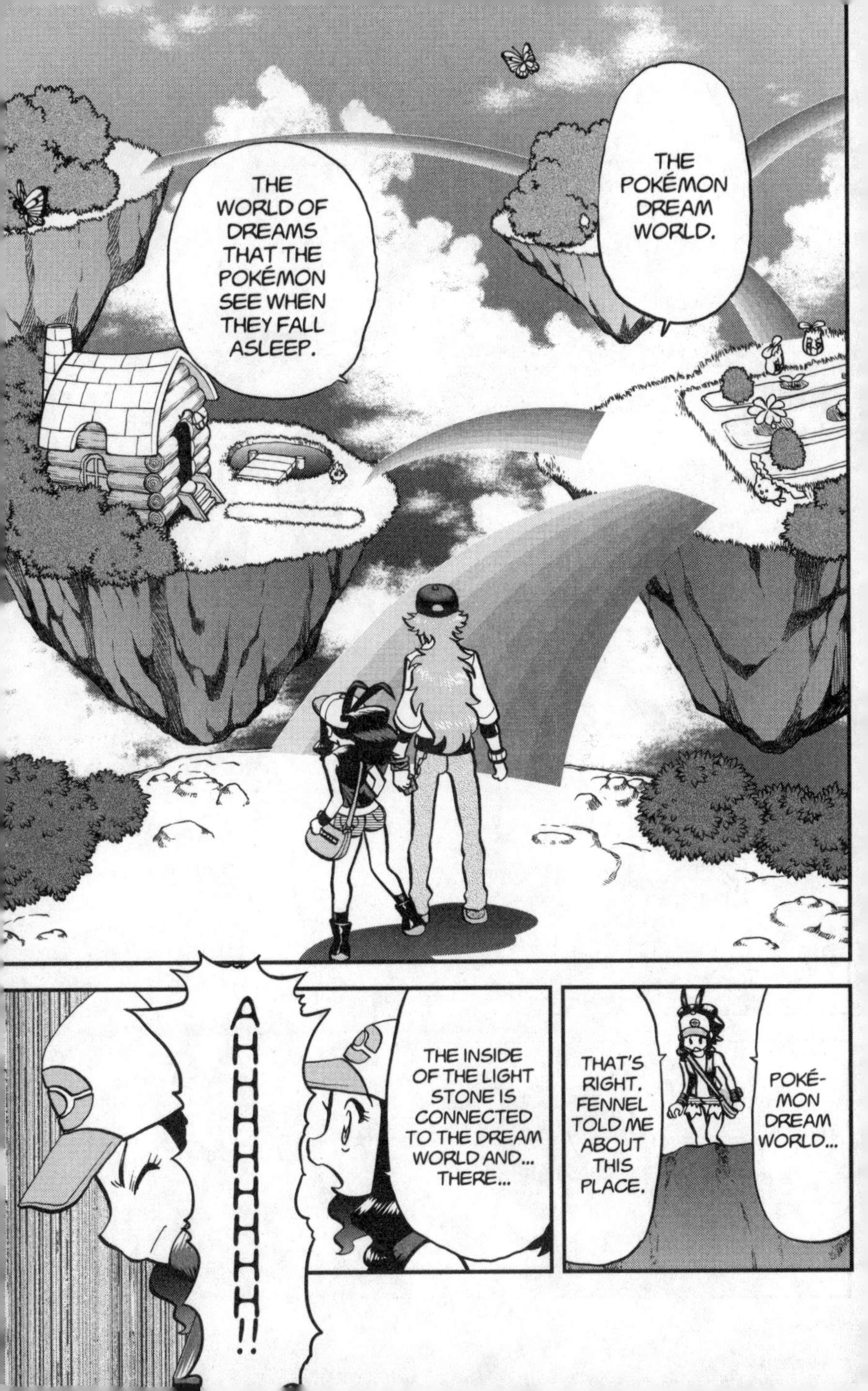
THE POKÉMON DREAM WORLD.
THE WORLD OF DREAMS THAT THE POKÉMON SEE WHEN THEY FALL ASLEEP.
POKÉ-MON DREAM WORLD...
THAT'S RIGHT. FENNEL TOLD ME ABOUT THIS PLACE.
THE INSIDE OF THE LIGHT STONE IS CONNECTED TO THE DREAM WORLD AND... THERE...
AHHHHHHHHH!!

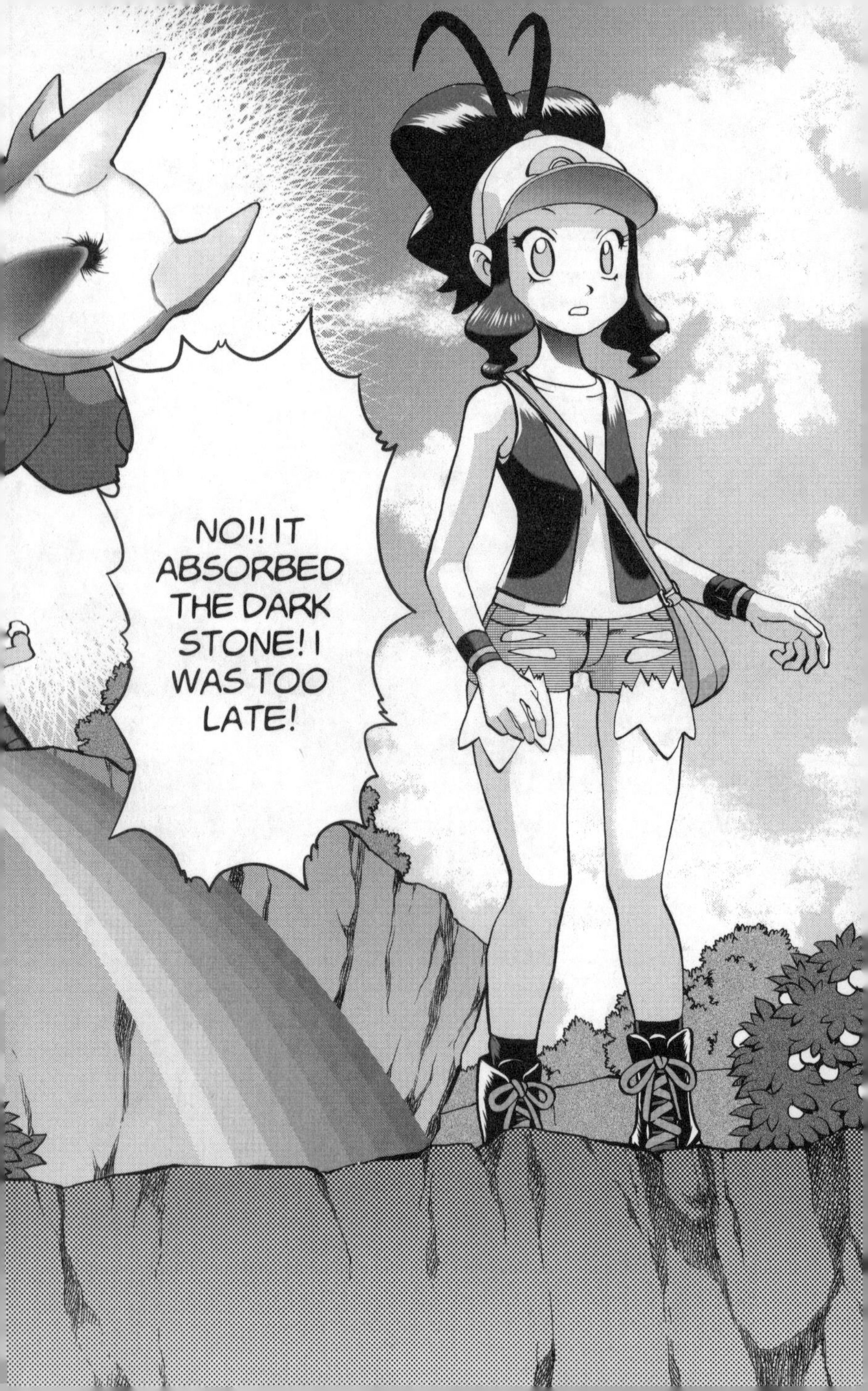
NO!! IT ABSORBED THE DARK STONE! I WAS TOO LATE!

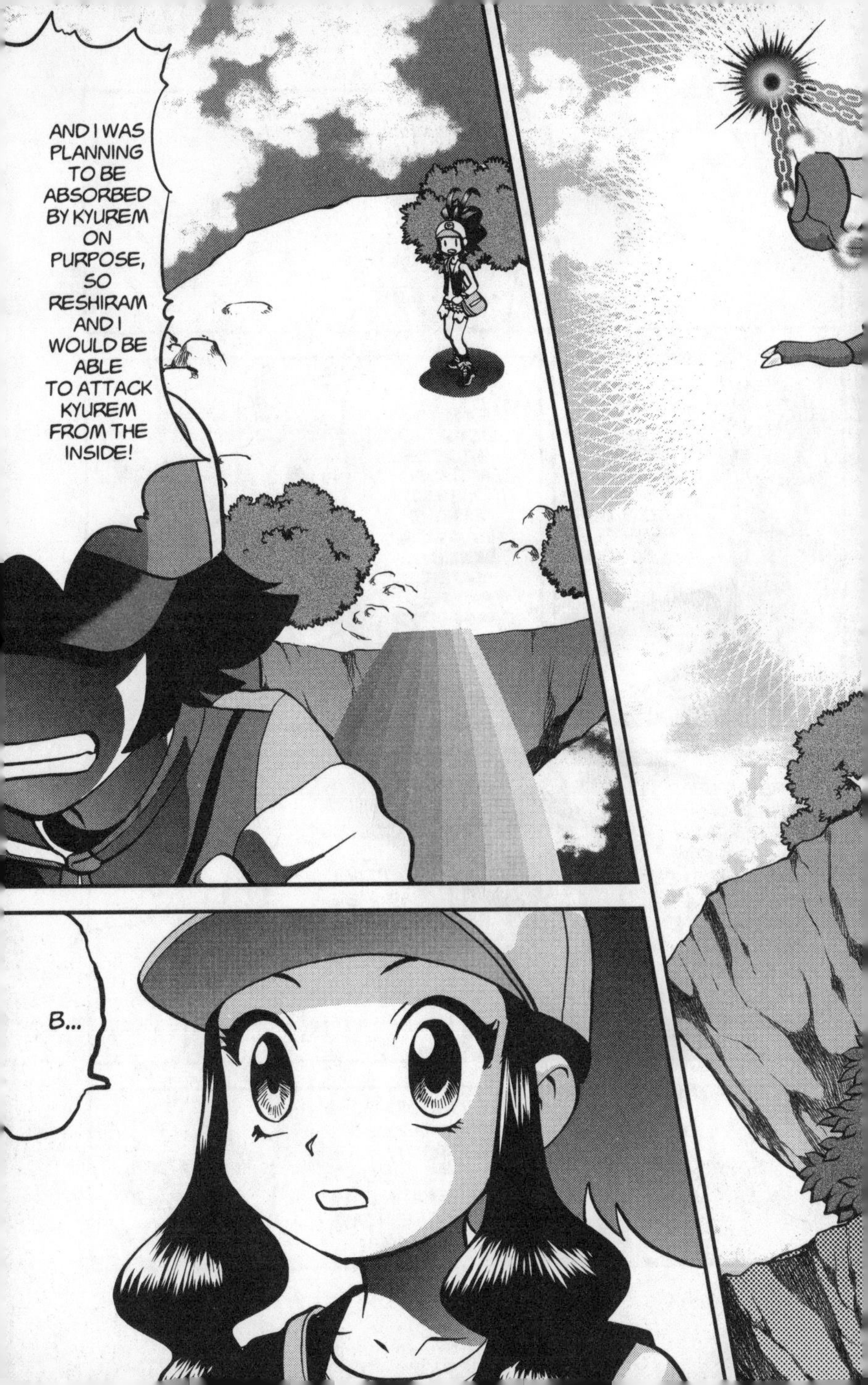
AND I WAS PLANNING TO BE ABSORBED BY KYUREM ON PURPOSE, SO RESHIRAM AND I WOULD BE ABLE TO ATTACK KYUREM FROM THE INSIDE!
B...

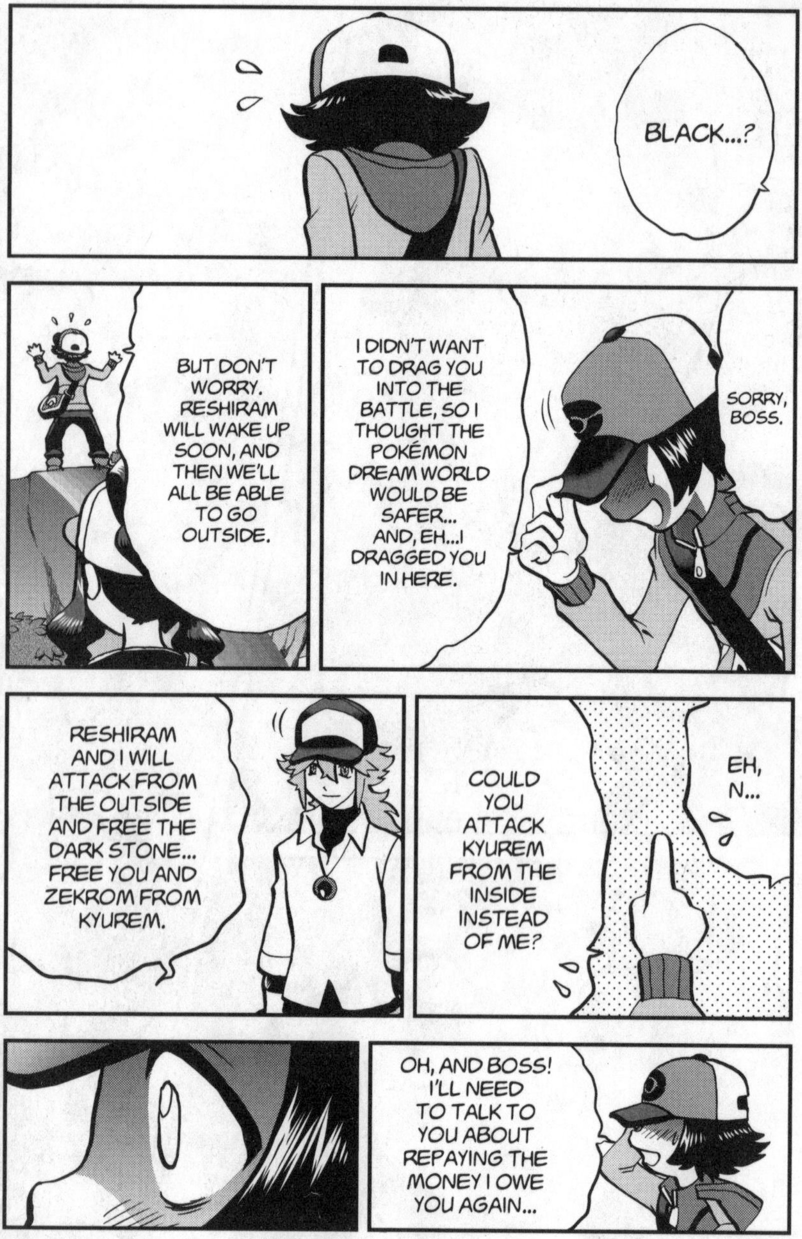

BLACK...?
SORRY, BOSS.
I DIDN'T WANT TO DRAG YOU INTO THE BATTLE, SO I THOUGHT THE POKÉMON DREAM WORLD WOULD BE SAFER... AND, EH...I DRAGGED YOU IN HERE.
BUT DON'T WORRY. RESHIRAM WILL WAKE UP SOON, AND THEN WE'LL ALL BE ABLE TO GO OUTSIDE.
EH, N...
COULD YOU ATTACK KYUREM FROM THE INSIDE INSTEAD OF ME?
RESHIRAM AND I WILL ATTACK FROM THE OUTSIDE AND FREE THE DARK STONE... FREE YOU AND ZEKROM FROM KYUREM.
OH, AND BOSS! I'LL NEED TO TALK TO YOU ABOUT REPAYING THE MONEY I OWE YOU AGAIN...

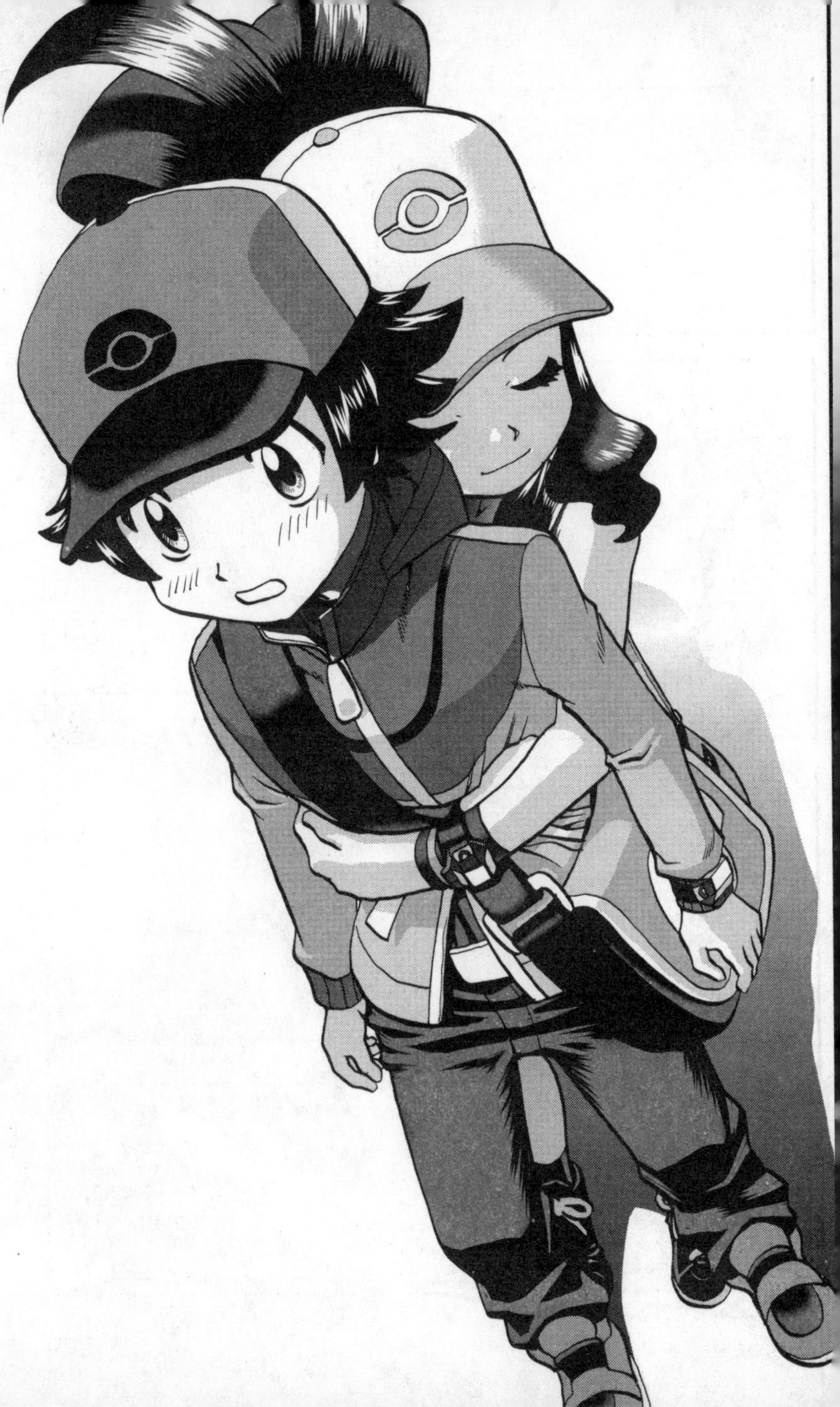

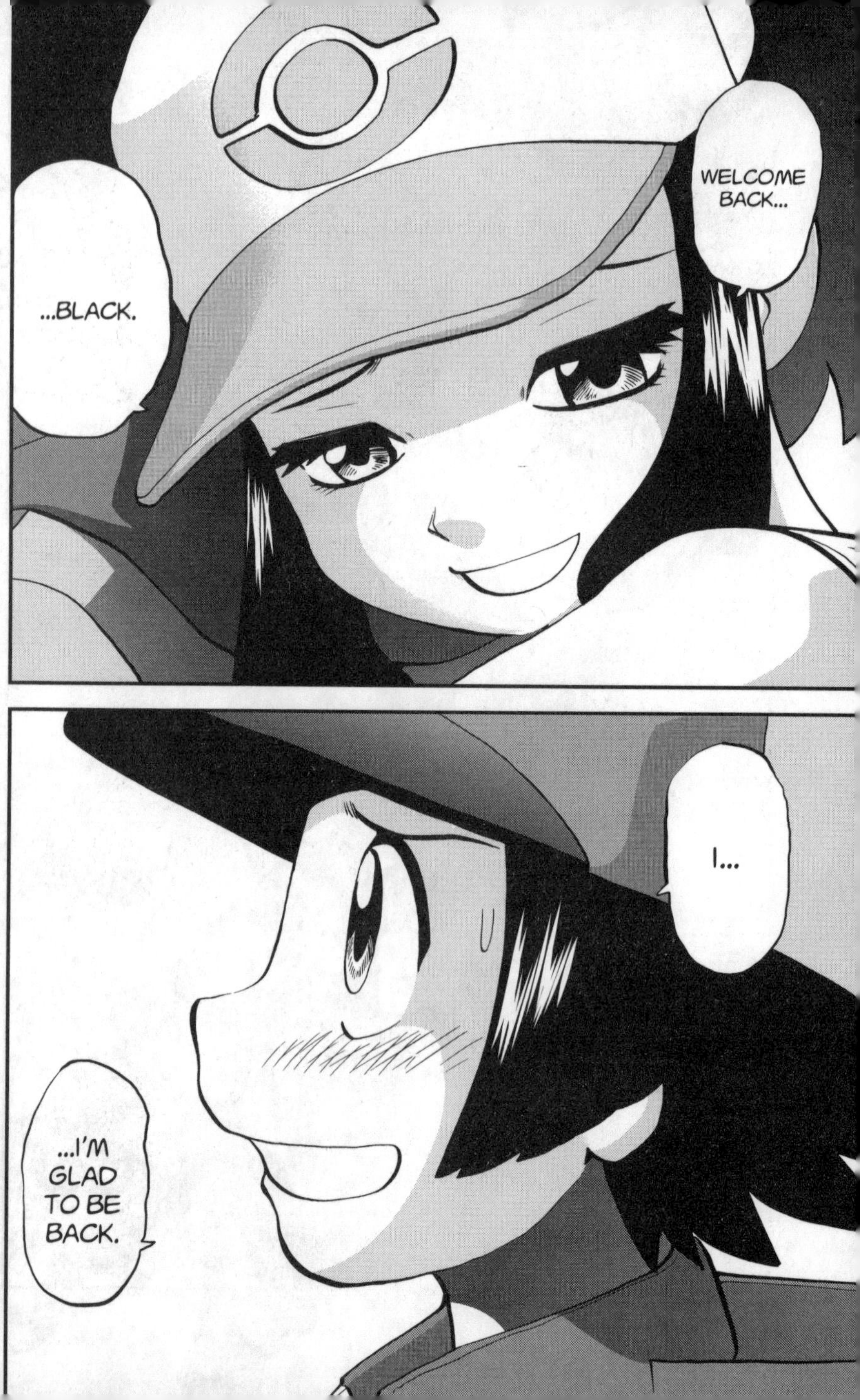
WELCOME BACK...
...BLACK.
I...
...I'M GLAD TO BE BACK.

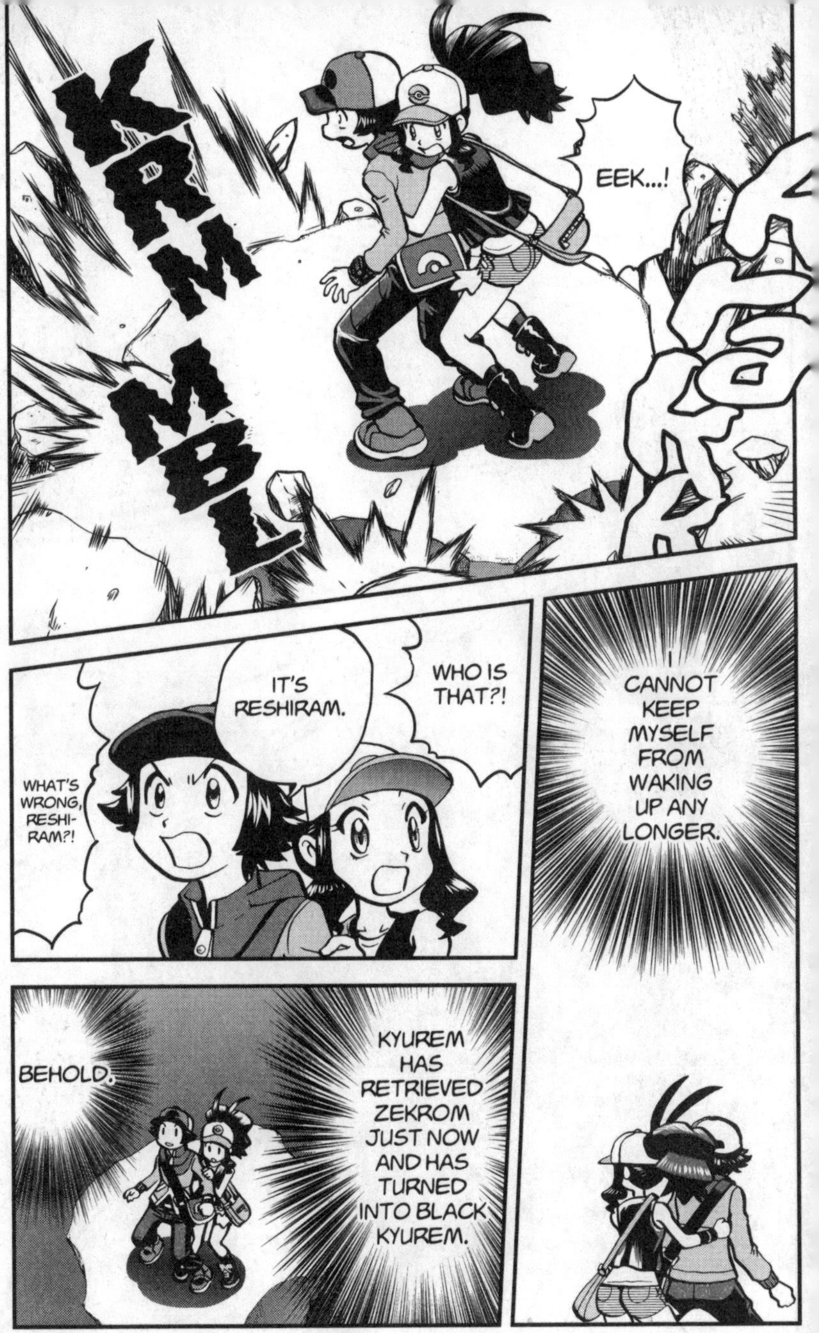
EEK...!
KRMMBL
I CANNOT KEEP MYSELF FROM WAKING UP ANY LONGER.
WHO IS THAT?!
IT'S RESHIRAM.
WHAT'S WRONG, RESHIRAM?!
KYUREM HAS RETRIEVED ZEKROM JUST NOW AND HAS TURNED INTO BLACK KYUREM.
BEHOLD.

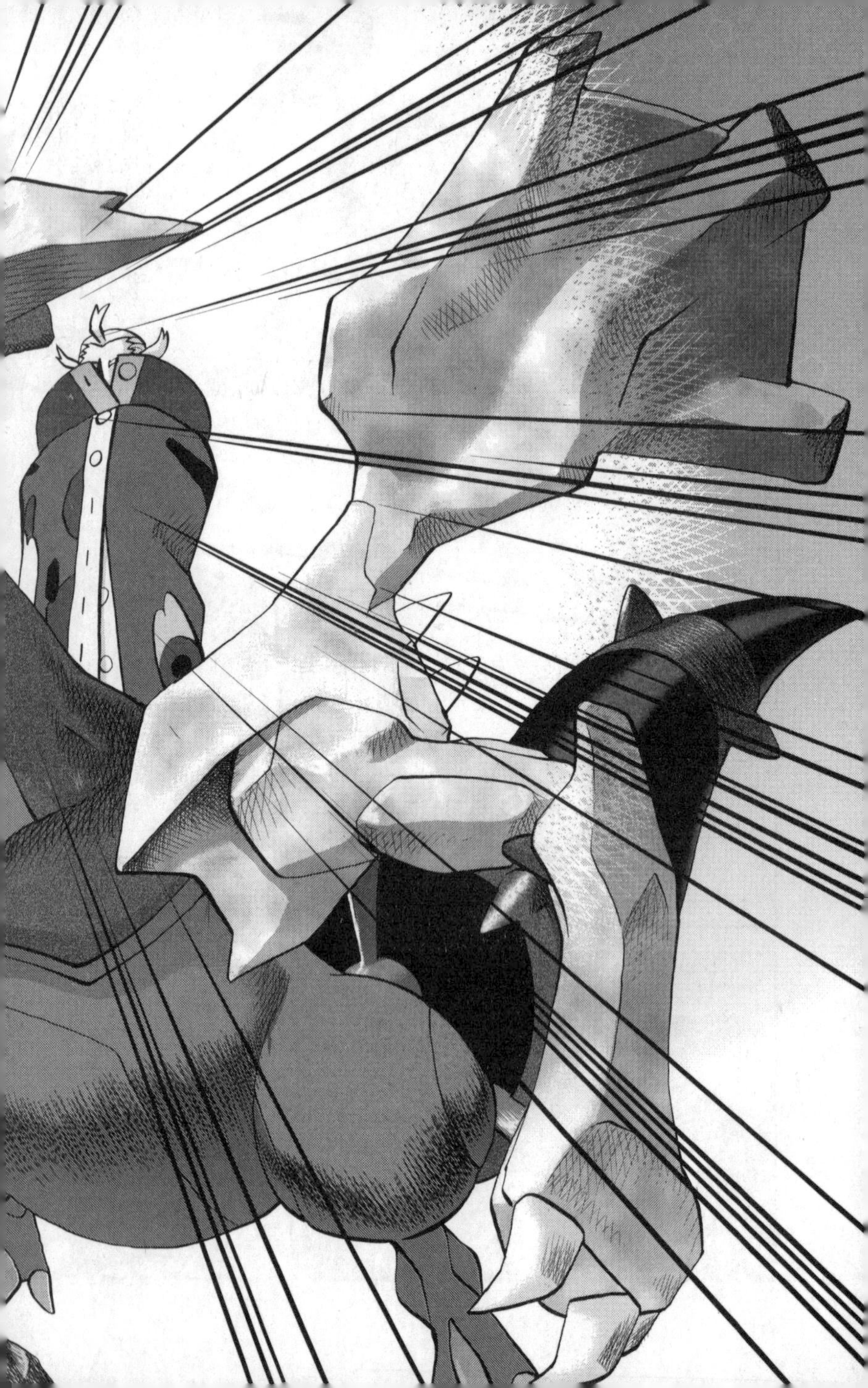

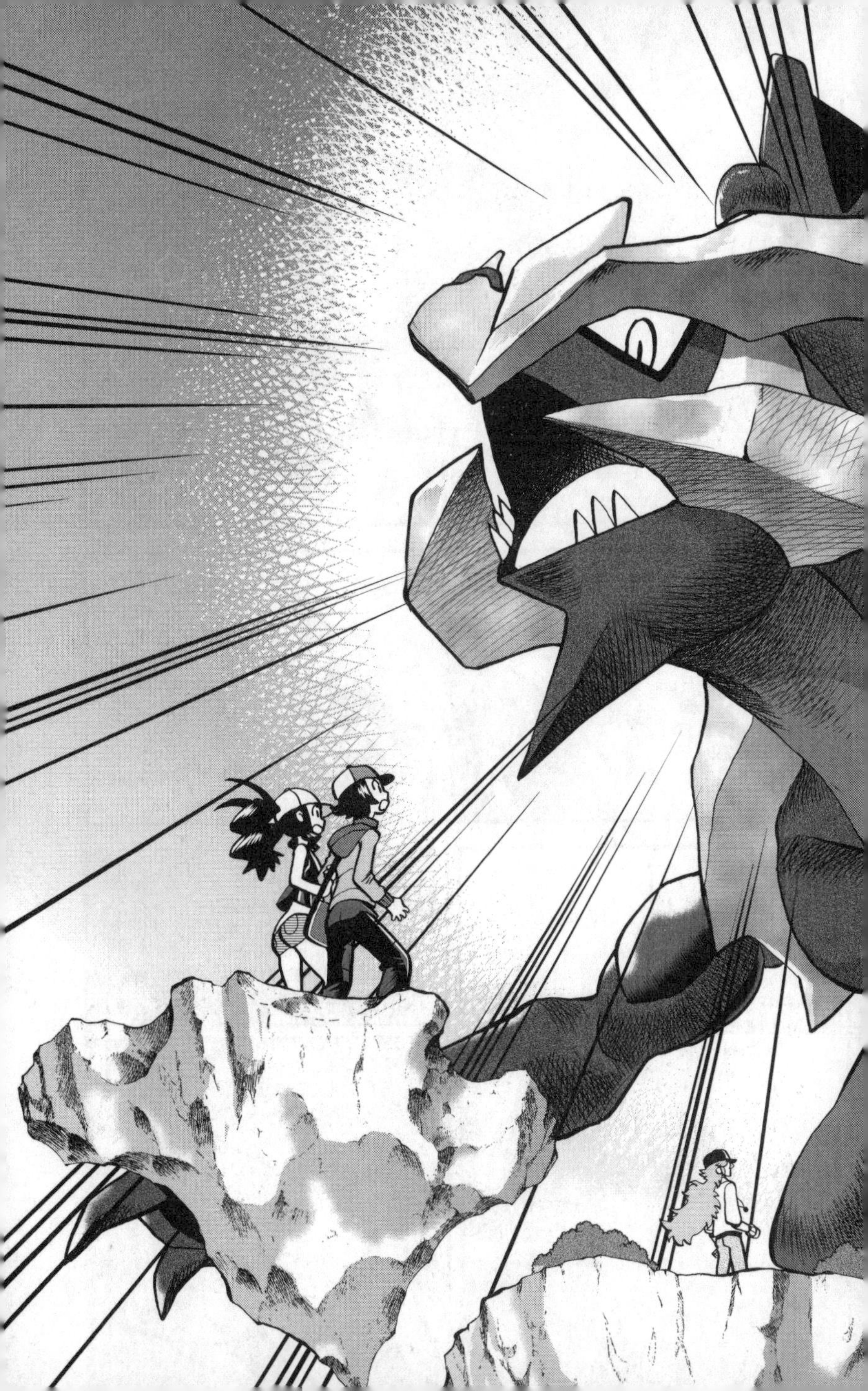

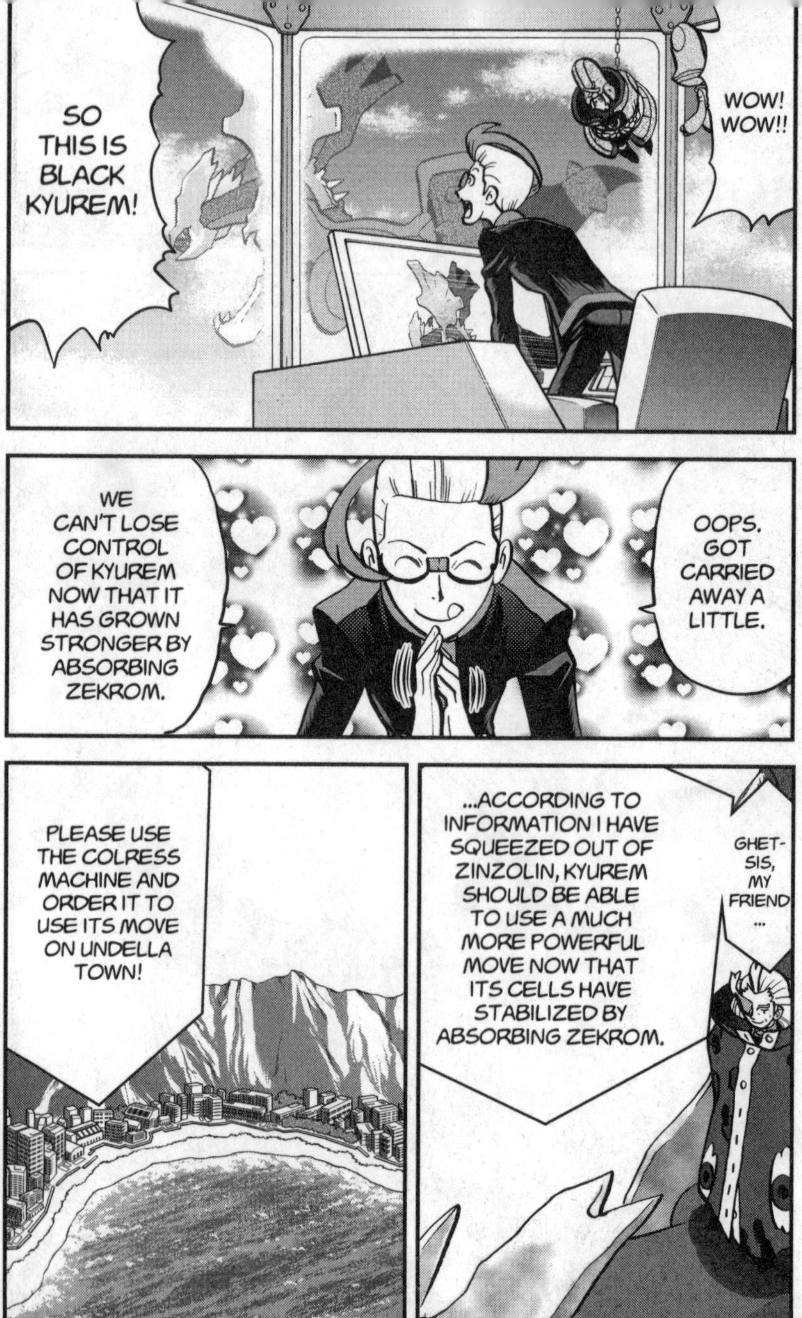
WOW! WOW!!
SO THIS IS BLACK KYUREM!
OOPS. GOT CARRIED AWAY A LITTLE.
WE CAN'T LOSE CONTROL OF KYUREM NOW THAT IT HAS GROWN STRONGER BY ABSORBING ZEKROM.
GHET-SIS, MY FRIEND...
...ACCORDING TO INFORMATION I HAVE SQUEEZED OUT OF ZINZOLIN, KYUREM SHOULD BE ABLE TO USE A MUCH MORE POWERFUL MOVE NOW THAT ITS CELLS HAVE STABILIZED BY ABSORBING ZEKROM.
PLEASE USE THE COLRESS MACHINE AND ORDER IT TO USE ITS MOVE ON UNDELLA TOWN!

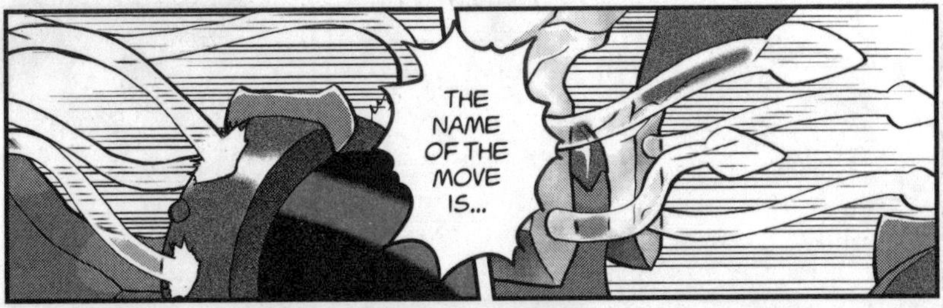
THE NAME OF THE MOVE IS...
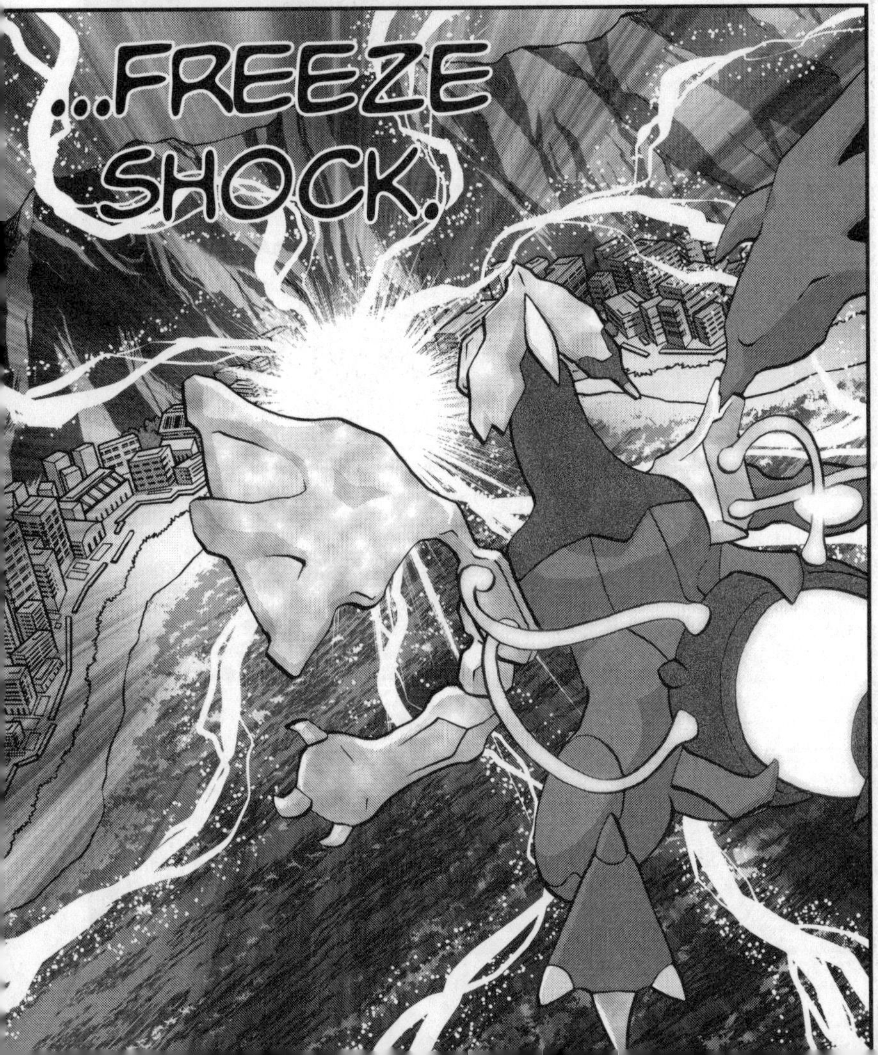
...FREEZE SHOCK.

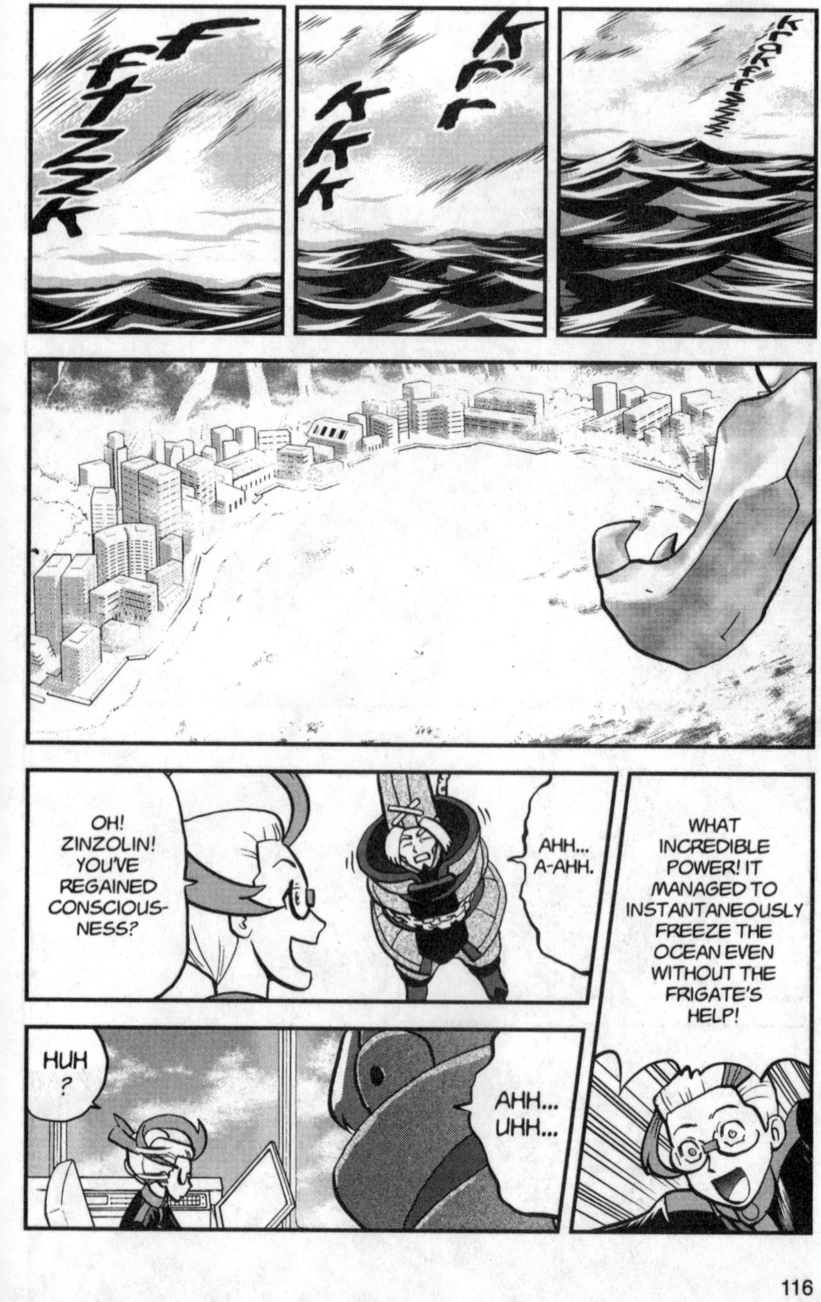
KRAKFFSZZZZZ
KRR KKK
FFTZZK
WHAT INCREDIBLE POWER! IT MANAGED TO INSTANTANEOUSLY FREEZE THE OCEAN EVEN WITHOUT THE FRIGATE'S HELP!
AHH... A-AHH.
OH! ZINZOLIN! YOU'VE REGAINED CONSCIOUS-NESS?
AHH... UHH...
HUH?

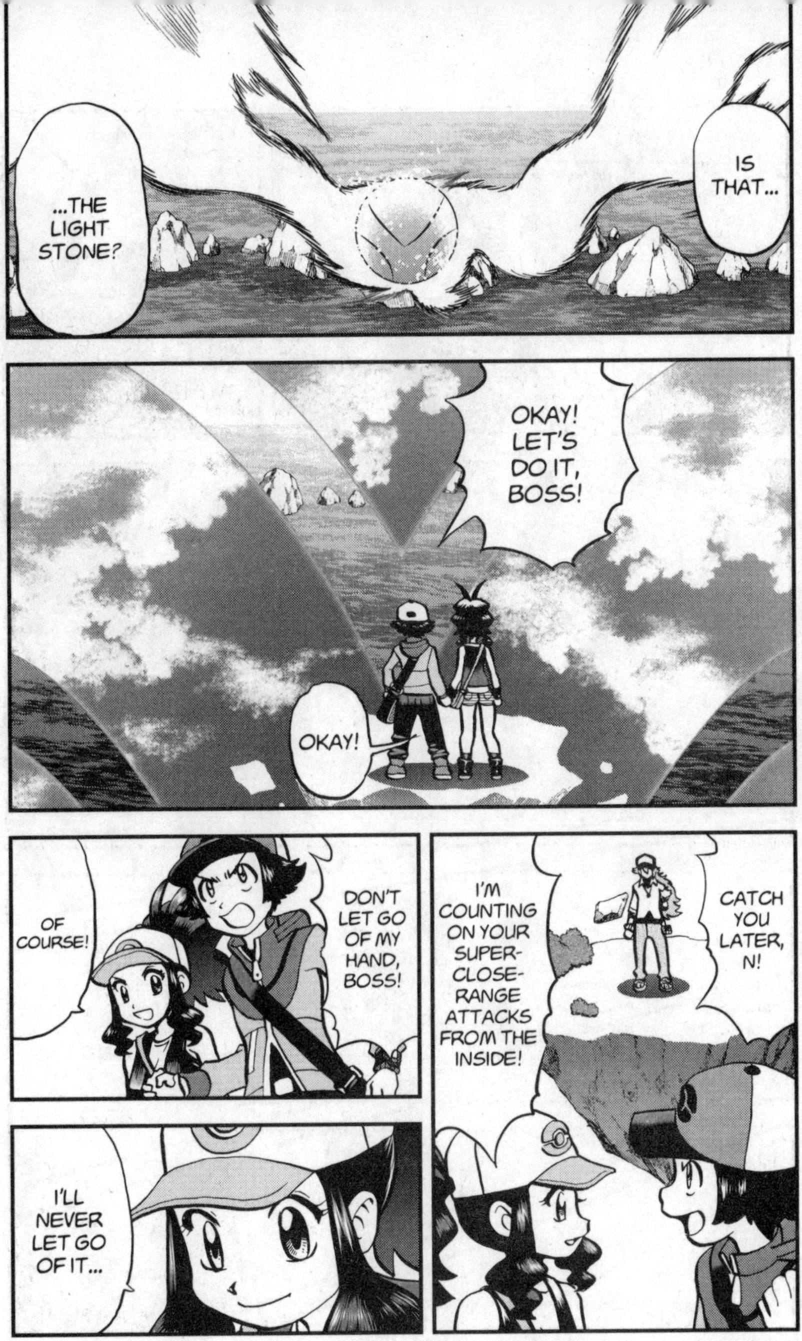
IS THAT...
...THE LIGHT STONE?
OKAY! LET'S DO IT, BOSS!
OKAY!
CATCH YOU LATER, N!
I'M COUNTING ON YOUR SUPER-CLOSE-RANGE ATTACKS FROM THE INSIDE!
DON'T LET GO OF MY HAND, BOSS!
OF COURSE!
I'LL NEVER LET GO OF IT...

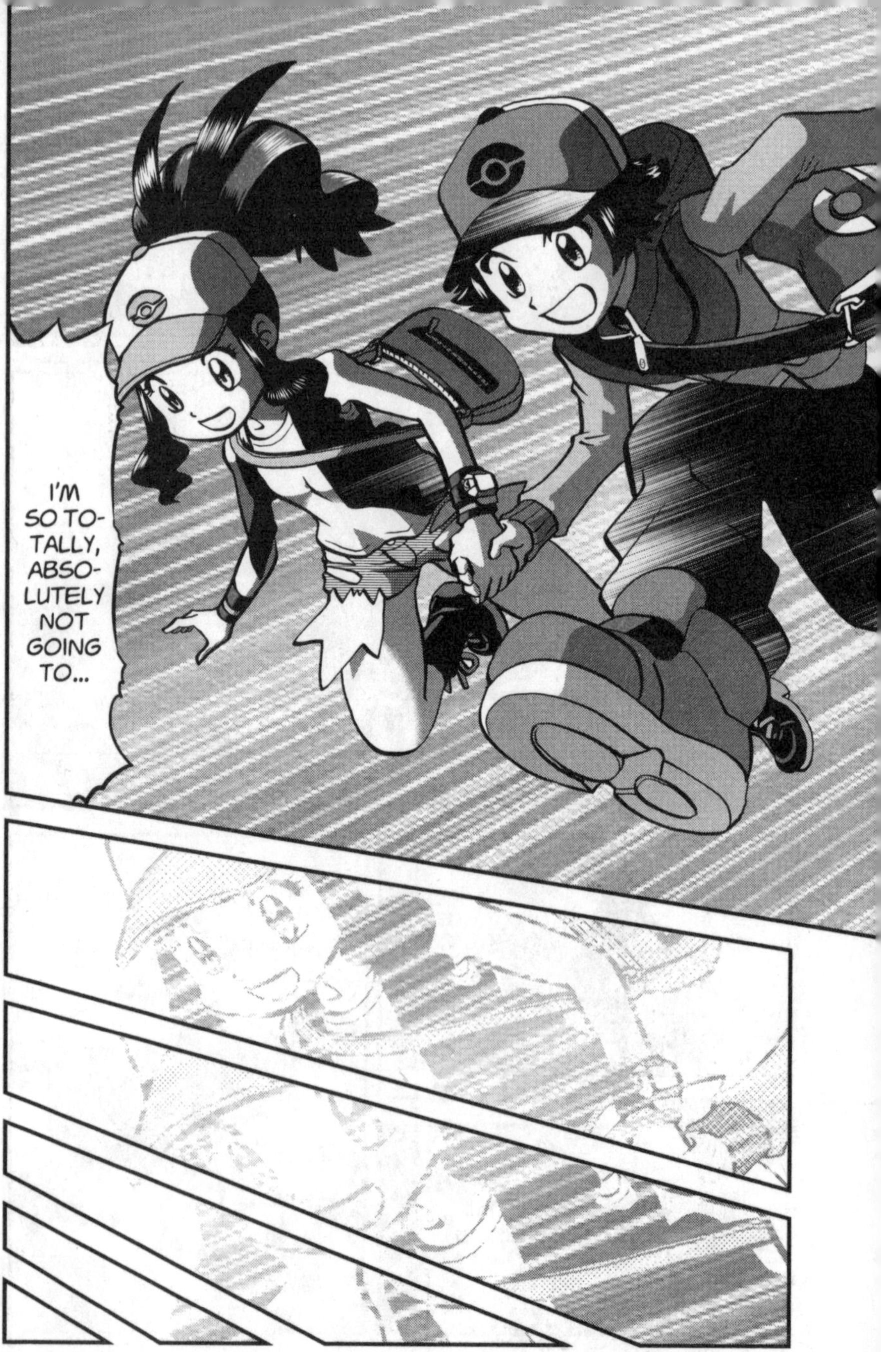
I'M SO TO-TALLY, ABSO-LUTELY NOT GOING TO...

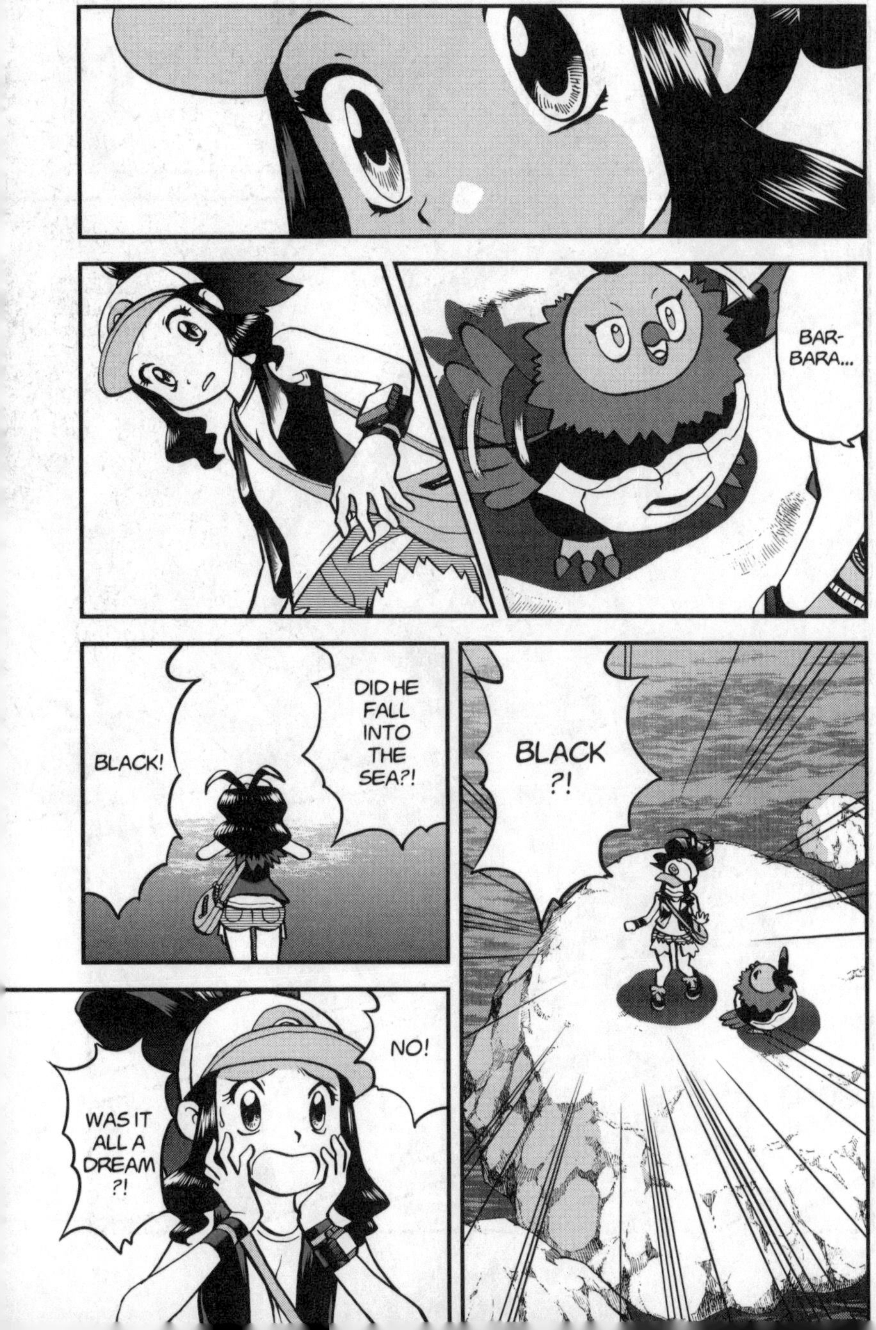
BAR-BARA...
BLACK ?!
DID HE FALL INTO THE SEA?!
BLACK!
NO!
WAS IT ALL A DREAM ?!

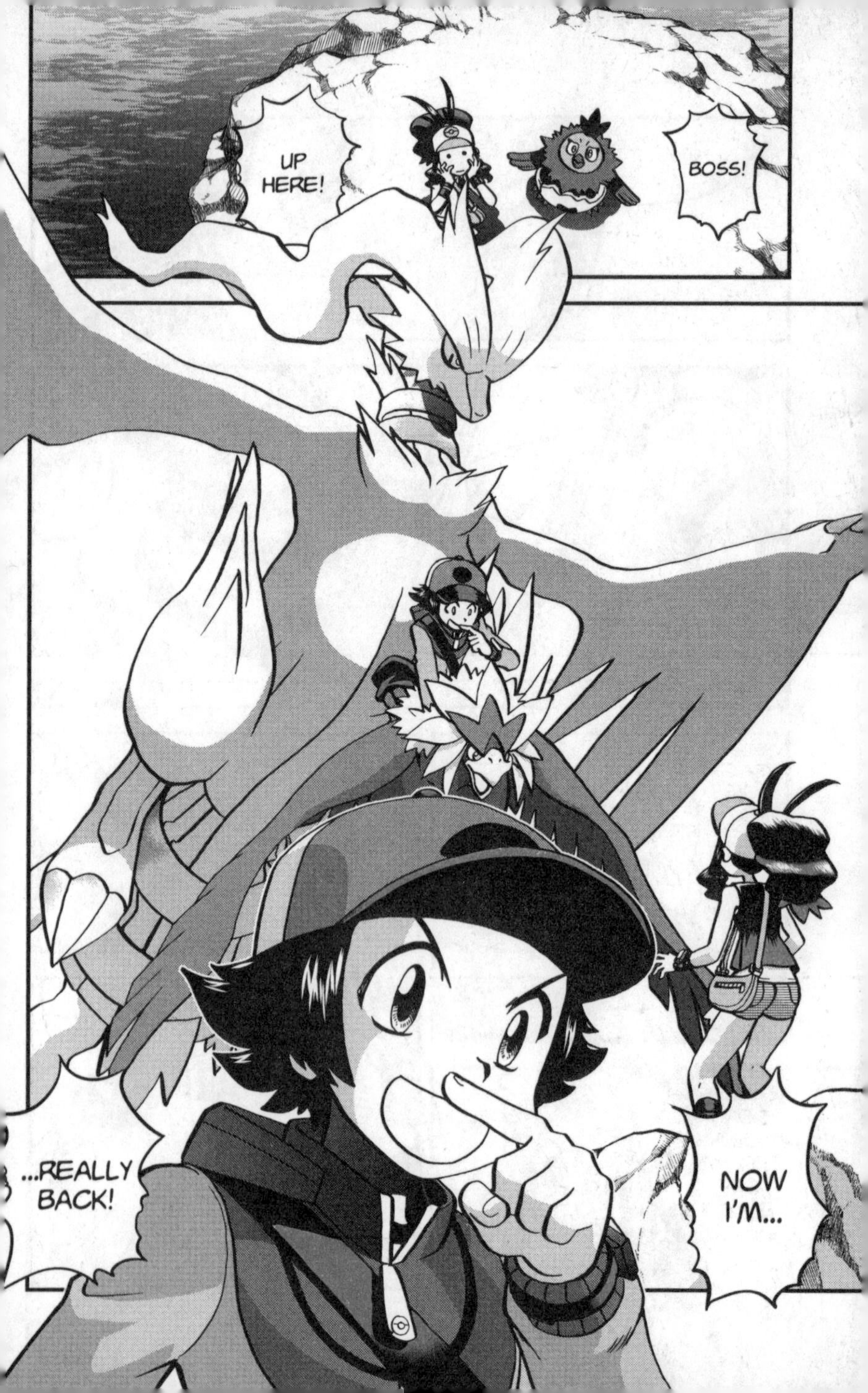
BOSS!
UP HERE!
NOW I'M...
...REALLY BACK!

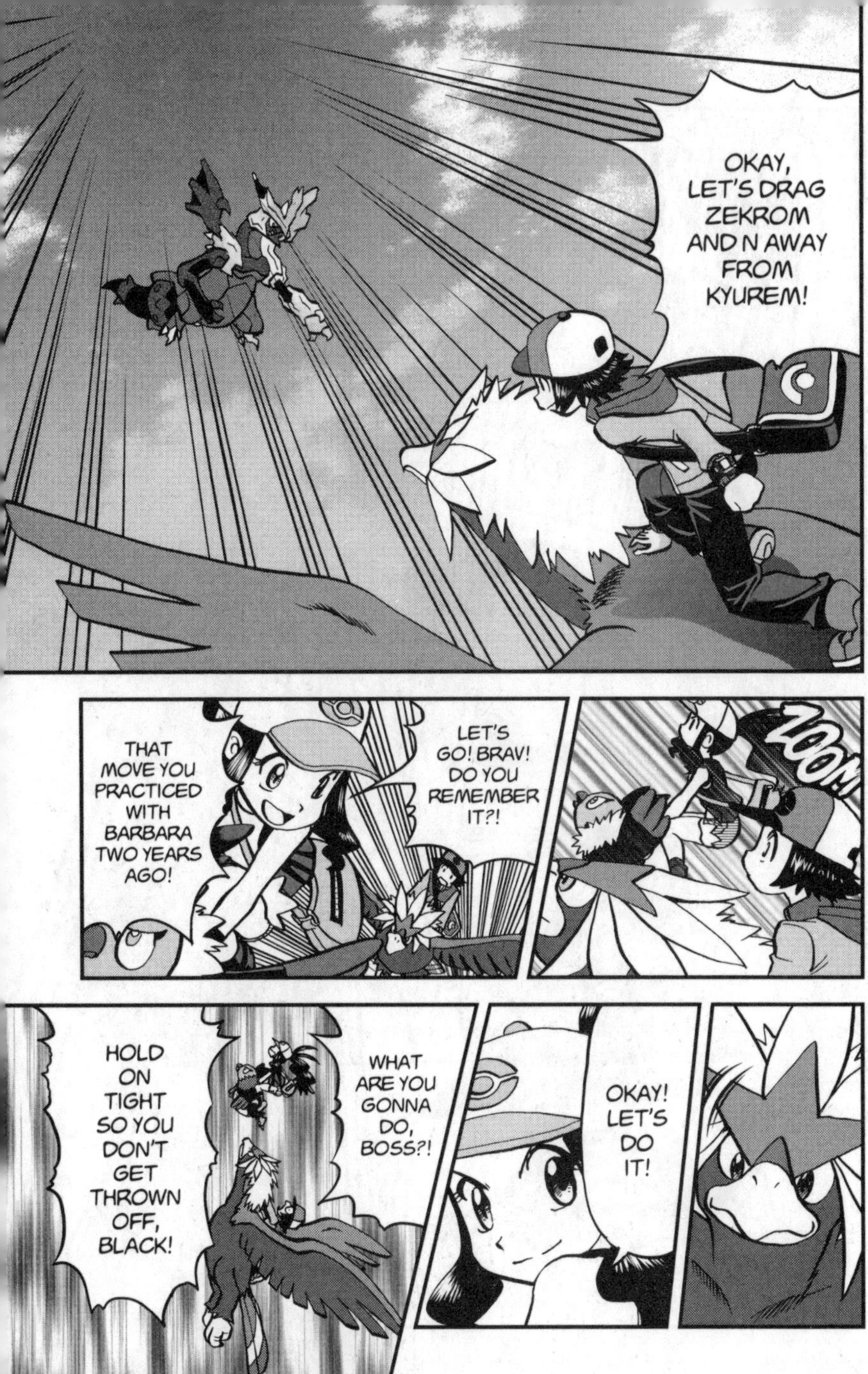
OKAY, LET'S DRAG ZEKROM AND N AWAY FROM KYUREM!
ZOOM
LET'S GO! BRAV! DO YOU REMEMBER IT?!
THAT MOVE YOU PRACTICED WITH BARBARA TWO YEARS AGO!
OKAY! LET'S DO IT!
WHAT ARE YOU GONNA DO, BOSS?!
HOLD ON TIGHT SO YOU DON'T GET THROWN OFF, BLACK!

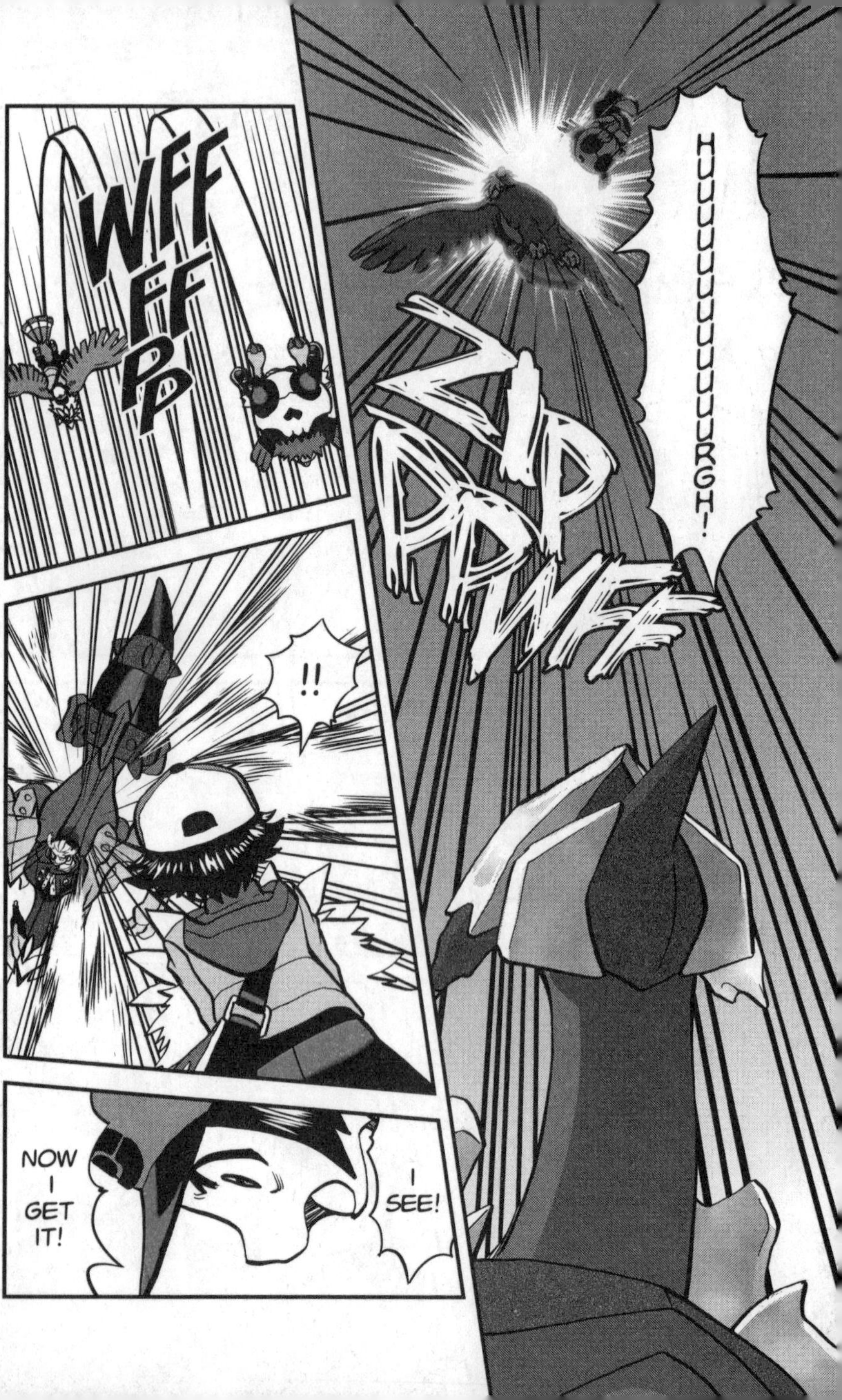
HUUUUUUUUUUUUURGH!
WFFFFPP
!!
I SEE!
NOW I GET IT!

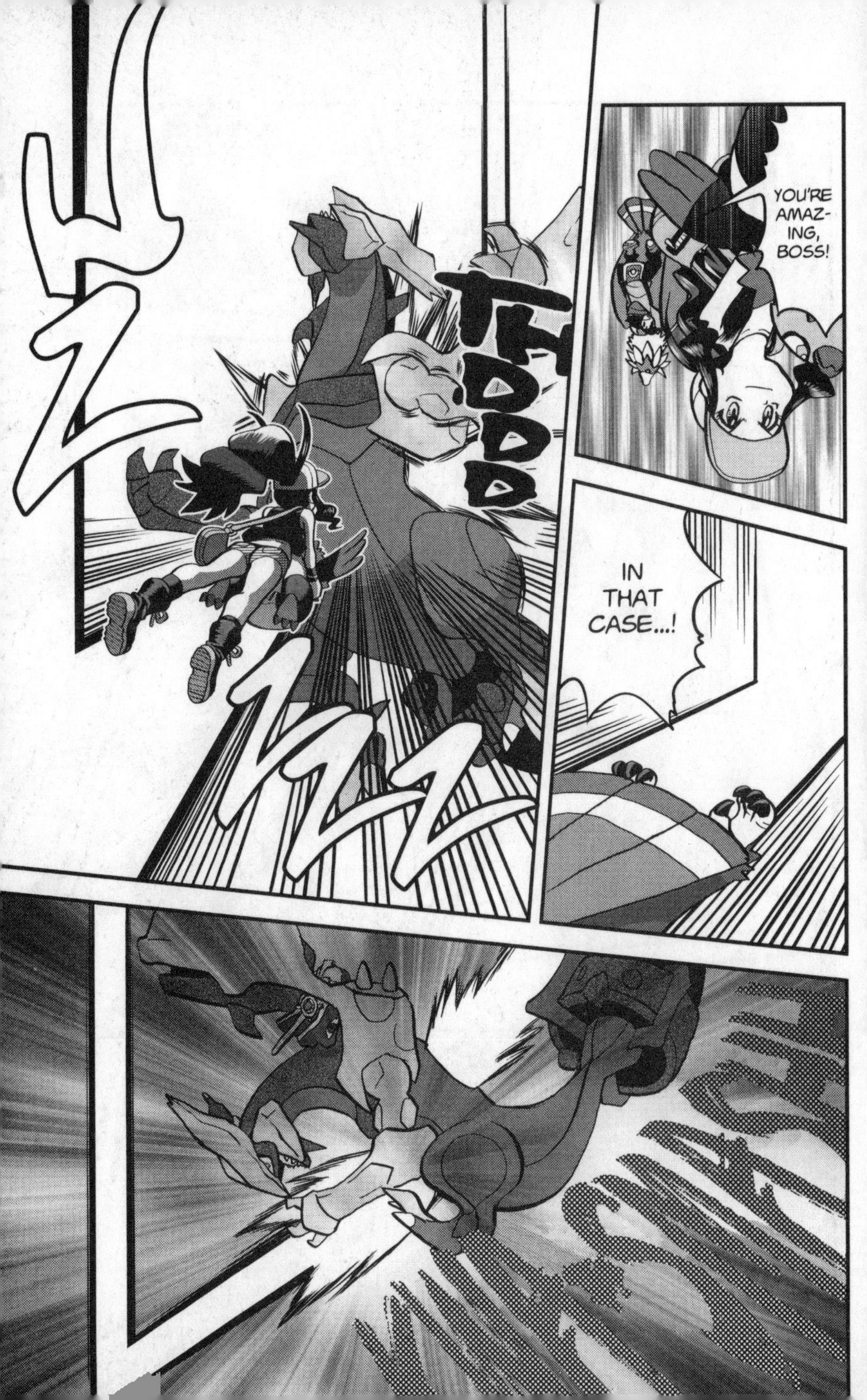
YOU'RE AMAZ-ING, BOSS!
IN THAT CASE...!
THDDDD

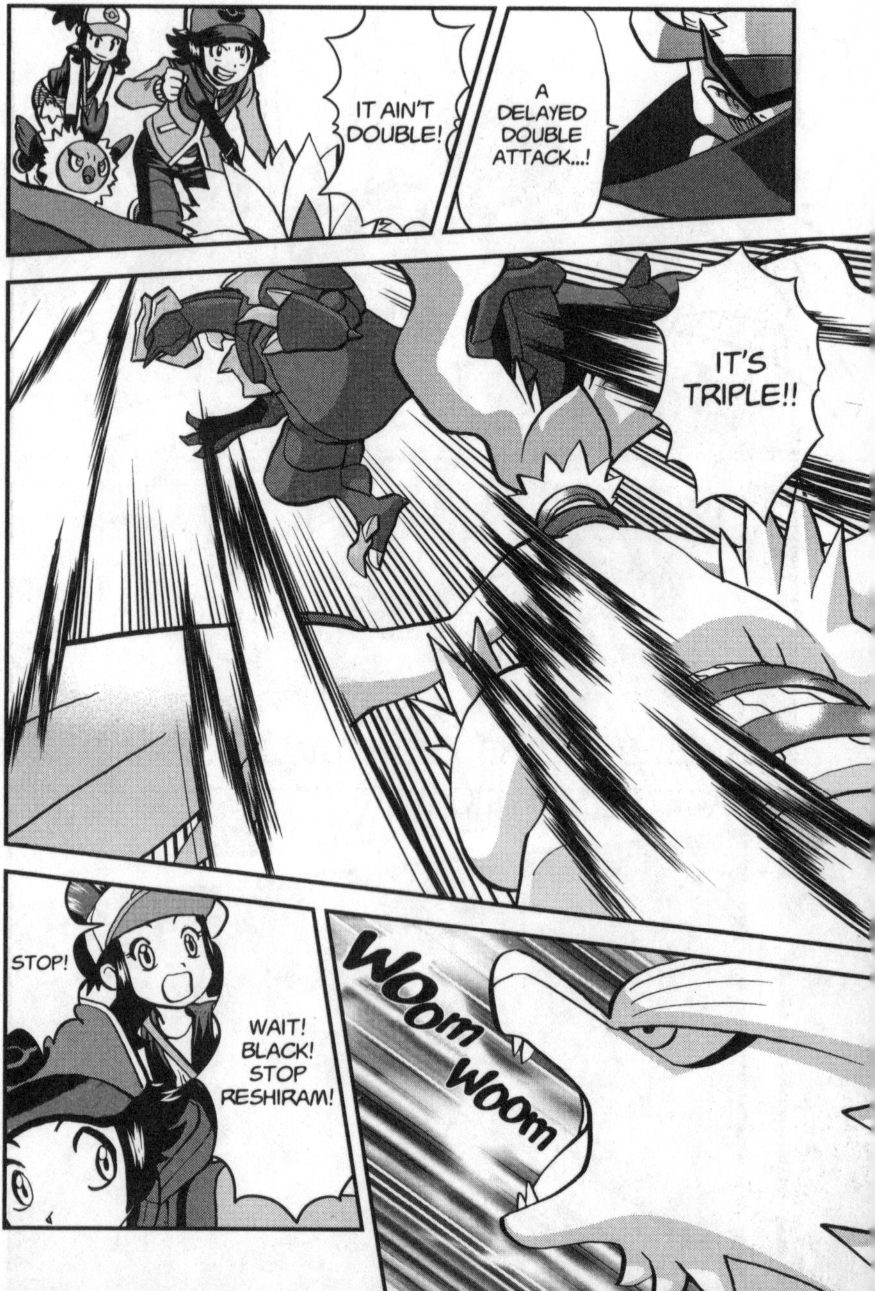
A DELAYED DOUBLE ATTACK...!
IT AIN'T DOUBLE!
IT'S TRIPLE!!
WOOM WOOM
WAIT! BLACK! STOP RESHIRAM!
STOP!

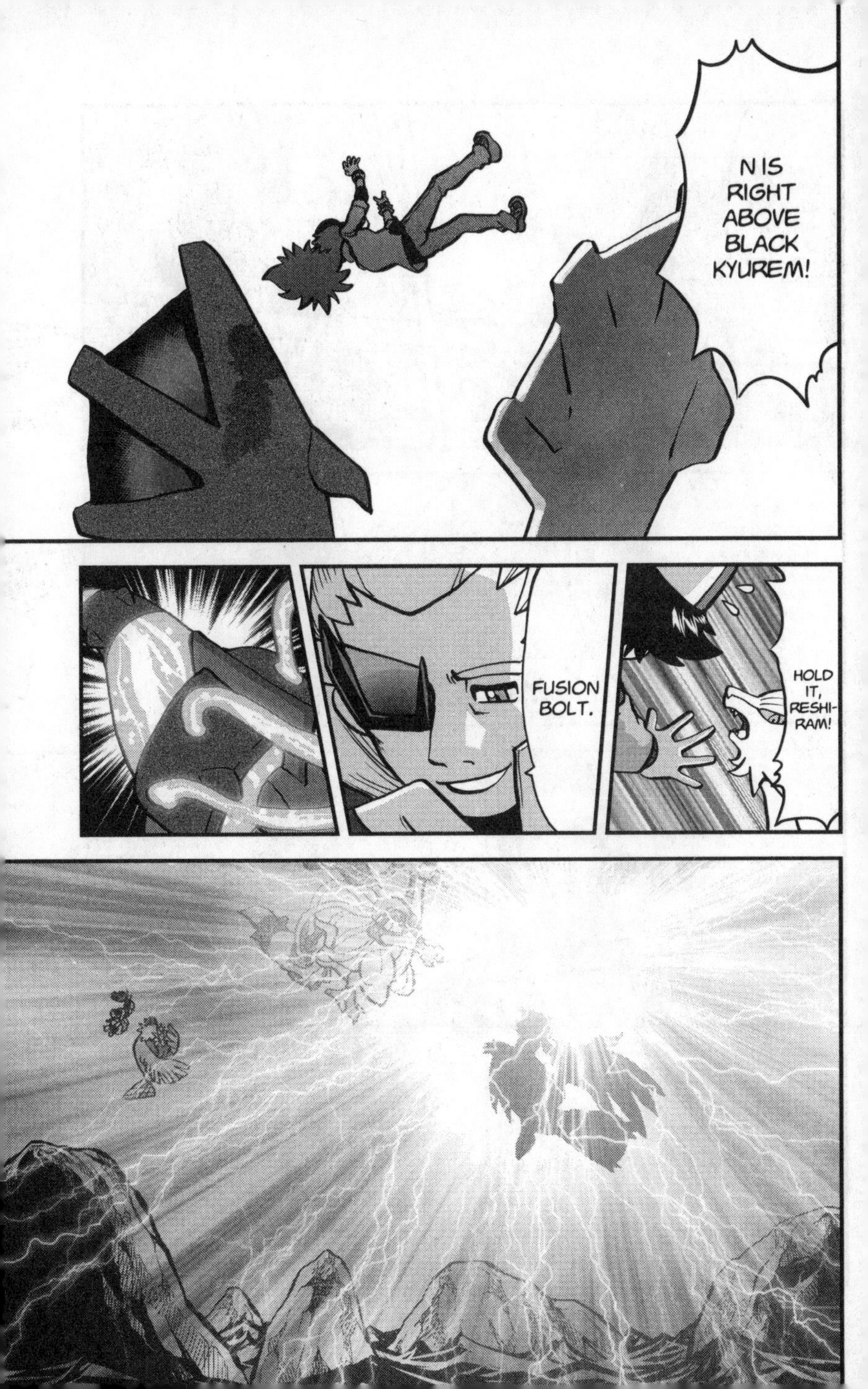
N IS RIGHT ABOVE BLACK KYUREM!
HOLD IT, RESHI-RAM!
FUSION BOLT.

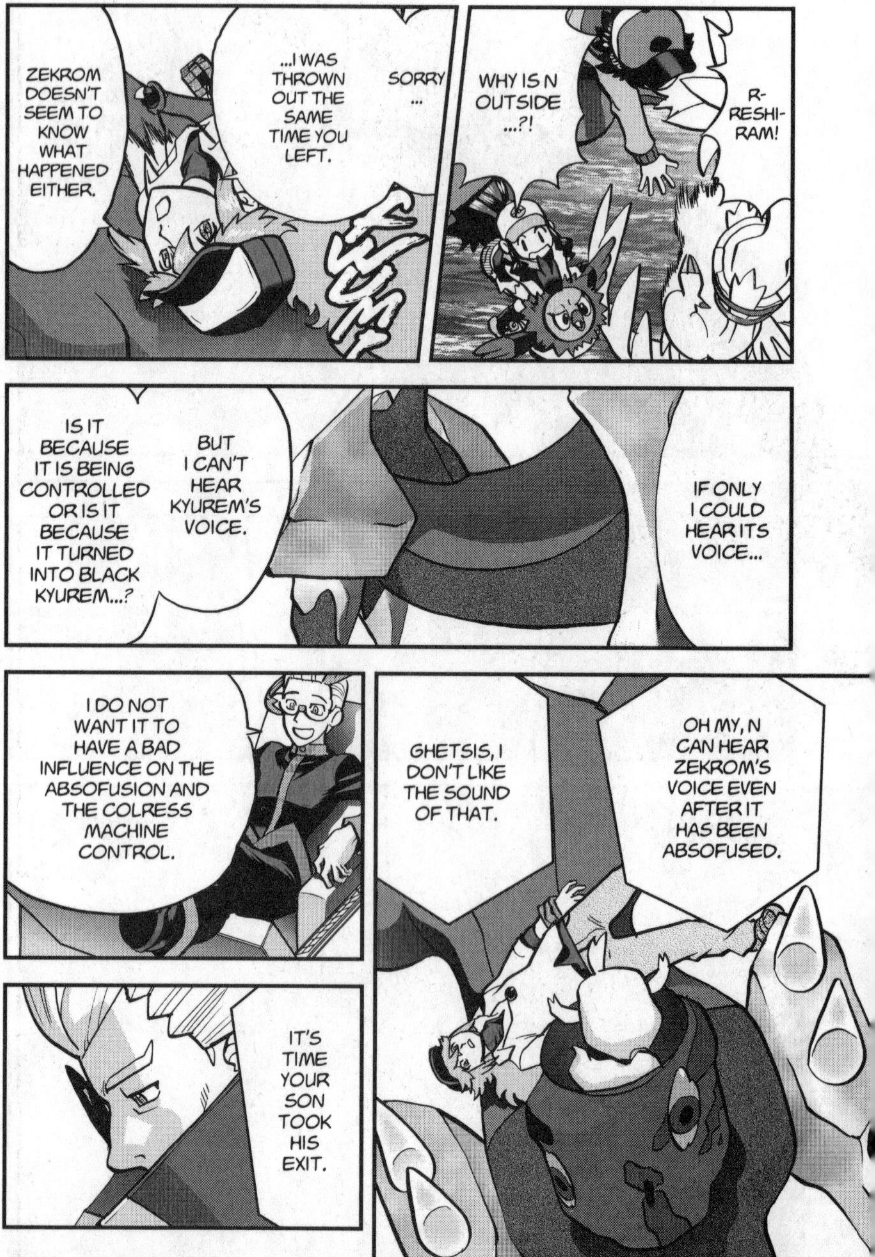
R-RESHIRAM!
WHY IS N OUTSIDE ...?!
SORRY ...
...I WAS THROWN OUT THE SAME TIME YOU LEFT.
ZEKROM DOESN'T SEEM TO KNOW WHAT HAPPENED EITHER.
BUT I CAN'T HEAR KYUREM'S VOICE.
IS IT BECAUSE IT IS BEING CONTROLLED OR IS IT BECAUSE IT TURNED INTO BLACK KYUREM...?
IF ONLY I COULD HEAR ITS VOICE...
OH MY, N CAN HEAR ZEKROM'S VOICE EVEN AFTER IT HAS BEEN ABSOFUSED.
GHETSIS, I DON'T LIKE THE SOUND OF THAT.
I DO NOT WANT IT TO HAVE A BAD INFLUENCE ON THE ABSOFUSION AND THE COLRESS MACHINE CONTROL.
IT'S TIME YOUR SON TOOK HIS EXIT.

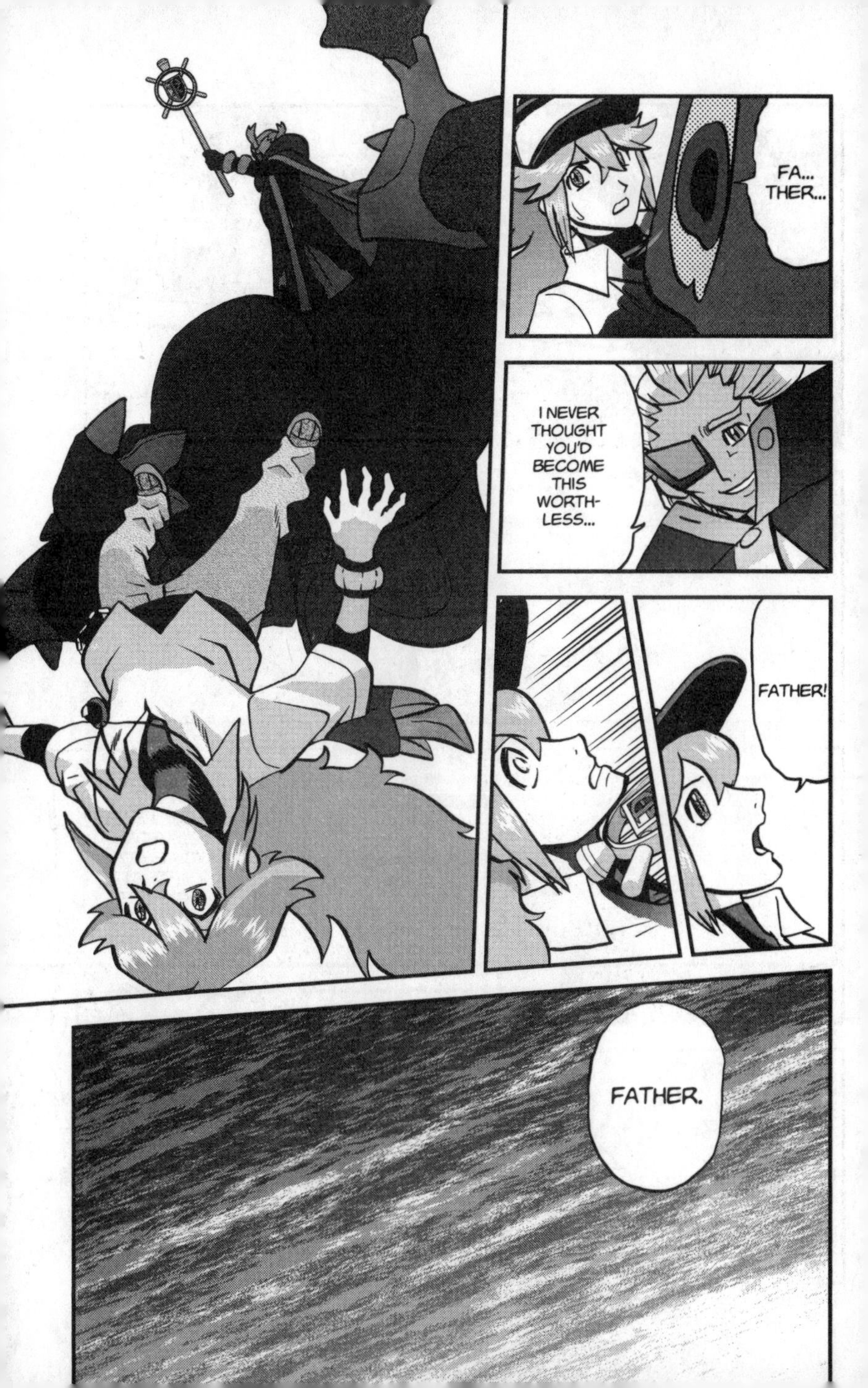
FA... THER...
I NEVER THOUGHT YOU'D BECOME THIS WORTH-LESS...
FATHER!
FATHER.

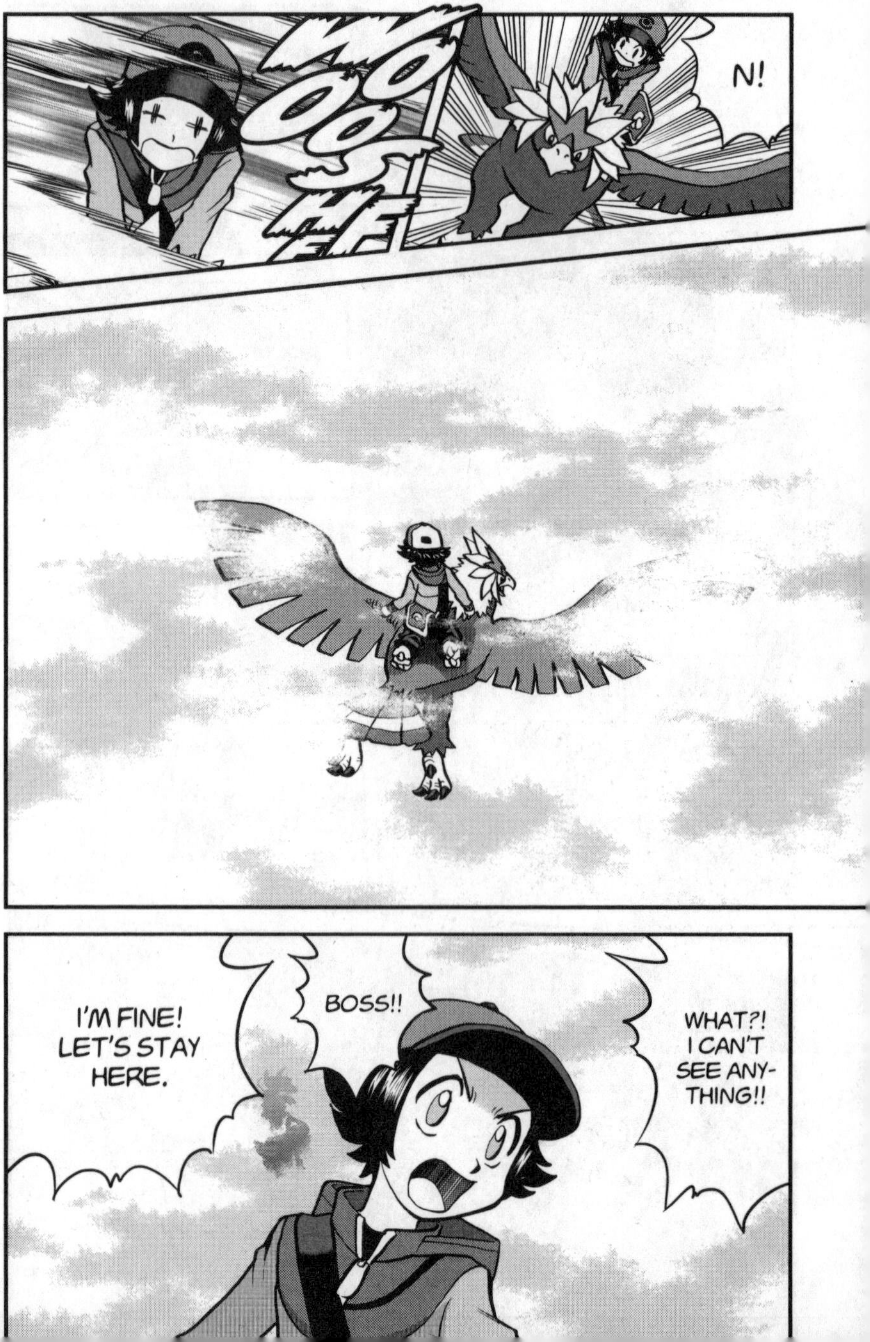
N!
WHAT?! I CAN'T SEE ANY-THING!!
BOSS!!
I'M FINE! LET'S STAY HERE.

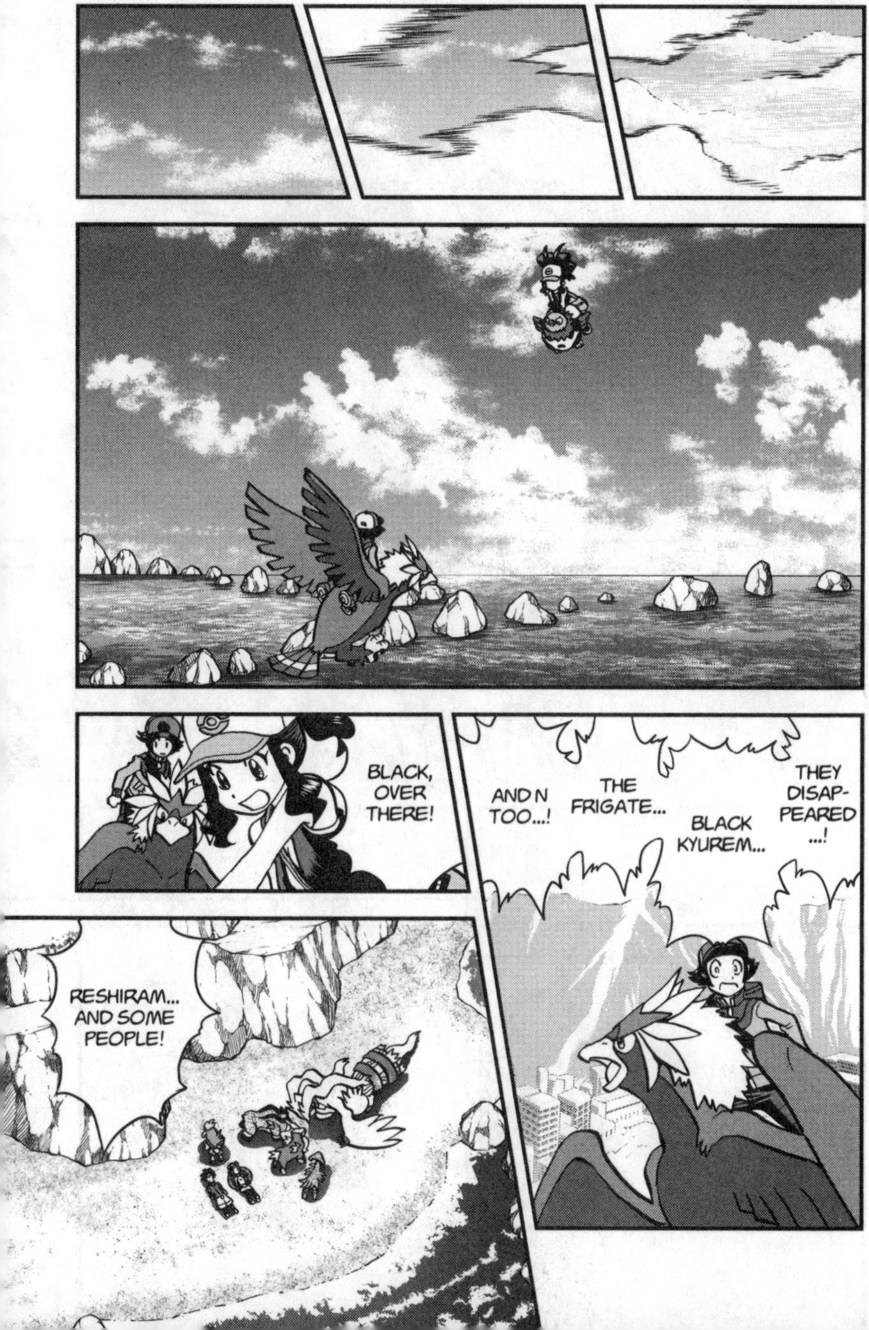
THEY DISAP-PEARED ...!
BLACK KYUREM...
THE FRIGATE...
AND N TOO...!
BLACK, OVER THERE!
RESHIRAM... AND SOME PEOPLE!

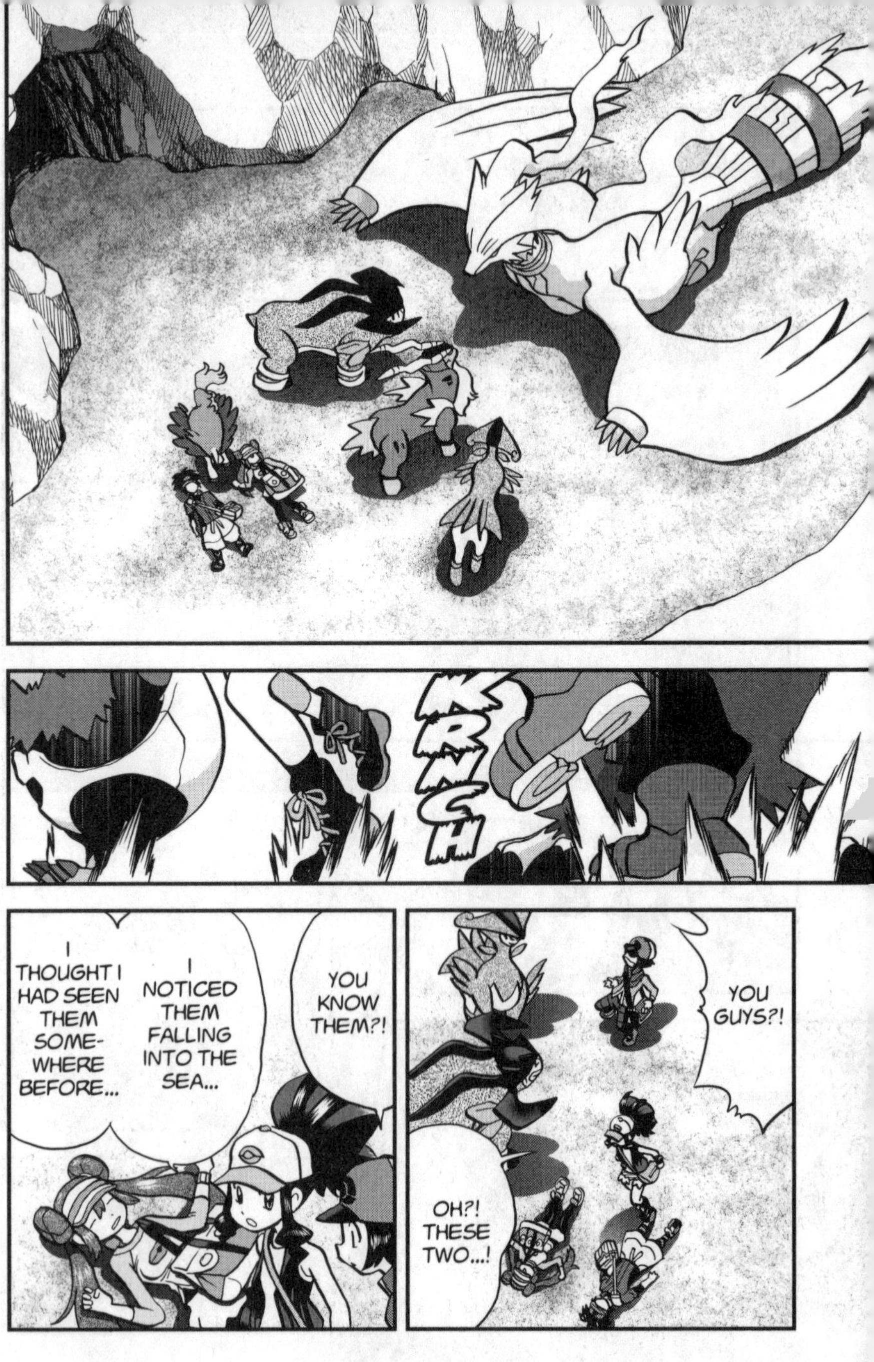
KRNCH
YOU GUYS?!
OH?! THESE TWO...!
YOU KNOW THEM?!
I NOTICED THEM FALLING INTO THE SEA...
I THOUGHT I HAD SEEN THEM SOME-WHERE BEFORE...

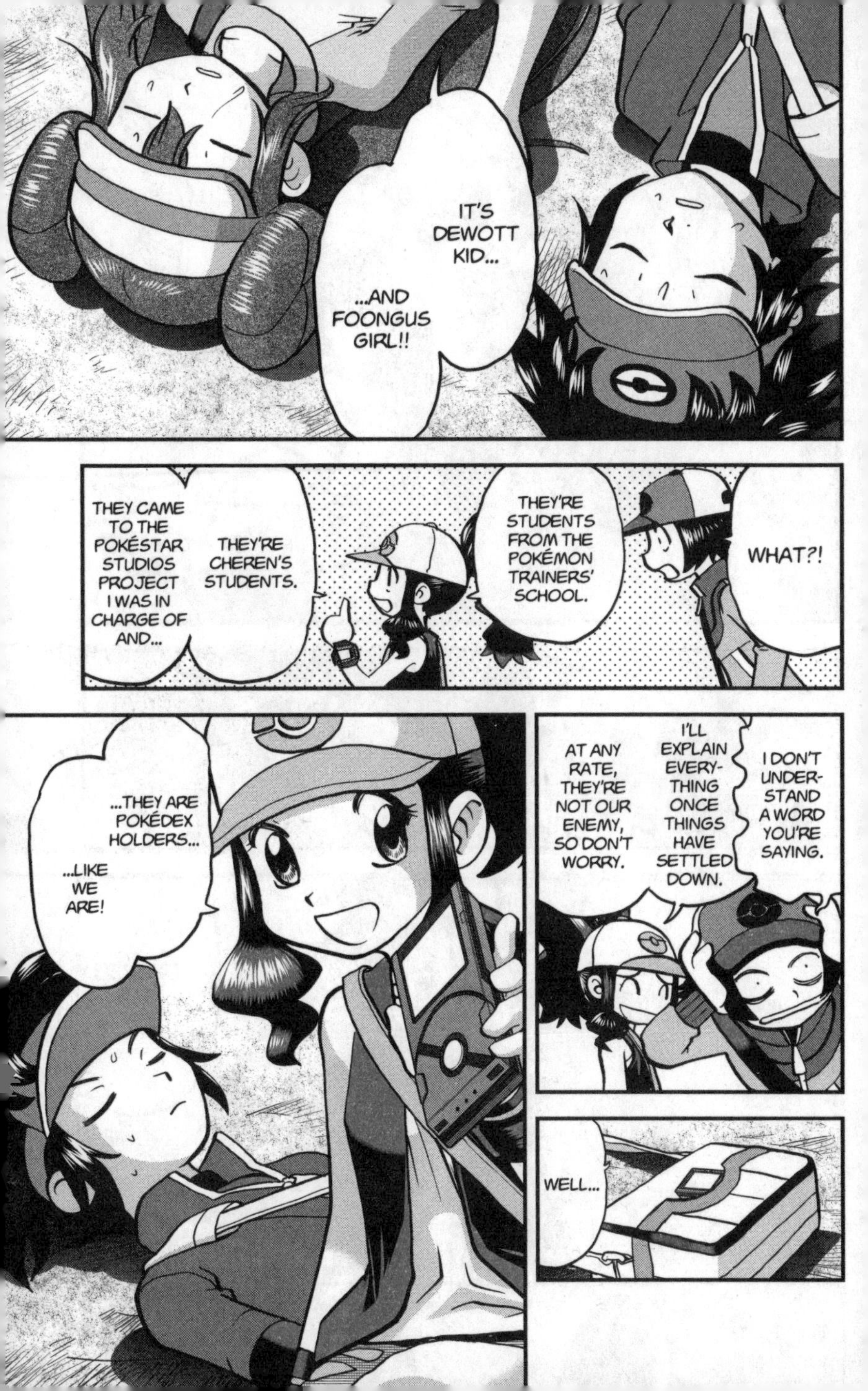
IT'S DEWOTT KID...
...AND FOONGUS GIRL!!
WHAT?!
THEY'RE STUDENTS FROM THE POKÉMON TRAINERS' SCHOOL.
THEY'RE CHEREN'S STUDENTS.
THEY CAME TO THE POKÉSTAR STUDIOS PROJECT I WAS IN CHARGE OF AND...
I DON'T UNDERSTAND A WORD YOU'RE SAYING.
I'LL EXPLAIN EVERYTHING ONCE THINGS HAVE SETTLED DOWN.
AT ANY RATE, THEY'RE NOT OUR ENEMY, SO DON'T WORRY.
WELL...
...THEY ARE POKÉDEX HOLDERS...
...LIKE WE ARE!

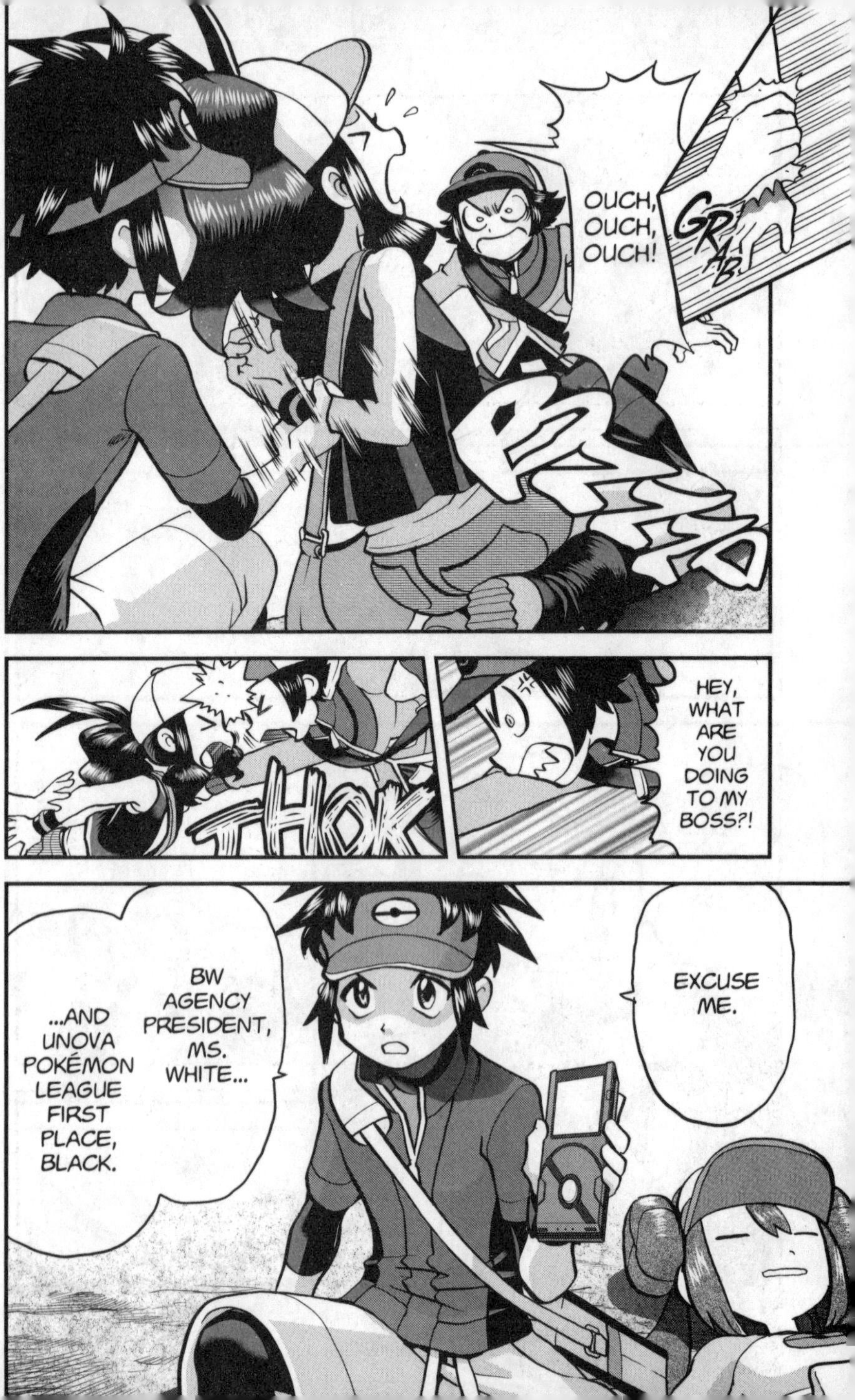
GRAB
OUCH, OUCH, OUCH!
FWUMP
HEY, WHAT ARE YOU DOING TO MY BOSS?!
THOK
EXCUSE ME.
BW AGENCY PRESIDENT, MS. WHITE...
...AND UNOVA POKÉMON LEAGUE FIRST PLACE, BLACK.

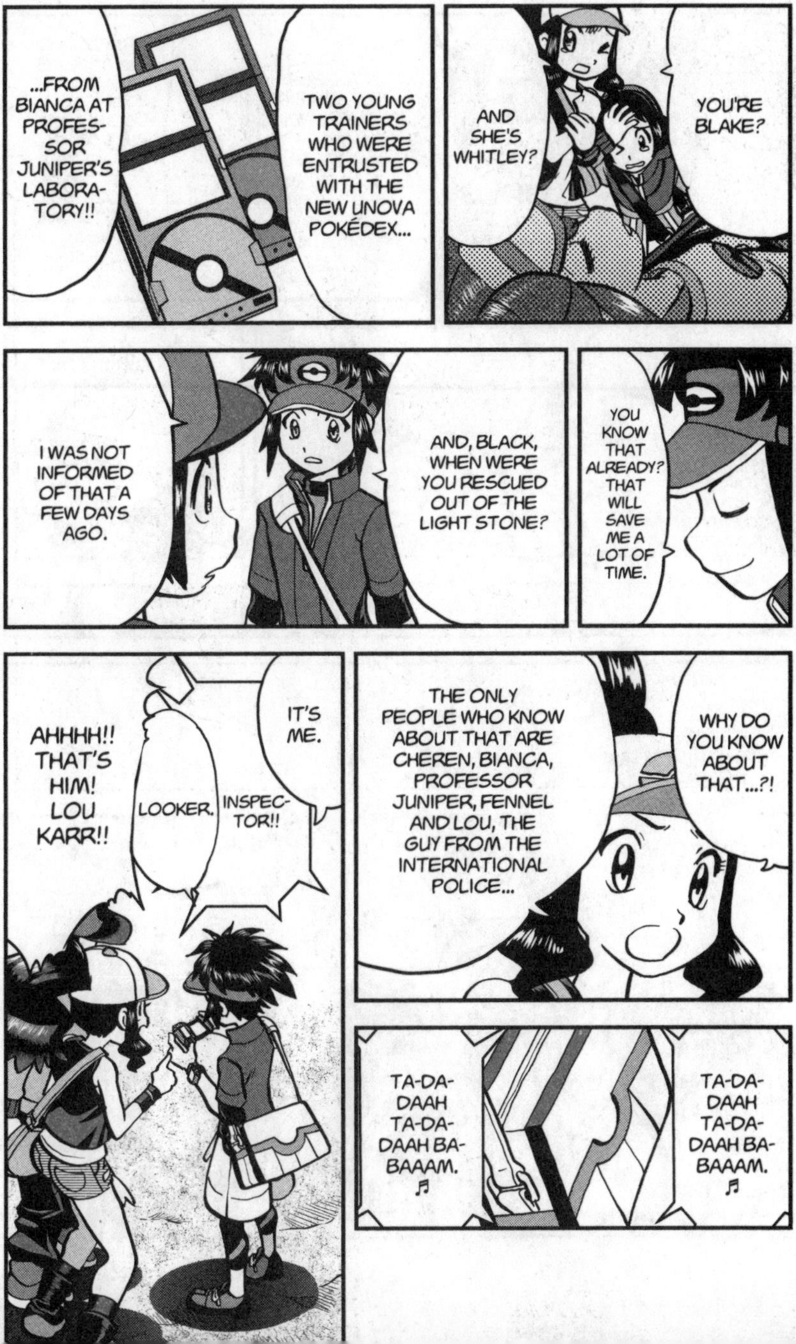
YOU'RE BLAKE?
AND SHE'S WHITLEY?
TWO YOUNG TRAINERS WHO WERE ENTRUSTED WITH THE NEW UNOVA POKÉDEX...
...FROM BIANCA AT PROFESSOR JUNIPER'S LABORATORY!!
YOU KNOW THAT ALREADY? THAT WILL SAVE ME A LOT OF TIME.
AND, BLACK, WHEN WERE YOU RESCUED OUT OF THE LIGHT STONE?
I WAS NOT INFORMED OF THAT A FEW DAYS AGO.
WHY DO YOU KNOW ABOUT THAT...?!
THE ONLY PEOPLE WHO KNOW ABOUT THAT ARE CHEREN, BIANCA, PROFESSOR JUNIPER, FENNEL AND LOU, THE GUY FROM THE INTERNATIONAL POLICE...
TA-DA-DAAH TA-DA-DAAH BA-BAAAM. ♬
TA-DA-DAAH TA-DA-DAAH BA-BAAAM. ♬
IT'S ME.
INSPECTOR!!
LOOKER.
AHHHH!! THAT'S HIM! LOU KARR!!

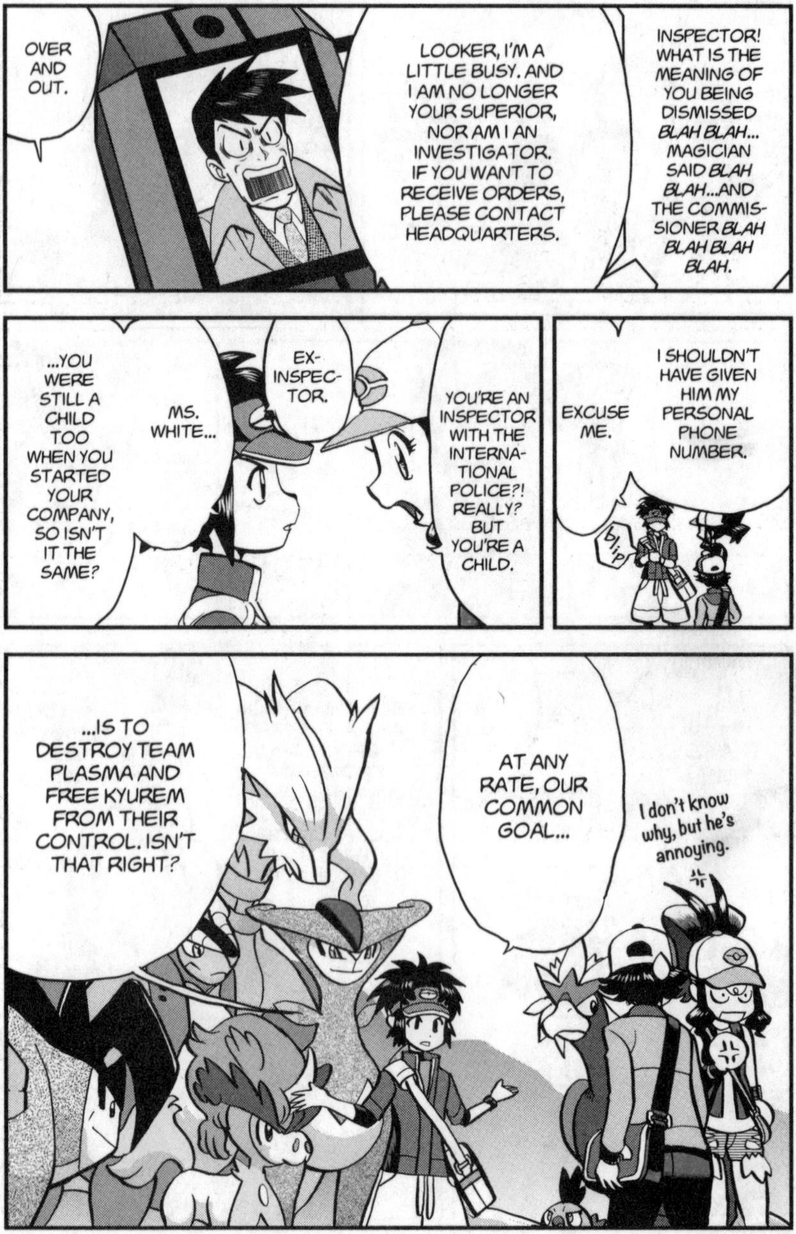
INSPECTOR! WHAT IS THE MEANING OF YOU BEING DISMISSED *BLAH BLAH*... MAGICIAN SAID *BLAH BLAH*...AND THE COMMISSIONER *BLAH BLAH BLAH BLAH*.
LOOKER, I'M A LITTLE BUSY. AND I AM NO LONGER YOUR SUPERIOR, NOR AM I AN INVESTIGATOR. IF YOU WANT TO RECEIVE ORDERS, PLEASE CONTACT HEADQUARTERS.
OVER AND OUT.
I SHOULDN'T HAVE GIVEN HIM MY PERSONAL PHONE NUMBER.
EXCUSE ME.
blip
YOU'RE AN INSPECTOR WITH THE INTERNATIONAL POLICE?! REALLY? BUT YOU'RE A CHILD.
EX-INSPECTOR.
MS. WHITE...
...YOU WERE STILL A CHILD TOO WHEN YOU STARTED YOUR COMPANY, SO ISN'T IT THE SAME?
I don't know why, but he's annoying.
AT ANY RATE, OUR COMMON GOAL...
...IS TO DESTROY TEAM PLASMA AND FREE KYUREM FROM THEIR CONTROL. ISN'T THAT RIGHT?

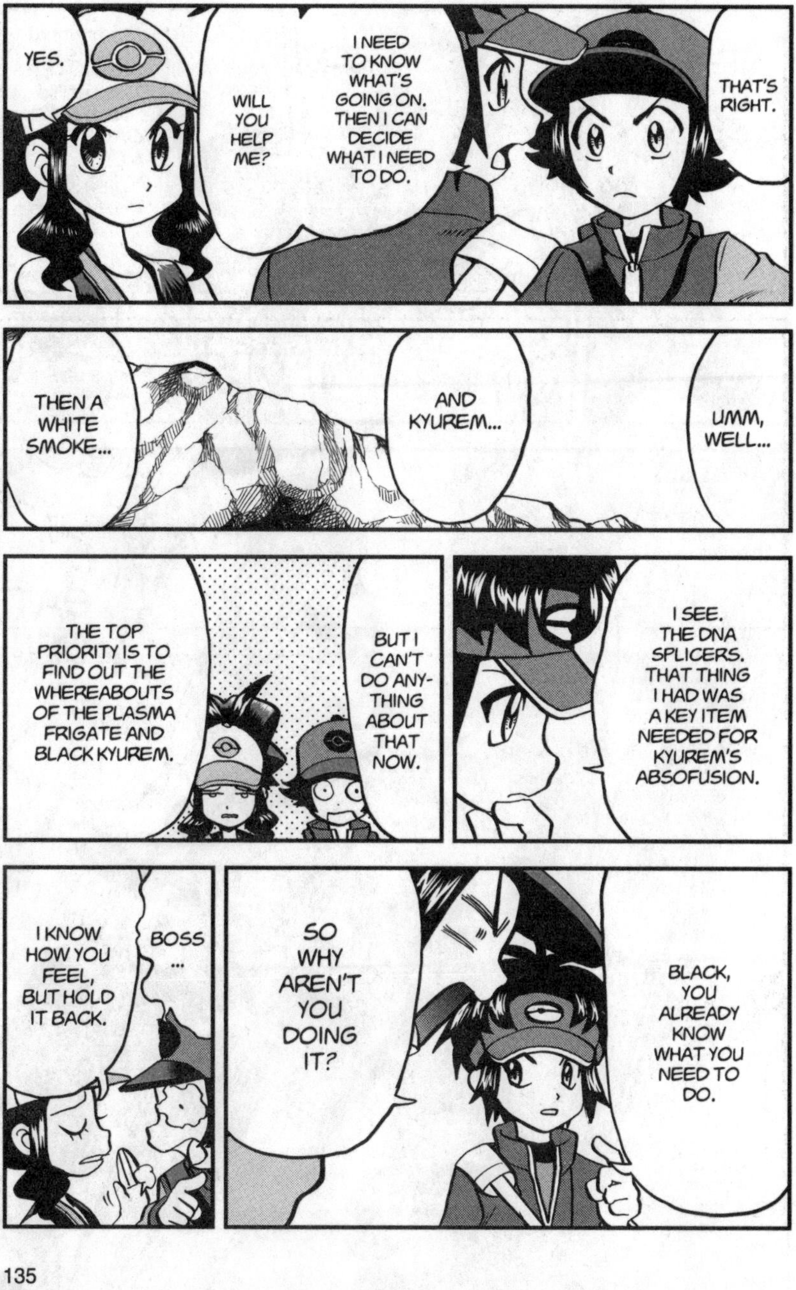
THAT'S RIGHT.
I NEED TO KNOW WHAT'S GOING ON. THEN I CAN DECIDE WHAT I NEED TO DO.
WILL YOU HELP ME?
YES.
UMM, WELL...
AND KYUREM...
THEN A WHITE SMOKE...
I SEE. THE DNA SPLICERS. THAT THING I HAD WAS A KEY ITEM NEEDED FOR KYUREM'S ABSOFUSION.
BUT I CAN'T DO ANYTHING ABOUT THAT NOW.
THE TOP PRIORITY IS TO FIND OUT THE WHEREABOUTS OF THE PLASMA FRIGATE AND BLACK KYUREM.
BLACK, YOU ALREADY KNOW WHAT YOU NEED TO DO.
SO WHY AREN'T YOU DOING IT?
BOSS...
I KNOW HOW YOU FEEL, BUT HOLD IT BACK.

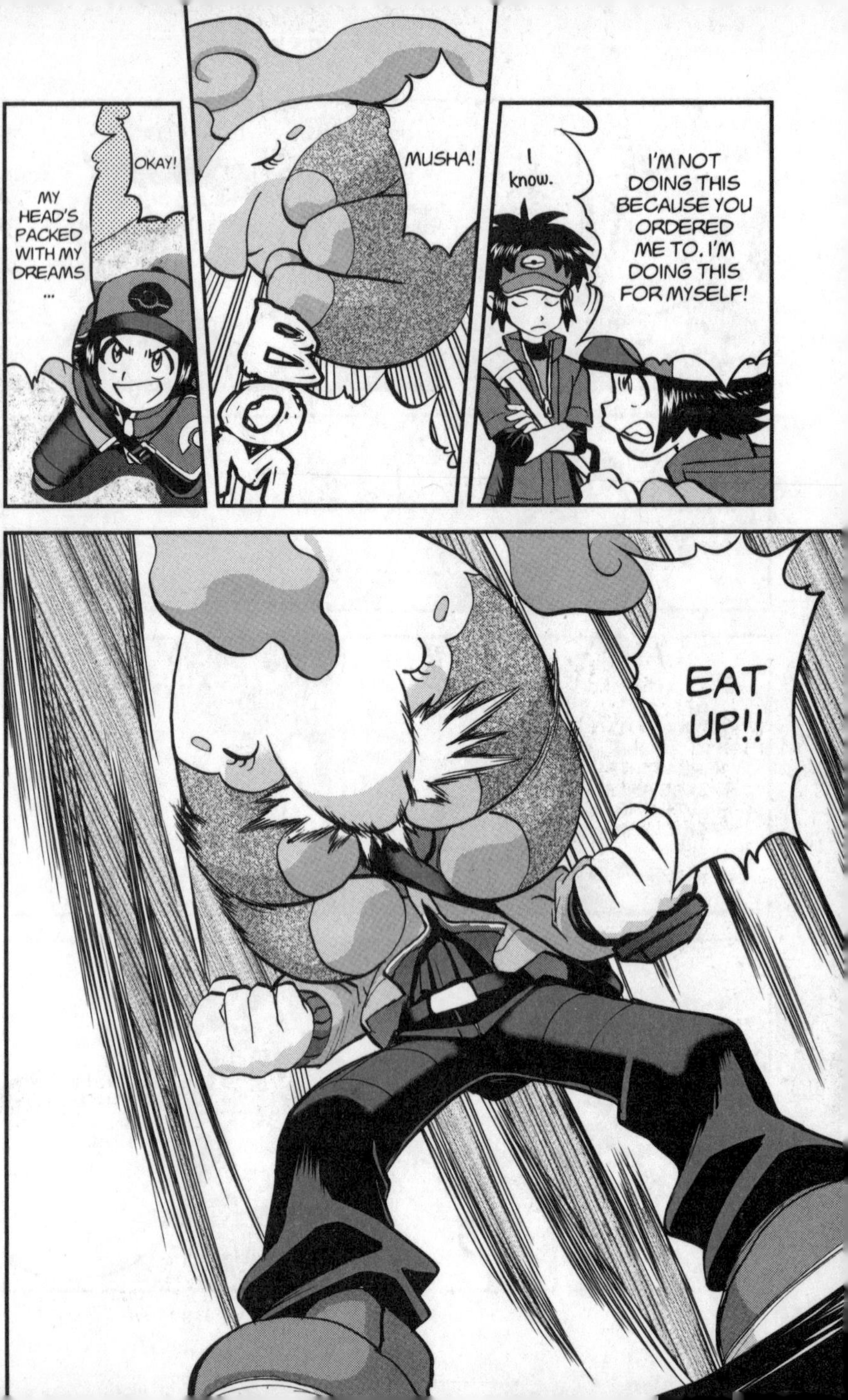
I'M NOT DOING THIS BECAUSE YOU ORDERED ME TO. I'M DOING THIS FOR MYSELF!
I know.
MUSHA!
OKAY!
MY HEAD'S PACKED WITH MY DREAMS ...
EAT UP!!

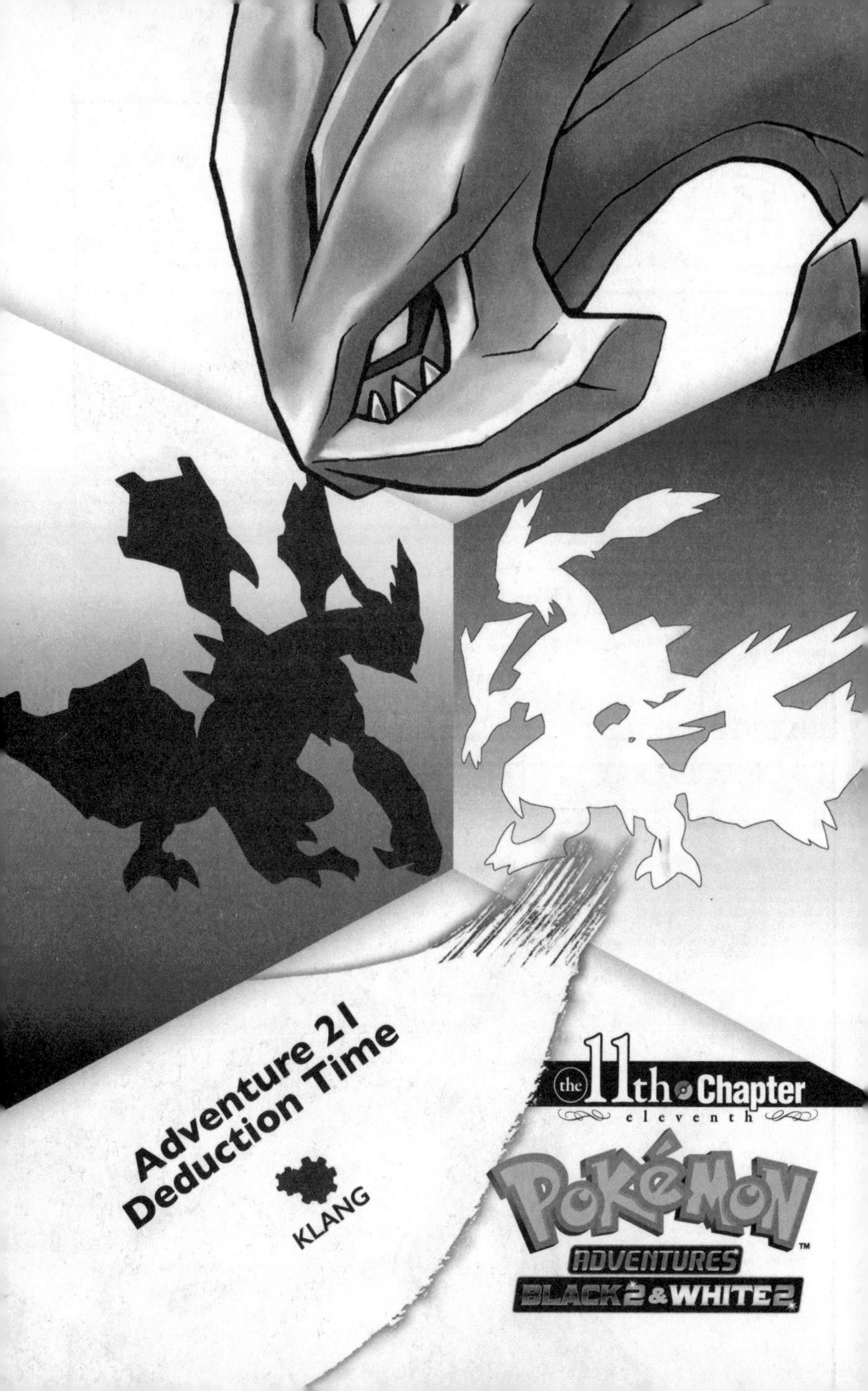
Adventure 21
Deduction Time
KLANG
the 11th Chapter
eleventh
POKÉMON
ADVENTURES
BLACK 2 & WHITE 2

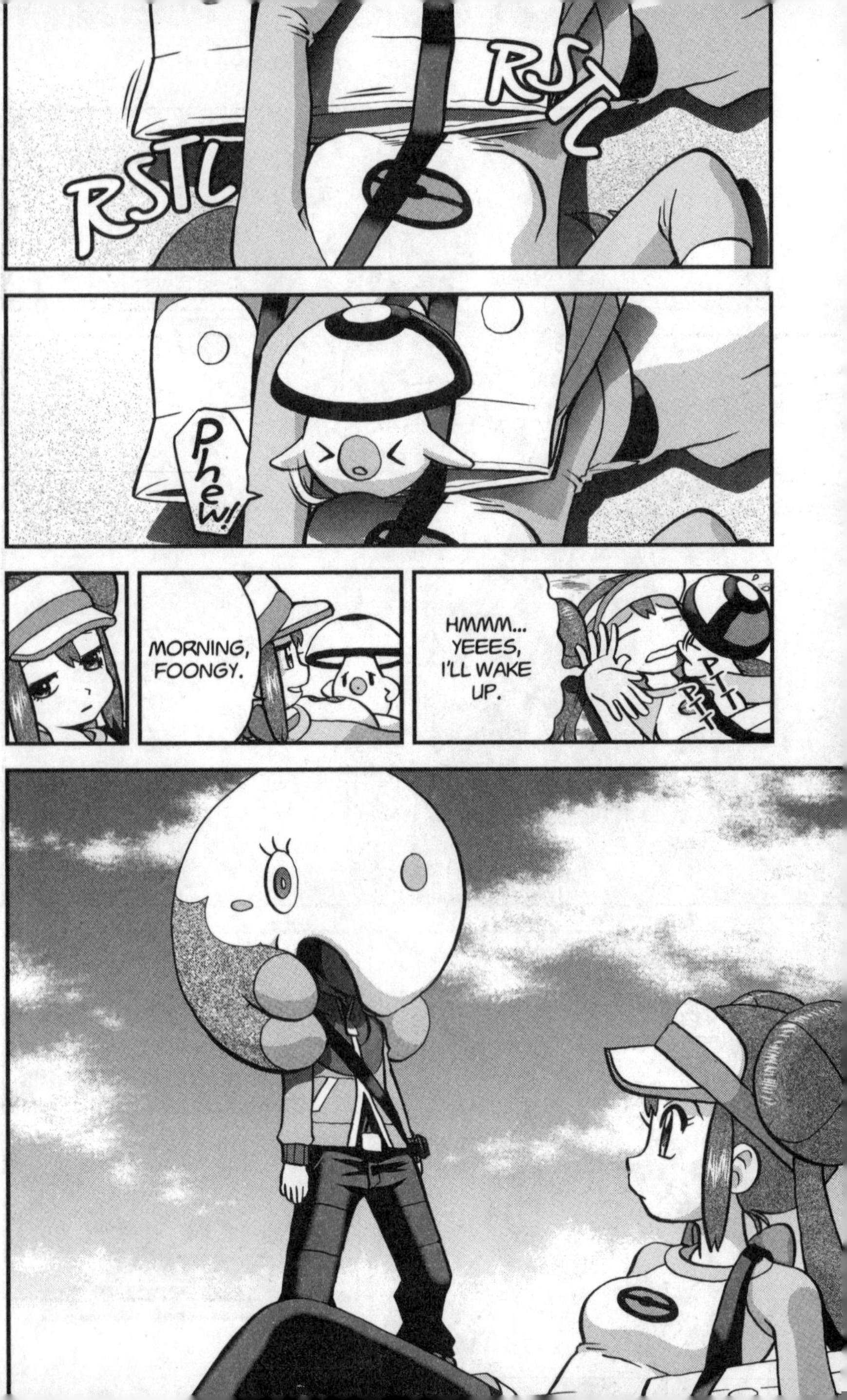
RSTL
RSTL
Phew!
HMMM... YEEES, I'LL WAKE UP.
PTTT
PTTT
MORNING, FOONGY.

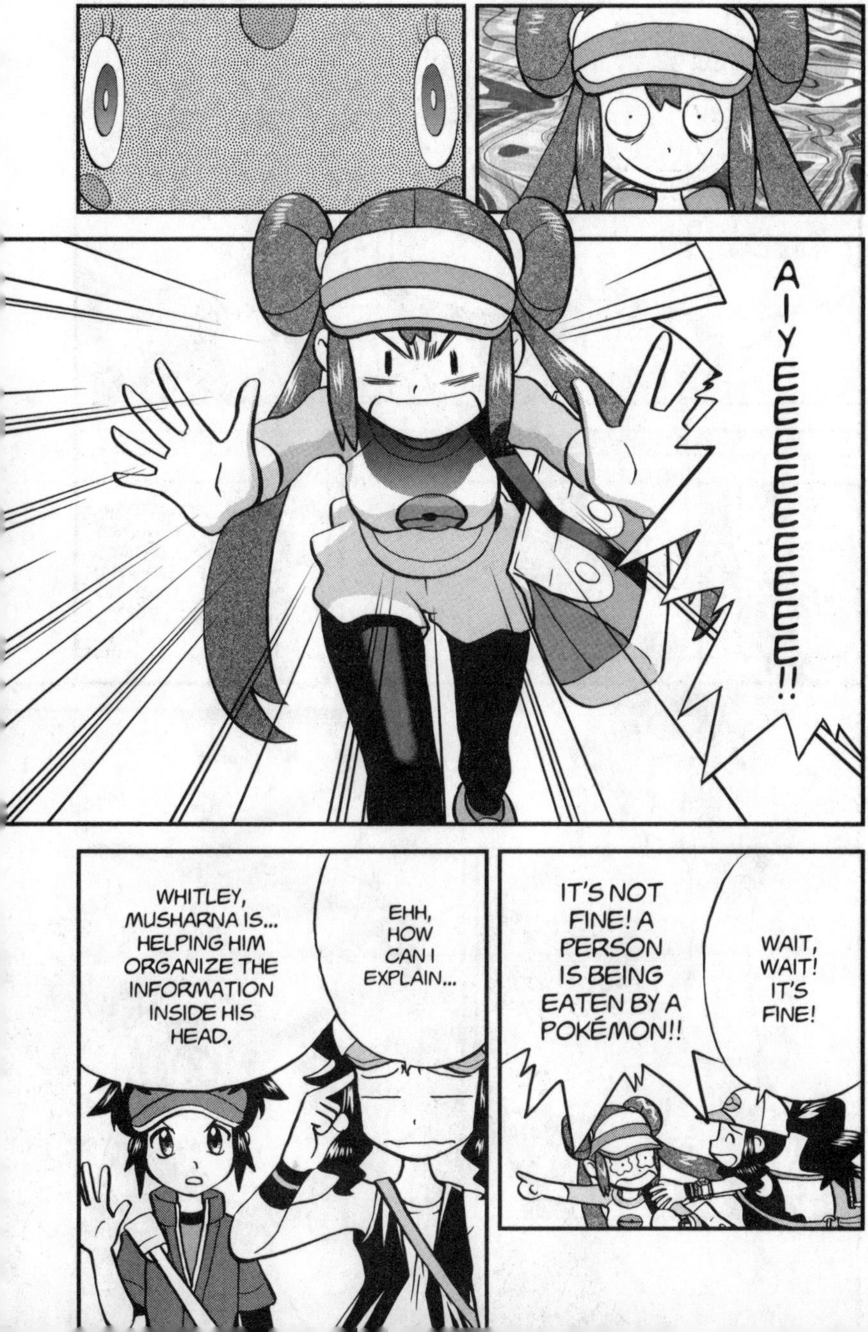
AIYEEEEEEEEEE!!
WAIT, WAIT! IT'S FINE!
IT'S NOT FINE! A PERSON IS BEING EATEN BY A POKÉMON!!
EHH, HOW CAN I EXPLAIN...
WHITLEY, MUSHARNA IS... HELPING HIM ORGANIZE THE INFORMATION INSIDE HIS HEAD.

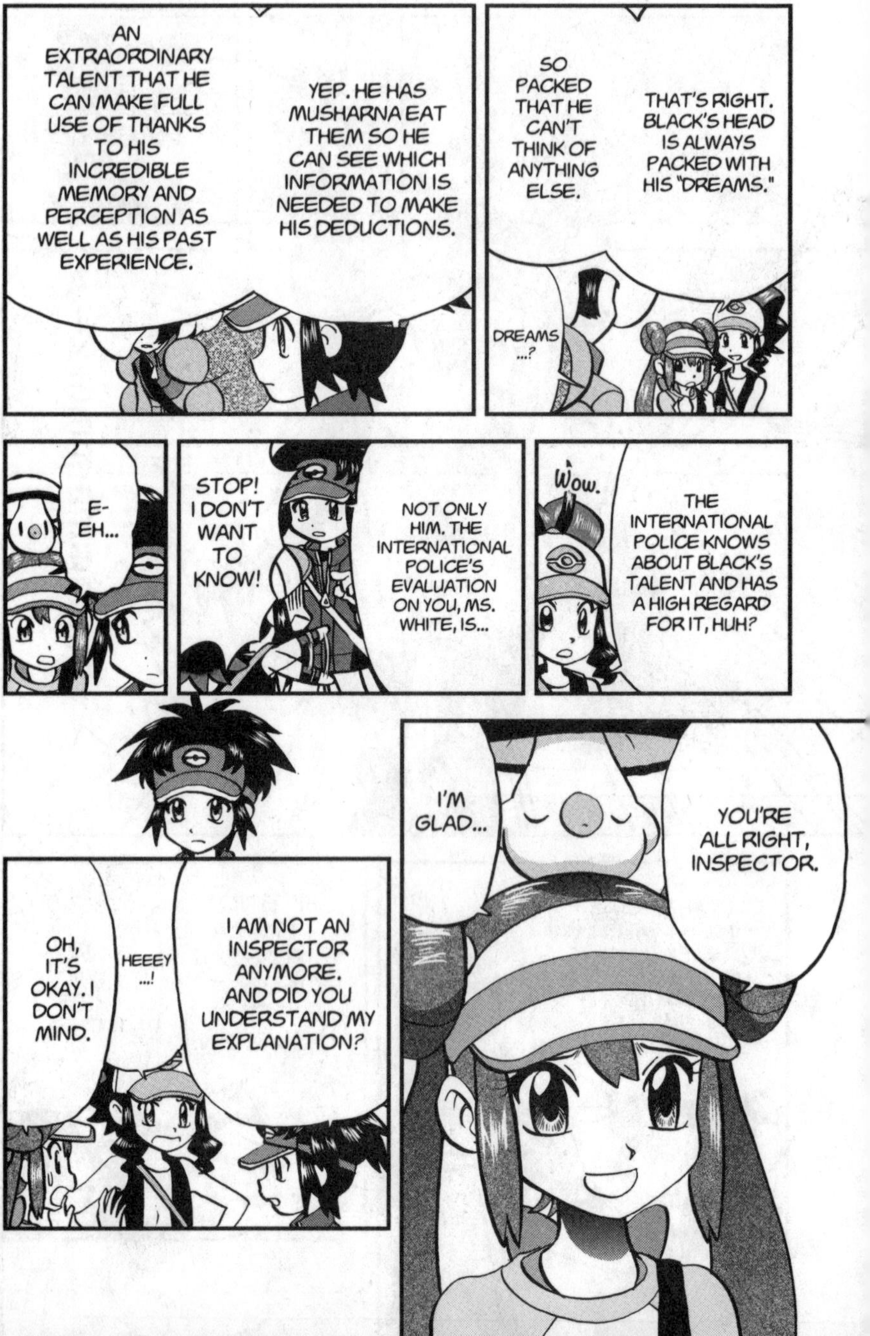
THAT'S RIGHT. BLACK'S HEAD IS ALWAYS PACKED WITH HIS "DREAMS."
SO PACKED THAT HE CAN'T THINK OF ANYTHING ELSE.
DREAMS ...?
YEP. HE HAS MUSHARNA EAT THEM SO HE CAN SEE WHICH INFORMATION IS NEEDED TO MAKE HIS DEDUCTIONS.
AN EXTRAORDINARY TALENT THAT HE CAN MAKE FULL USE OF THANKS TO HIS INCREDIBLE MEMORY AND PERCEPTION AS WELL AS HIS PAST EXPERIENCE.
THE INTERNATIONAL POLICE KNOWS ABOUT BLACK'S TALENT AND HAS A HIGH REGARD FOR IT, HUH?
WOW.
NOT ONLY HIM. THE INTERNATIONAL POLICE'S EVALUATION ON YOU, MS. WHITE, IS...
STOP! I DON'T WANT TO KNOW!
E- EH...
YOU'RE ALL RIGHT, INSPECTOR.
I'M GLAD...
I AM NOT AN INSPECTOR ANYMORE. AND DID YOU UNDERSTAND MY EXPLANATION?
HEEEY ...!
OH, IT'S OKAY. I DON'T MIND.

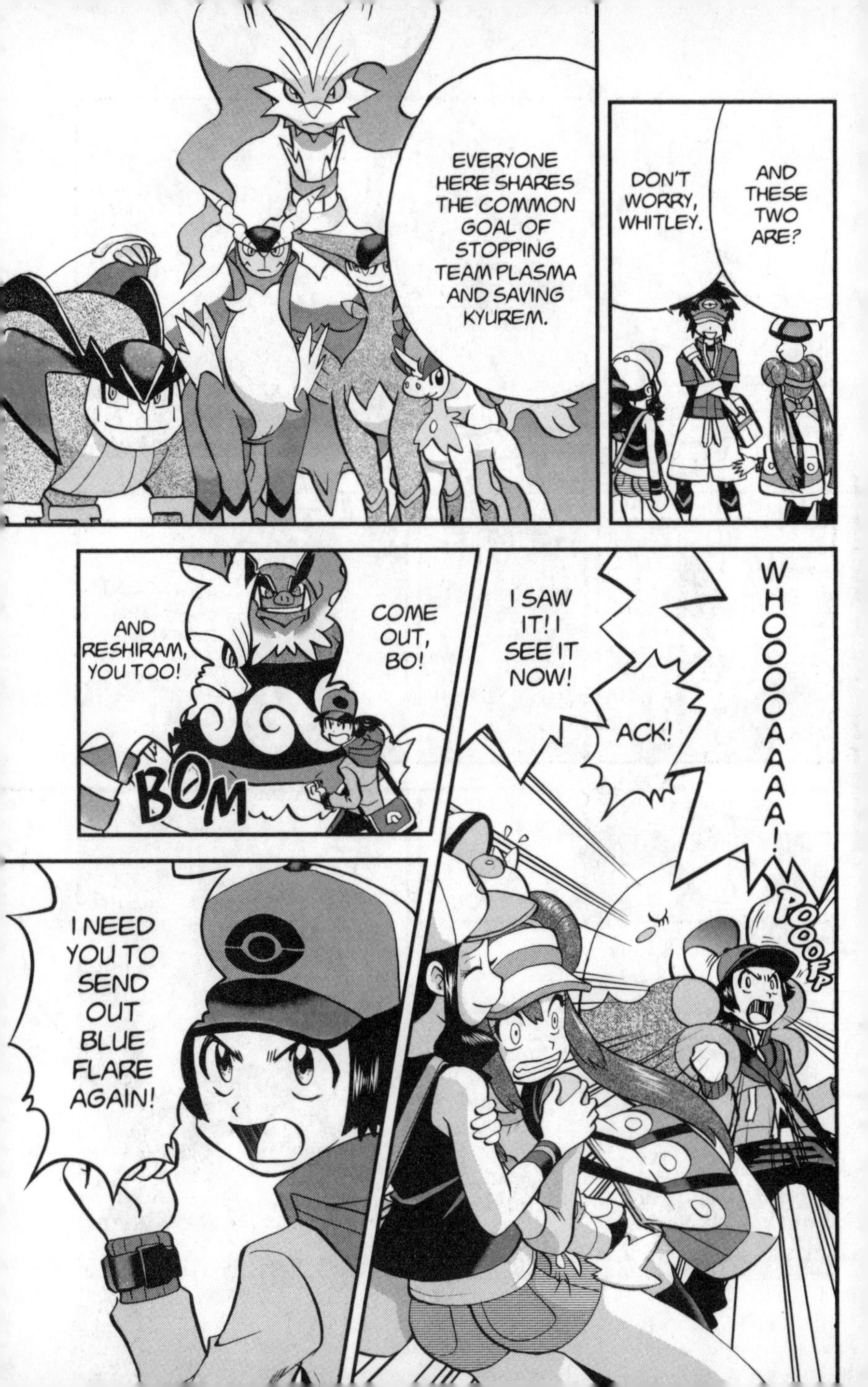
AND THESE TWO ARE?
DON'T WORRY, WHITLEY.
EVERYONE HERE SHARES THE COMMON GOAL OF STOPPING TEAM PLASMA AND SAVING KYUREM.
WHOOOOOAAAAA!
I SAW IT! I SEE IT NOW!
ACK!
POOOF
COME OUT, BO!
AND RESHIRAM, YOU TOO!
BOM
I NEED YOU TO SEND OUT BLUE FLARE AGAIN!

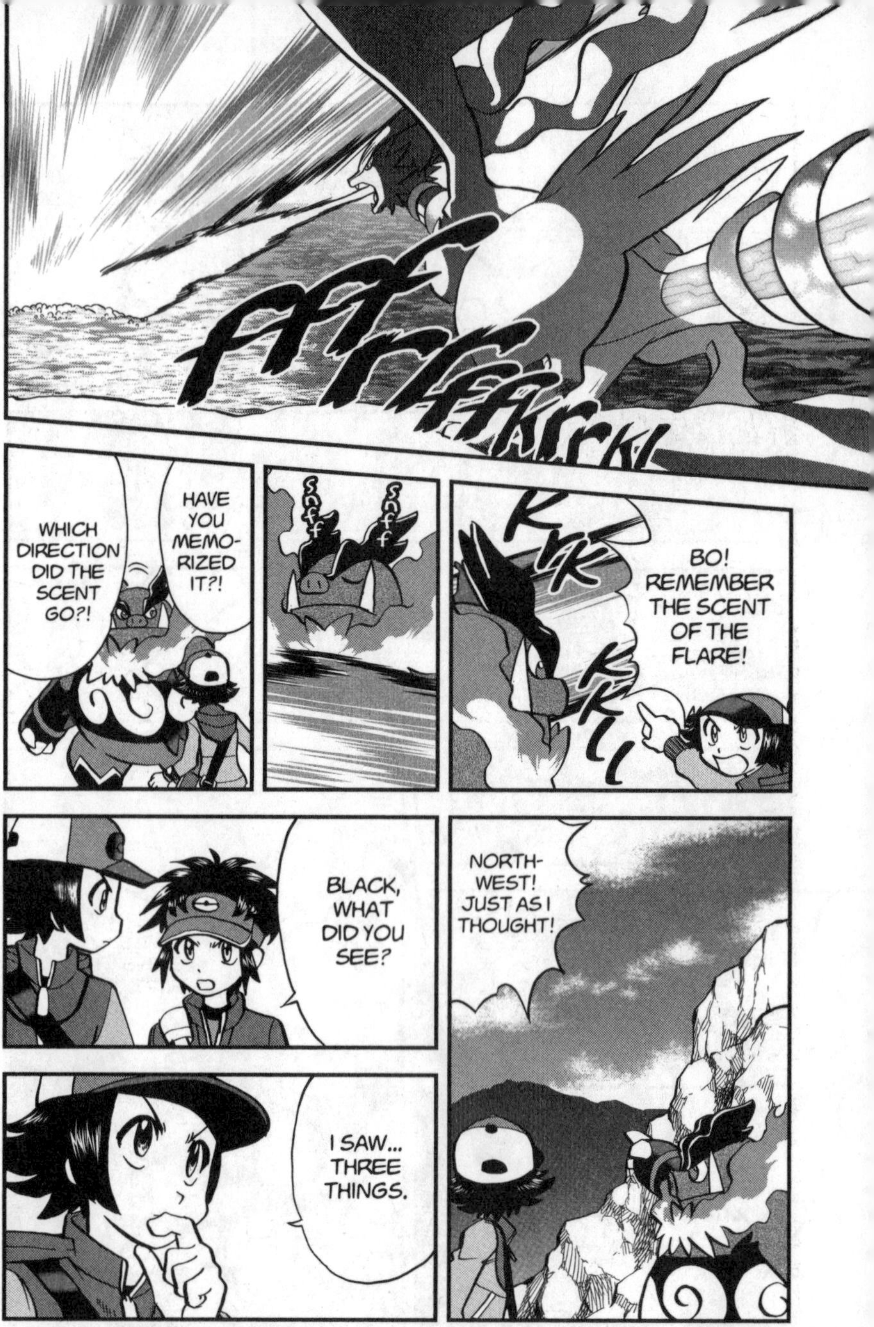
BO! REMEMBER THE SCENT OF THE FLARE!
snff
snff
HAVE YOU MEMO-RIZED IT?!
WHICH DIRECTION DID THE SCENT GO?!
NORTH-WEST! JUST AS I THOUGHT!
BLACK, WHAT DID YOU SEE?
I SAW... THREE THINGS.

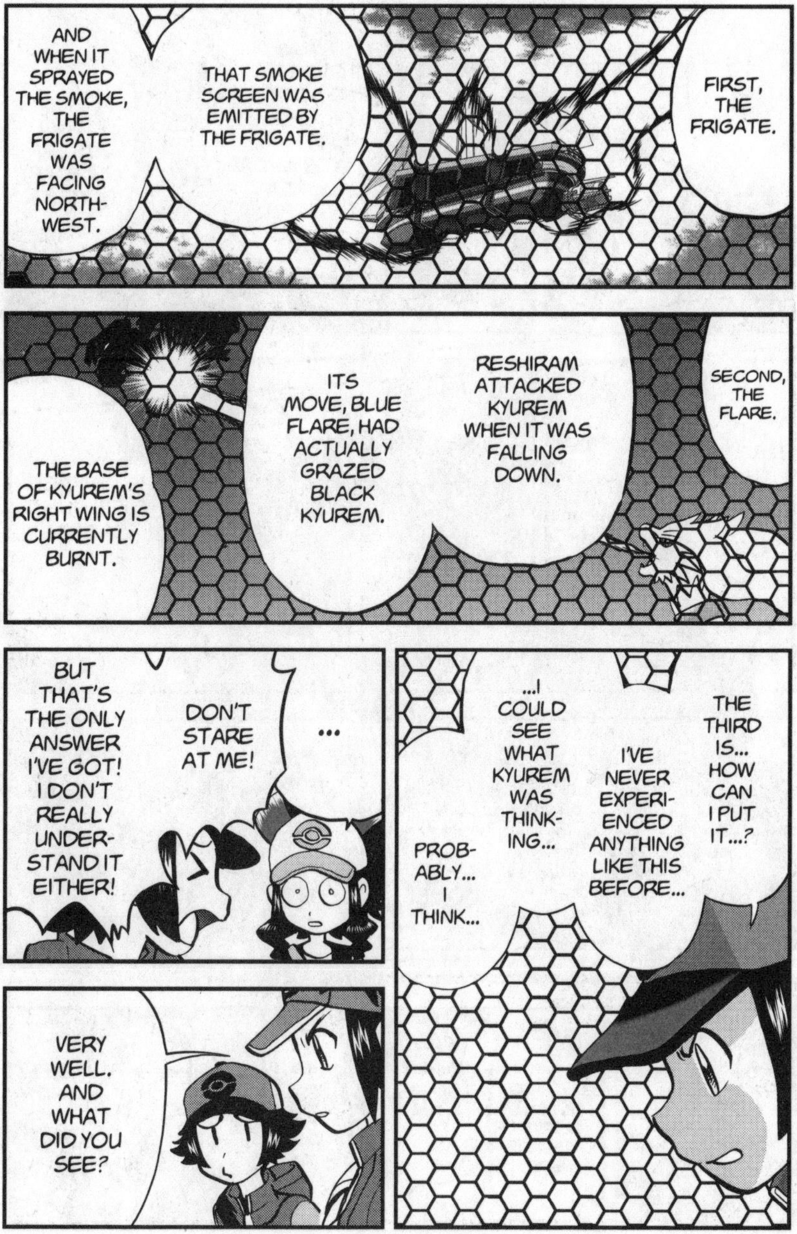
FIRST, THE FRIGATE.
THAT SMOKE SCREEN WAS EMITTED BY THE FRIGATE.
AND WHEN IT SPRAYED THE SMOKE, THE FRIGATE WAS FACING NORTH-WEST.
SECOND, THE FLARE.
RESHIRAM ATTACKED KYUREM WHEN IT WAS FALLING DOWN.
ITS MOVE, BLUE FLARE, HAD ACTUALLY GRAZED BLACK KYUREM.
THE BASE OF KYUREM'S RIGHT WING IS CURRENTLY BURNT.
THE THIRD IS... HOW CAN I PUT IT...?
I'VE NEVER EXPERIENCED ANYTHING LIKE THIS BEFORE...
...I COULD SEE WHAT KYUREM WAS THINKING...
PROBABLY... I THINK...
...
DON'T STARE AT ME!
BUT THAT'S THE ONLY ANSWER I'VE GOT! I DON'T REALLY UNDERSTAND IT EITHER!
VERY WELL. AND WHAT DID YOU SEE?

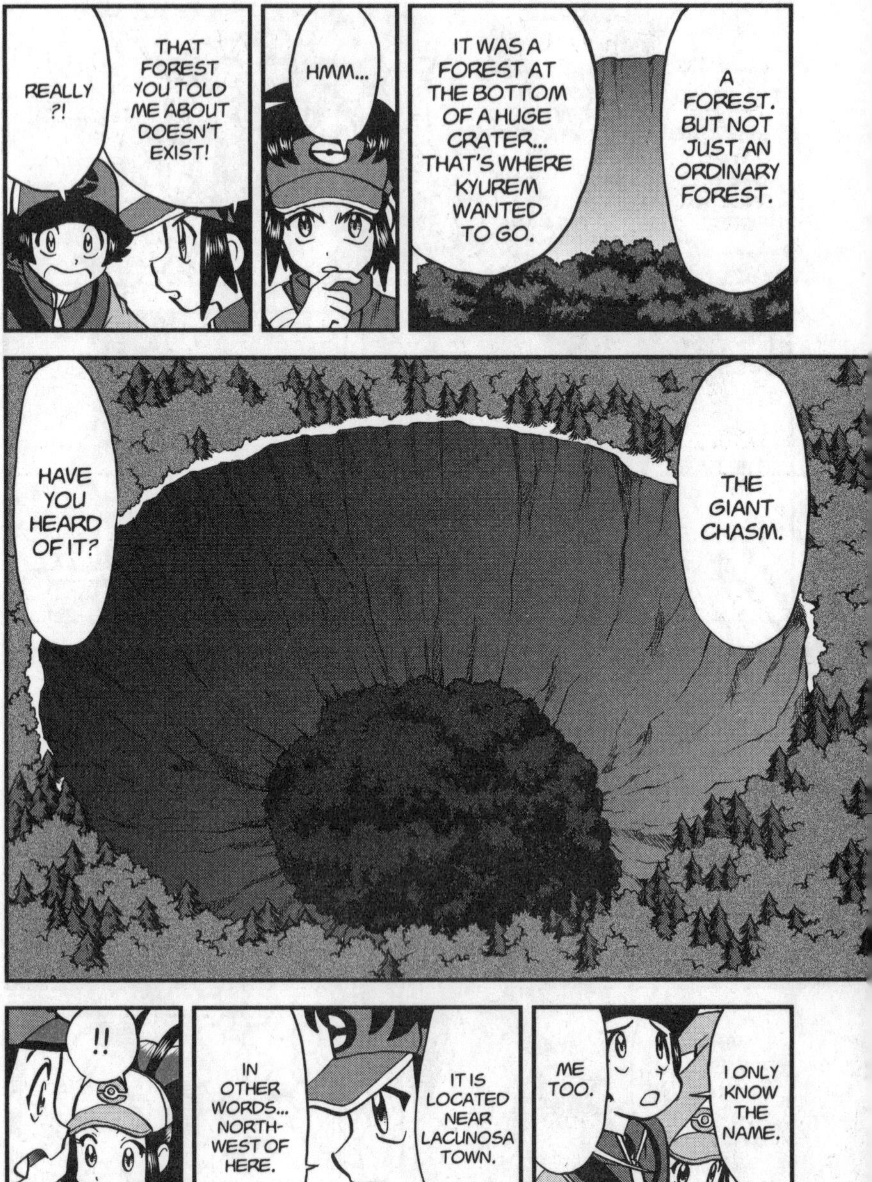
A FOREST. BUT NOT JUST AN ORDINARY FOREST.
IT WAS A FOREST AT THE BOTTOM OF A HUGE CRATER... THAT'S WHERE KYUREM WANTED TO GO.
HMM...
THAT FOREST YOU TOLD ME ABOUT DOESN'T EXIST!
REALLY ?!
THE GIANT CHASM.
HAVE YOU HEARD OF IT?
I ONLY KNOW THE NAME.
ME TOO.
IT IS LOCATED NEAR LACUNOSA TOWN.
IN OTHER WORDS... NORTH-WEST OF HERE.
!!

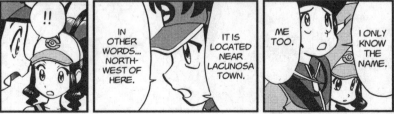

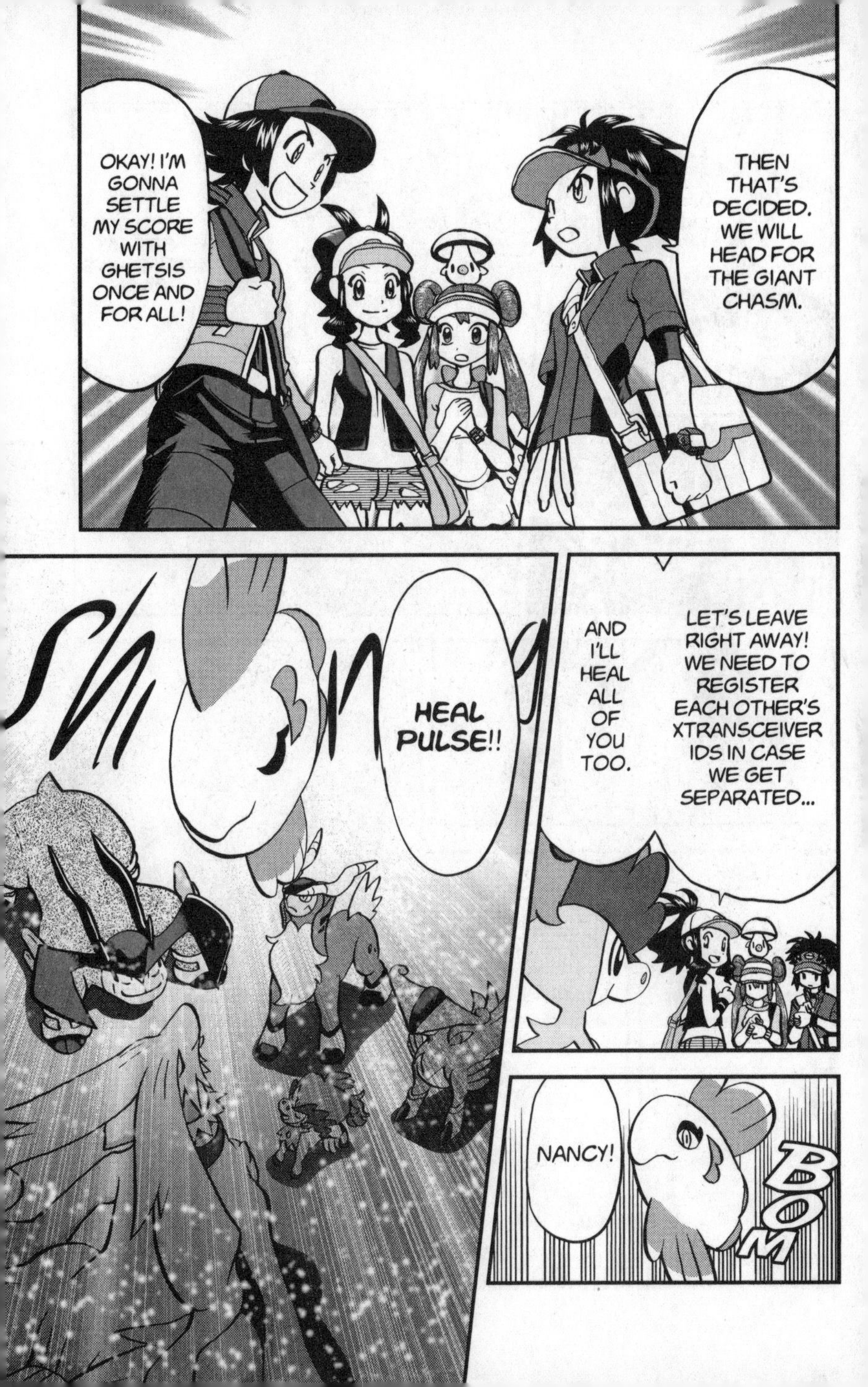
THEN THAT'S DECIDED. WE WILL HEAD FOR THE GIANT CHASM.
OKAY! I'M GONNA SETTLE MY SCORE WITH GHETSIS ONCE AND FOR ALL!
LET'S LEAVE RIGHT AWAY! WE NEED TO REGISTER EACH OTHER'S XTRANSCEIVER IDS IN CASE WE GET SEPARATED...
AND I'LL HEAL ALL OF YOU TOO.
BOOM
NANCY!
HEAL PULSE!!

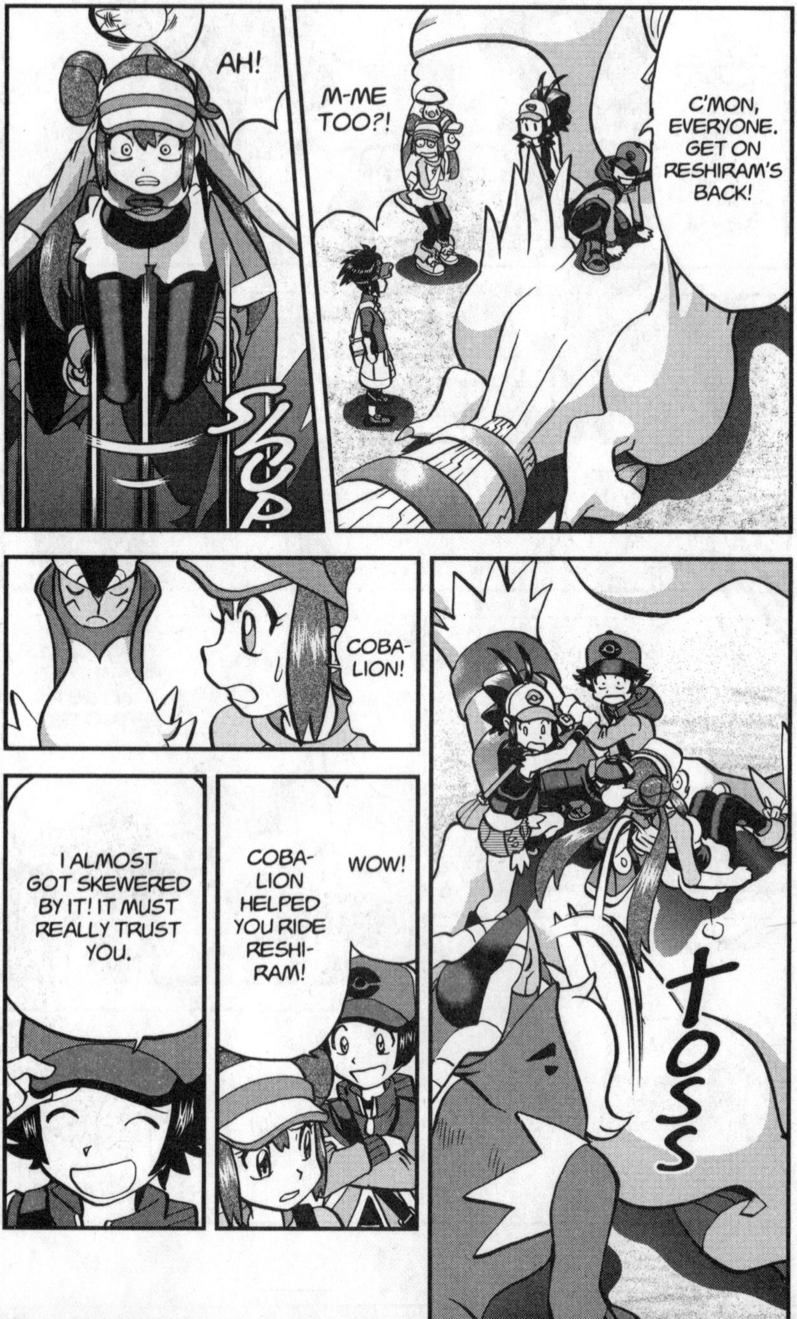
C'MON, EVERYONE. GET ON RESHIRAM'S BACK!
M-ME TOO?!
AH!
SHUP
TOSS
COBA-LION!
WOW!
COBA-LION HELPED YOU RIDE RESHI-RAM!
I ALMOST GOT SKEWERED BY IT! IT MUST REALLY TRUST YOU.

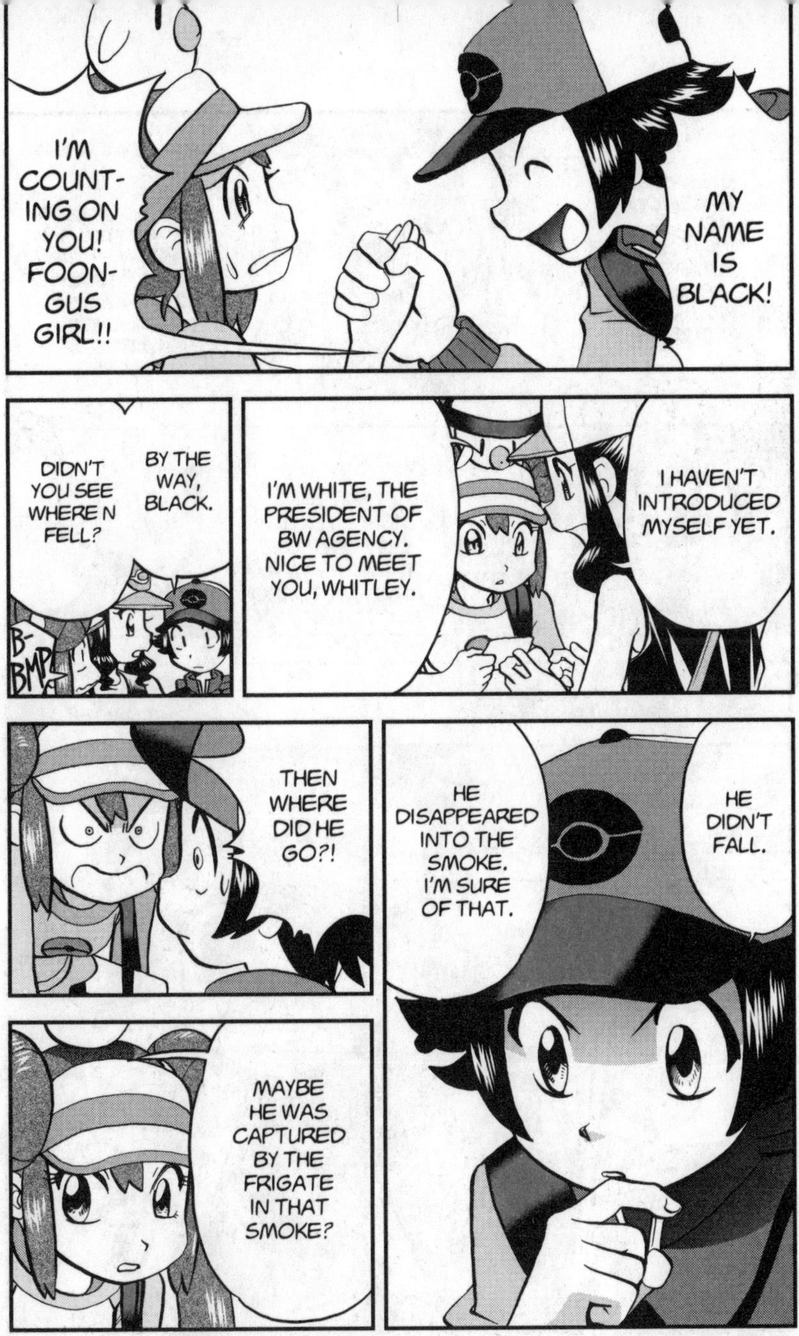
MY NAME IS BLACK!
I'M COUNTING ON YOU! FOONGUS GIRL!!
I HAVEN'T INTRODUCED MYSELF YET.
I'M WHITE, THE PRESIDENT OF BW AGENCY. NICE TO MEET YOU, WHITLEY.
BY THE WAY, BLACK.
DIDN'T YOU SEE WHERE N FELL?
B-BMP!
HE DIDN'T FALL.
HE DISAPPEARED INTO THE SMOKE. I'M SURE OF THAT.
THEN WHERE DID HE GO?!
MAYBE HE WAS CAPTURED BY THE FRIGATE IN THAT SMOKE?

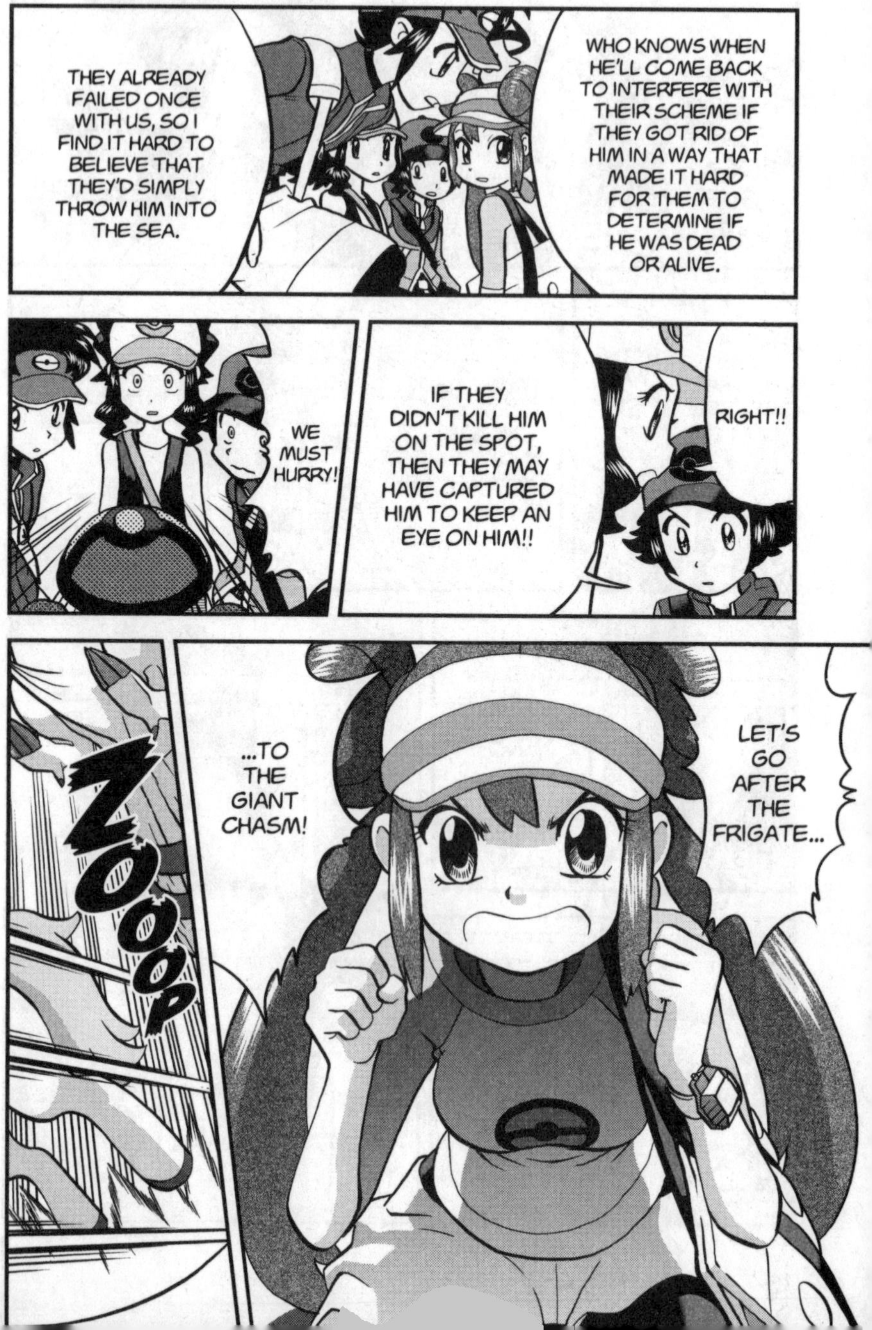
WHO KNOWS WHEN HE'LL COME BACK TO INTERFERE WITH THEIR SCHEME IF THEY GOT RID OF HIM IN A WAY THAT MADE IT HARD FOR THEM TO DETERMINE IF HE WAS DEAD OR ALIVE.
THEY ALREADY FAILED ONCE WITH US, SO I FIND IT HARD TO BELIEVE THAT THEY'D SIMPLY THROW HIM INTO THE SEA.
RIGHT!!
IF THEY DIDN'T KILL HIM ON THE SPOT, THEN THEY MAY HAVE CAPTURED HIM TO KEEP AN EYE ON HIM!!
WE MUST HURRY!
LET'S GO AFTER THE FRIGATE...
...TO THE GIANT CHASM!
ZOOOP

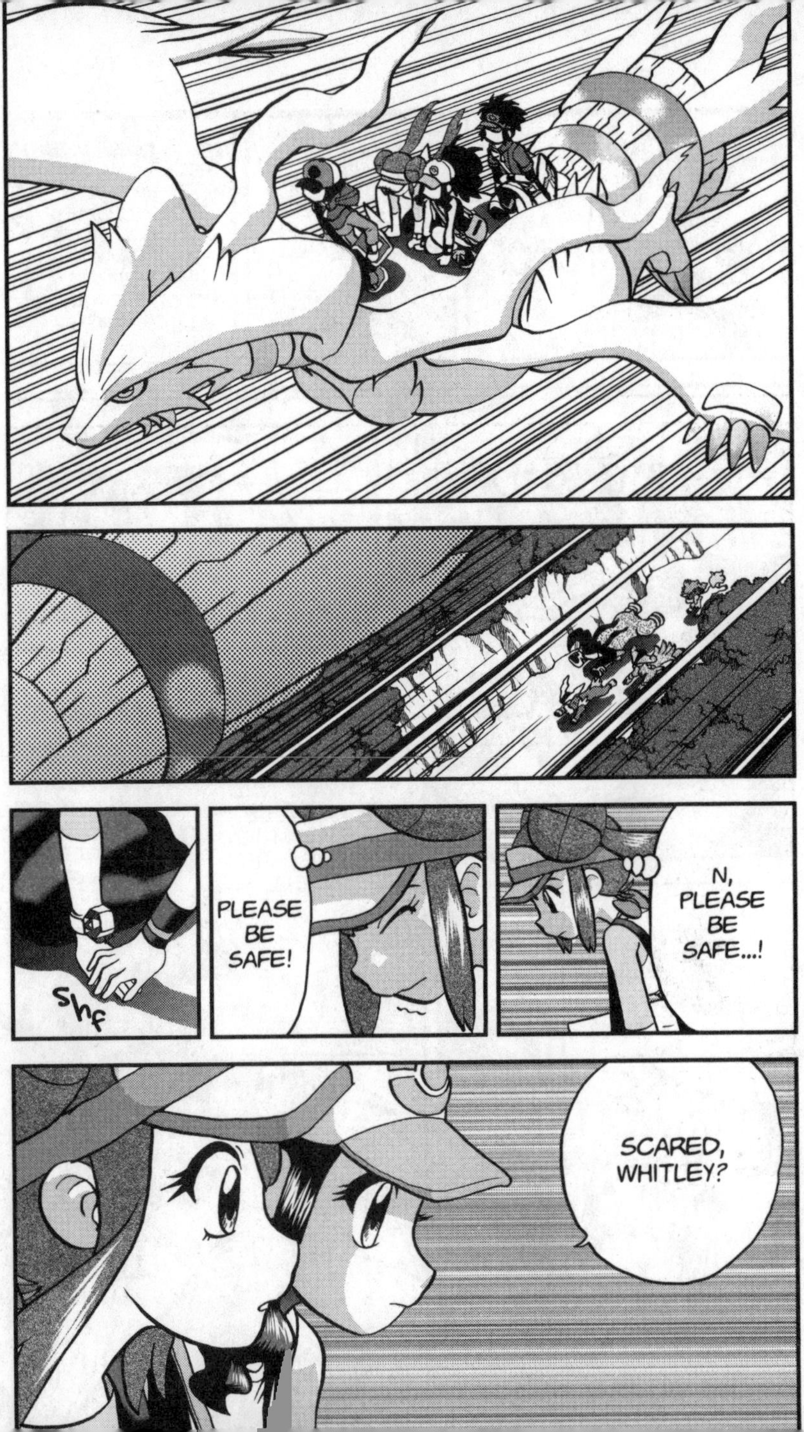
N, PLEASE BE SAFE...!
PLEASE BE SAFE!
SHF
SCARED, WHITLEY?

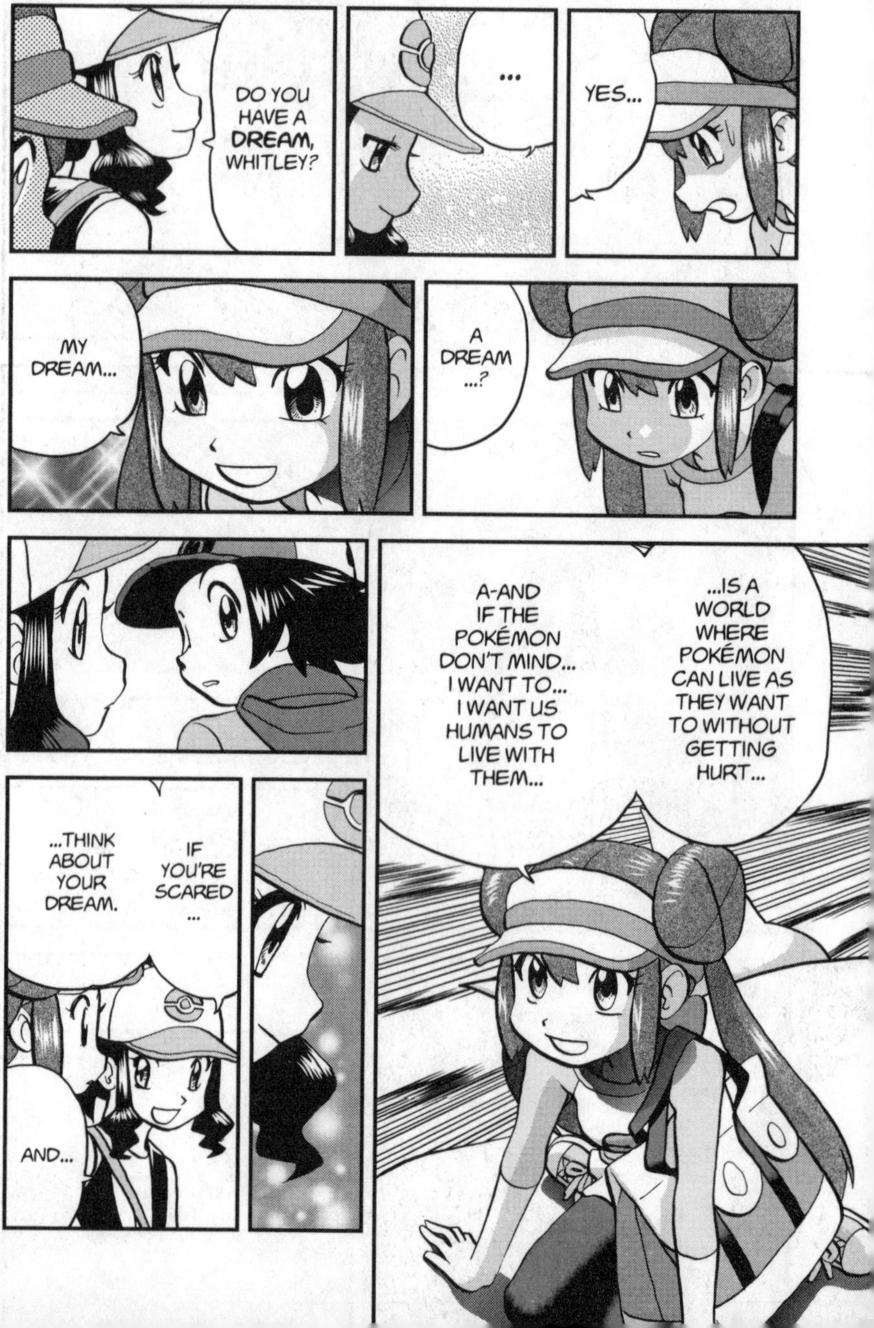
YES...
...
DO YOU HAVE A DREAM, WHITLEY?
A DREAM ...?
MY DREAM...
...IS A WORLD WHERE POKÉMON CAN LIVE AS THEY WANT TO WITHOUT GETTING HURT...
A-AND IF THE POKÉMON DON'T MIND... I WANT TO... I WANT US HUMANS TO LIVE WITH THEM...
IF YOU'RE SCARED ...
...THINK ABOUT YOUR DREAM.
AND...

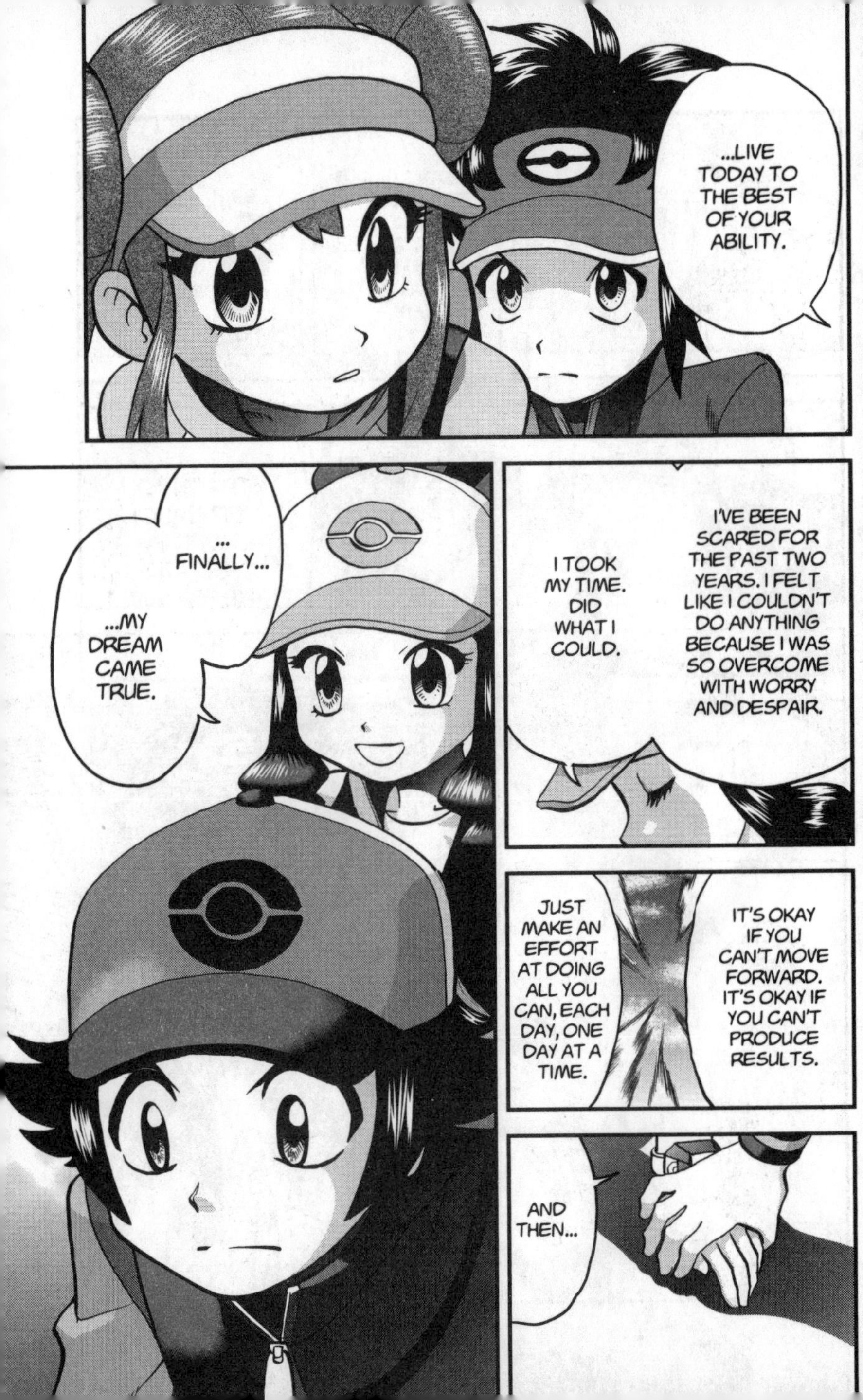

...LIVE TODAY TO THE BEST OF YOUR ABILITY.
I'VE BEEN SCARED FOR THE PAST TWO YEARS. I FELT LIKE I COULDN'T DO ANYTHING BECAUSE I WAS SO OVERCOME WITH WORRY AND DESPAIR.
I TOOK MY TIME. DID WHAT I COULD.
IT'S OKAY IF YOU CAN'T MOVE FORWARD. IT'S OKAY IF YOU CAN'T PRODUCE RESULTS.
JUST MAKE AN EFFORT AT DOING ALL YOU CAN, EACH DAY, ONE DAY AT A TIME.
AND THEN...
... FINALLY...
...MY DREAM CAME TRUE.

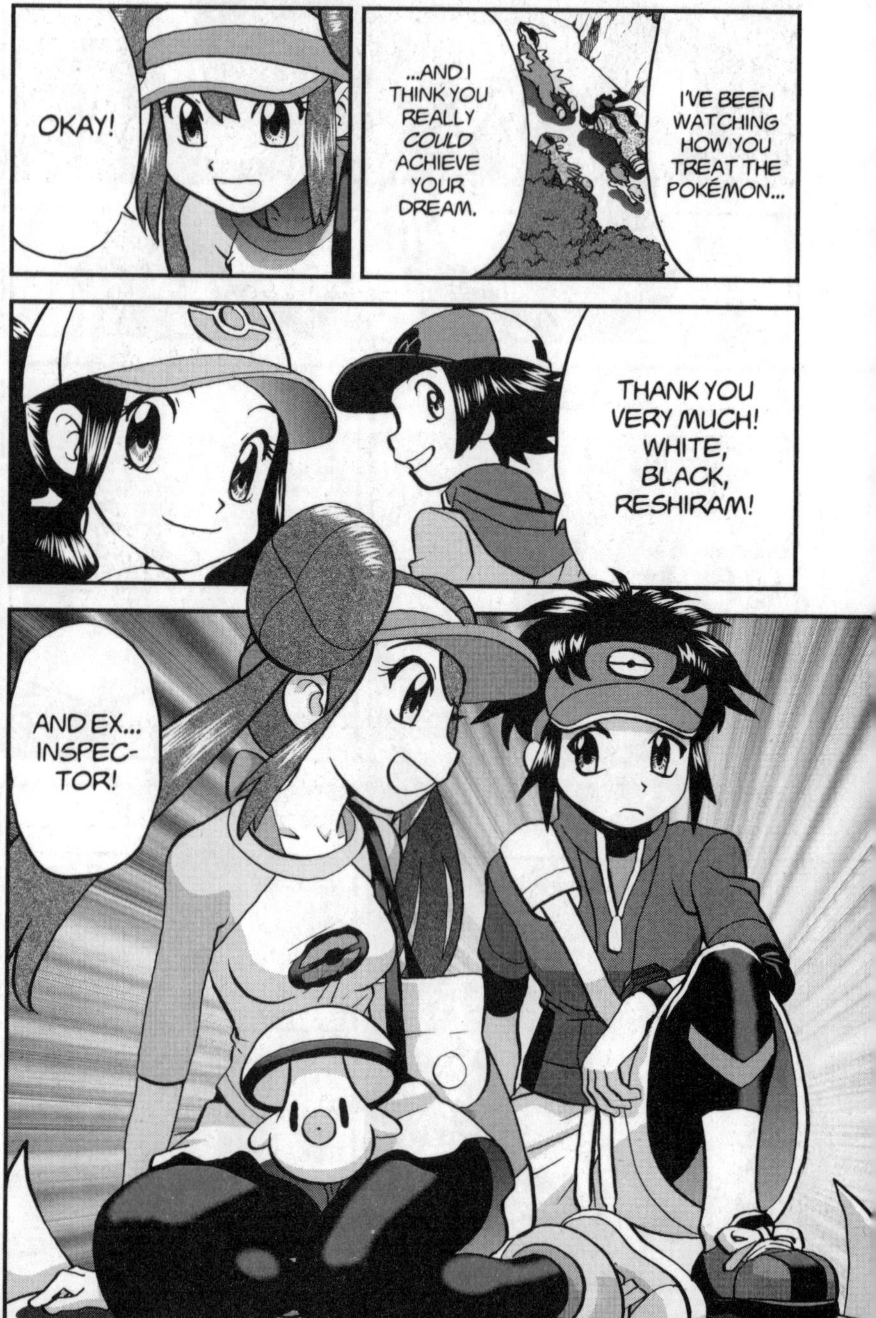
I'VE BEEN WATCHING HOW YOU TREAT THE POKÉMON...
...AND I THINK YOU REALLY *COULD* ACHIEVE YOUR DREAM.
OKAY!
THANK YOU VERY MUCH! WHITE, BLACK, RESHIRAM!
AND EX... INSPEC-TOR!

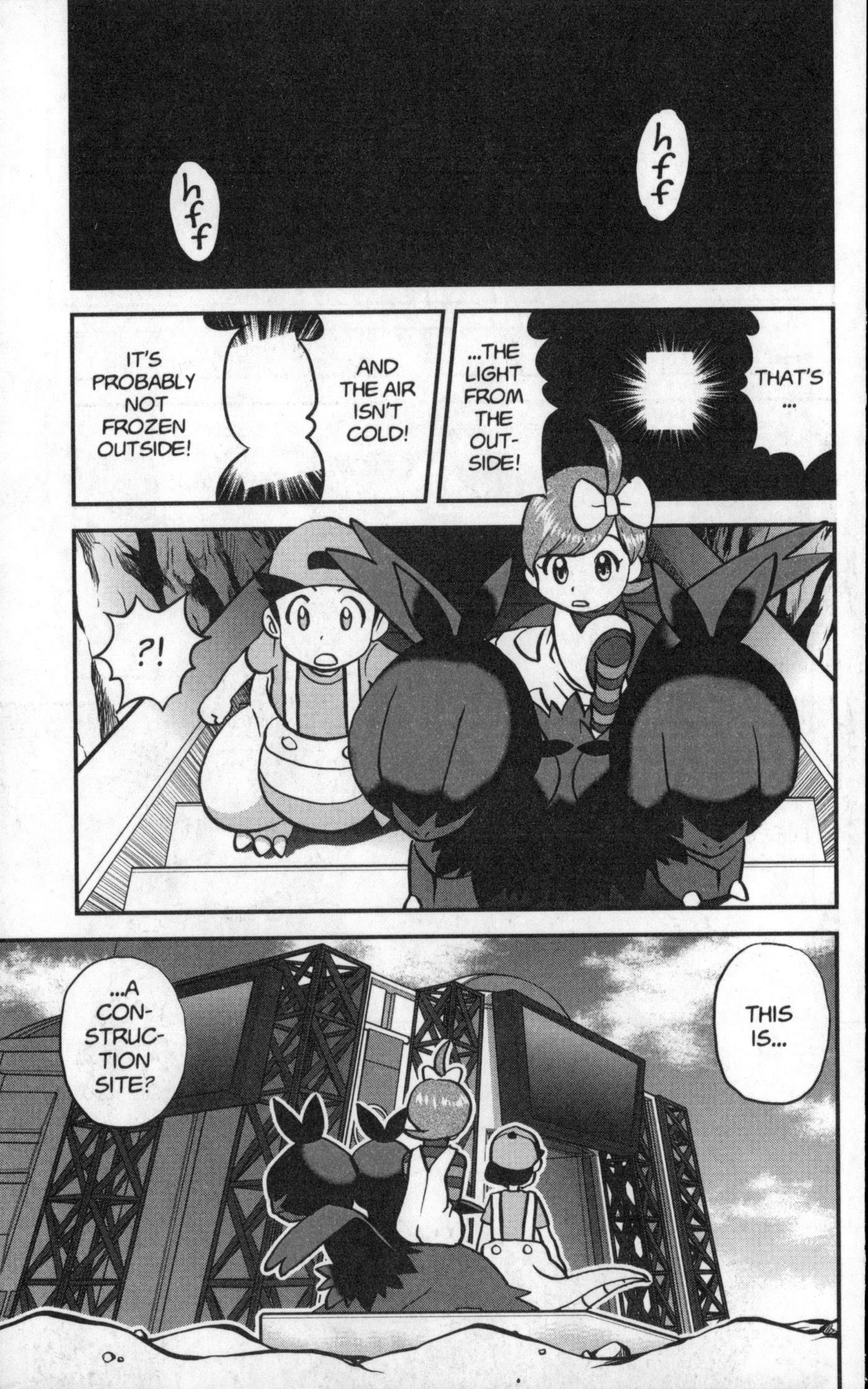
hff
hff
THAT'S ...
...THE LIGHT FROM THE OUT-SIDE!
AND THE AIR ISN'T COLD!
IT'S PROBABLY NOT FROZEN OUTSIDE!
?!
THIS IS...
...A CON-STRUC-TION SITE?

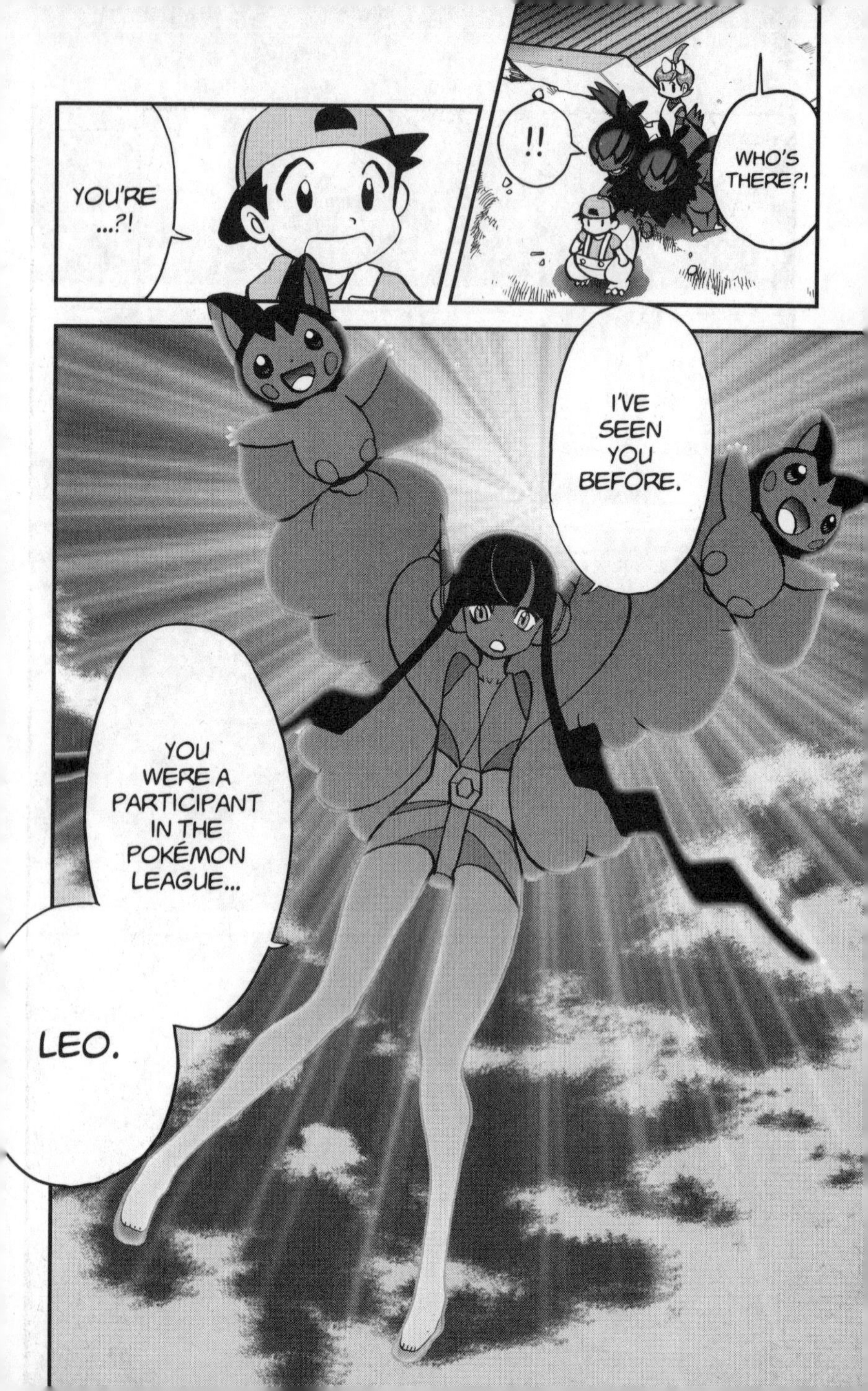
WHO'S THERE?!
!!
YOU'RE ...?!
I'VE SEEN YOU BEFORE.
YOU WERE A PARTICIPANT IN THE POKÉMON LEAGUE...
LEO.

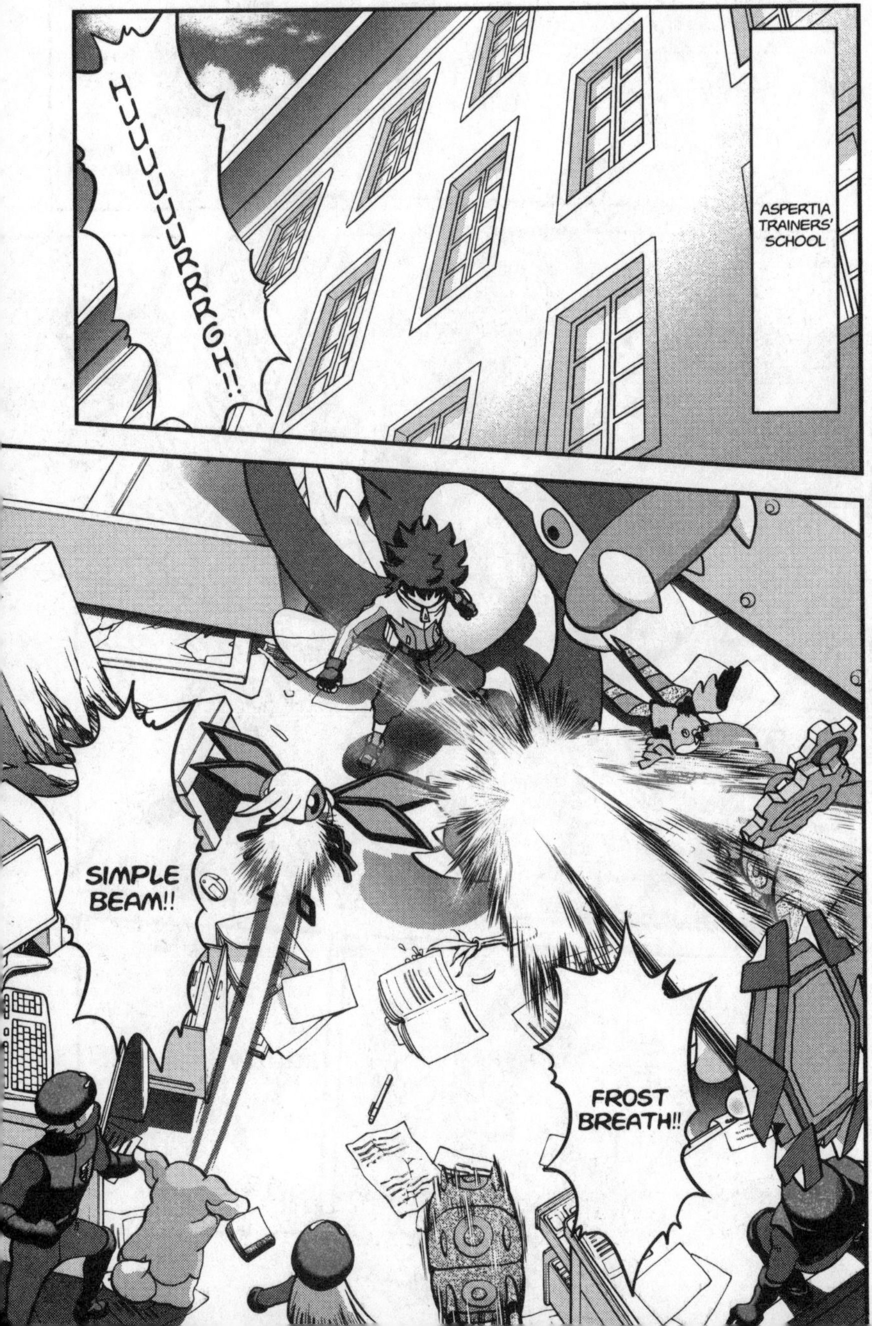
ASPERTIA TRAINERS' SCHOOL
HUUUUUURRRGH!!
SIMPLE BEAM!!
FROST BREATH!!

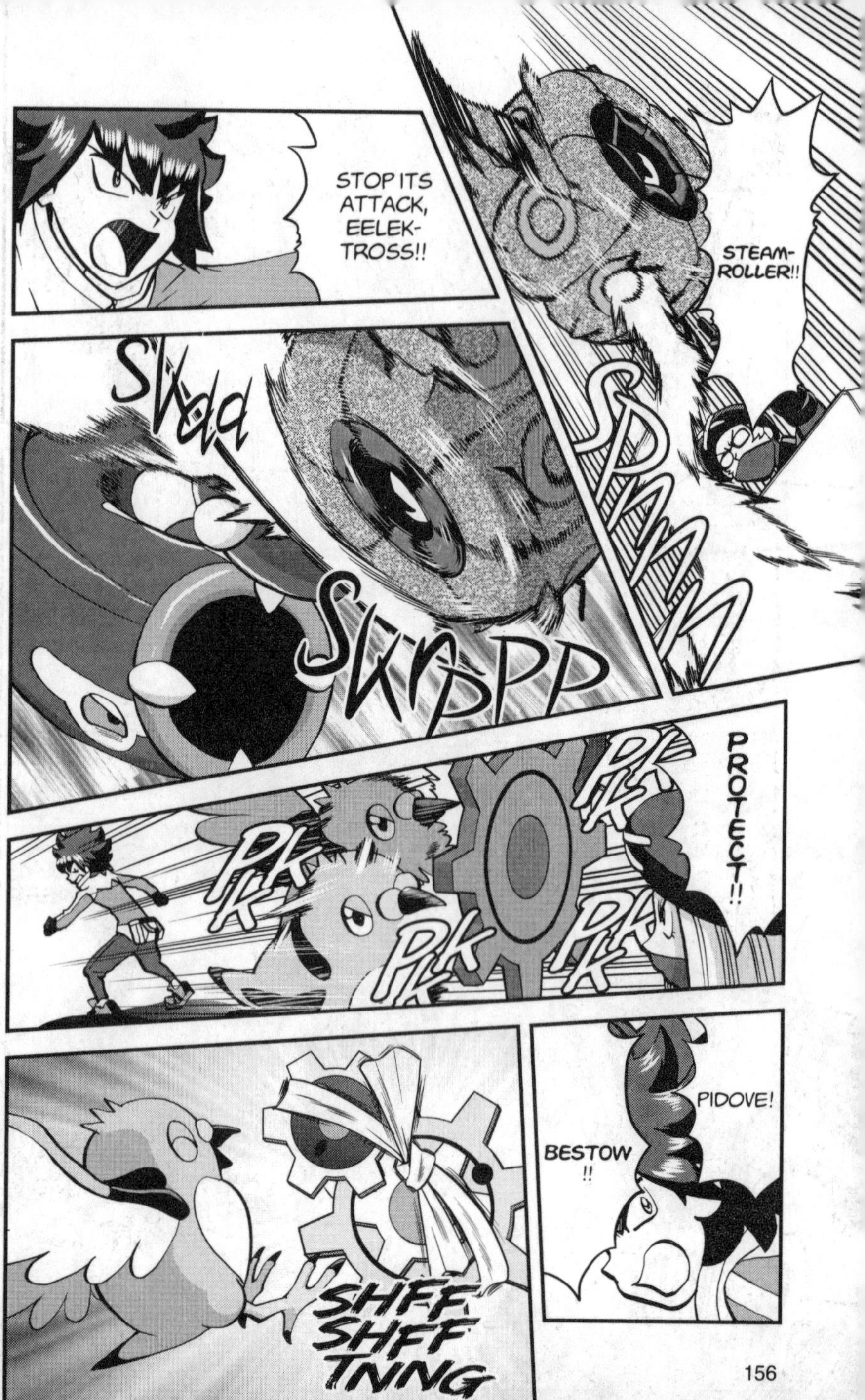
STEAM-ROLLER!!
STOP ITS ATTACK, EELEK-TROSS!!
PROTECT!!
PIDOVE!
BESTOW!!
SHFF SHFF TNNG

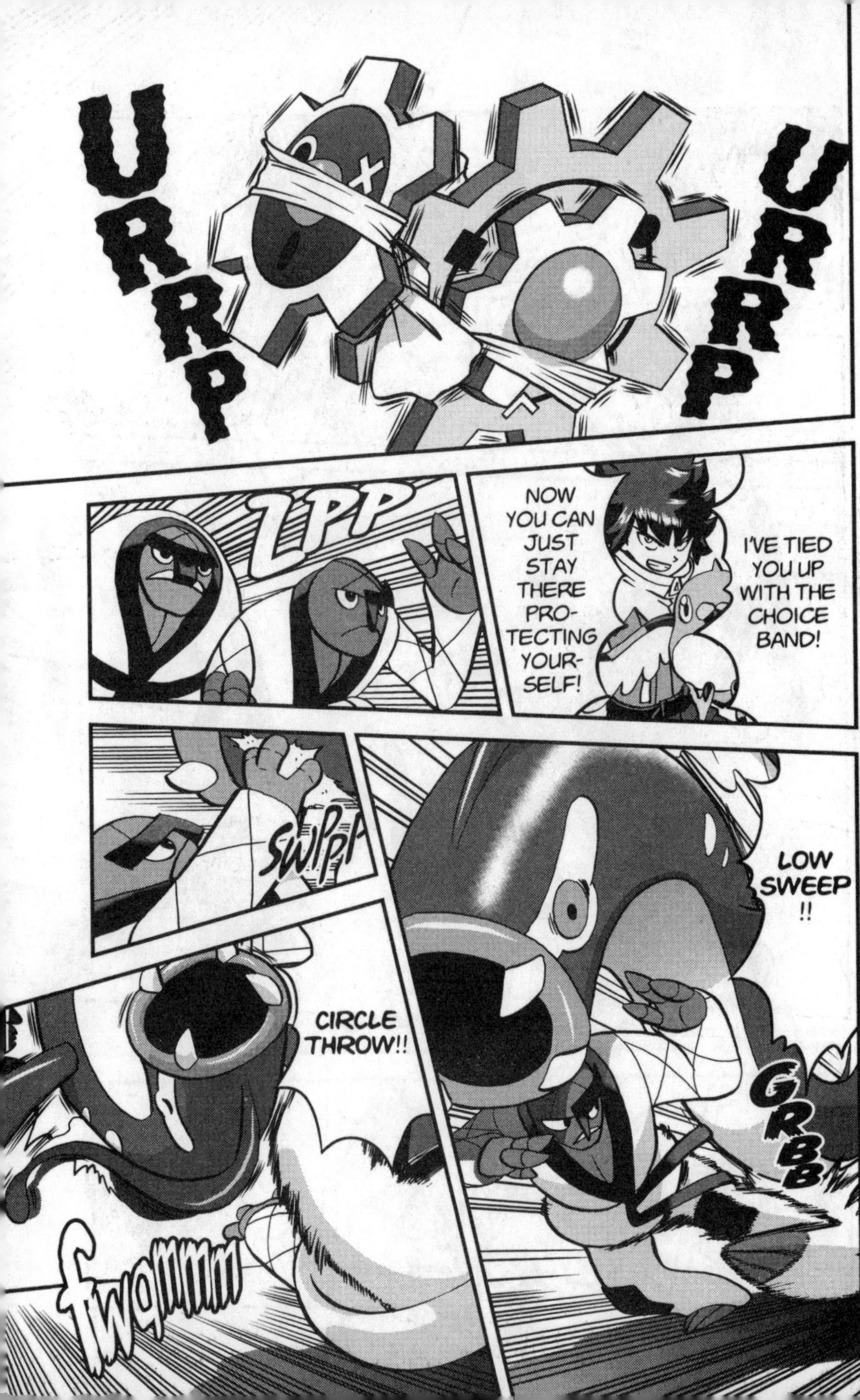
URRP
URRP
I'VE TIED YOU UP WITH THE CHOICE BAND!
NOW YOU CAN JUST STAY THERE PRO-TECTING YOUR-SELF!
ZPP
LOW SWEEP!!
GRBB
SWPP
CIRCLE THROW!!
fwommm

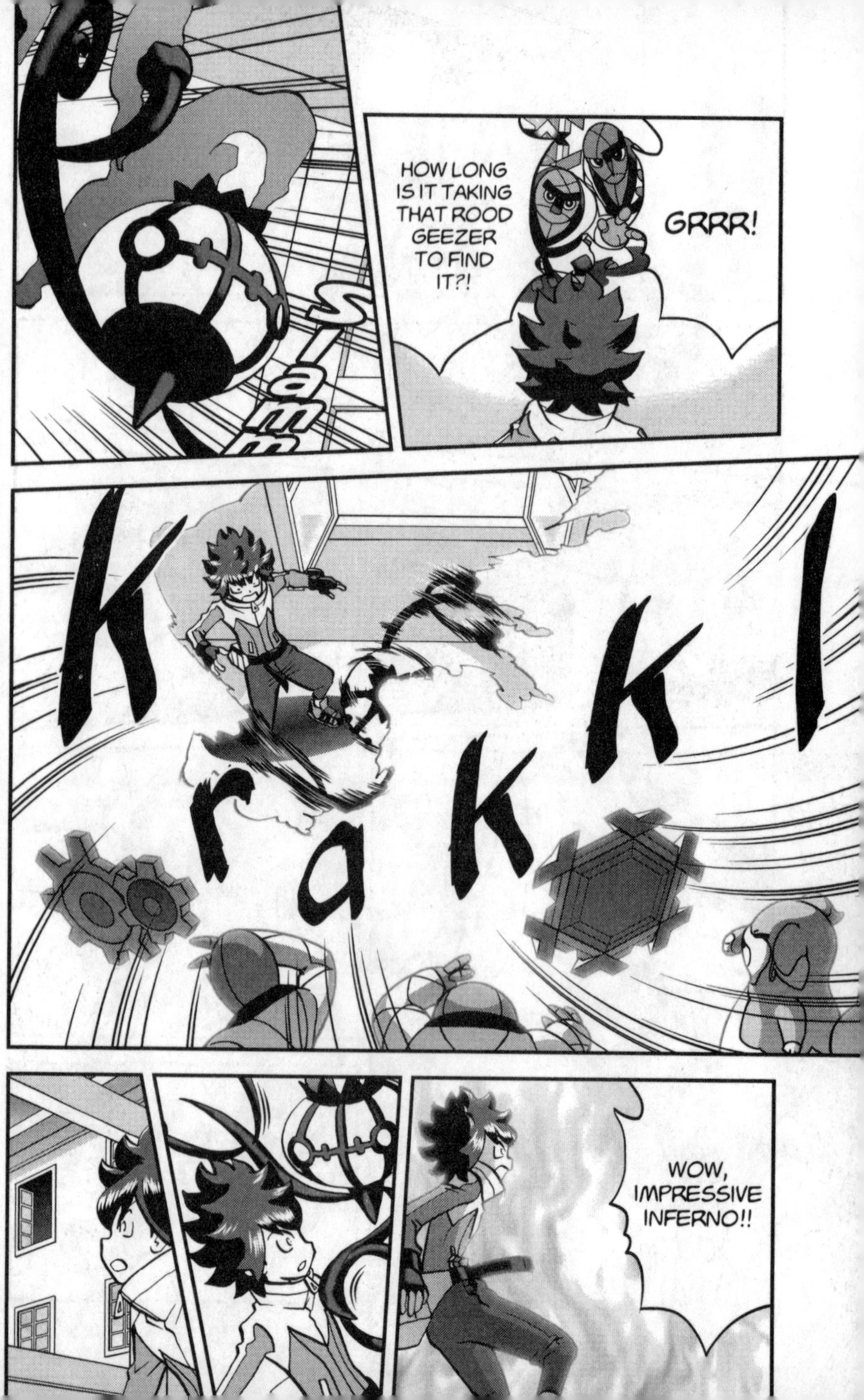

Slamm
HOW LONG IS IT TAKING THAT ROOD GEEZER TO FIND IT?!
GRRR!
Krakkl
WOW, IMPRESSIVE INFERNO!!

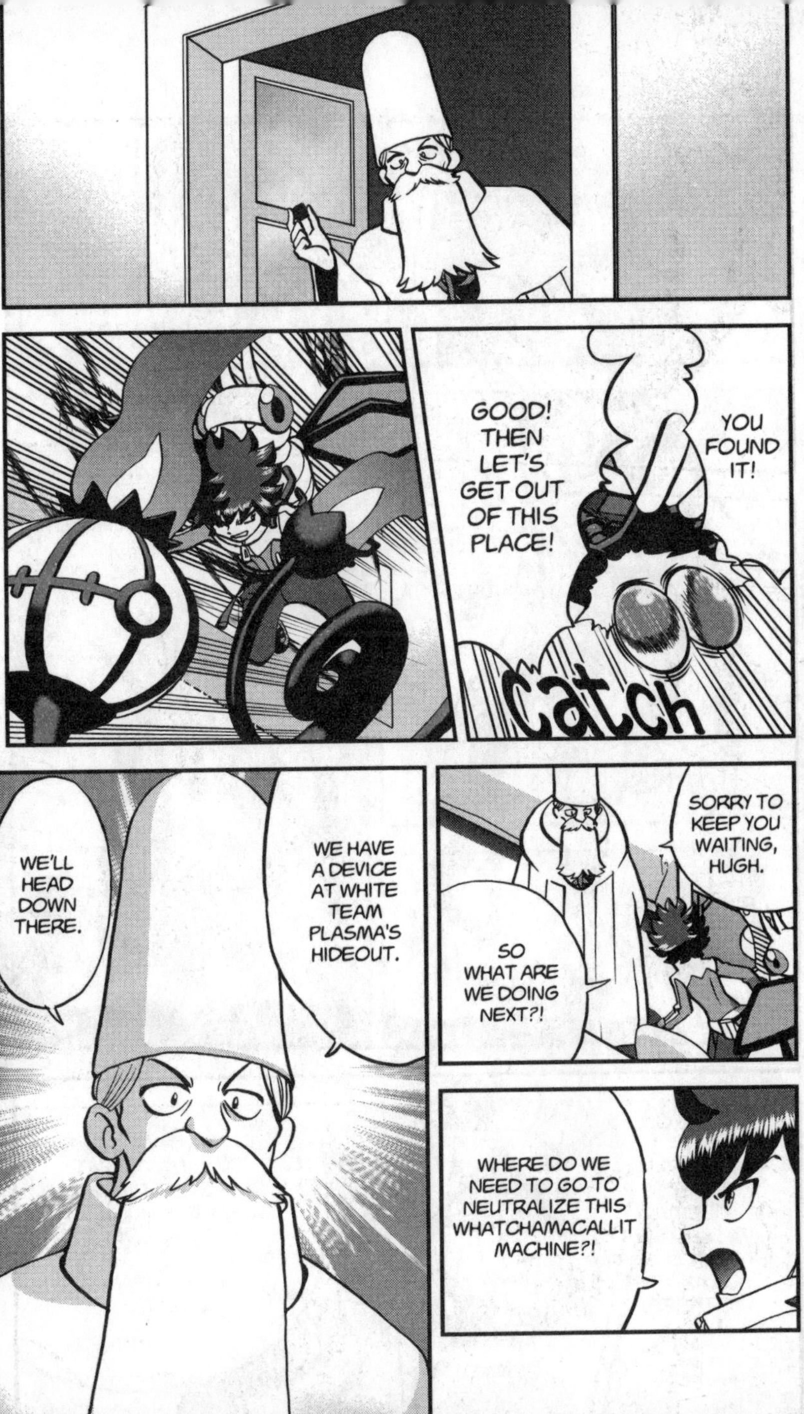
YOU FOUND IT!
GOOD! THEN LET'S GET OUT OF THIS PLACE!
catch
SORRY TO KEEP YOU WAITING, HUGH.
SO WHAT ARE WE DOING NEXT?!
WHERE DO WE NEED TO GO TO NEUTRALIZE THIS WHATCHAMACALLIT MACHINE?!
WE HAVE A DEVICE AT WHITE TEAM PLASMA'S HIDEOUT.
WE'LL HEAD DOWN THERE.

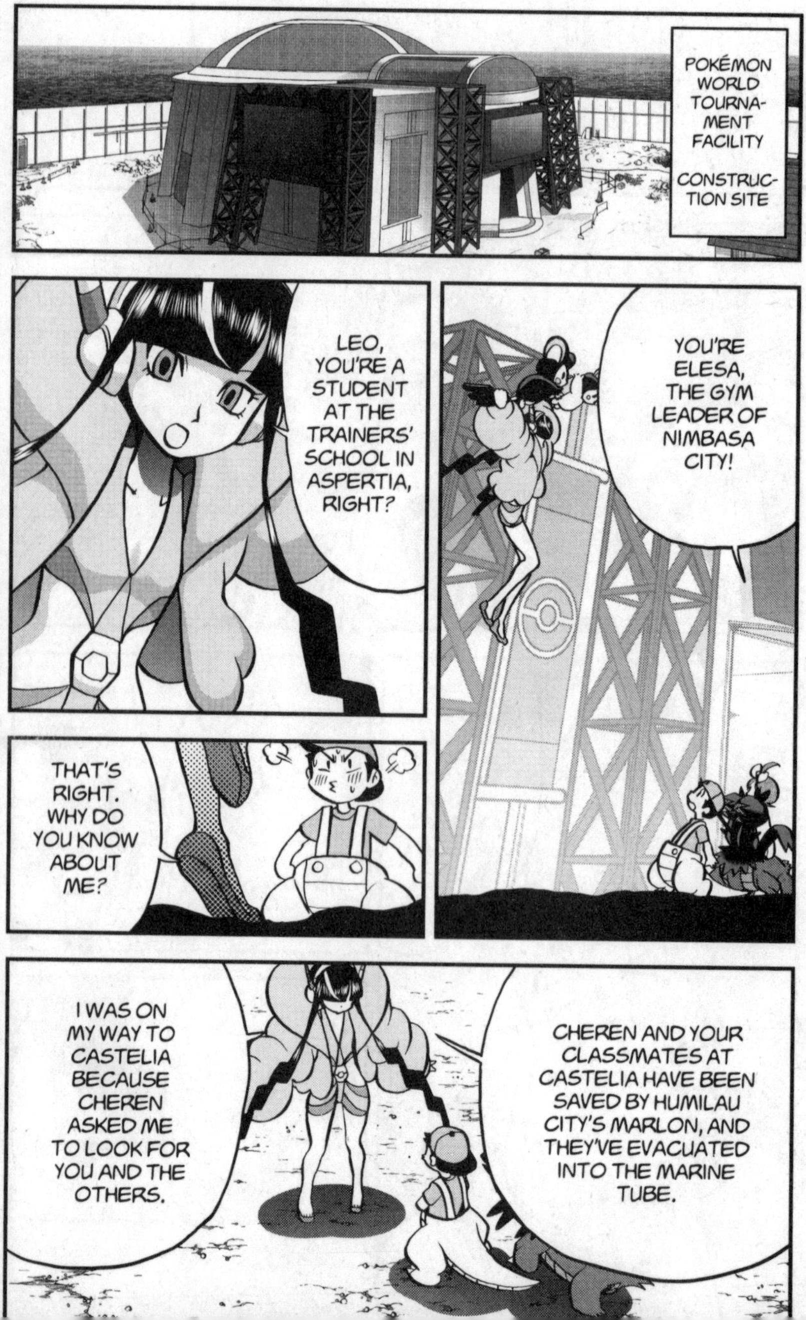
POKÉMON WORLD TOURNAMENT FACILITY
CONSTRUCTION SITE
YOU'RE ELESA, THE GYM LEADER OF NIMBASA CITY!
LEO, YOU'RE A STUDENT AT THE TRAINERS' SCHOOL IN ASPERTIA, RIGHT?
THAT'S RIGHT. WHY DO YOU KNOW ABOUT ME?
CHEREN AND YOUR CLASSMATES AT CASTELIA HAVE BEEN SAVED BY HUMILAU CITY'S MARLON, AND THEY'VE EVACUATED INTO THE MARINE TUBE.
I WAS ON MY WAY TO CASTELIA BECAUSE CHEREN ASKED ME TO LOOK FOR YOU AND THE OTHERS.

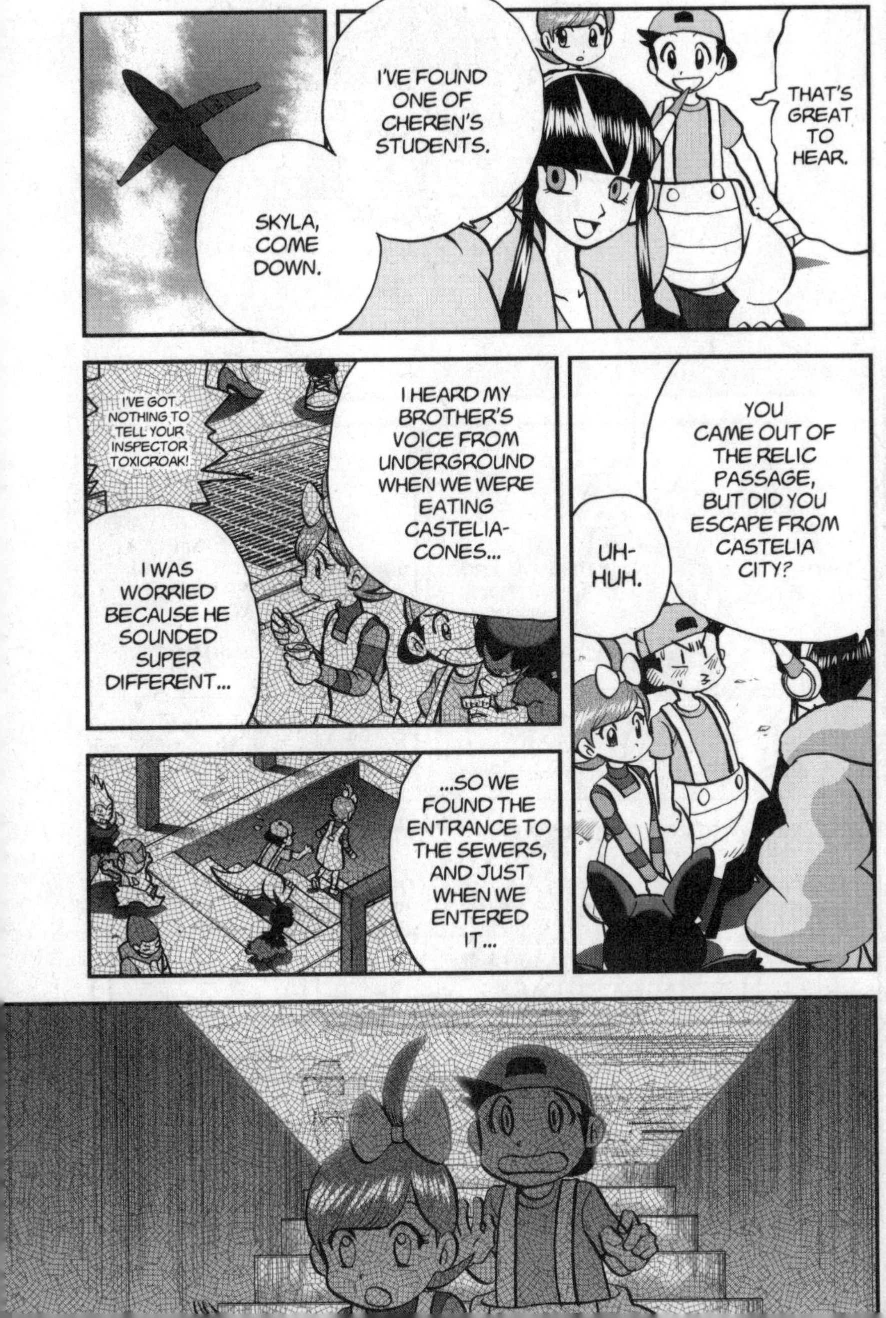
I'VE FOUND ONE OF CHEREN'S STUDENTS.
THAT'S GREAT TO HEAR.
SKYLA, COME DOWN.
YOU CAME OUT OF THE RELIC PASSAGE, BUT DID YOU ESCAPE FROM CASTELIA CITY?
UH-HUH.
I HEARD MY BROTHER'S VOICE FROM UNDERGROUND WHEN WE WERE EATING CASTELIA-CONES...
I'VE GOT NOTHING TO TELL YOUR INSPECTOR TOXICROAK!
I WAS WORRIED BECAUSE HE SOUNDED SUPER DIFFERENT...
...SO WE FOUND THE ENTRANCE TO THE SEWERS, AND JUST WHEN WE ENTERED IT...

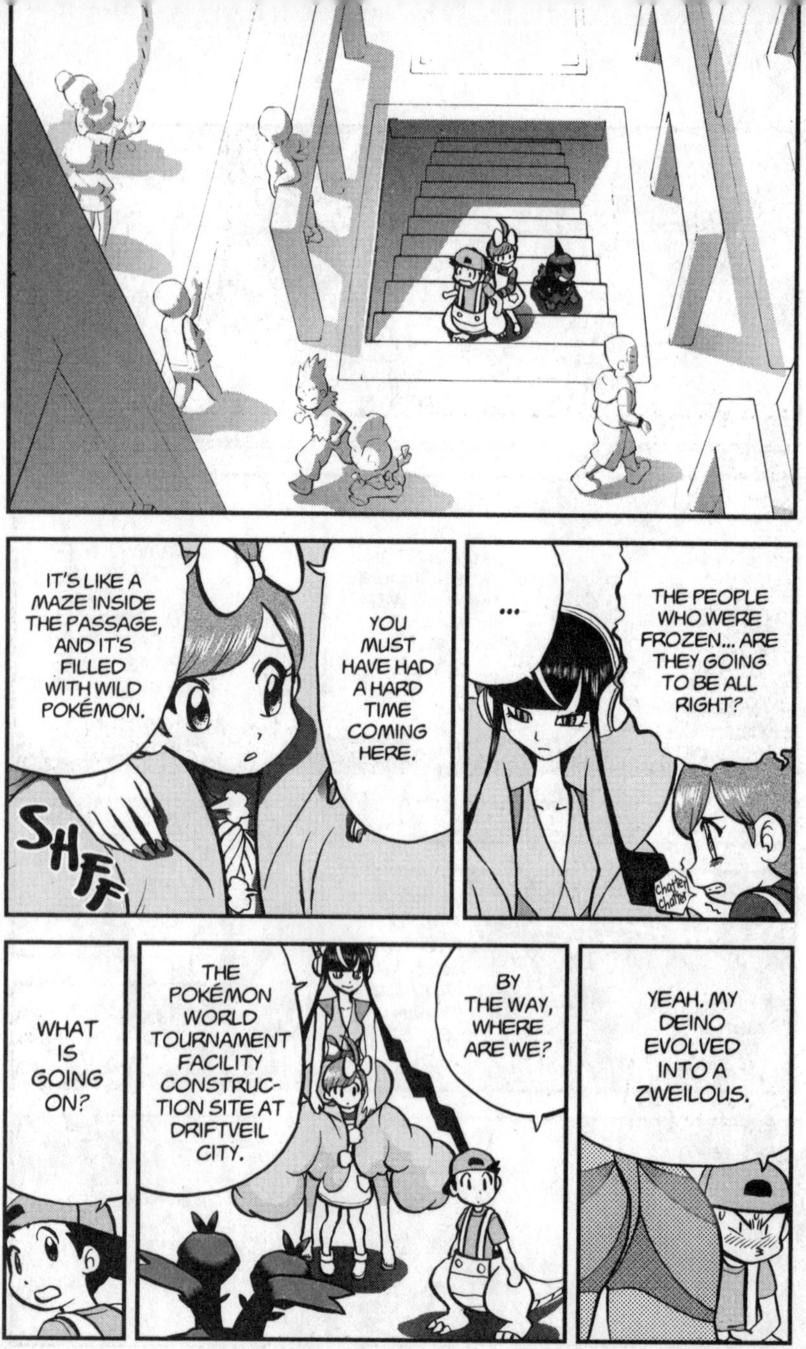
THE PEOPLE WHO WERE FROZEN... ARE THEY GOING TO BE ALL RIGHT?
...
Chatter Chatter
YOU MUST HAVE HAD A HARD TIME COMING HERE.
IT'S LIKE A MAZE INSIDE THE PASSAGE, AND IT'S FILLED WITH WILD POKÉMON.
SHFF
YEAH. MY DEINO EVOLVED INTO A ZWEILOUS.
BY THE WAY, WHERE ARE WE?
THE POKÉMON WORLD TOURNAMENT FACILITY CONSTRUCTION SITE AT DRIFTVEIL CITY.
WHAT IS GOING ON?

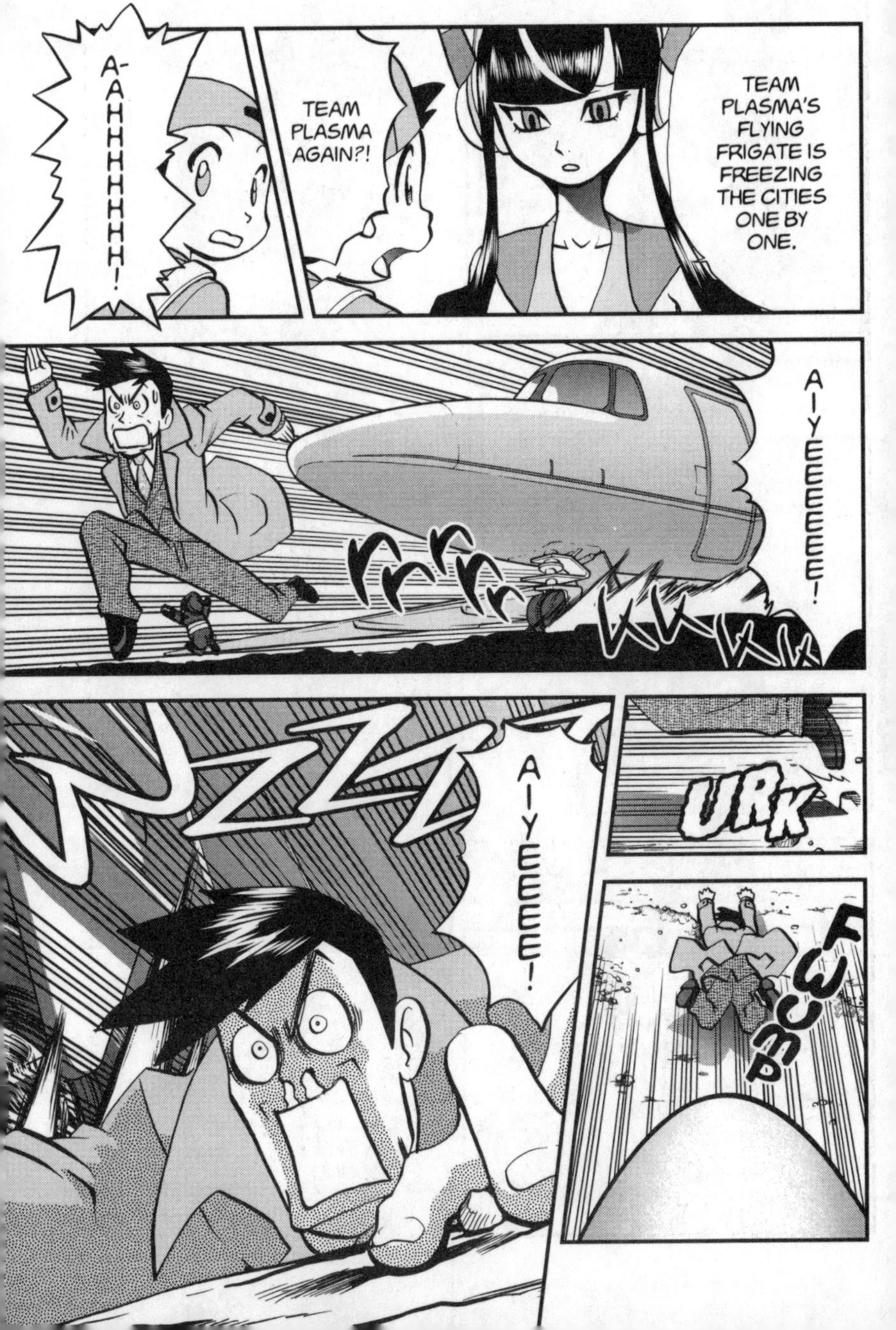
TEAM PLASMA'S FLYING FRIGATE IS FREEZING THE CITIES ONE BY ONE.
TEAM PLASMA AGAIN?!
A-AHHHHHHHH!
AIYEEEEEEE!
AIYEEEE!
URK
FWUMP

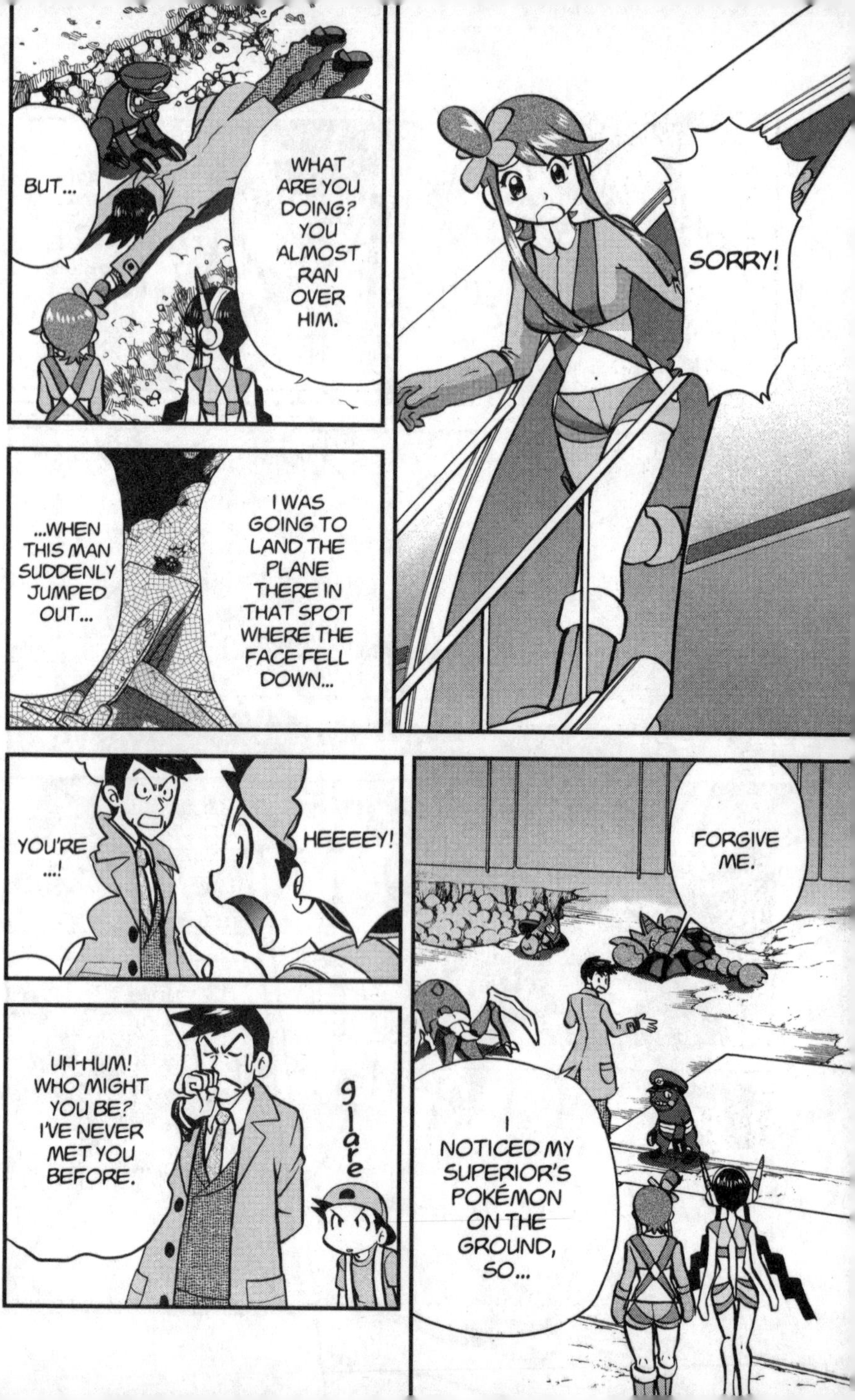
SORRY!
WHAT ARE YOU DOING? YOU ALMOST RAN OVER HIM.
BUT...
I WAS GOING TO LAND THE PLANE THERE IN THAT SPOT WHERE THE FACE FELL DOWN...
...WHEN THIS MAN SUDDENLY JUMPED OUT...
FORGIVE ME.
I NOTICED MY SUPERIOR'S POKÉMON ON THE GROUND, SO...
HEEEEY!
YOU'RE ...!
glare
UH-HUM! WHO MIGHT YOU BE? I'VE NEVER MET YOU BEFORE.

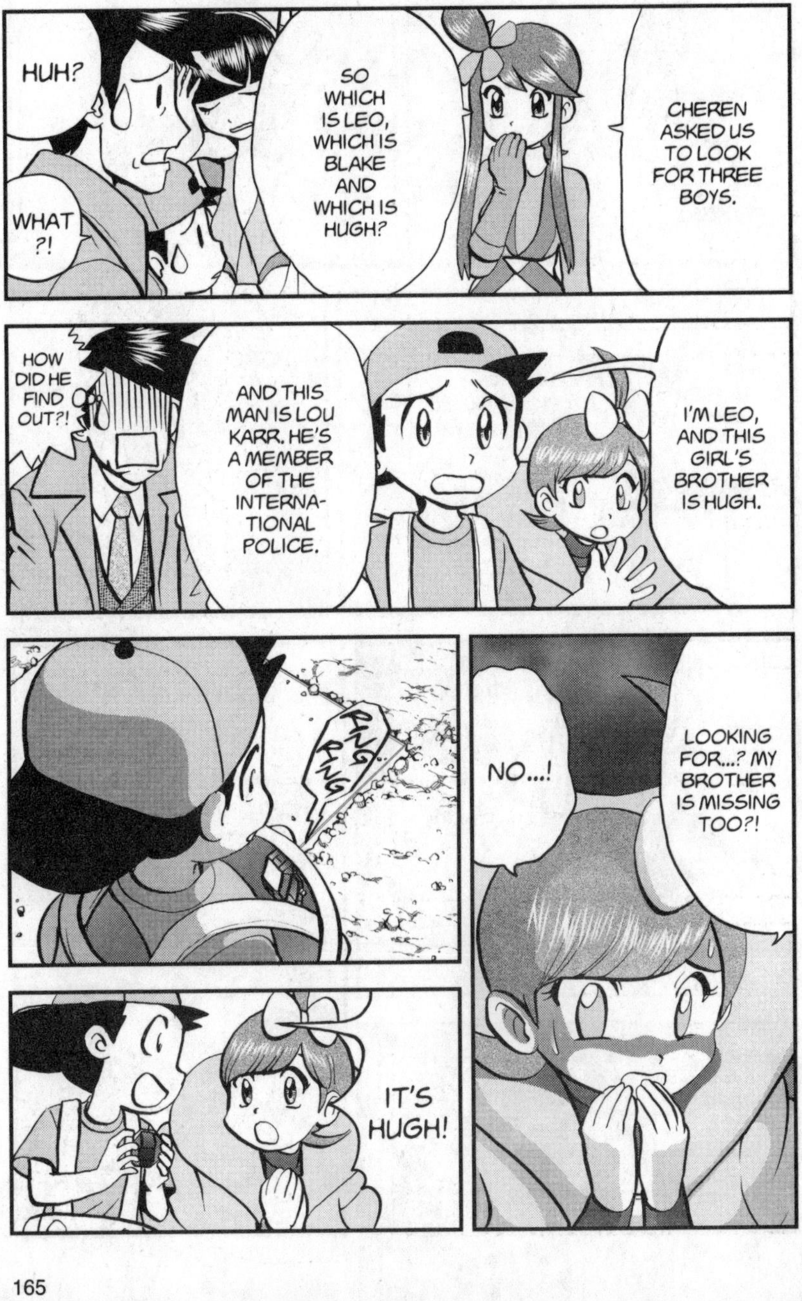
CHEREN ASKED US TO LOOK FOR THREE BOYS.
SO WHICH IS LEO, WHICH IS BLAKE AND WHICH IS HUGH?
HUH?
WHAT?!
I'M LEO, AND THIS GIRL'S BROTHER IS HUGH.
AND THIS MAN IS LOU KARR. HE'S A MEMBER OF THE INTERNATIONAL POLICE.
HOW DID HE FIND OUT?!
LOOKING FOR...? MY BROTHER IS MISSING TOO?!
NO...!
RING RING
IT'S HUGH!

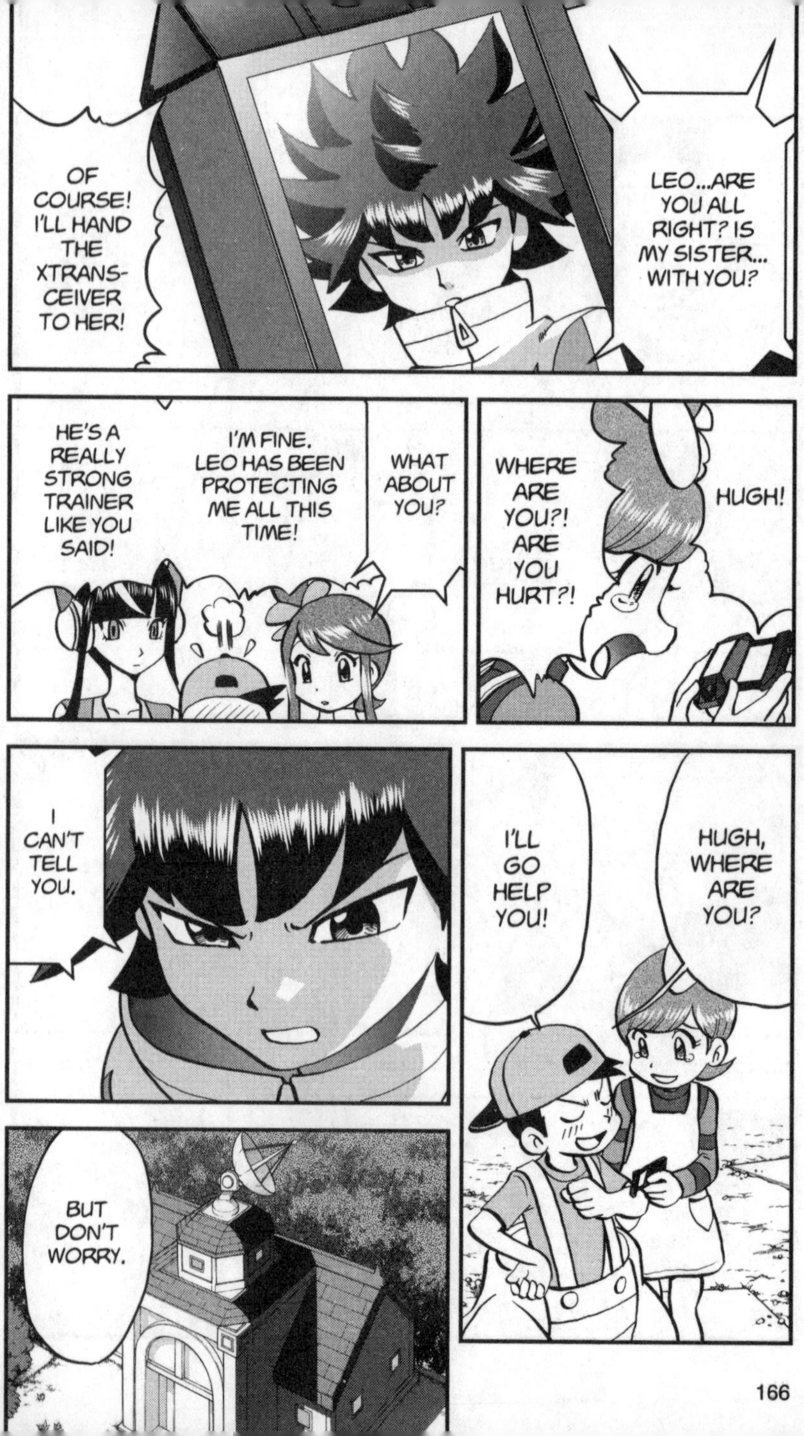
LEO...ARE YOU ALL RIGHT? IS MY SISTER... WITH YOU?
OF COURSE! I'LL HAND THE XTRANS-CEIVER TO HER!
HUGH!
WHERE ARE YOU?! ARE YOU HURT?!
WHAT ABOUT YOU?
I'M FINE. LEO HAS BEEN PROTECTING ME ALL THIS TIME!
HE'S A REALLY STRONG TRAINER LIKE YOU SAID!
HUGH, WHERE ARE YOU?
I'LL GO HELP YOU!
I CAN'T TELL YOU.
BUT DON'T WORRY.

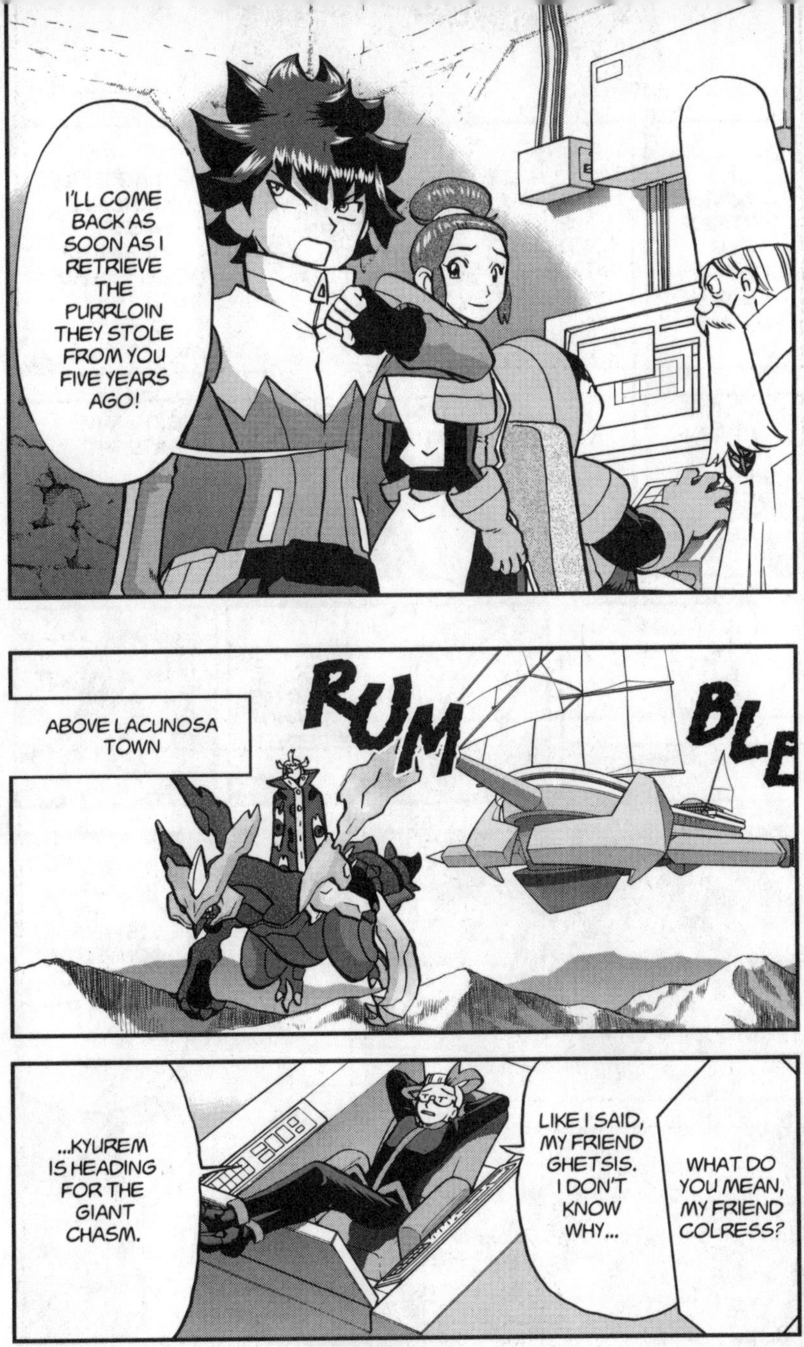
I'LL COME BACK AS SOON AS I RETRIEVE THE PURRLOIN THEY STOLE FROM YOU FIVE YEARS AGO!
RUMBLE
ABOVE LACUNOSA TOWN
WHAT DO YOU MEAN, MY FRIEND COLRESS?
LIKE I SAID, MY FRIEND GHETSIS. I DON'T KNOW WHY...
...KYUREM IS HEADING FOR THE GIANT CHASM.

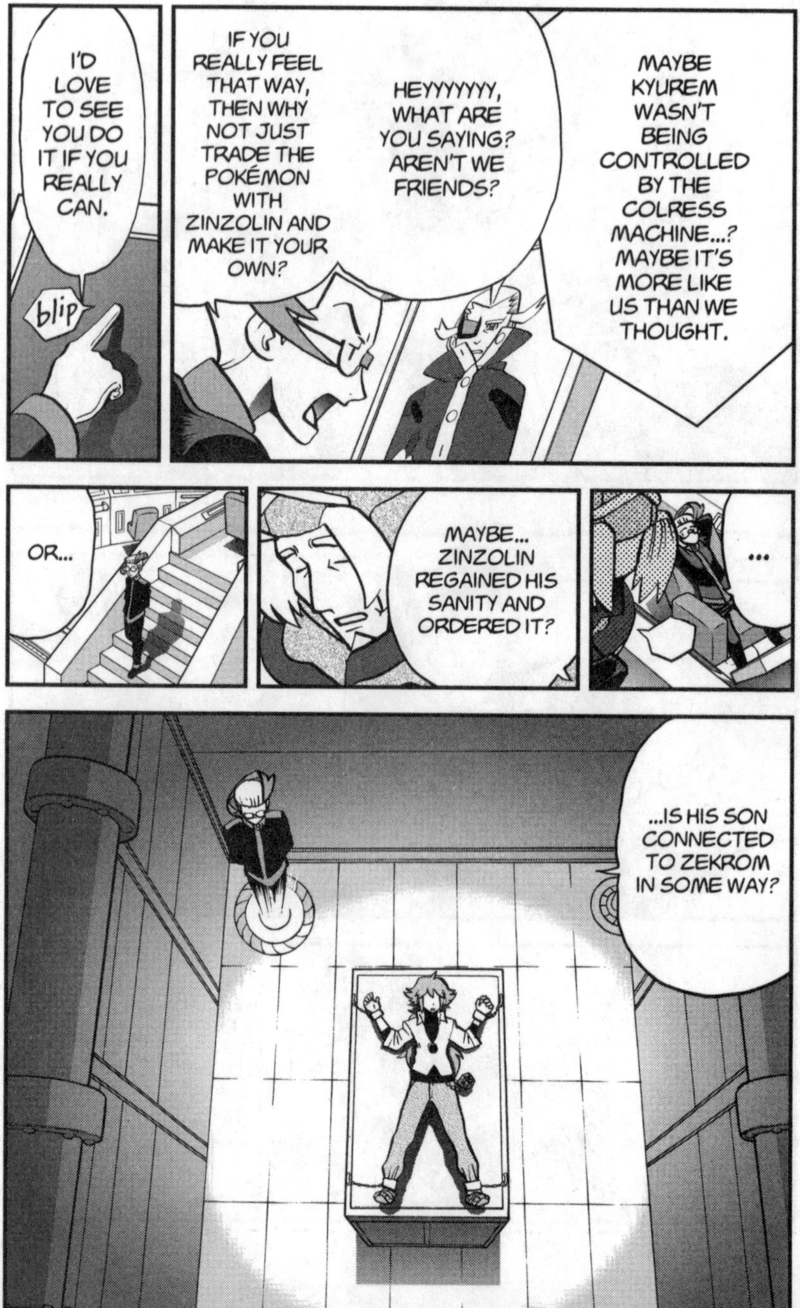
MAYBE KYUREM WASN'T BEING CONTROLLED BY THE COLRESS MACHINE...? MAYBE IT'S MORE LIKE US THAN WE THOUGHT.
HEYYYYYYY, WHAT ARE YOU SAYING? AREN'T WE FRIENDS?
IF YOU REALLY FEEL THAT WAY, THEN WHY NOT JUST TRADE THE POKÉMON WITH ZINZOLIN AND MAKE IT YOUR OWN?
I'D LOVE TO SEE YOU DO IT IF YOU REALLY CAN.
blip
...
MAYBE... ZINZOLIN REGAINED HIS SANITY AND ORDERED IT?
OR...
...IS HIS SON CONNECTED TO ZEKROM IN SOME WAY?

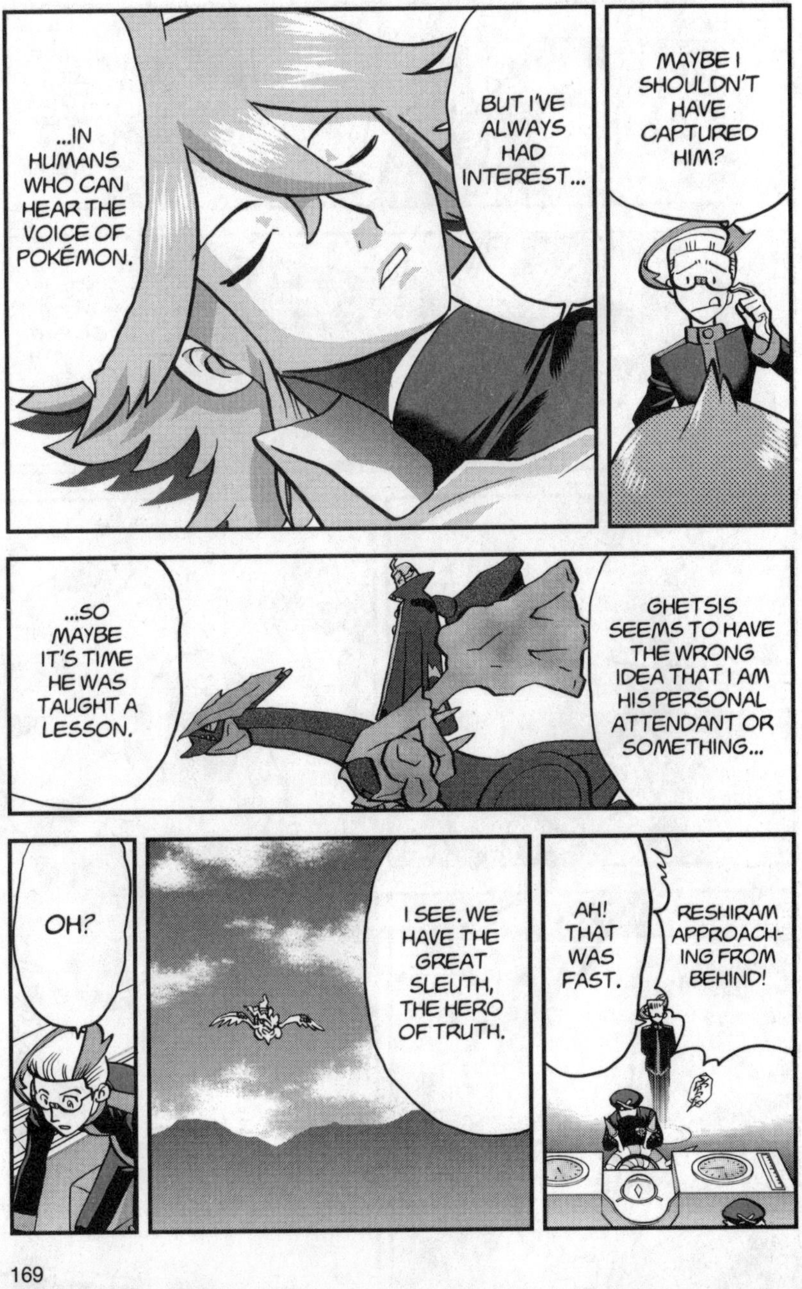
MAYBE I SHOULDN'T HAVE CAPTURED HIM?
BUT I'VE ALWAYS HAD INTEREST...
...IN HUMANS WHO CAN HEAR THE VOICE OF POKÉMON.
GHETSIS SEEMS TO HAVE THE WRONG IDEA THAT I AM HIS PERSONAL ATTENDANT OR SOMETHING...
...SO MAYBE IT'S TIME HE WAS TAUGHT A LESSON.
RESHIRAM APPROACH-ING FROM BEHIND!
AH! THAT WAS FAST.
I SEE. WE HAVE THE GREAT SLEUTH, THE HERO OF TRUTH.
OH?

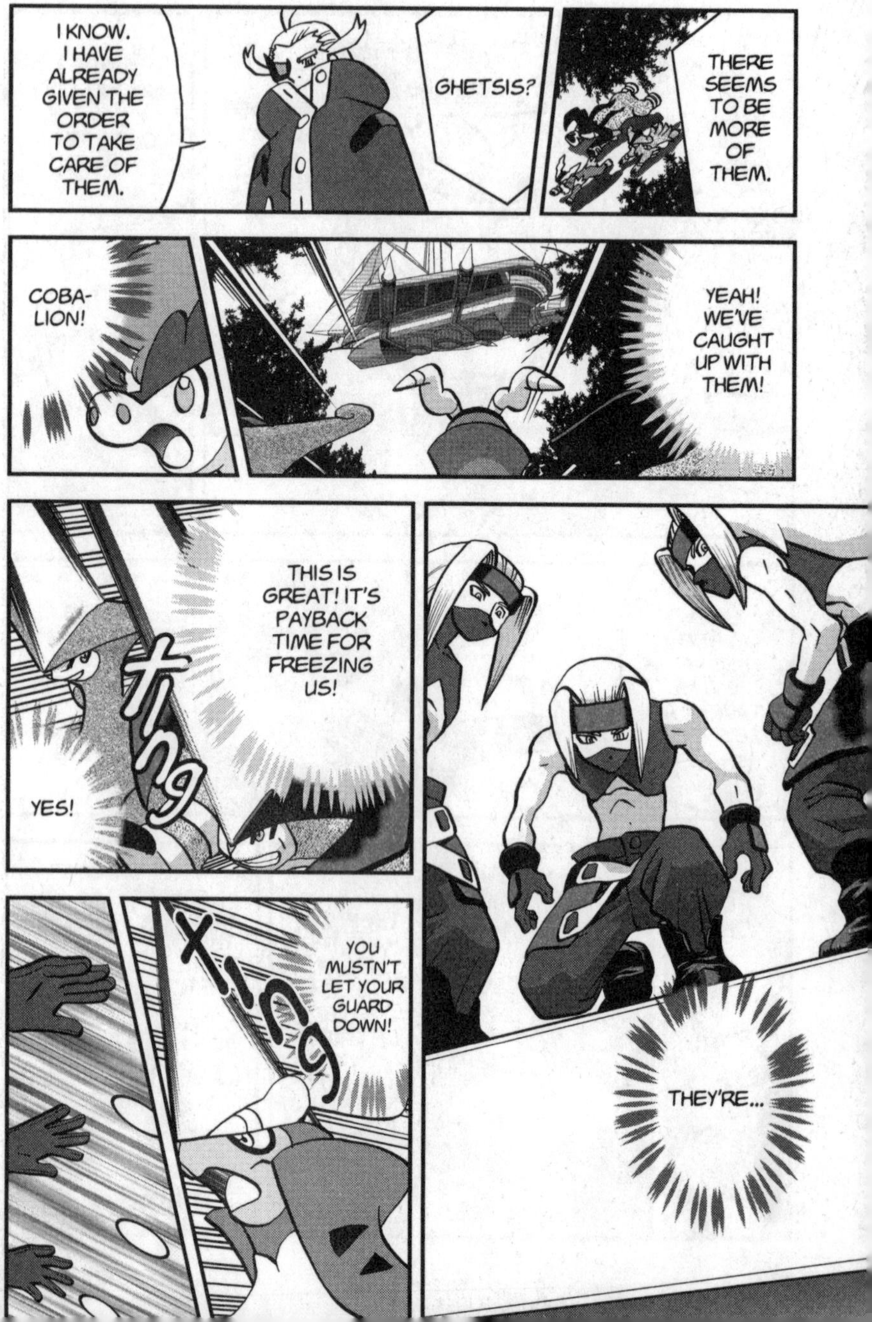
THERE SEEMS TO BE MORE OF THEM.
GHETSIS?
I KNOW. I HAVE ALREADY GIVEN THE ORDER TO TAKE CARE OF THEM.
YEAH! WE'VE CAUGHT UP WITH THEM!
COBA-LION!
THEY'RE...
THIS IS GREAT! IT'S PAYBACK TIME FOR FREEZING US!
ting
YES!
XING
YOU MUSTN'T LET YOUR GUARD DOWN!

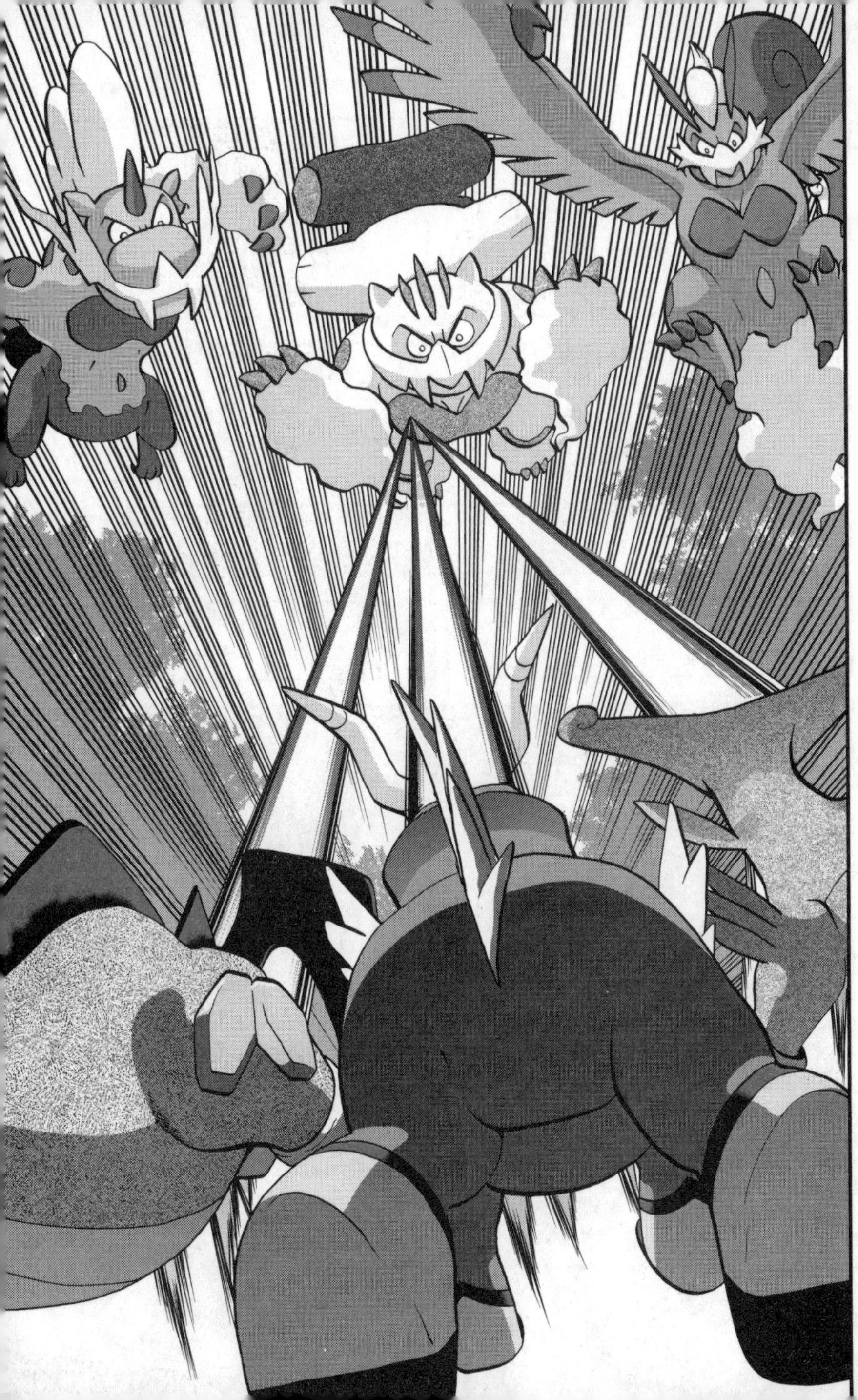

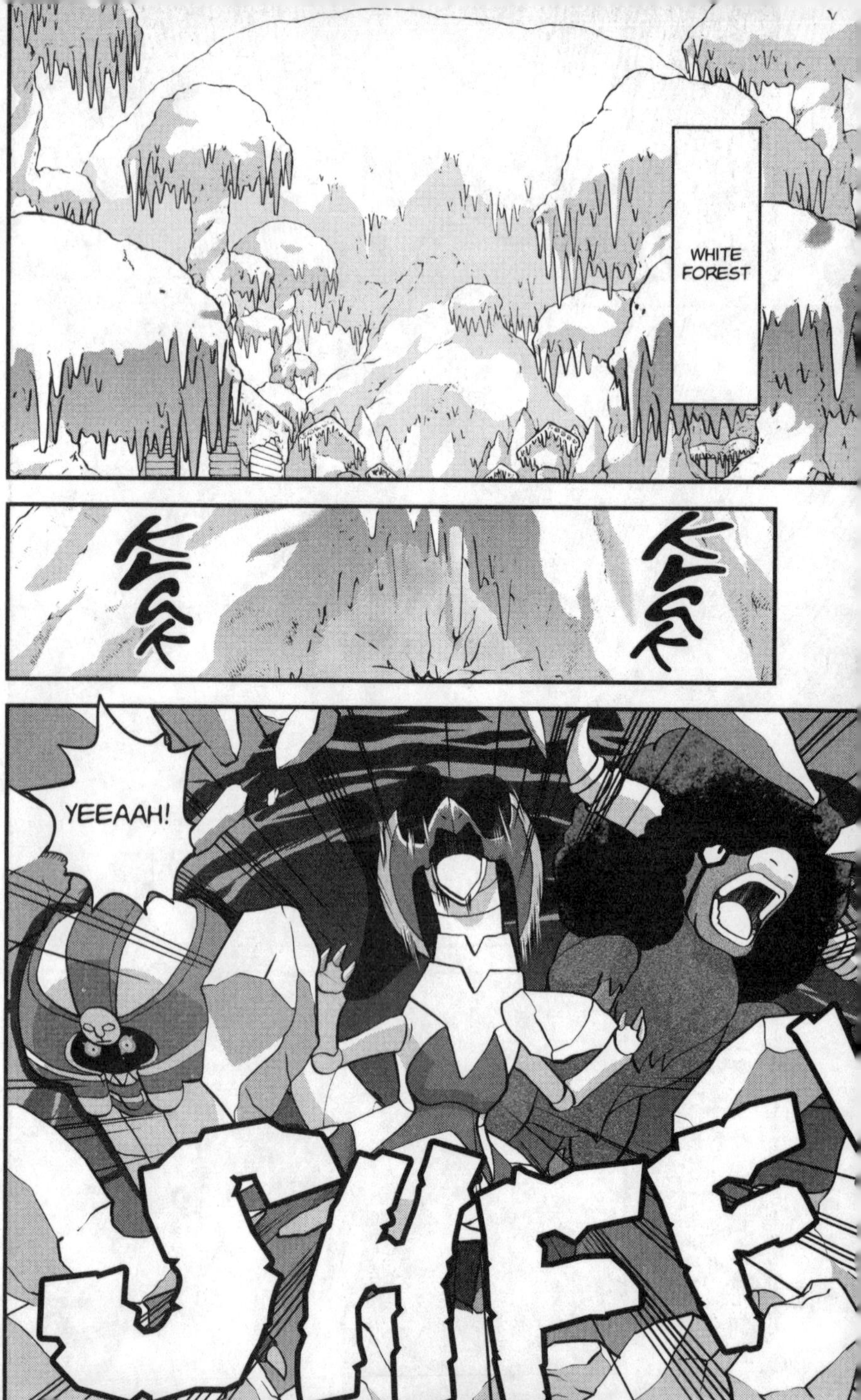
WHITE FOREST
KRAK
KRAK
YEEAAH!

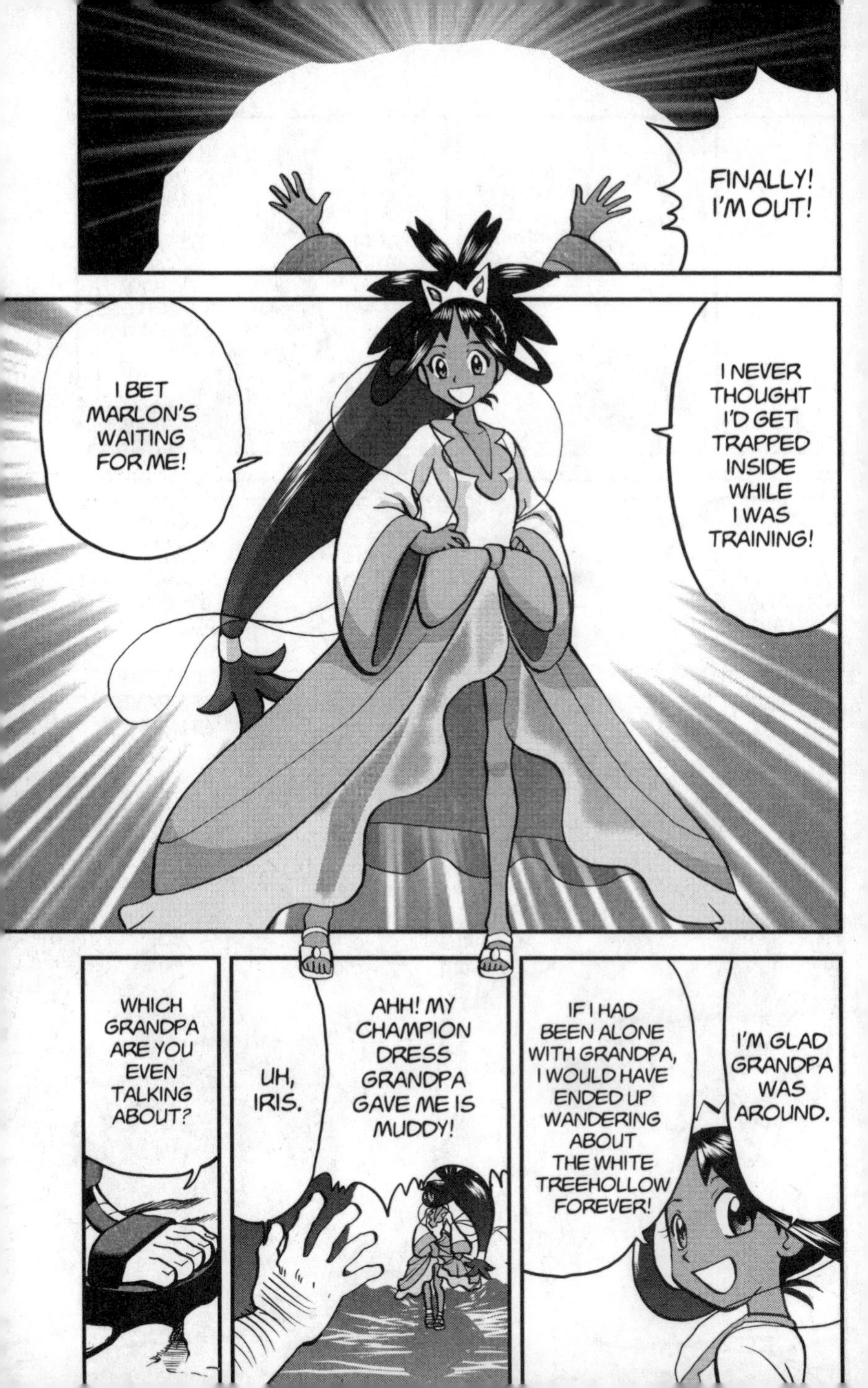
FINALLY! I'M OUT!
I NEVER THOUGHT I'D GET TRAPPED INSIDE WHILE I WAS TRAINING!
I BET MARLON'S WAITING FOR ME!
I'M GLAD GRANDPA WAS AROUND.
IF I HAD BEEN ALONE WITH GRANDPA, I WOULD HAVE ENDED UP WANDERING ABOUT THE WHITE TREEHOLLOW FOREVER!
AHH! MY CHAMPION DRESS GRANDPA GAVE ME IS MUDDY!
UH, IRIS.
WHICH GRANDPA ARE YOU EVEN TALKING ABOUT?

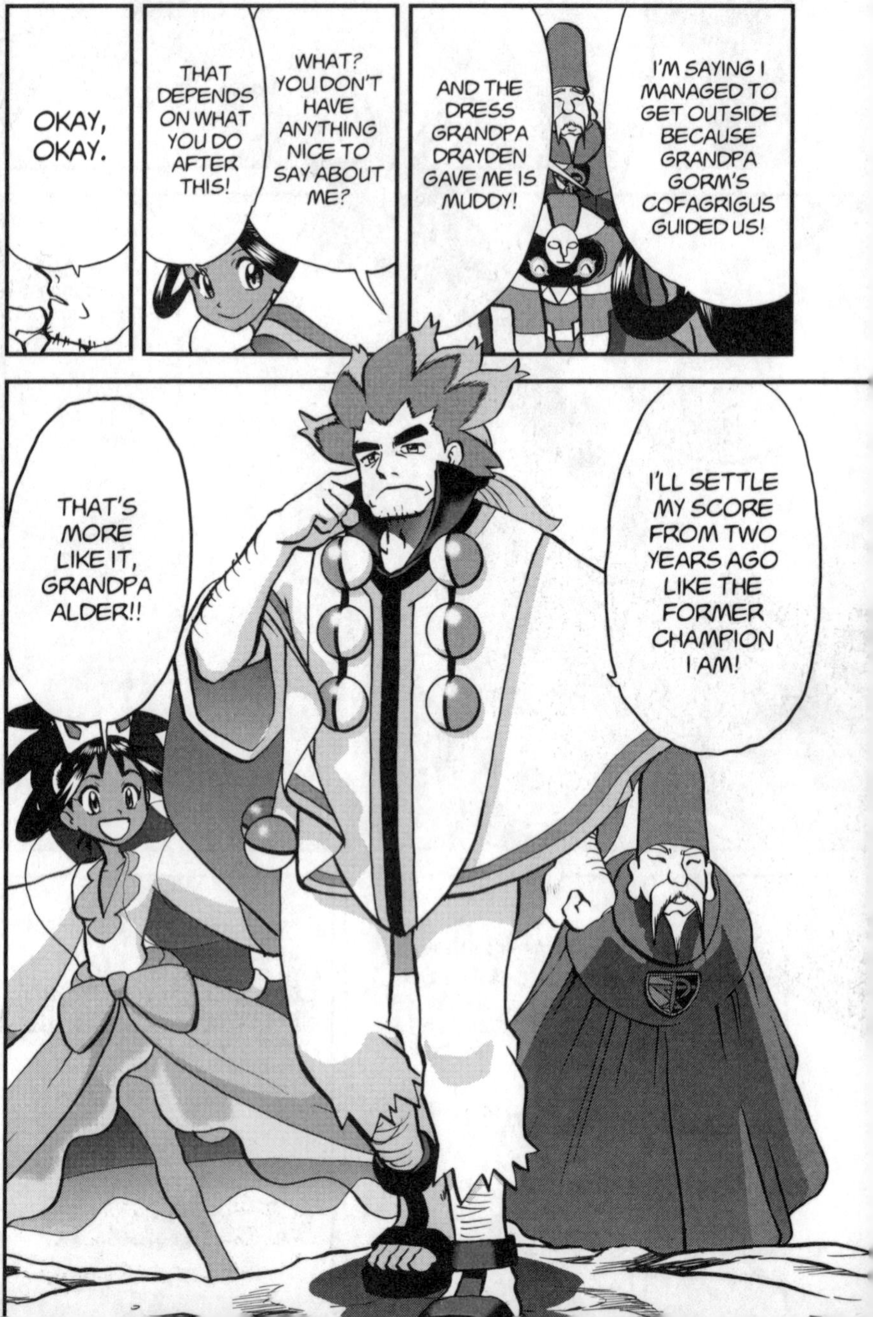
I'M SAYING I MANAGED TO GET OUTSIDE BECAUSE GRANDPA GORM'S COFAGRIGUS GUIDED US!
AND THE DRESS GRANDPA DRAYDEN GAVE ME IS MUDDY!
WHAT? YOU DON'T HAVE ANYTHING NICE TO SAY ABOUT ME?
THAT DEPENDS ON WHAT YOU DO AFTER THIS!
OKAY, OKAY.
I'LL SETTLE MY SCORE FROM TWO YEARS AGO LIKE THE FORMER CHAMPION I AM!
THAT'S MORE LIKE IT, GRANDPA ALDER!!

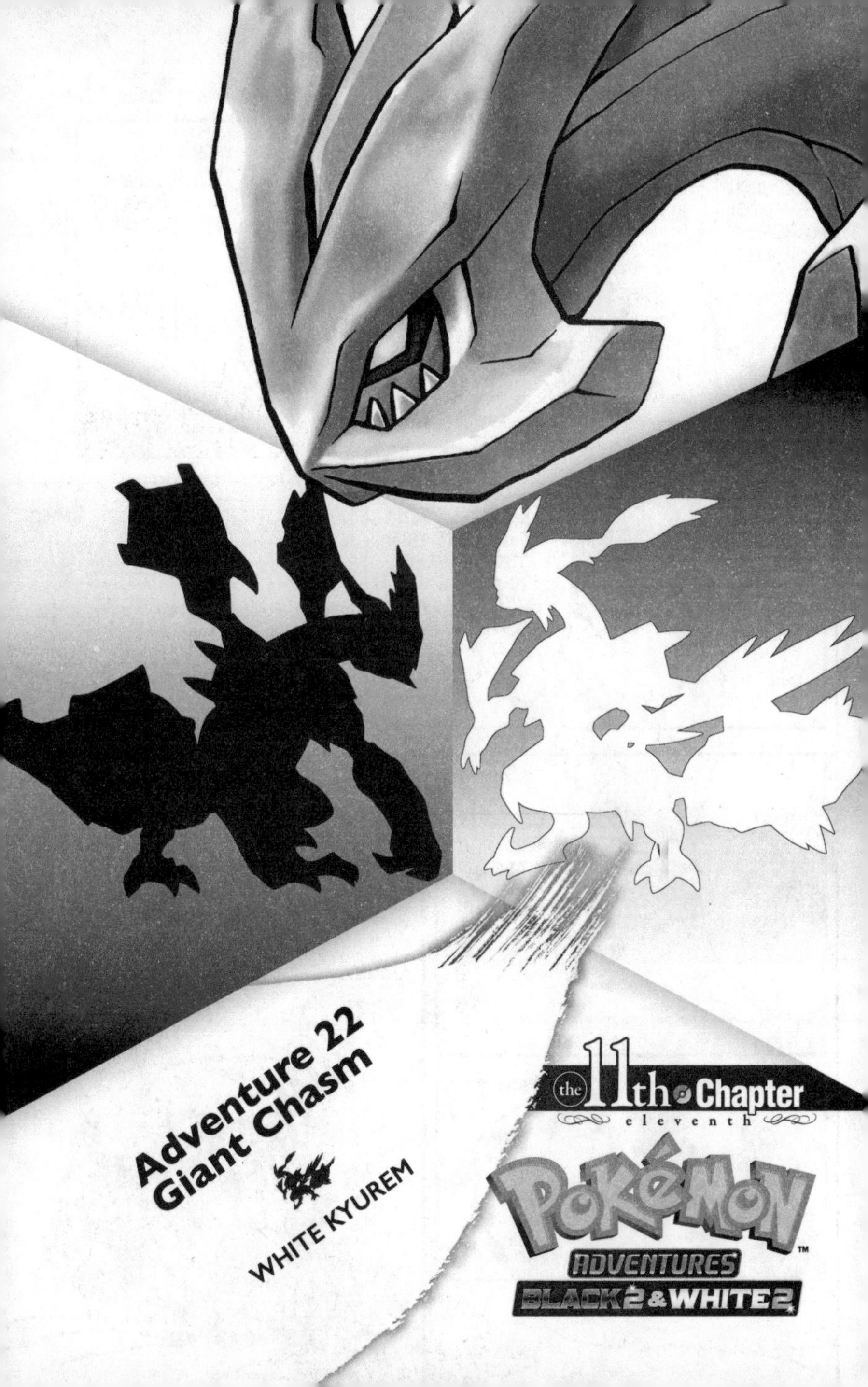
Adventure 22
Giant Chasm
WHITE KYUREM
the 11th Chapter
eleventh
POKÉMON™
ADVENTURES
BLACK 2 & WHITE 2

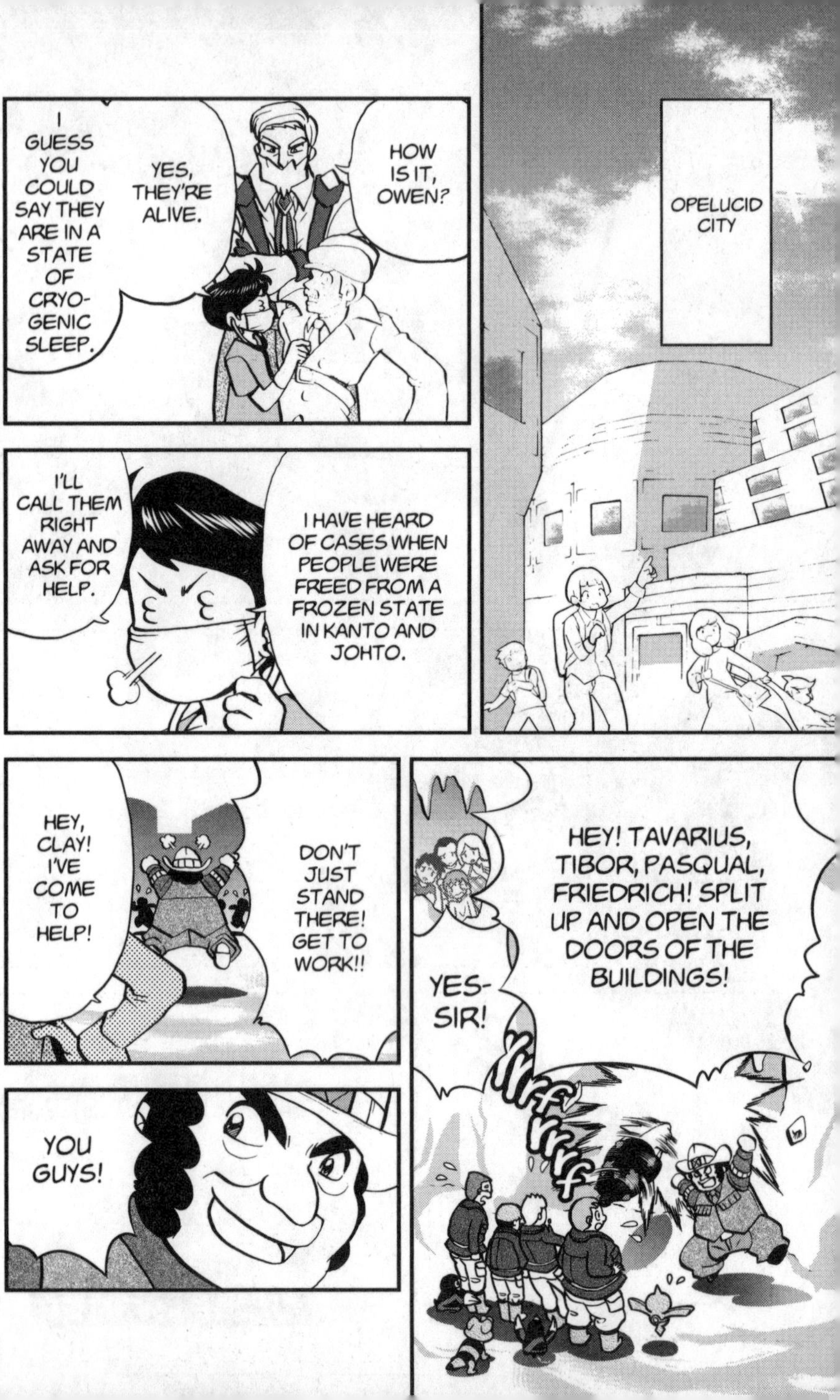
OPELUCID CITY
HOW IS IT, OWEN?
YES, THEY'RE ALIVE.
I GUESS YOU COULD SAY THEY ARE IN A STATE OF CRYO-GENIC SLEEP.
I HAVE HEARD OF CASES WHEN PEOPLE WERE FREED FROM A FROZEN STATE IN KANTO AND JOHTO.
I'LL CALL THEM RIGHT AWAY AND ASK FOR HELP.
HEY! TAVARIUS, TIBOR, PASQUAL, FRIEDRICH! SPLIT UP AND OPEN THE DOORS OF THE BUILDINGS!
YES-SIR!
DON'T JUST STAND THERE! GET TO WORK!!
HEY, CLAY! I'VE COME TO HELP!
YOU GUYS!

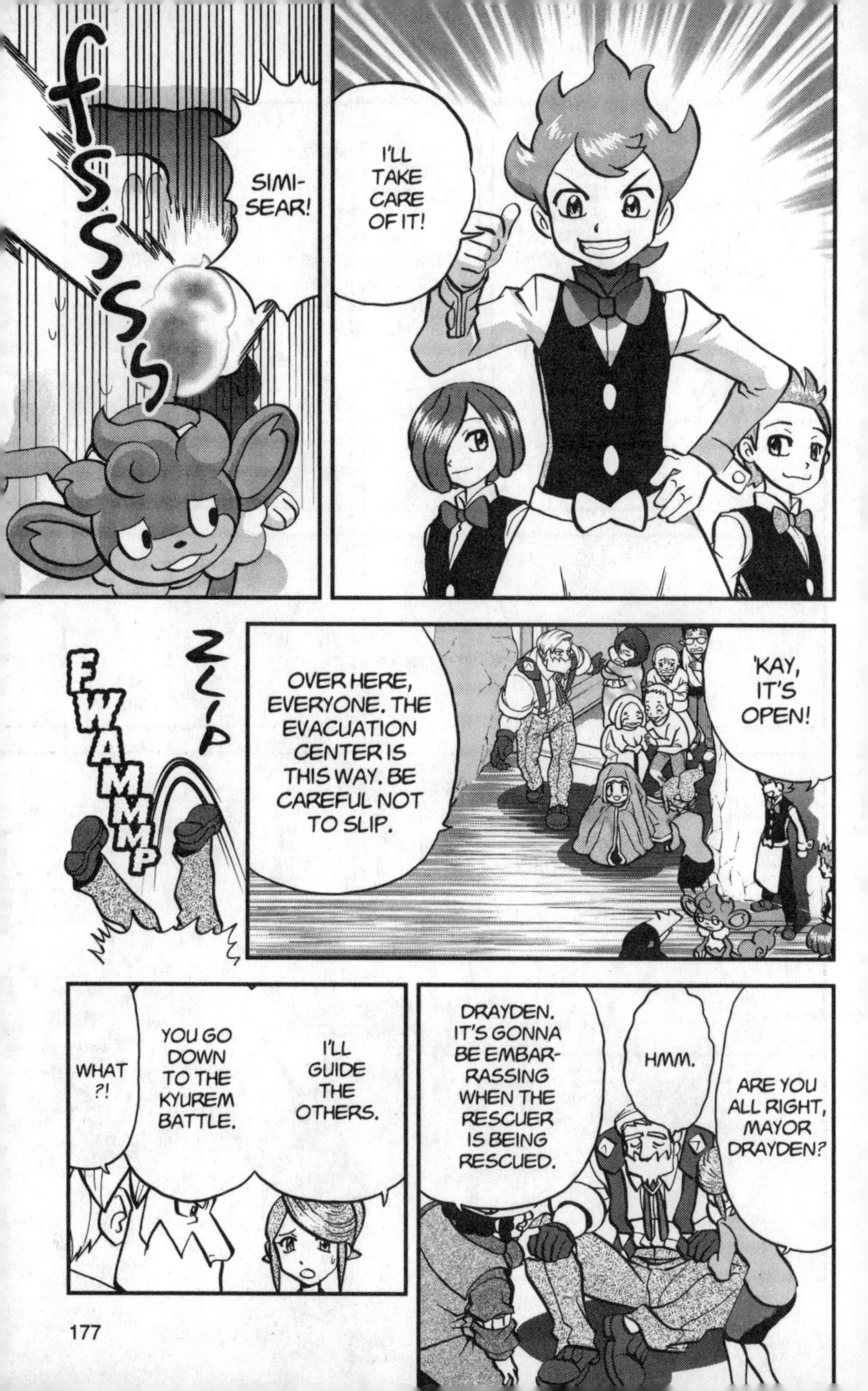
I'LL TAKE CARE OF IT!
SIMI-SEAR!
fSSSSS
'KAY, IT'S OPEN!
OVER HERE, EVERYONE. THE EVACUATION CENTER IS THIS WAY. BE CAREFUL NOT TO SLIP.
ZLIP
FWAMMMP
ARE YOU ALL RIGHT, MAYOR DRAYDEN?
HMM.
DRAYDEN. IT'S GONNA BE EMBAR-RASSING WHEN THE RESCUER IS BEING RESCUED.
I'LL GUIDE THE OTHERS.
YOU GO DOWN TO THE KYUREM BATTLE.
WHAT?!

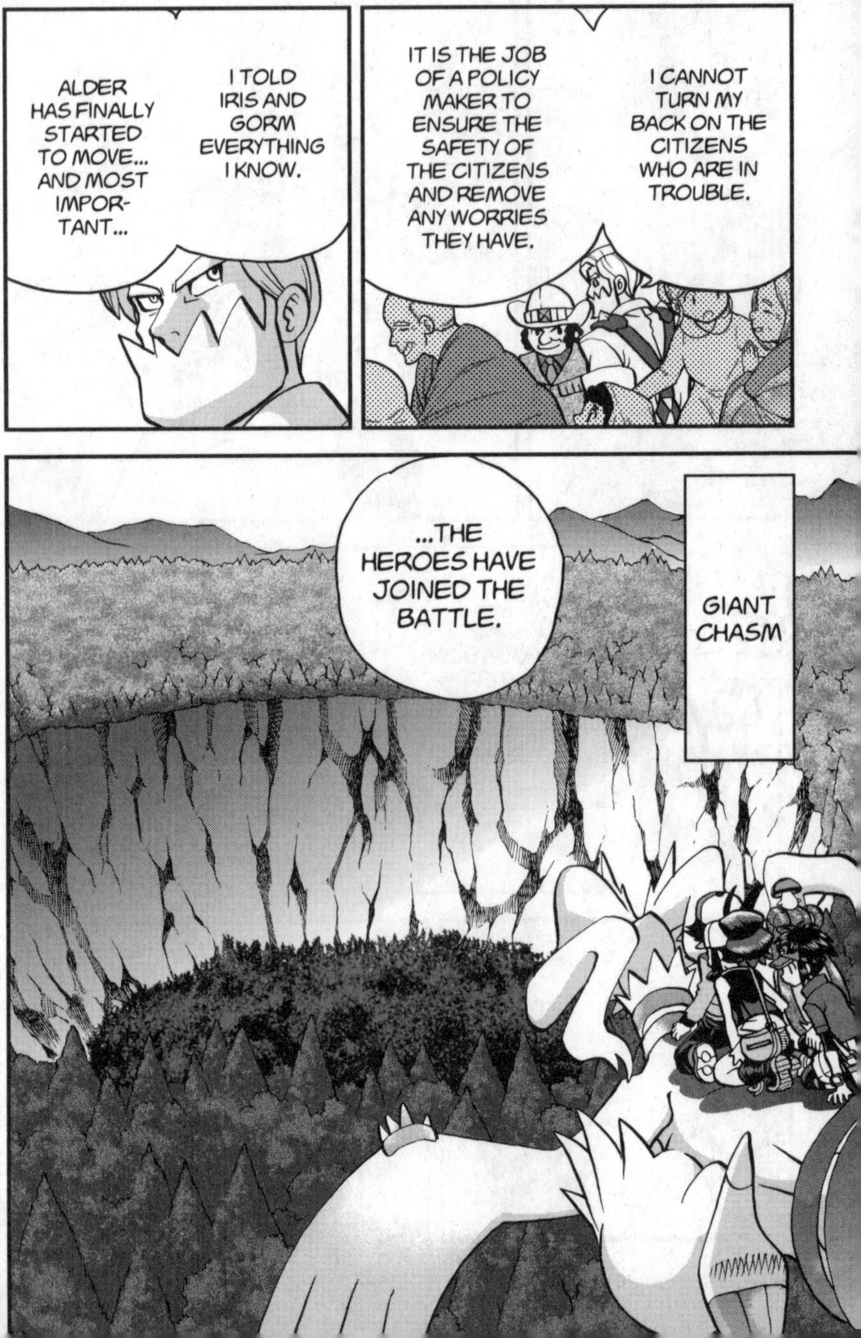
I CANNOT TURN MY BACK ON THE CITIZENS WHO ARE IN TROUBLE.
IT IS THE JOB OF A POLICY MAKER TO ENSURE THE SAFETY OF THE CITIZENS AND REMOVE ANY WORRIES THEY HAVE.
I TOLD IRIS AND GORM EVERYTHING I KNOW.
ALDER HAS FINALLY STARTED TO MOVE... AND MOST IMPOR-TANT...
GIANT CHASM
...THE HEROES HAVE JOINED THE BATTLE.

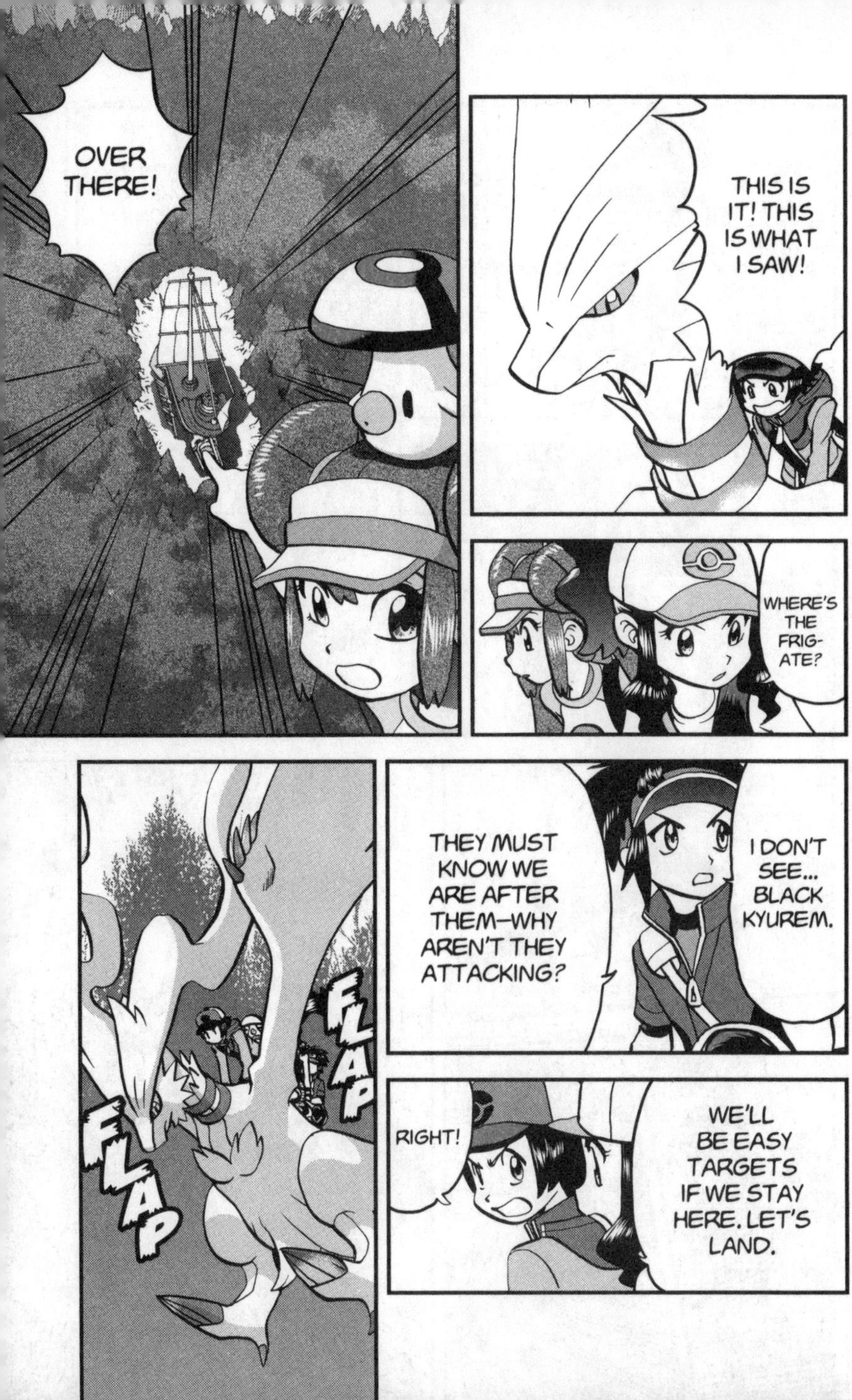
THIS IS IT! THIS IS WHAT I SAW!
WHERE'S THE FRIGATE?
OVER THERE!
I DON'T SEE... BLACK KYUREM.
THEY MUST KNOW WE ARE AFTER THEM—WHY AREN'T THEY ATTACKING?
WE'LL BE EASY TARGETS IF WE STAY HERE. LET'S LAND.
RIGHT!
FLAP
FLAP

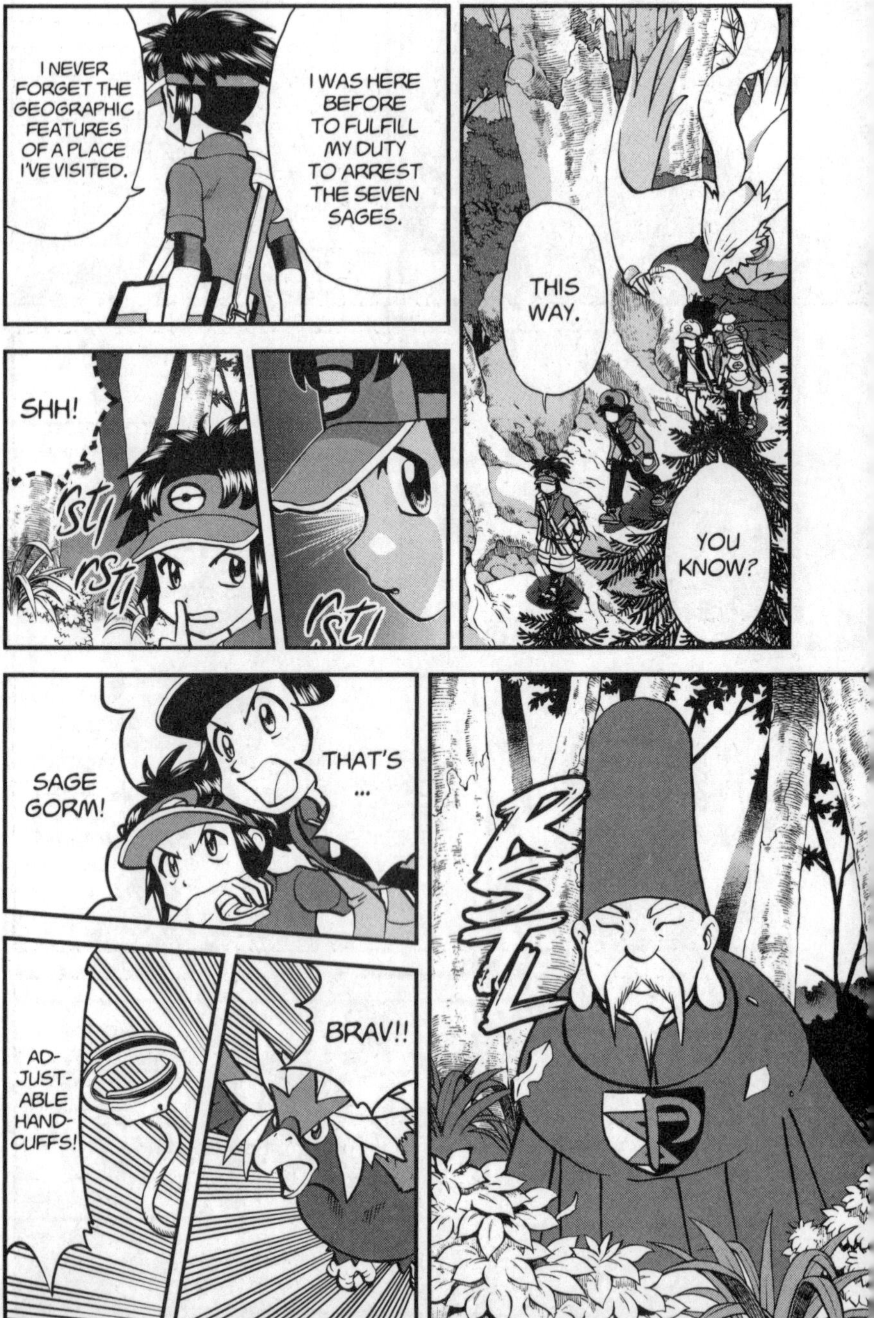
THIS WAY.
YOU KNOW?
I WAS HERE BEFORE TO FULFILL MY DUTY TO ARREST THE SEVEN SAGES.
I NEVER FORGET THE GEOGRAPHIC FEATURES OF A PLACE I'VE VISITED.
rstl
SHH!
rstl
rstl
RSTL
THAT'S ...
SAGE GORM!
BRAV!!
AD-JUST-ABLE HAND-CUFFS!

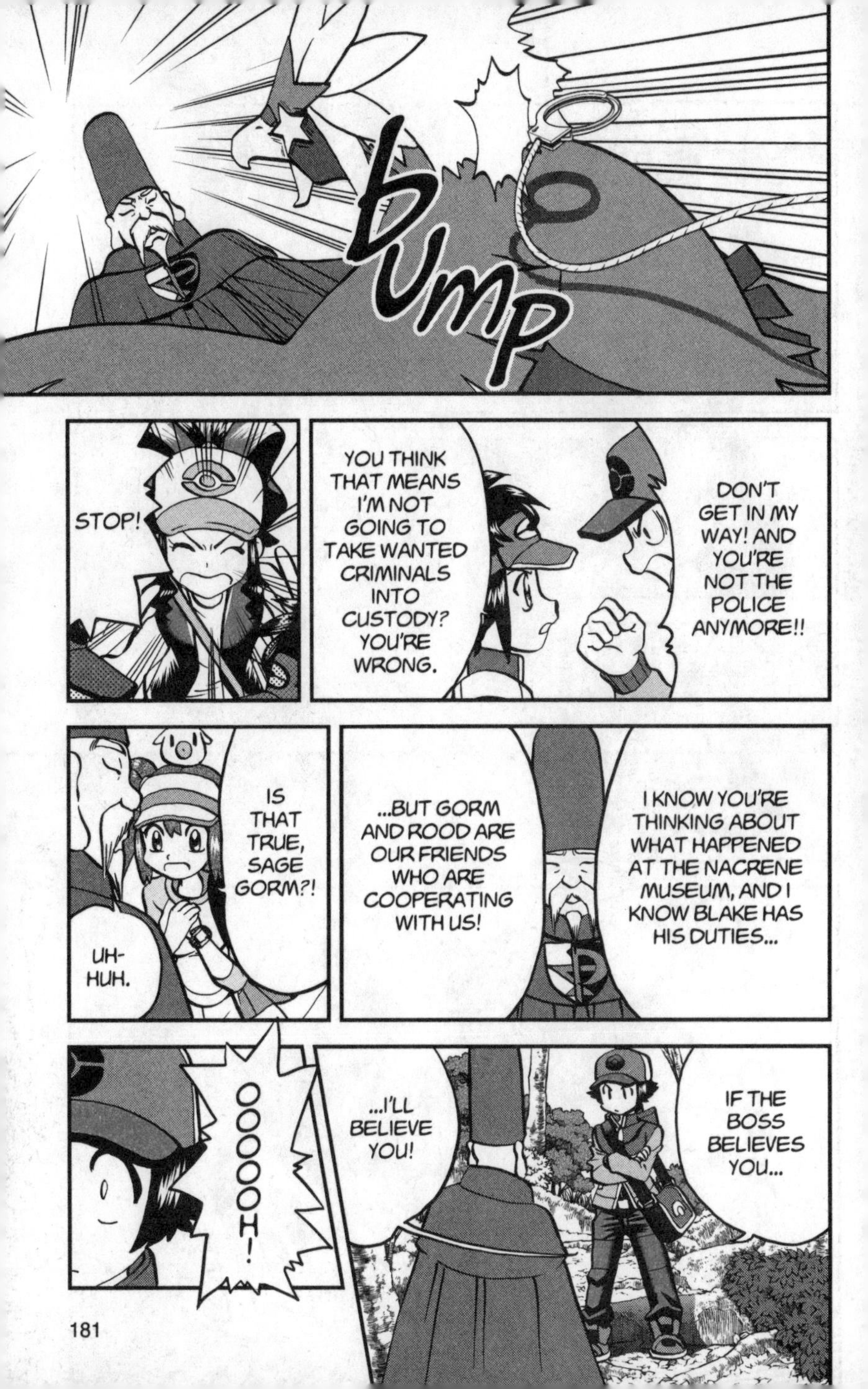
BUMP
DON'T GET IN MY WAY! AND YOU'RE NOT THE POLICE ANYMORE!!
YOU THINK THAT MEANS I'M NOT GOING TO TAKE WANTED CRIMINALS INTO CUSTODY? YOU'RE WRONG.
STOP!
I KNOW YOU'RE THINKING ABOUT WHAT HAPPENED AT THE NACRENE MUSEUM, AND I KNOW BLAKE HAS HIS DUTIES...
...BUT GORM AND ROOD ARE OUR FRIENDS WHO ARE COOPERATING WITH US!
IS THAT TRUE, SAGE GORM?!
UH-HUH.
IF THE BOSS BELIEVES YOU...
...I'LL BELIEVE YOU!
OOOOOOH!

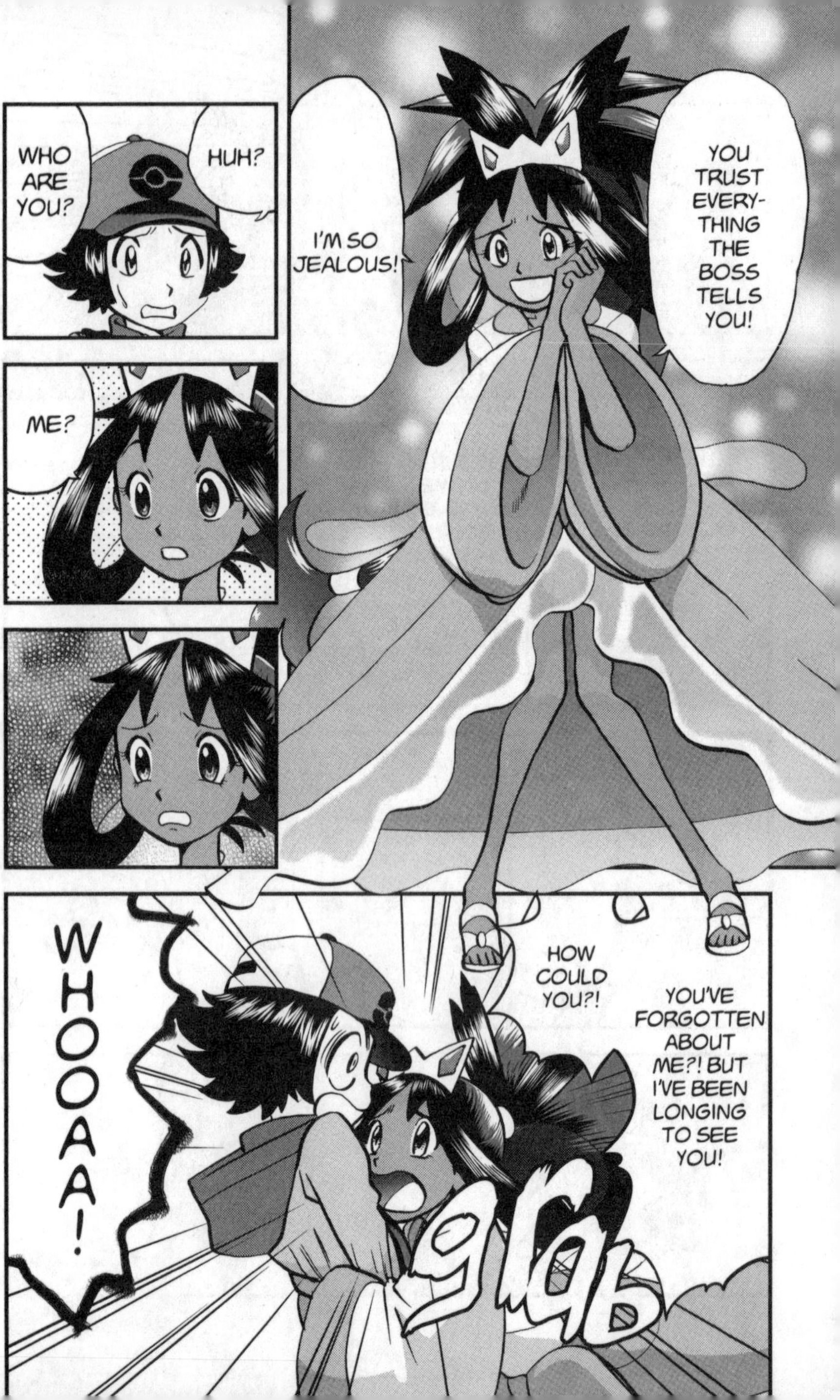
YOU TRUST EVERY-THING THE BOSS TELLS YOU!
I'M SO JEALOUS!
HUH?
WHO ARE YOU?
ME?
HOW COULD YOU?!
YOU'VE FORGOTTEN ABOUT ME?! BUT I'VE BEEN LONGING TO SEE YOU!
WHOOAA!
grab

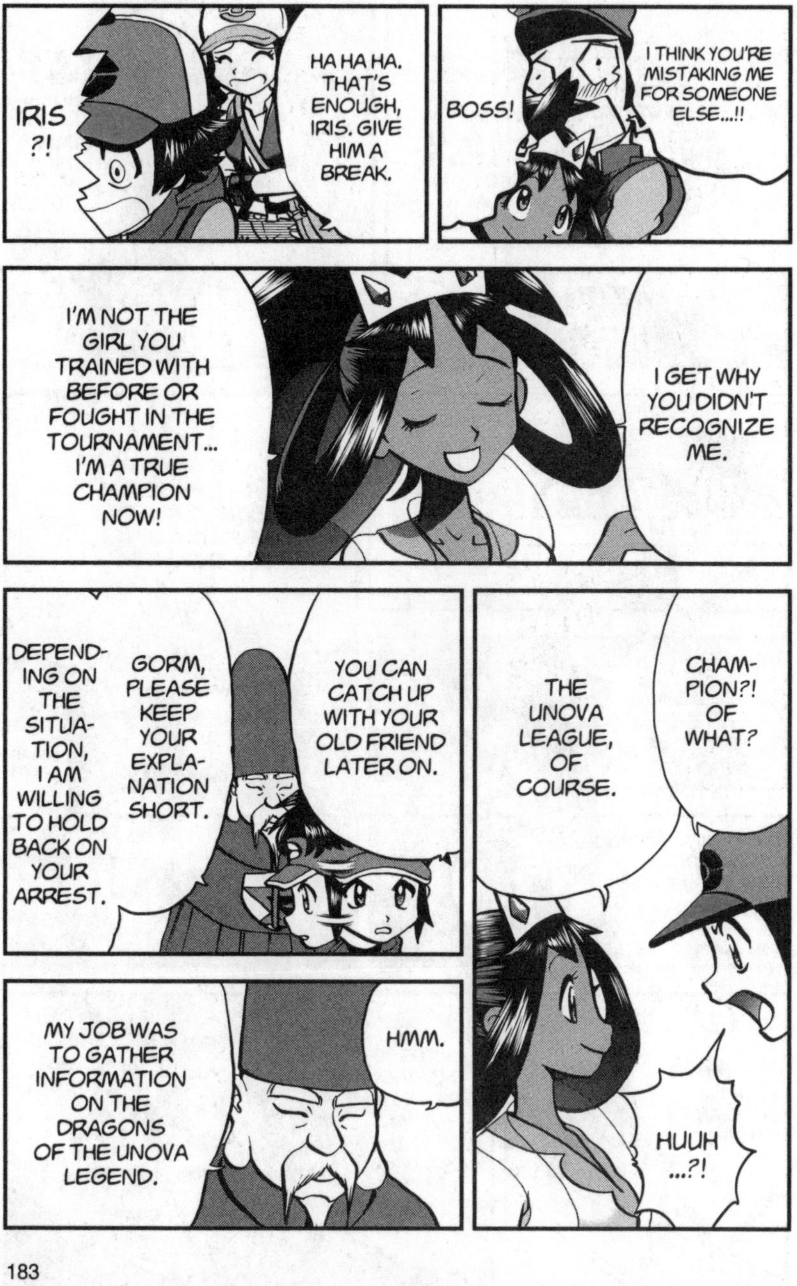
I THINK YOU'RE MISTAKING ME FOR SOMEONE ELSE...!!
BOSS!
HA HA HA. THAT'S ENOUGH, IRIS. GIVE HIM A BREAK.
IRIS ?!
I GET WHY YOU DIDN'T RECOGNIZE ME.
I'M NOT THE GIRL YOU TRAINED WITH BEFORE OR FOUGHT IN THE TOURNAMENT... I'M A TRUE CHAMPION NOW!
CHAMPION?! OF WHAT?
THE UNOVA LEAGUE, OF COURSE.
HUUH ...?!
YOU CAN CATCH UP WITH YOUR OLD FRIEND LATER ON.
GORM, PLEASE KEEP YOUR EXPLANATION SHORT.
DEPENDING ON THE SITUATION, I AM WILLING TO HOLD BACK ON YOUR ARREST.
HMM.
MY JOB WAS TO GATHER INFORMATION ON THE DRAGONS OF THE UNOVA LEGEND.

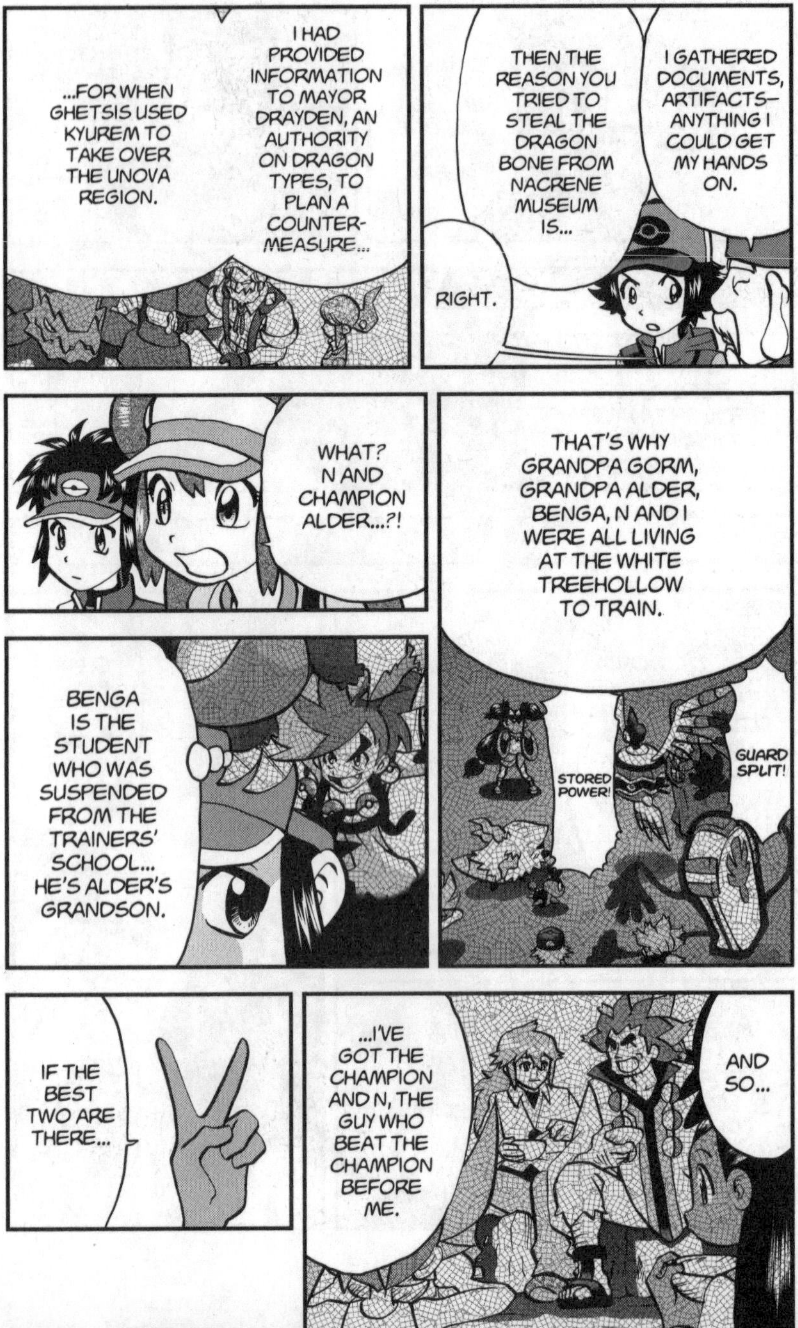
I GATHERED DOCUMENTS, ARTIFACTS—ANYTHING I COULD GET MY HANDS ON.
THEN THE REASON YOU TRIED TO STEAL THE DRAGON BONE FROM NACRENE MUSEUM IS...
RIGHT.
I HAD PROVIDED INFORMATION TO MAYOR DRAYDEN, AN AUTHORITY ON DRAGON TYPES, TO PLAN A COUNTER-MEASURE...
...FOR WHEN GHETSIS USED KYUREM TO TAKE OVER THE UNOVA REGION.
THAT'S WHY GRANDPA GORM, GRANDPA ALDER, BENGA, N AND I WERE ALL LIVING AT THE WHITE TREEHOLLOW TO TRAIN.
GUARD SPLIT!
STORED POWER!
WHAT? N AND CHAMPION ALDER...?!
BENGA IS THE STUDENT WHO WAS SUSPENDED FROM THE TRAINERS' SCHOOL... HE'S ALDER'S GRANDSON.
AND SO...
...I'VE GOT THE CHAMPION AND N, THE GUY WHO BEAT THE CHAMPION BEFORE ME.
IF THE BEST TWO ARE THERE...

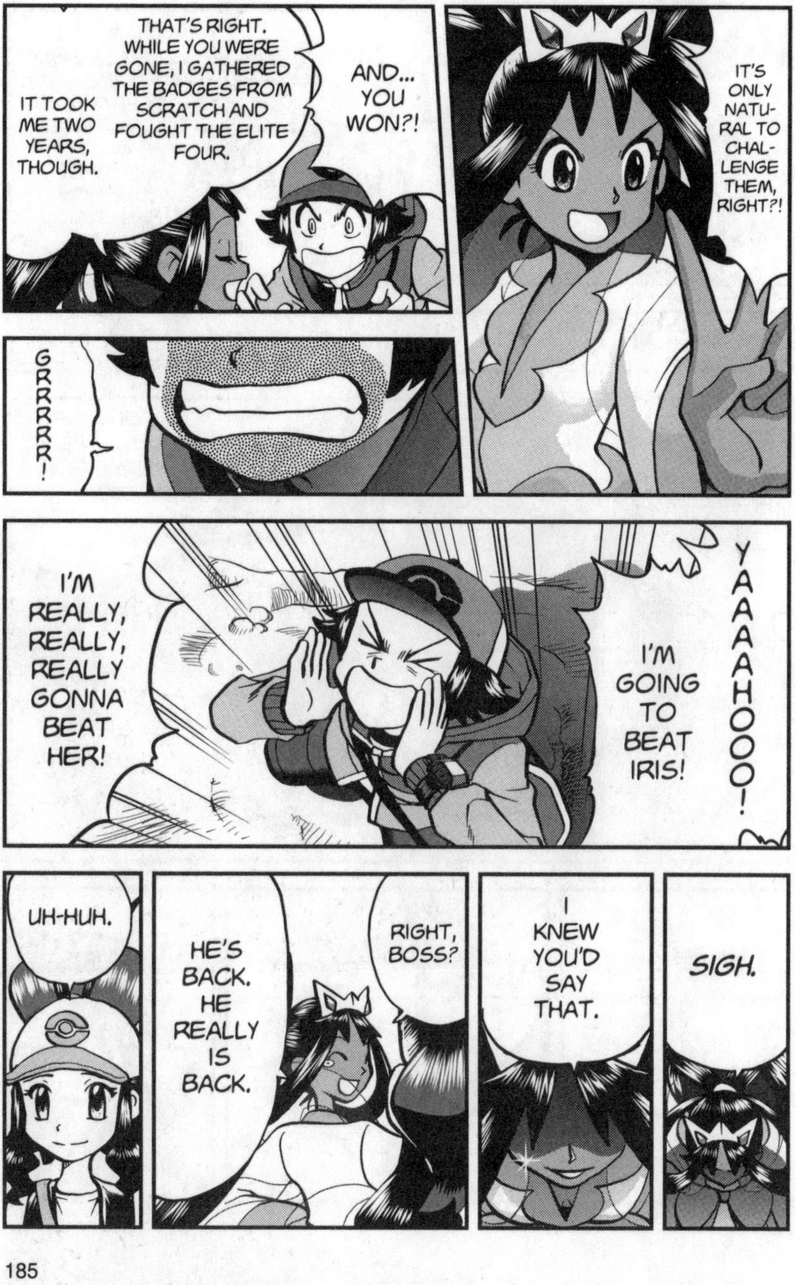
IT'S ONLY NATURAL TO CHALLENGE THEM, RIGHT?!
AND... YOU WON?!
THAT'S RIGHT. WHILE YOU WERE GONE, I GATHERED THE BADGES FROM SCRATCH AND FOUGHT THE ELITE FOUR.
IT TOOK ME TWO YEARS, THOUGH.
GRRRRR!
YAAAAHOOOO!
I'M GOING TO BEAT IRIS!
I'M REALLY, REALLY, REALLY GONNA BEAT HER!
SIGH.
I KNEW YOU'D SAY THAT.
RIGHT, BOSS?
HE'S BACK. HE REALLY IS BACK.
UH-HUH.

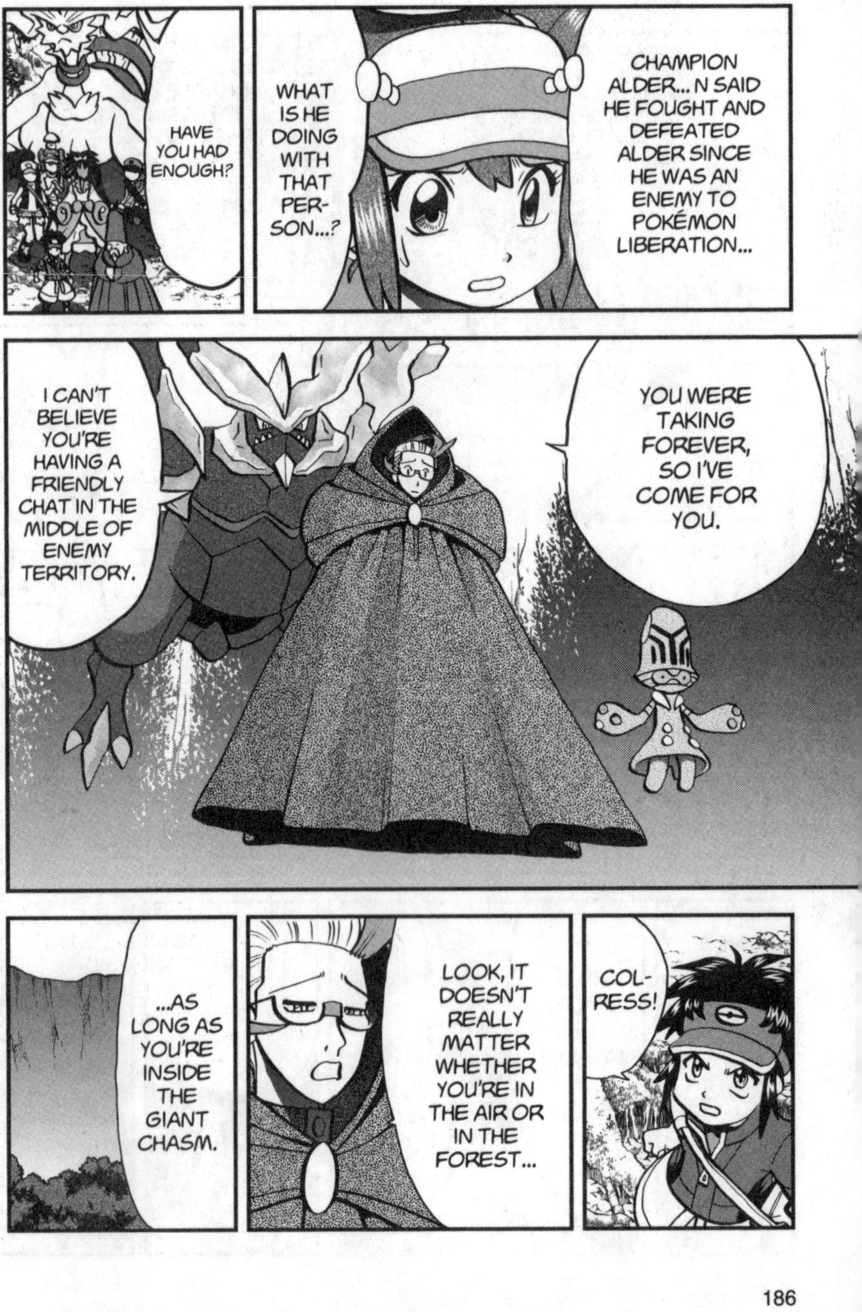
CHAMPION ALDER... N SAID HE FOUGHT AND DEFEATED ALDER SINCE HE WAS AN ENEMY TO POKÉMON LIBERATION...
WHAT IS HE DOING WITH THAT PER-SON...?
HAVE YOU HAD ENOUGH?
YOU WERE TAKING FOREVER, SO I'VE COME FOR YOU.
I CAN'T BELIEVE YOU'RE HAVING A FRIENDLY CHAT IN THE MIDDLE OF ENEMY TERRITORY.
COL-RESS!
LOOK, IT DOESN'T REALLY MATTER WHETHER YOU'RE IN THE AIR OR IN THE FOREST...
...AS LONG AS YOU'RE INSIDE THE GIANT CHASM.

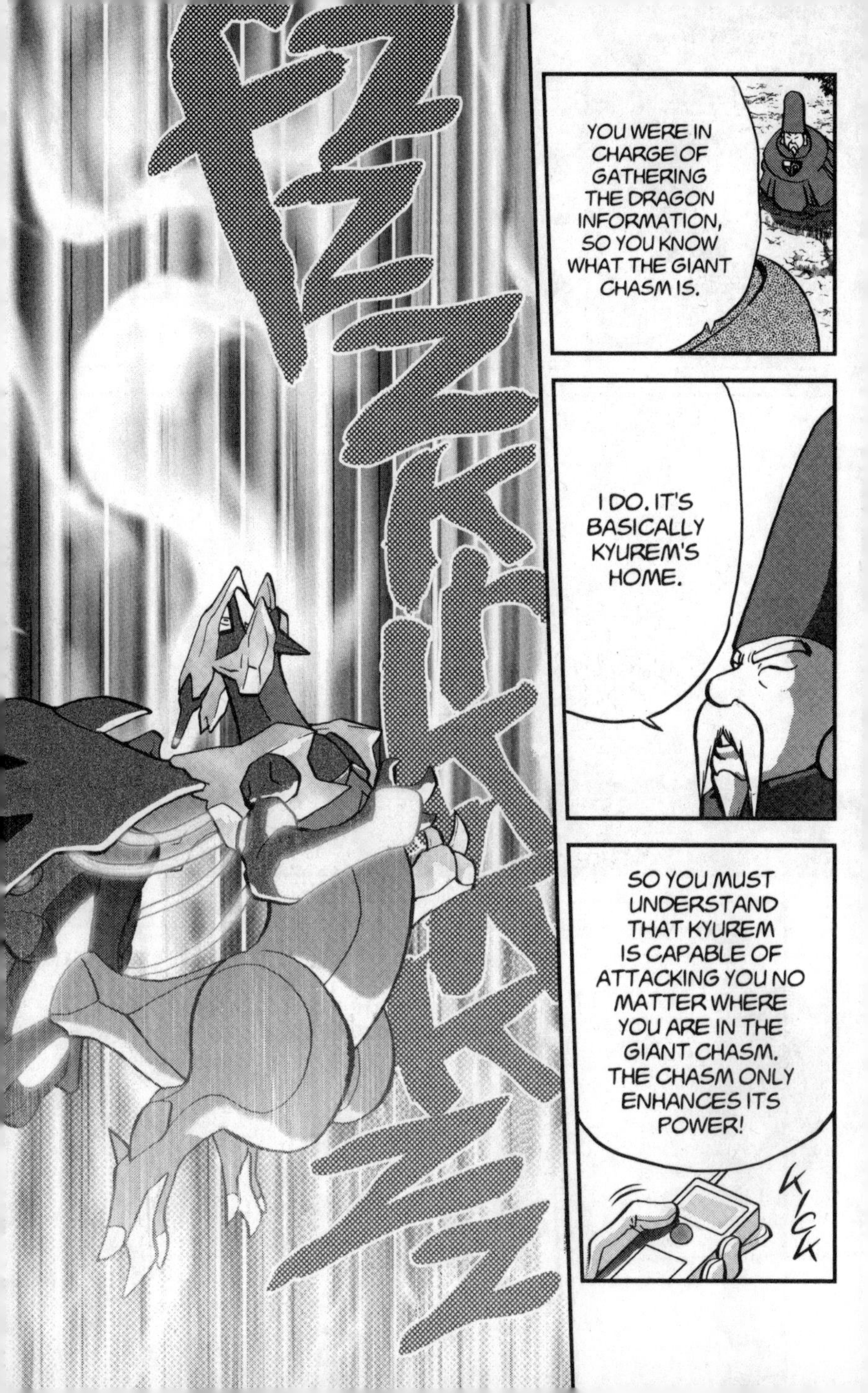
YOU WERE IN CHARGE OF GATHERING THE DRAGON INFORMATION, SO YOU KNOW WHAT THE GIANT CHASM IS.
I DO. IT'S BASICALLY KYUREM'S HOME.
SO YOU MUST UNDERSTAND THAT KYUREM IS CAPABLE OF ATTACKING YOU NO MATTER WHERE YOU ARE IN THE GIANT CHASM. THE CHASM ONLY ENHANCES ITS POWER!
KICK

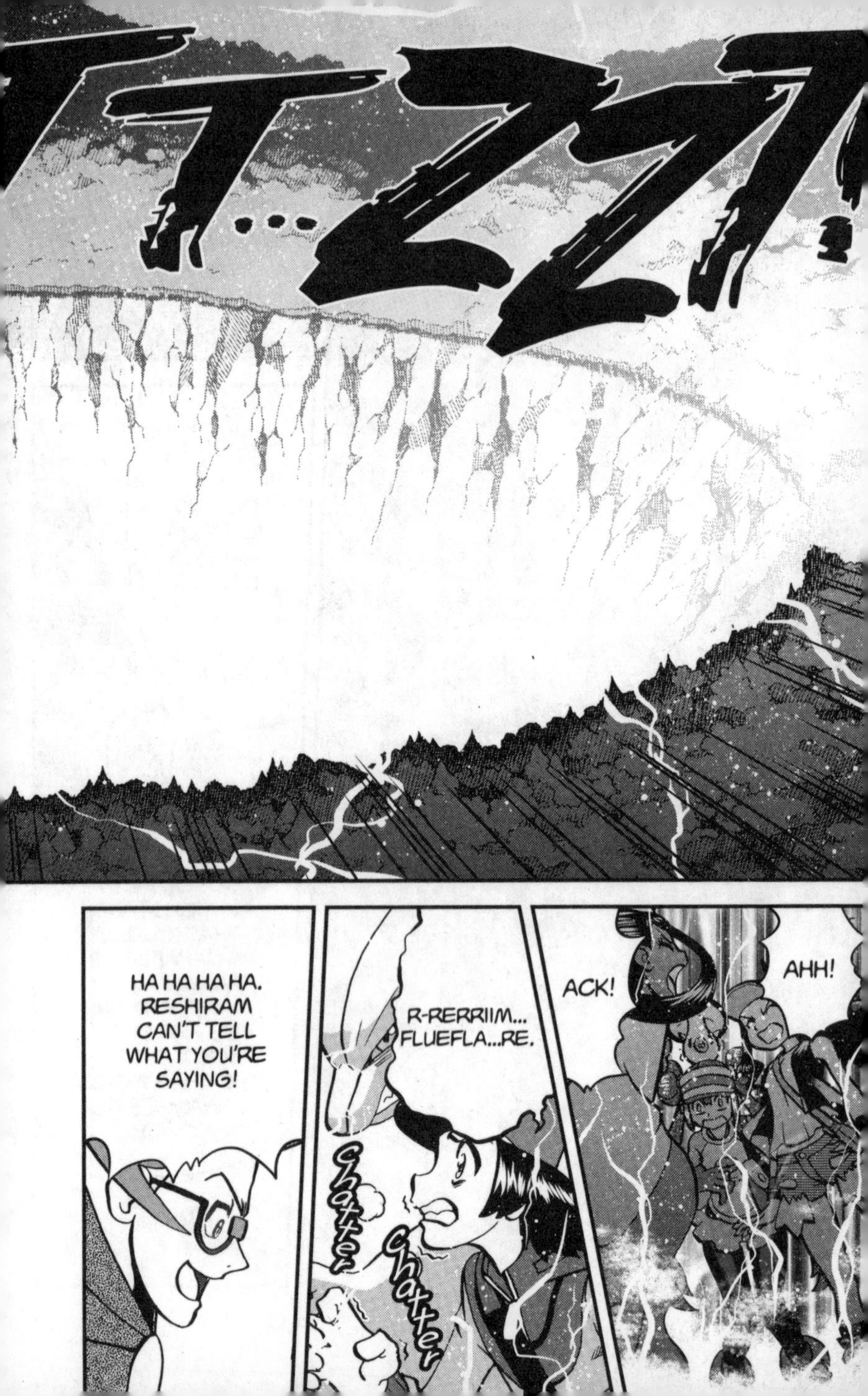
AHH!
ACK!
R-RERRIIM... FLUEFLA...RE.
chatter chatter
HA HA HA HA. RESHIRAM CAN'T TELL WHAT YOU'RE SAYING!

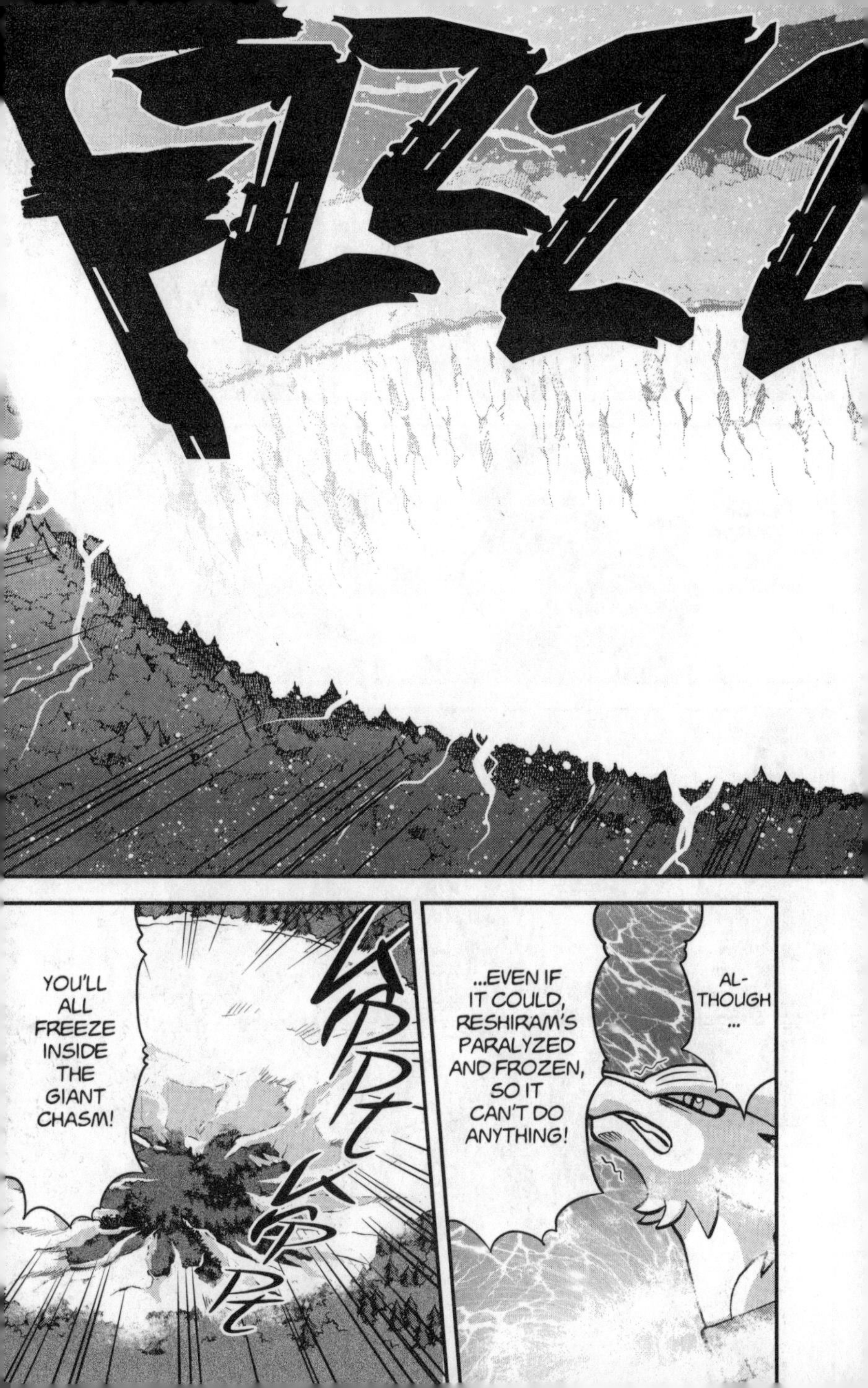
FZZZ
AL-THOUGH...
...EVEN IF IT COULD, RESHIRAM'S PARALYZED AND FROZEN, SO IT CAN'T DO ANYTHING!
YOU'LL ALL FREEZE INSIDE THE GIANT CHASM!

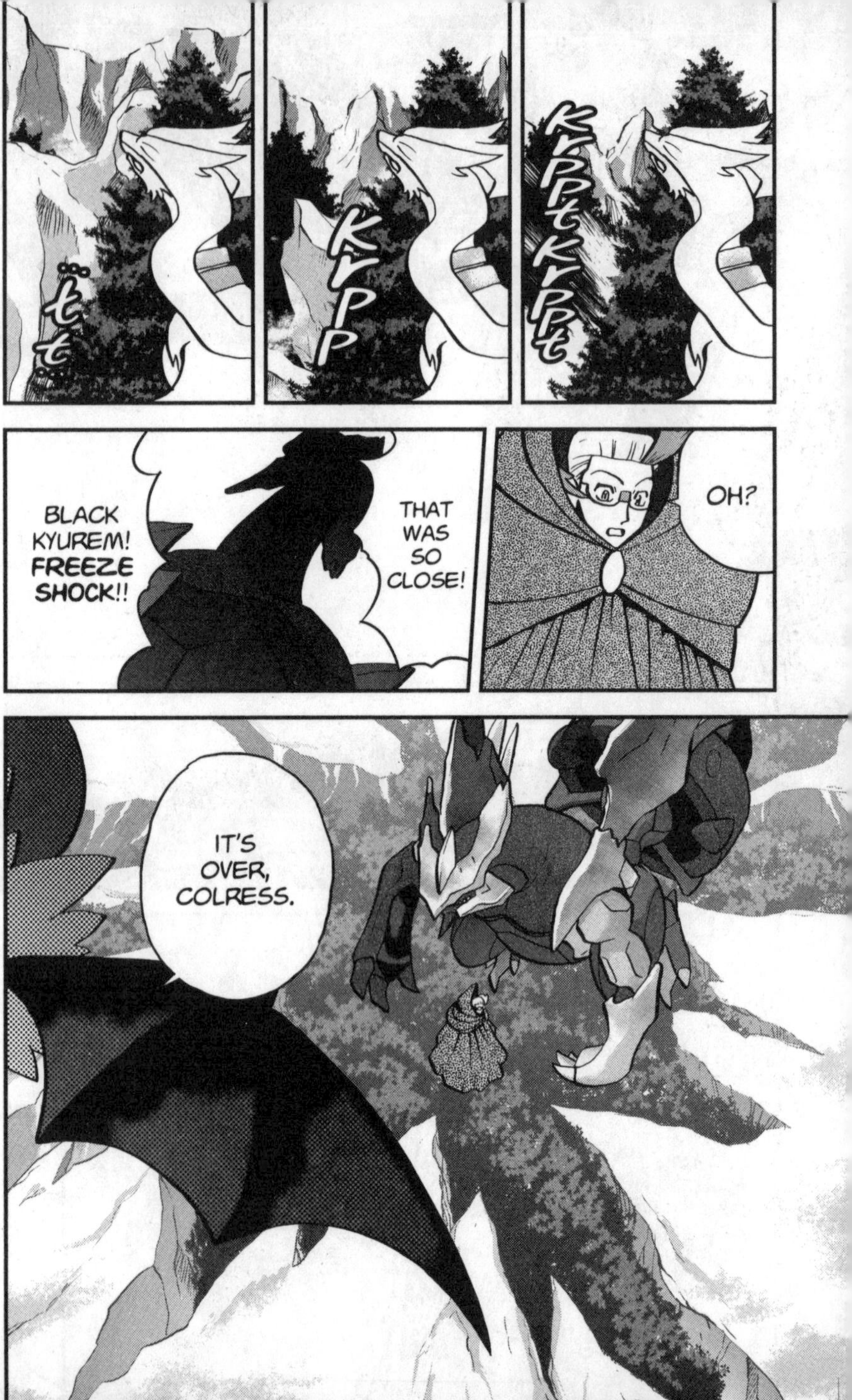
KYPPtKYPPt
KYPP
...tt...
OH?
THAT WAS SO CLOSE!
BLACK KYUREM! FREEZE SHOCK!!
IT'S OVER, COLRESS.

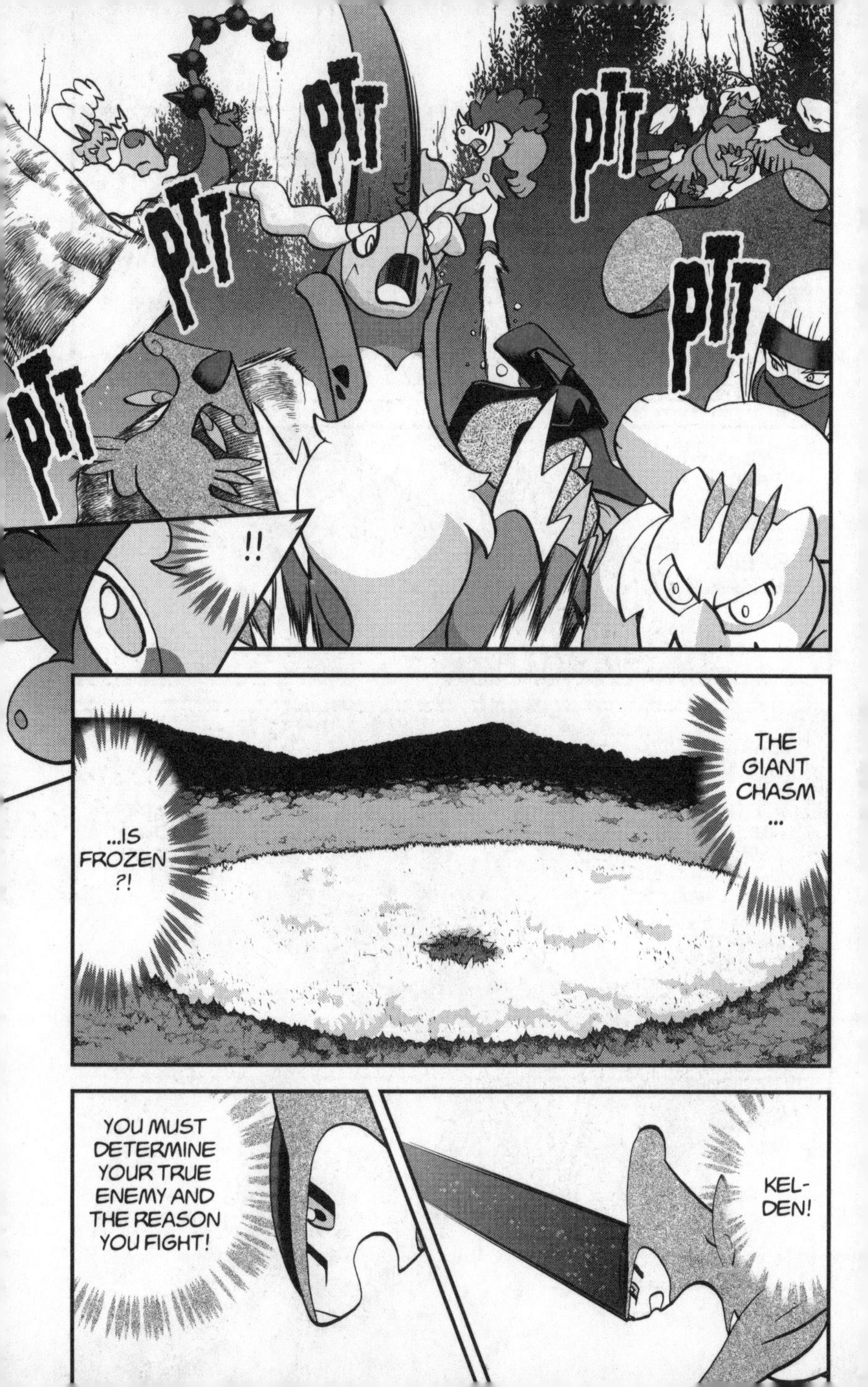
PTT
PTT
PTT
PTT
PTT
!!
THE GIANT CHASM ...
...IS FROZEN ?!
KEL-DEN!
YOU MUST DETERMINE YOUR TRUE ENEMY AND THE REASON YOU FIGHT!

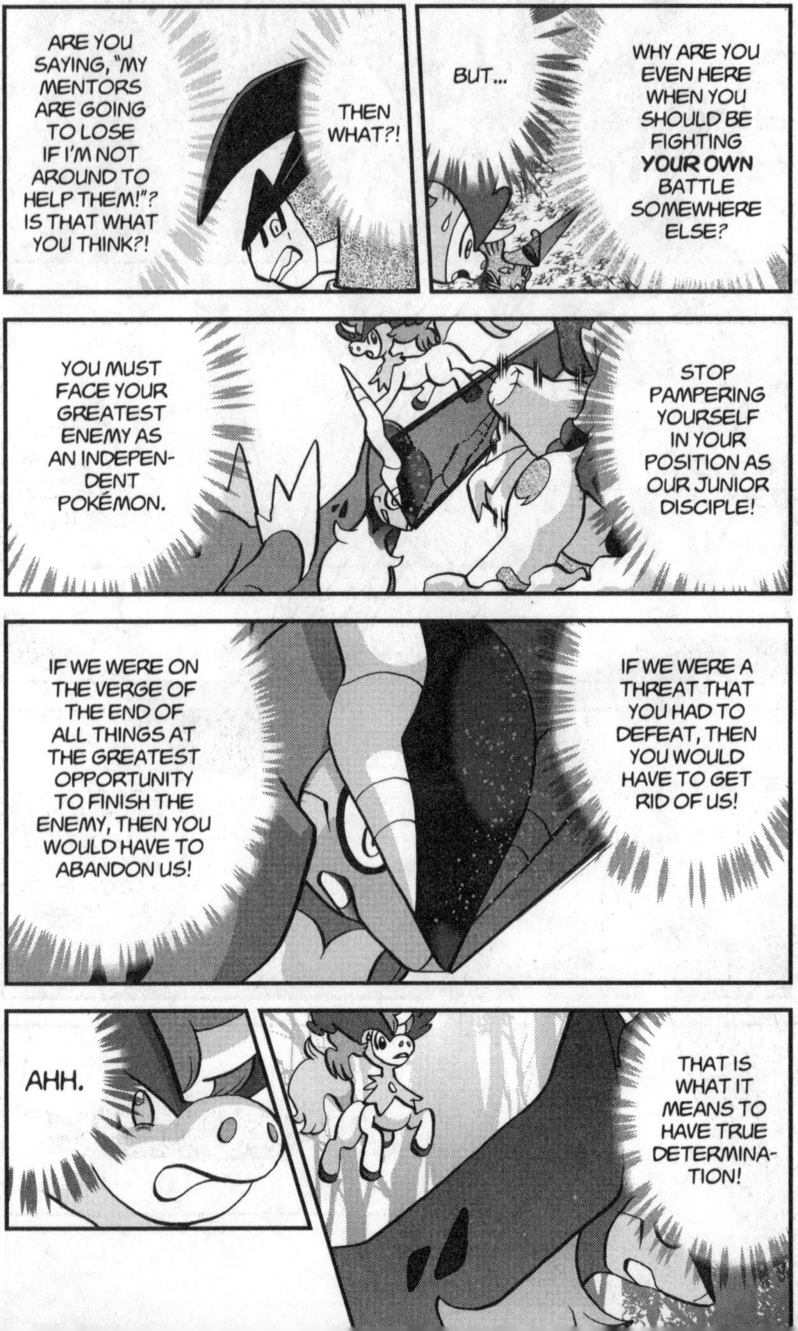
WHY ARE YOU EVEN HERE WHEN YOU SHOULD BE FIGHTING **YOUR OWN** BATTLE SOMEWHERE ELSE?
BUT...
THEN WHAT?!
ARE YOU SAYING, "MY MENTORS ARE GOING TO LOSE IF I'M NOT AROUND TO HELP THEM!"? IS THAT WHAT YOU THINK?!
STOP PAMPERING YOURSELF IN YOUR POSITION AS OUR JUNIOR DISCIPLE!
YOU MUST FACE YOUR GREATEST ENEMY AS AN INDEPEN-DENT POKÉMON.
IF WE WERE A THREAT THAT YOU HAD TO DEFEAT, THEN YOU WOULD HAVE TO GET RID OF US!
IF WE WERE ON THE VERGE OF THE END OF ALL THINGS AT THE GREATEST OPPORTUNITY TO FINISH THE ENEMY, THEN YOU WOULD HAVE TO ABANDON US!
THAT IS WHAT IT MEANS TO HAVE TRUE DETERMINA-TION!
AHH.

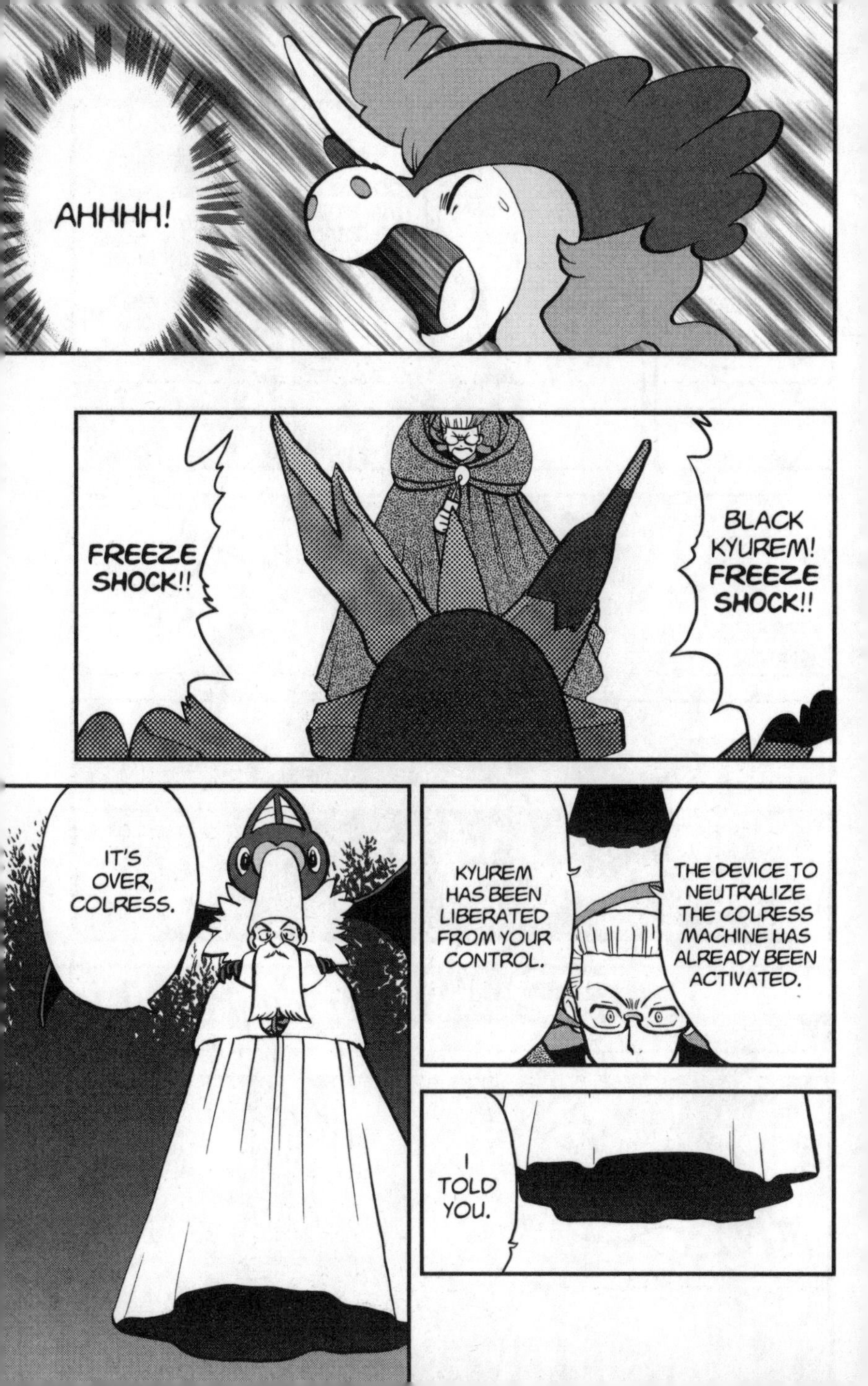
AHHHH!
BLACK KYUREM! FREEZE SHOCK!!
FREEZE SHOCK!!
THE DEVICE TO NEUTRALIZE THE COLRESS MACHINE HAS ALREADY BEEN ACTIVATED.
KYUREM HAS BEEN LIBERATED FROM YOUR CONTROL.
IT'S OVER, COLRESS.
I TOLD YOU.

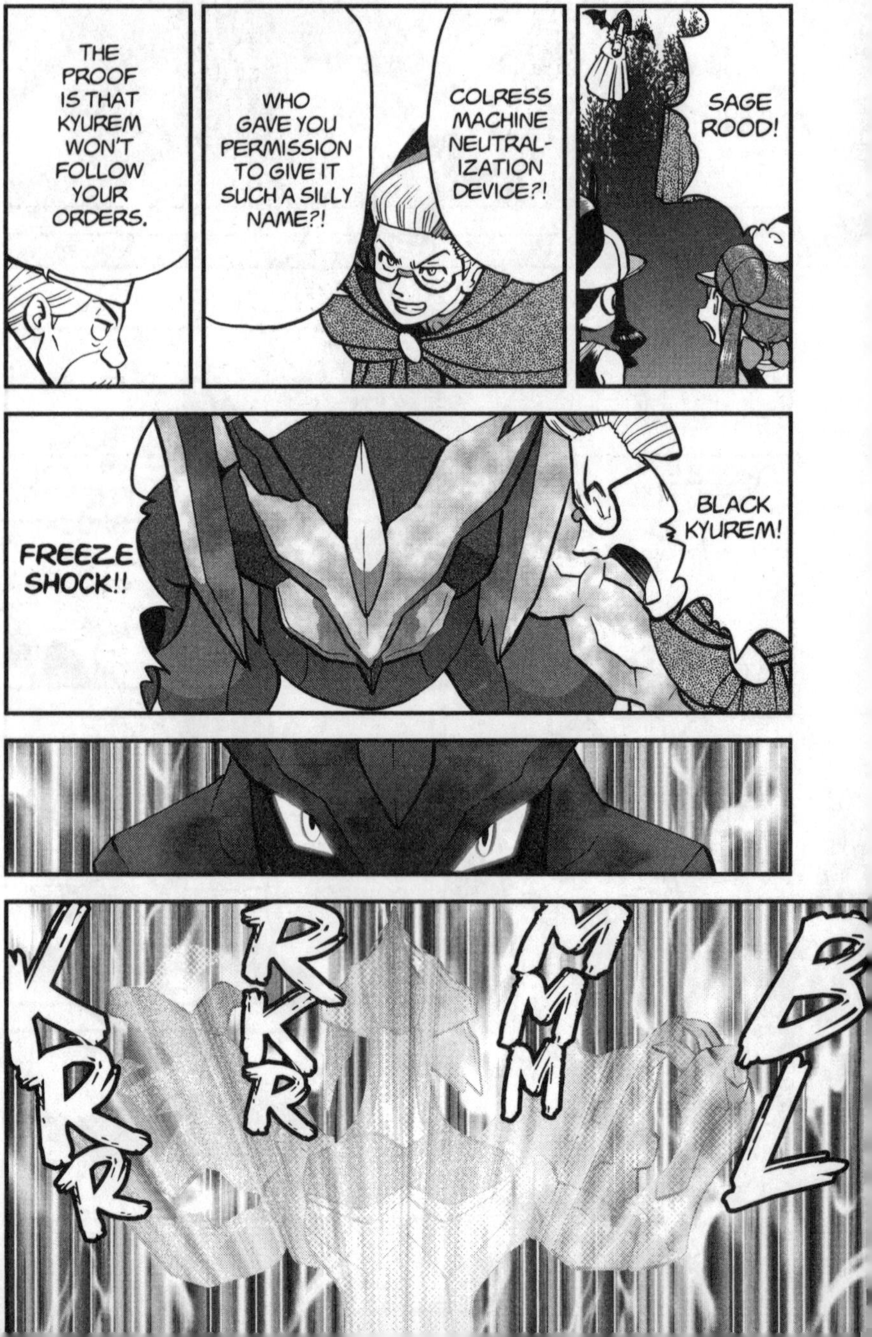
SAGE ROOD!
COLRESS MACHINE NEUTRAL-IZATION DEVICE?!
WHO GAVE YOU PERMISSION TO GIVE IT SUCH A SILLY NAME?!
THE PROOF IS THAT KYUREM WON'T FOLLOW YOUR ORDERS.
BLACK KYUREM!
FREEZE SHOCK!!
BL
MMM
RKR
KRRR

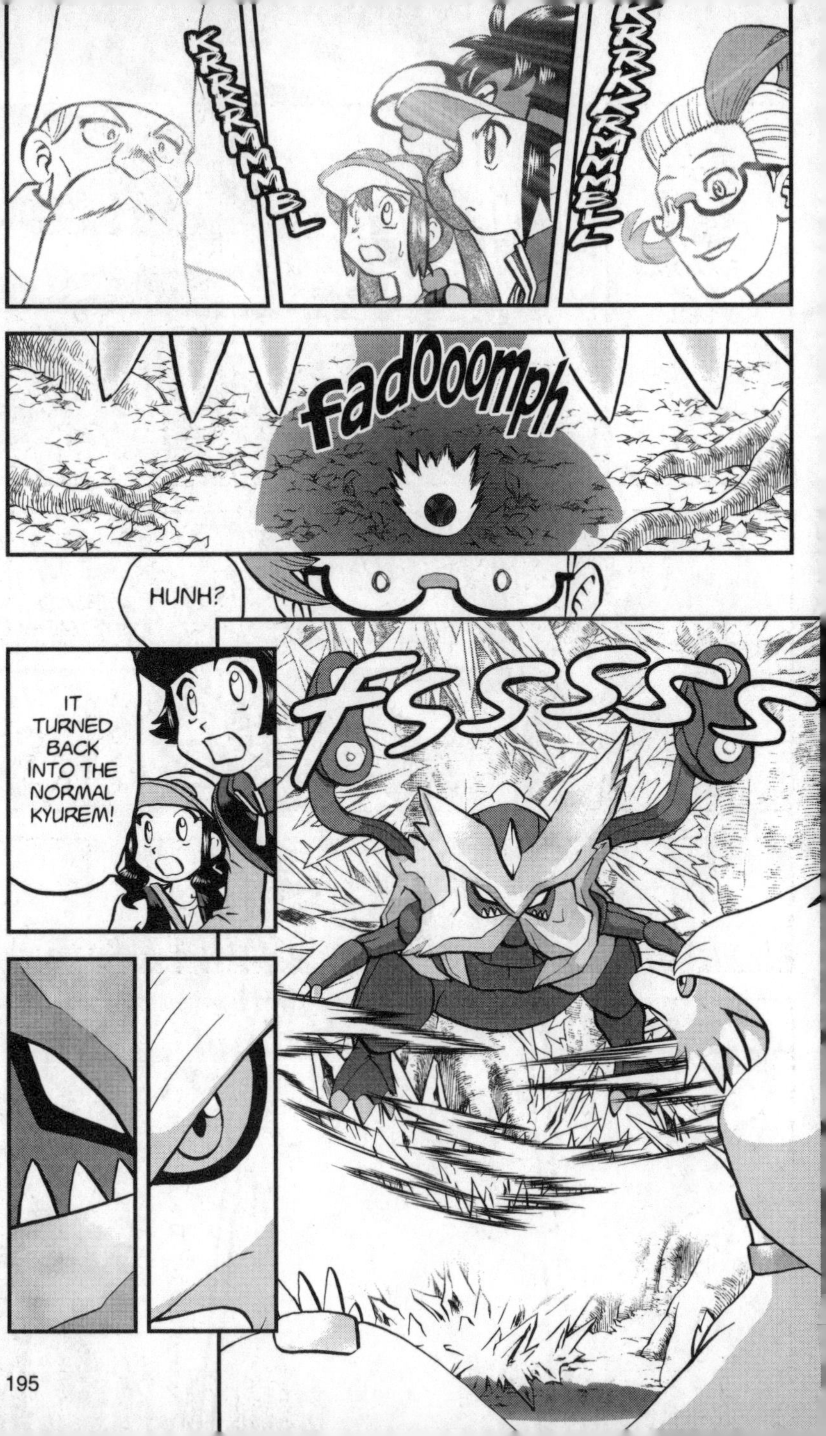
KRRRKRRRMMMBL
KRRKRMMMBL
fadOooomph
HUNH?
fsssss
IT TURNED BACK INTO THE NORMAL KYUREM!

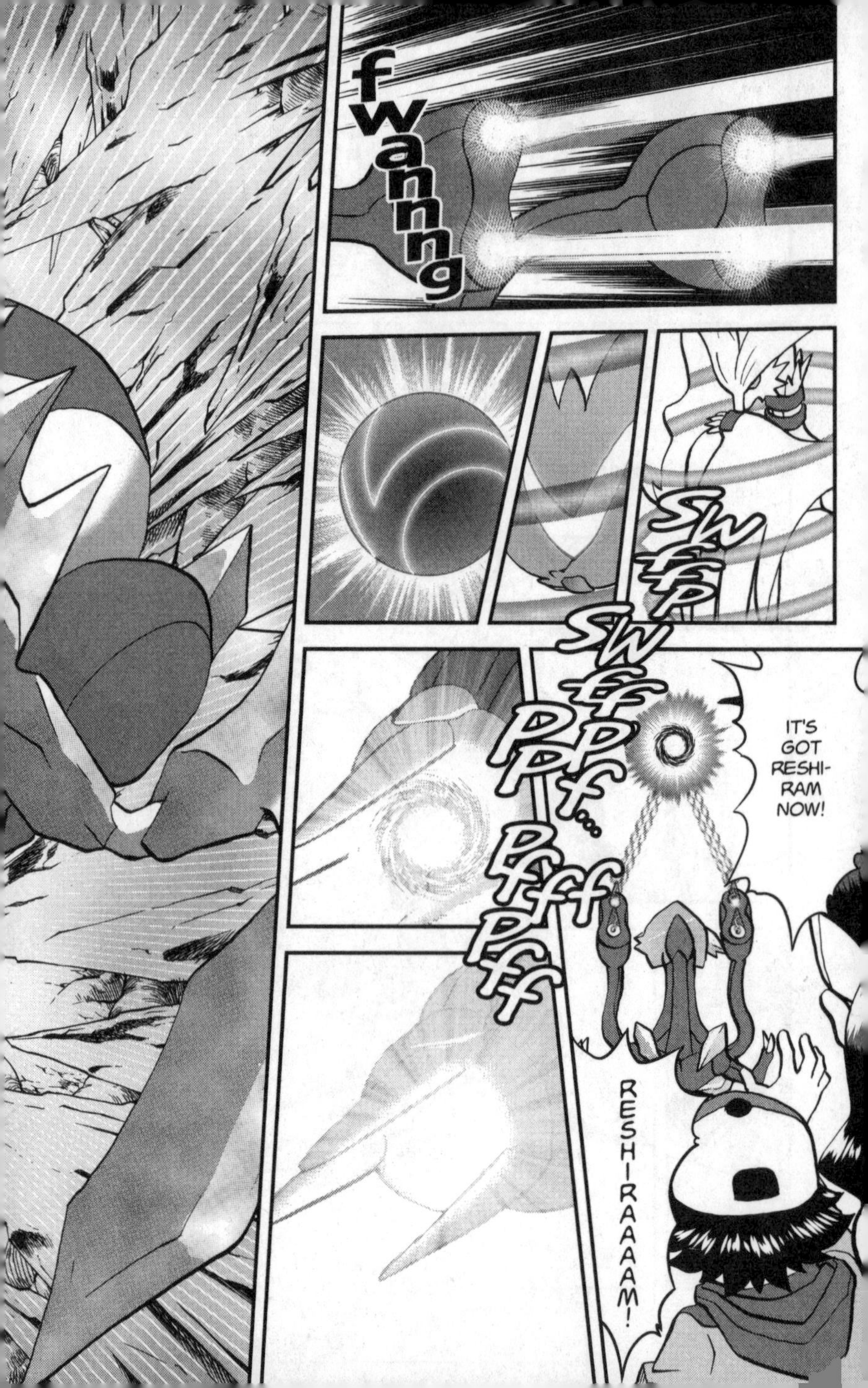
fwanng
SWFFP
SWFFP
PFF...
PFFF
PFFF
IT'S GOT RESHI-RAM NOW!
RESHIRAAAAAM!

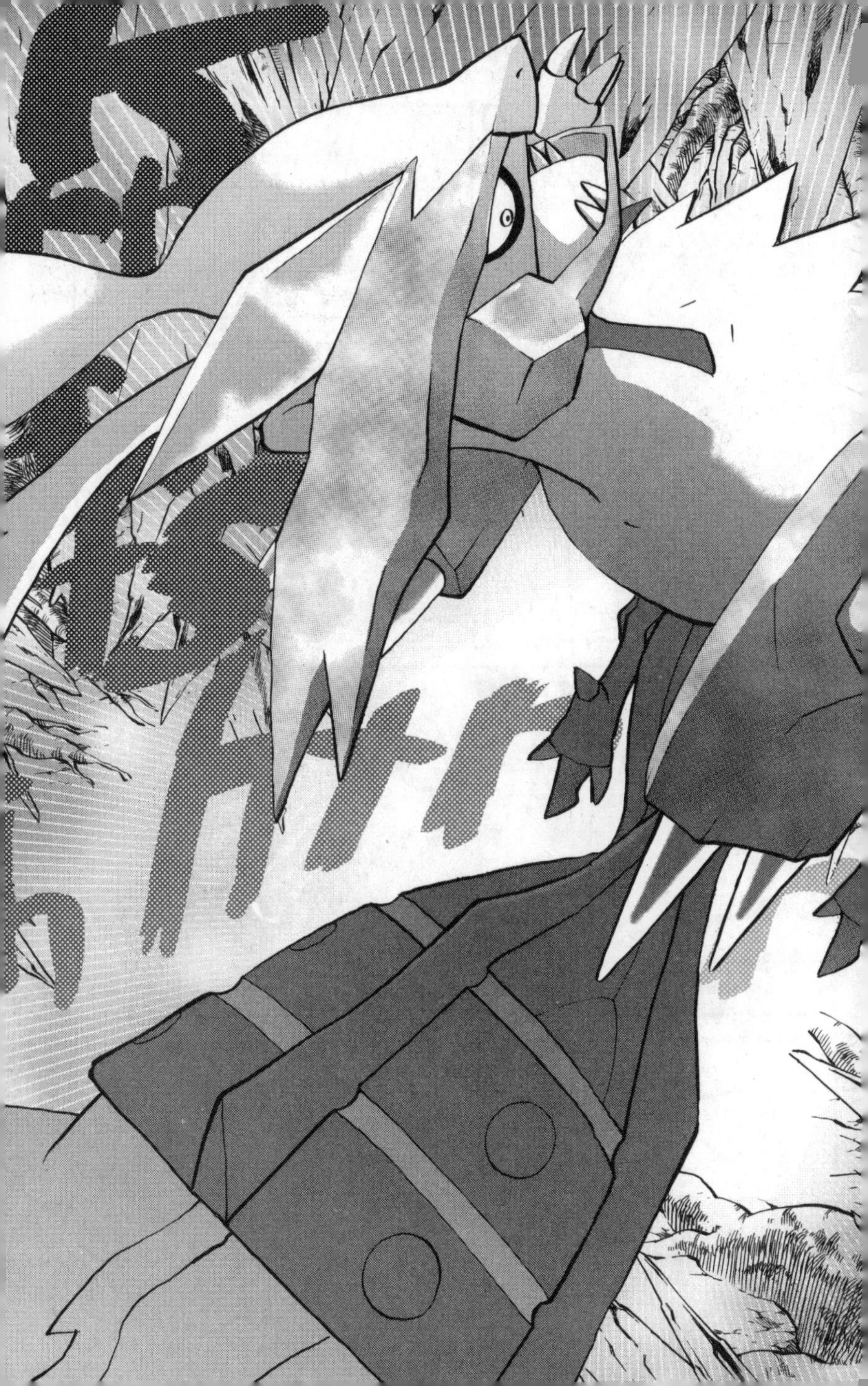

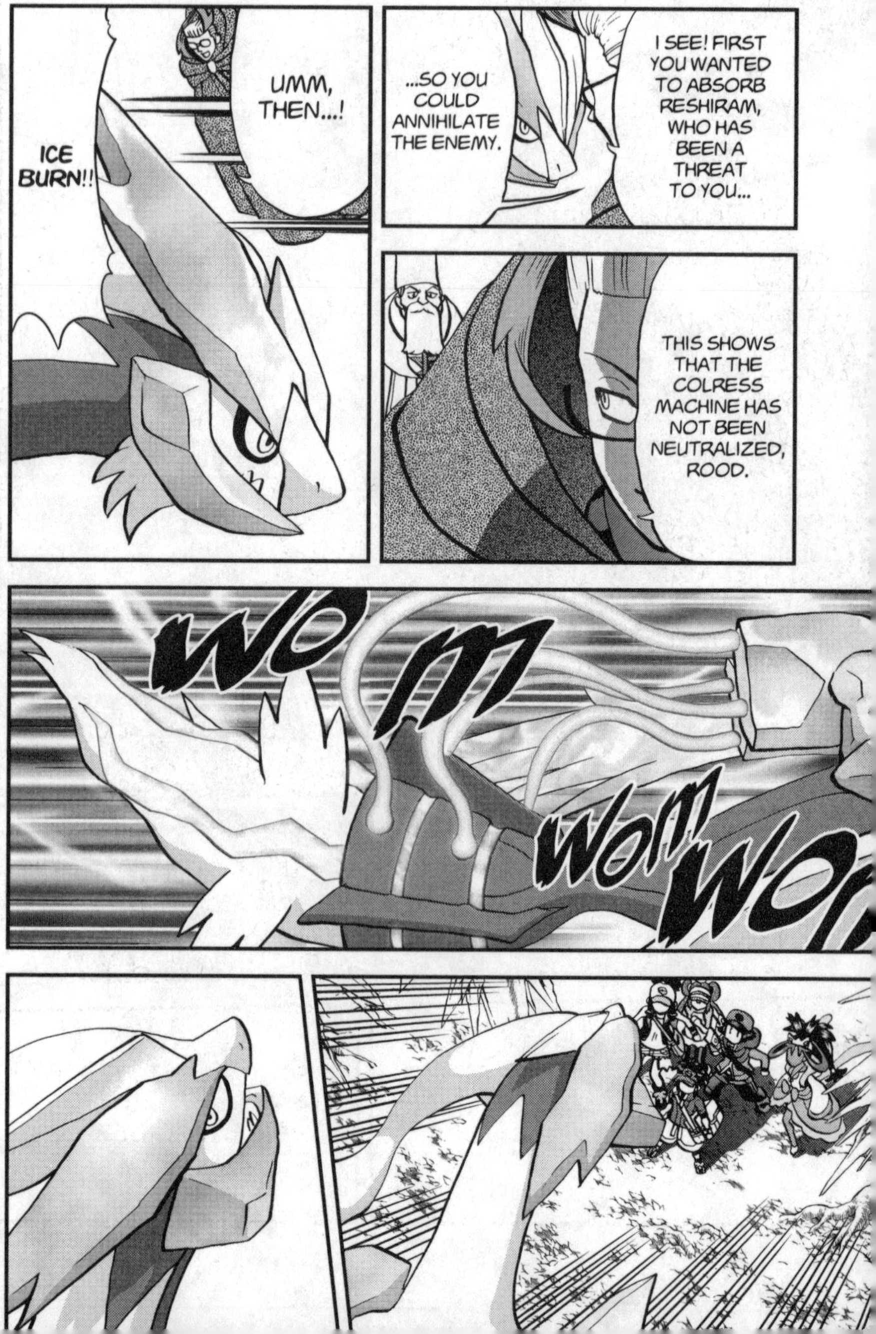
I SEE! FIRST YOU WANTED TO ABSORB RESHIRAM, WHO HAS BEEN A THREAT TO YOU...
...SO YOU COULD ANNIHILATE THE ENEMY.
THIS SHOWS THAT THE COLRESS MACHINE HAS NOT BEEN NEUTRALIZED, ROOD.
UMM, THEN...!
ICE BURN!!
WOM
WOM
WO

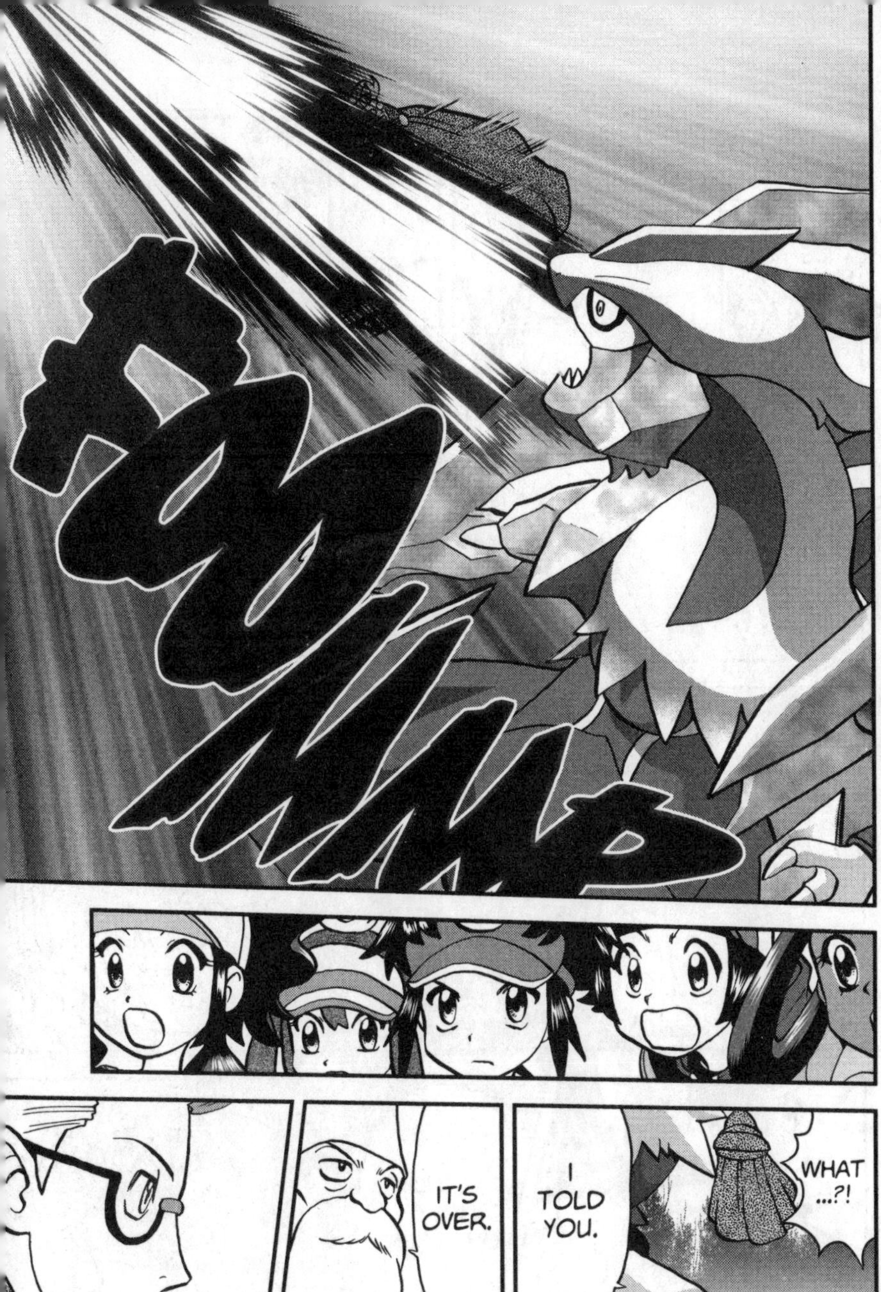
THUMP
WHAT ...?!
I TOLD YOU.
IT'S OVER.

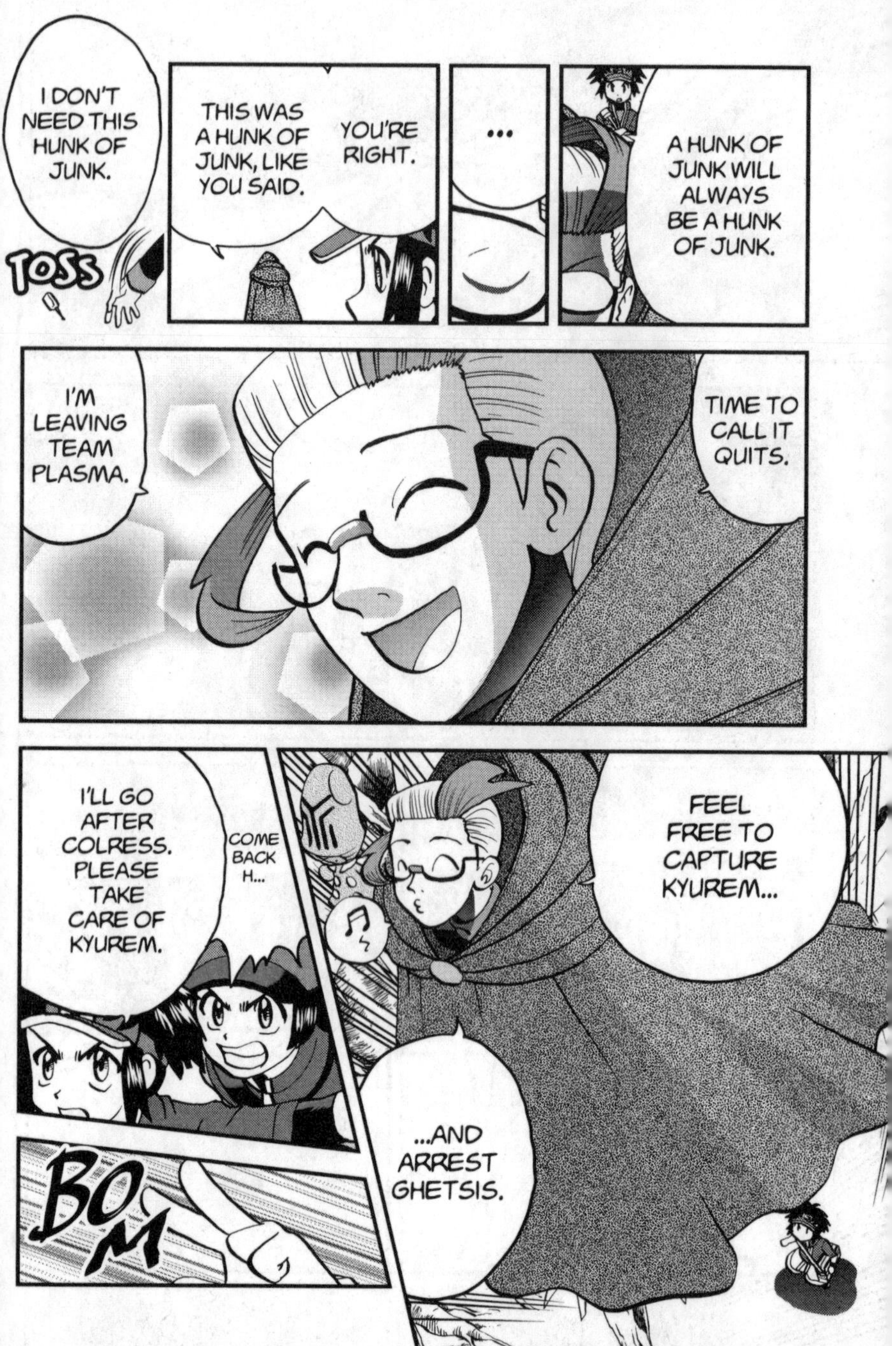
A HUNK OF JUNK WILL ALWAYS BE A HUNK OF JUNK.
...
YOU'RE RIGHT.
THIS WAS A HUNK OF JUNK, LIKE YOU SAID.
I DON'T NEED THIS HUNK OF JUNK.
TOSS
TIME TO CALL IT QUITS.
I'M LEAVING TEAM PLASMA.
FEEL FREE TO CAPTURE KYUREM...
...AND ARREST GHETSIS.
COME BACK H...
I'LL GO AFTER COLRESS. PLEASE TAKE CARE OF KYUREM.
BOOM

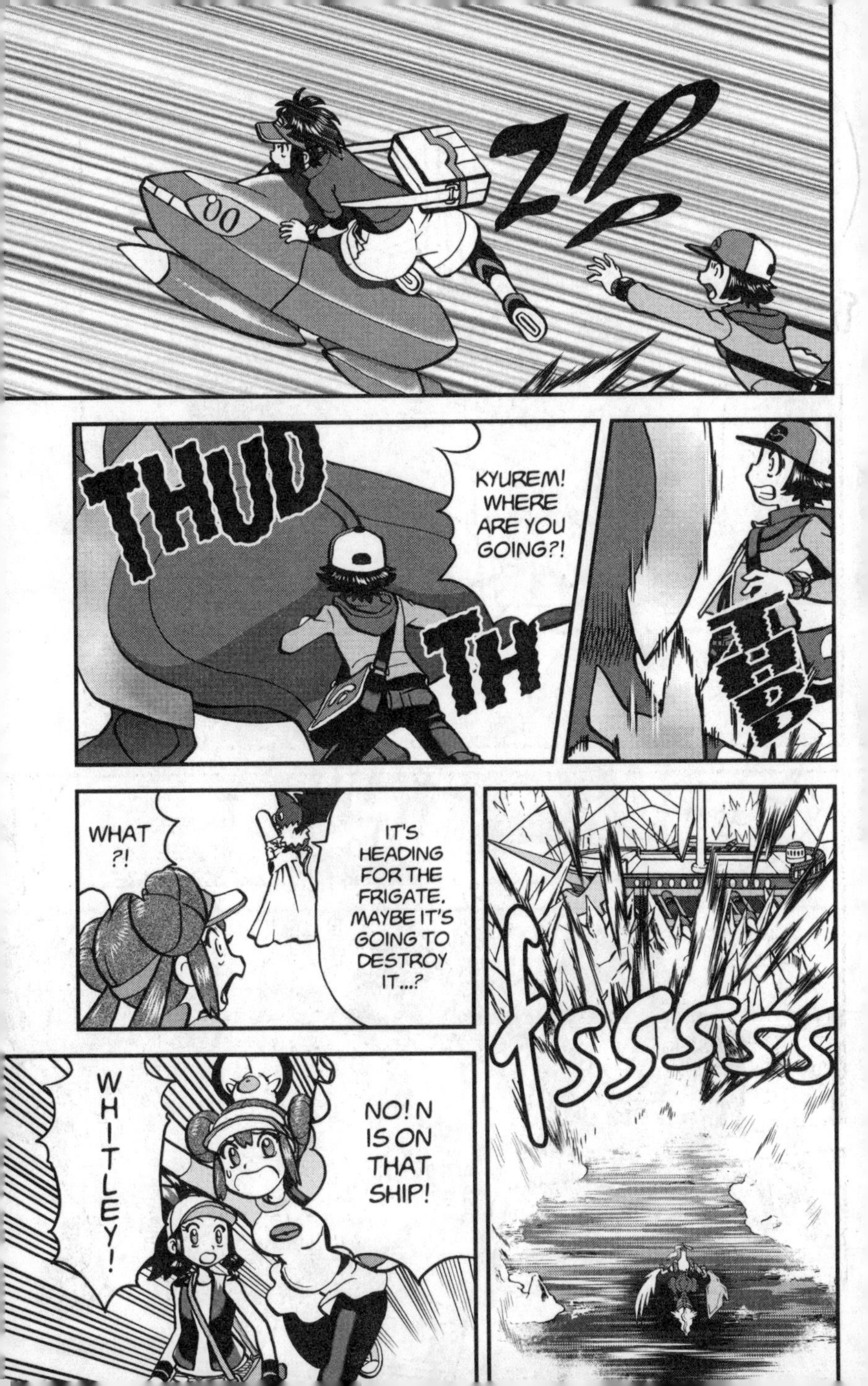
ZIP
THUD
KYUREM! WHERE ARE YOU GOING?!
TH
fssssss
IT'S HEADING FOR THE FRIGATE. MAYBE IT'S GOING TO DESTROY IT...?
WHAT?!
NO! N IS ON THAT SHIP!
WHITLEY!

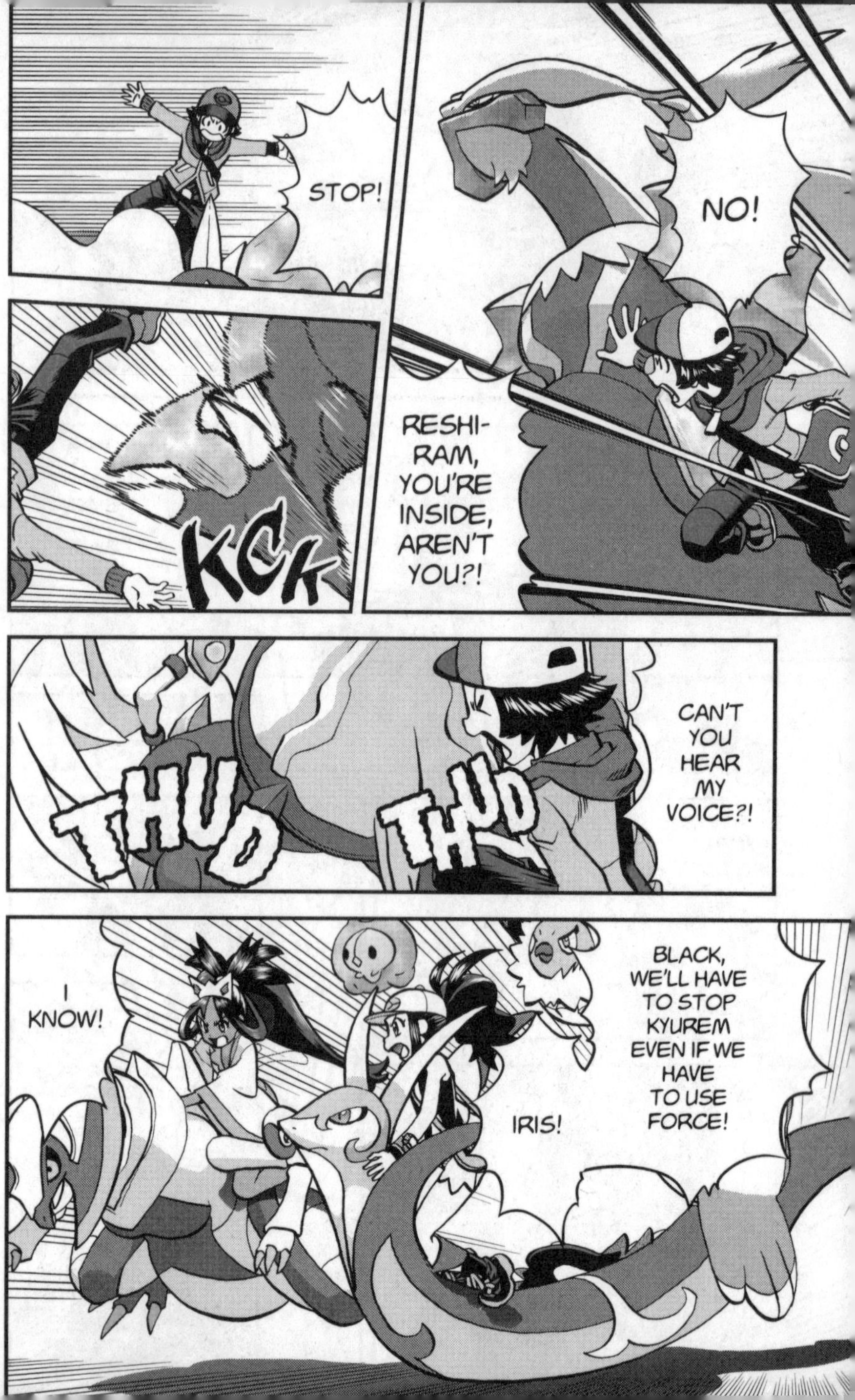
NO!
RESHIRAM, YOU'RE INSIDE, AREN'T YOU?!
STOP!
KCK
CAN'T YOU HEAR MY VOICE?!
THUD
THUD
BLACK, WE'LL HAVE TO STOP KYUREM EVEN IF WE HAVE TO USE FORCE!
IRIS!
I KNOW!

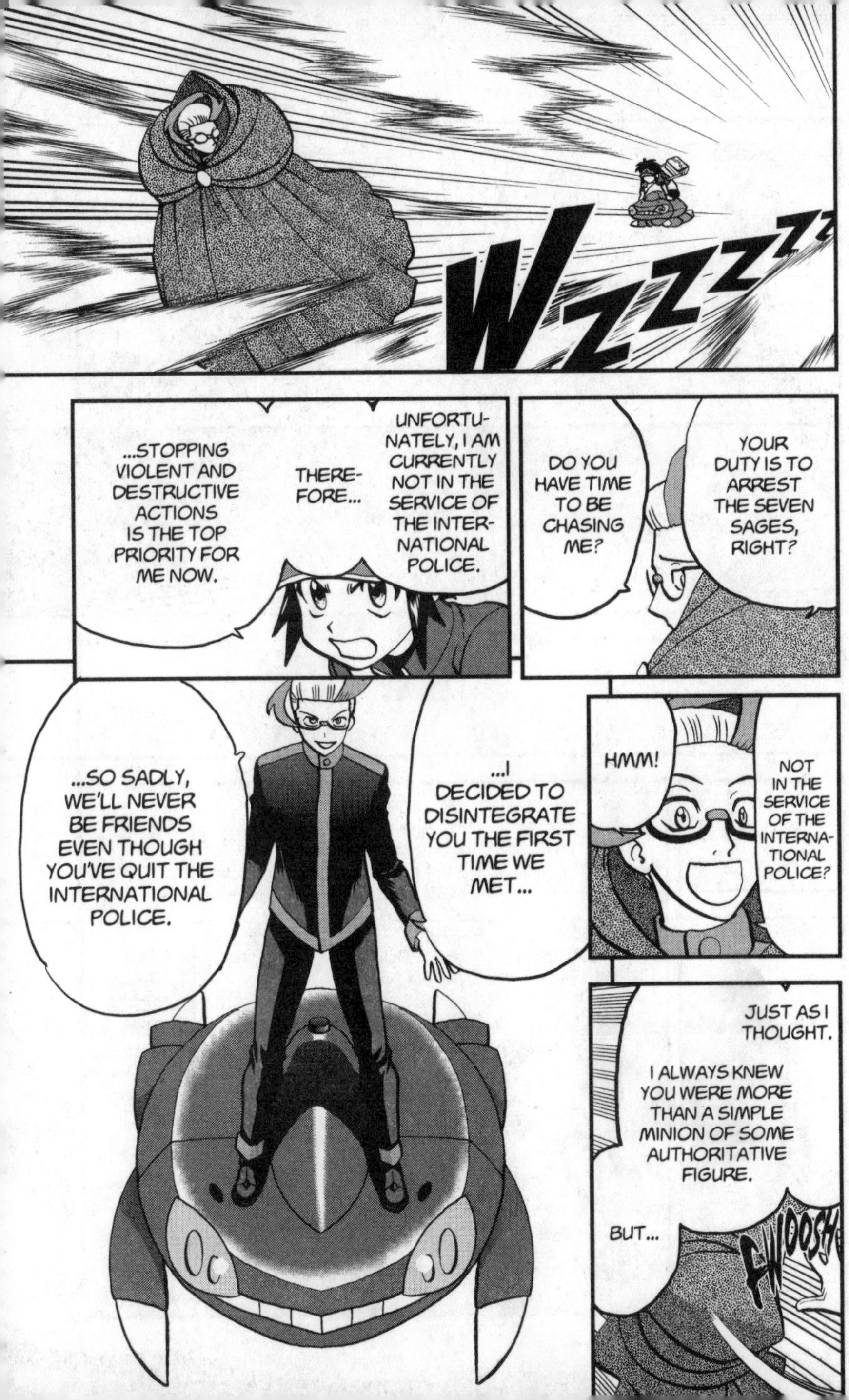
WZZZZZ
YOUR DUTY IS TO ARREST THE SEVEN SAGES, RIGHT?
DO YOU HAVE TIME TO BE CHASING ME?
UNFORTUNATELY, I AM CURRENTLY NOT IN THE SERVICE OF THE INTERNATIONAL POLICE.
THEREFORE...
...STOPPING VIOLENT AND DESTRUCTIVE ACTIONS IS THE TOP PRIORITY FOR ME NOW.
NOT IN THE SERVICE OF THE INTERNATIONAL POLICE?
HMM!
JUST AS I THOUGHT.
I ALWAYS KNEW YOU WERE MORE THAN A SIMPLE MINION OF SOME AUTHORITATIVE FIGURE.
BUT...
FWOOSH
...I DECIDED TO DISINTEGRATE YOU THE FIRST TIME WE MET...
...SO SADLY, WE'LL NEVER BE FRIENDS EVEN THOUGH YOU'VE QUIT THE INTERNATIONAL POLICE.

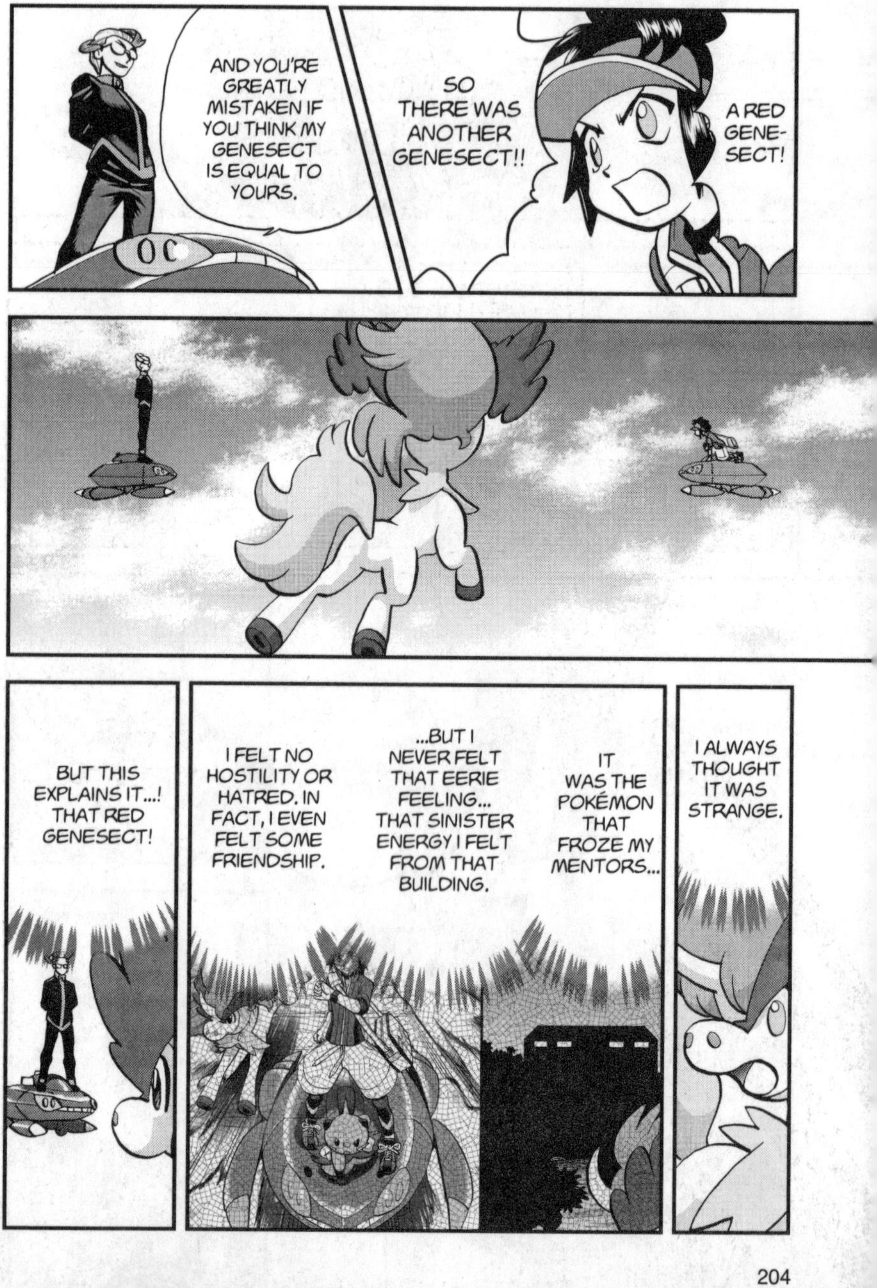
A RED GENE-SECT!
SO THERE WAS ANOTHER GENESECT!!
AND YOU'RE GREATLY MISTAKEN IF YOU THINK MY GENESECT IS EQUAL TO YOURS.
I ALWAYS THOUGHT IT WAS STRANGE.
IT WAS THE POKÉMON THAT FROZE MY MENTORS...
...BUT I NEVER FELT THAT EERIE FEELING... THAT SINISTER ENERGY I FELT FROM THAT BUILDING.
I FELT NO HOSTILITY OR HATRED. IN FACT, I EVEN FELT SOME FRIENDSHIP.
BUT THIS EXPLAINS IT...! THAT RED GENESECT!

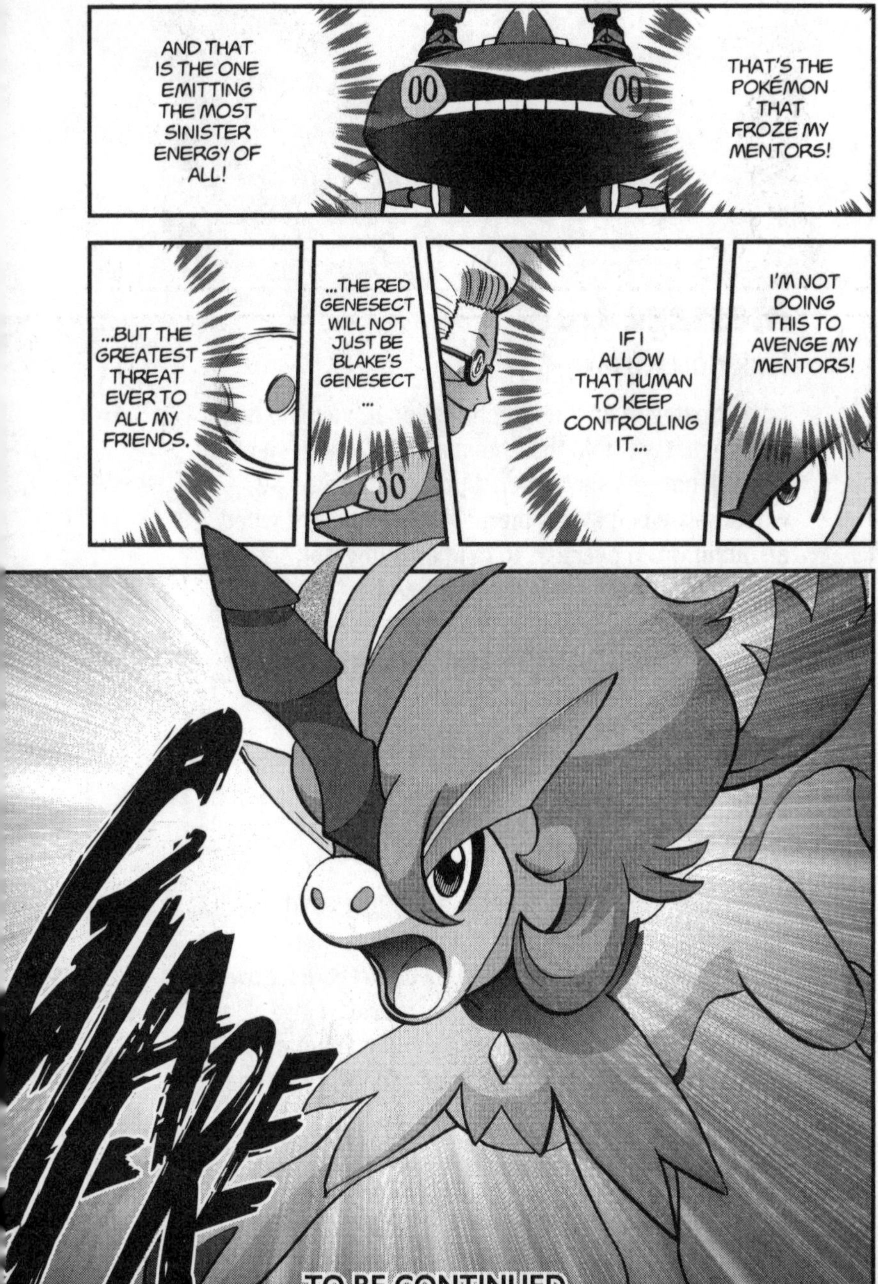
THAT'S THE POKÉMON THAT FROZE MY MENTORS!
AND THAT IS THE ONE EMITTING THE MOST SINISTER ENERGY OF ALL!
I'M NOT DOING THIS TO AVENGE MY MENTORS!
IF I ALLOW THAT HUMAN TO KEEP CONTROLLING IT...
...THE RED GENESECT WILL NOT JUST BE BLAKE'S GENESECT ...
...BUT THE GREATEST THREAT EVER TO ALL MY FRIENDS.
TO BE CONTINUED...

Message from
Hidenori Kusaka

I participated in an autograph session in Vietnam two years ago. I was told that the manga culture in Vietnam was still not very developed, but I was shocked by what I saw when I went there! They had never invited an author from overseas to hold an autograph session before. As a result, we were welcomed as "the first overseas authors who held an autograph session in Vietnam." It was a surprise, but I also felt honored to be a part of a "first time in history."

Message from
Satoshi Yamamoto

In order to work on each of the adventures that lead toward the climax, I watched Tatsuya Mori's documentary films *Fake*, *A* and *A2* and read a follow-up book that is a conclusion to the movies. I also watched a nonfiction Fuji Television documentary called *Branded as the Son of a Murderer* and the TV drama Dexter.